"*The Lost Daughter* delivers the goods: flawed but sympathetic characters and a plot that will keep readers turning the pages voraciously."
—WALLY LAMB, *NEW YORK TIMES* BESTSELLING AUTHOR

"With spellbinding attentiveness and intimacy, it explores what a husband and wife can be sure they know about each other but also, in prose wearing night-vision glasses, the inaccessible places where the hidden past lies threateningly coiled, and which love must also find a way to reach."
—FRANCISCO GOLDMAN, AUTHOR OF *SAY HER NAME*

"In her well-crafted novel, Ferriss considers the tender moments that shape our choices and challenge our most sacred bonds."
—ELIZABETH BRUNDAGE, AUTHOR OF *A STRANGER LIKE YOU* AND *THE DOCTOR'S WIFE*

"[A] moving tale of sin and redemption, motherhood and second chances, that is sure to touch the reader's heart."
—ERIC GOODMAN, AUTHOR OF *TWELFTH AND RACE* AND *CHILD OF MY RIGHT HAND*

Acclaim for the work of Lucy Ferriss

"*The Lost Daughter* delivers the goods: flawed but sympathetic characters and a plot that will keep readers turning the pages voraciously. From its harrowing prologue to its final sentences, I was emotionally engaged with this fine novel. Ferriss is a masterful storyteller."

—Wally Lamb, *New York Times* bestselling author of
She's Come Undone and *The Hour I First Believed*

"This achingly beautiful novel about marriage and love, pulsing with complex life, is the work of a master American realist, up there with Richard Yates or anyone else. With spellbinding attentiveness and intimacy it explores what a husband and wife can be sure they know about each other but also, in prose wearing night-vision glasses, the inaccessible places where the hidden past lies threateningly coiled, and which love must also find a way to reach."

—Francisco Goldman, author of *Say Her Name*

"In her well-crafted novel, Ferriss considers the tender moments that shape our choices and challenge our most sacred bonds. Her story reminds us how vulnerable our destinies are to the mistakes of our pasts."

—Elizabeth Brundage, author of *A Stranger Like You* and
The Doctor's Wife

"In *The Lost Daughter*, Lucy Ferriss has crafted a moving tale of sin and redemption, motherhood and second chances, that is sure to touch the reader's heart. This is a plot fully loaded, with flawed, compelling characters, in whom we recognize our best dreams of ourselves."

—Eric Goodman, author of *Twelfth and Race* and
Child of My Right Hand

continued . . .

"Ah, motherhood—who can know your bliss, your ache, your secrets? Lucy Ferriss knows and tells in this fast-paced, engrossing, and sometimes gruesome tale of mothers and daughters who are not what anyone expected."

—Deb Olin Unferth, author of *Vacation* and *Revolution: The Year I Fell in Love and Went to Join the War*

"Lucy Ferriss holds a mirror to today's headlines, smashes it, and turns the splintered shards into a tension-filled, beautifully written story of the moment, when a deadly secret takes on a life of its own."

—Mary-Ann Tirone Smith, author of *Girls of Tender Age*

"A hugely affecting meditation on the fragility of even the strongest bonds, when it comes to marriage . . . a beautifully constructed and moving novel."   —Jim Shepard, author of *You Think That's Bad*

"*The Lost Daughter* is an intelligent, entertaining, and deeply moving book about three courageous people who think they have escaped the past—'with its small-town gossip and strip malls and mistakes'—only to find that they are still deeply entangled with it and with each other. This is my favorite of Lucy Ferriss's novels and I read it with great pleasure."

—Molly Giles, author of *Iron Shoes* and *Creek Walk*

"This is the voice of a major writer."   —*St. Louis Post-Dispatch*

"Ferriss precisely traces the evolution of feeling."

—*The New York Times Book Review*

"Tough, grave, and sweet . . . a book that will stay with me for a long time."   —Lee Smith, author of *Mrs. Darcy and the Blue-Eyed Stranger*

"Beautiful . . . sympathetic, well-defined characters."   —*The Advocate*

"Sad and soaring and sexy, . . . lyrical, honest prose."
—Susan Straight, author of *Take One Candle Light a Room*

"Bittersweet but often laugh-out-loud funny."   —*ForeWord*

"Sharp humor and dazzling writing . . . one of the best books of the year, period."   —*St. Louis Riverfront Times*

"Thought-provoking and disturbing . . . subtle and original."
—*Contra Costa Times*

"If in this novel Ferriss makes you think, she will also make you feel."
—*Publishers Weekly* (starred review)

"Elegant and fearless."
—Mark Winegardner, author of *Crooked River Burning*

"Ferriss's strength as an author is her uncanny ability to layer so many emotions in her fiction. . . . This is a beautifully written collection, worthy of winning a prize."   —*St. Paul Pioneer Press*

"A powerful, painful book."
—Frederick Busch, author of *Rescue Missions*

"A gripping coming-of-age story . . . dense and richly evocative."
—*The Washington Times*

"A complex, satisfying work."   —*Ms.*

continued . . .

"A beautiful novel about family and love, from one of the best writers around." —Oscar Hijuelos, author of *Beautiful Maria of My Soul*

"Ferriss writes with mesmerizing power and confidence. Her characters throb with life, and her story takes turns that alternately fire and chill the blood." —Knight Ridder

"Tight, cleanly structured, and polished . . . The author's voice is intelligent and her analysis shrewd. . . . Interiors—the parts that matter—are brilliantly drawn, and the prose itself is often superb."
—*St. Louis Post-Dispatch*

The Lost Daughter

Lucy Ferriss

BERKLEY BOOKS, NEW YORK

THE BERKLEY PUBLISHING GROUP
Published by the Penguin Group
Penguin Group (USA) Inc.
375 Hudson Street, New York, New York 10014, USA
Penguin Group (Canada), 90 Eglinton Avenue East, Suite 700, Toronto, Ontario M4P 2Y3, Canada
(a division of Pearson Penguin Canada Inc.) • Penguin Books Ltd., 80 Strand, London WC2R 0RL,
England • Penguin Group Ireland, 25 St. Stephen's Green, Dublin 2, Ireland (a division of Penguin
Books Ltd.) • Penguin Group (Australia), 250 Camberwell Road, Camberwell, Victoria 3124, Australia
(a division of Pearson Australia Group Pty. Ltd.) • Penguin Books India Pvt. Ltd., 11 Community
Centre, Panchsheel Park, New Delhi—110 017, India • Penguin Group (NZ), 67 Apollo Drive,
Rosedale, Auckland 0632, New Zealand (a division of Pearson New Zealand Ltd.) • Penguin Books
(South Africa) (Pty.) Ltd., 24 Sturdee Avenue, Rosebank, Johannesburg 2196, South Africa

Penguin Books Ltd., Registered Offices: 80 Strand, London WC2R 0RL, England

Lines from "Thirteen Ways of Looking at a Blackbird" are taken from *Harmonium* by Wallace Stevens.
Lines from "The Disquieting Muses" are taken from *The Collected Poems* © Sylvia Plath and reprinted
by permission of Faber and Faber Ltd. Lines from "Daddy" are taken from *Ariel* by Sylvia Plath © Ted
Hughes and reprinted by permission of Faber and Faber Ltd. Lines from "Nature the Gentlest
Mother Is" are by Emily Dickinson.

This book is an original publication of The Berkley Publishing Group.

This is a work of fiction. Names, characters, places, and incidents either are the product of the author's
imagination or are used fictitiously, and any resemblance to actual persons, living or dead, business
establishments, events, or locales is entirely coincidental. The publisher does not have any control over
and does not assume any responsibility for author or third-party websites or their content.

PUBLISHING HISTORY
Berkley trade paperback edition / February 2012

Library of Congress Cataloging-in-Publication Data

Ferriss, Lucy, 1954–
The lost daughter / Lucy Ferriss. — Berkley trade paperback ed.
p. cm.
ISBN 978-0-425-24556-9
1. Marriage—Fiction. 2. Family secrets—Fiction. 3. Triangles (Interpersonal relations)—
Fiction. I. Title.
PS3556.E754L67 2012
813'.54—dc23
2011023502

PRINTED IN THE UNITED STATES OF AMERICA

10 9 8 7 6 5 4 3

For Don

Many believers breathed life into the sparks of this story. Fellow writers Eric Goodman and Irene Papoulis helped keep the fire burning. Al Zuckerman, my agent, gave his immense vitality and insight to the forging of characters and their all-too-human actions. Don Moon kept seeing the possibilities in one glowing ember or another. The acumen of my editor, Jackie Cantor, along with copyeditor Amy Schneider, brought both light and warmth to the project. For help on issues of disability in school and in the family, I am grateful to Jeffrey Kittay, as well as to Jonathan Mooney's *The Short Bus: A Journey Beyond Normal* and Jane Bernstein's *Rachel in the World*. I offer humble and enduring thanks to all.

What seas what shores what granite islands towards my timbers
And woodthrush calling through the fog
My daughter.

—T. S. Eliot, "Marina"

Prologue

1993

Even as Brooke signed the guest register at the motel, she was try-ing to remember whose idea this had been. Alex had had fifty bucks in his wallet, and she'd had thirty-five, which she'd handed to him before they walked through the glass doors of the lobby. It was Alex who'd driven away from Daisy's Kitchen, away from Windermere toward Scranton. It was Brooke who'd spotted the Econo Lodge sign. "We'll just get to the room," Alex had said when he parked the car, "and then we'll have time to think."

There was an old box of Kleenex on the dash of his car. She'd shoved maybe a dozen tissues into her panties, and they were all soaked now, a warm wet load. At first she'd thought of telling Alex that sometimes nothing happened for a day or two after your water broke, but then the cramps had started, in the car, and she'd gritted her teeth and let him bring her here.

The room was on the third floor, toward the back. "I told them," Alex said in a stage whisper as he steered her down the dim hallway, "that we wanted quiet."

"Didn't he think it was weird that we didn't have luggage?"

"Sure. He thinks we're here to screw."

"Done that," said Brooke feebly.

"Here," said Alex when he'd gotten the card key to work. "Just lie down. We'll figure this out."

"I want a bath," she said.

"Bath? Oh, right. Bath. Warm bath. Coming up." He was going around the room, flicking on lights. In their unnatural light his face looked bleached, almost powdery. Brooke wondered if he was going to faint. She sank to the edge of the bed. It felt like period cramps, only coming and going. Reaching between her legs, she scooped out the wet wad of Kleenex. Immediately there was a new rush of water. She stepped quickly to the bathroom, where Alex was kneeling by the shallow tub. Dumping the wad in the toilet, she grabbed a towel.

"We're going to make a mess," she said, hearing her mother's tone in her own voice.

"We can't think about that. We can't think about that," said Alex.

"Why are you saying things twice?"

"Because I'm nervous, all right? Because I don't know if we should even be here. We oughta call someone, or get you to a hospital—"

"Get me in the bath, first. Here, step out of the way."

He stepped away. When she gave him a look, he stepped out of the bathroom altogether. But he didn't shut the door behind him, and she didn't shut it in his face. A new cramp came. She caught herself on the edge of the sink and bit her lip. Then quickly she slid out of the jean jacket and oversized T-shirt and leggings, and stepped into the bath. There was blood on her legs now, like first-day period. She grabbed a washcloth from the metal rack over the toilet and slid down. Cramp. One, she counted, two three four five six. Up to twenty-five, then it slacked off. Gingerly she slid the washcloth between her legs, as if she were touching a wound. It felt the same, only the area above it lay heavier and lower than ever, a metal pot between her legs. Cramp. She shut her eyes, leaned back, counted.

"Brooke? You okay?"

"Yeah." She sat up. She was in a sea of dark pink. God, oh God, the blood hadn't stopped, the way it did when you had your period and took a bath.

"You want to stay here, or go?"

"Go where?" She pulled the plug and ran fresh water in.

"You know. The hospital."

"Give me a minute, Lex."

"Are you in labor?"

"A *minute*, I said."

Fresh water, another cramp. He knocked on the door, but her teeth were gritted. Finally she saw his head, poking in. "Jesus fucking Christ," he said.

"It's what happens, Alex. I think."

"Don't you fucking *know*?"

"I thought it'd happen at three months, remember? When I'd finished drinking Isadora's tea? She said it'd be like a big period."

"You want a doctor?" He came and knelt by the side of the white tub. He looked so young, his face wide open. Brooke felt the sweetness of the first time his face had hovered so close and she had kissed his mouth, drenched with desire.

"I don't know," Brooke said. She began to weep. Overhead, the ceiling fan whirred; you couldn't turn it off. She whispered, "Don't cry, don't cry," aloud to herself, the way she did when she was alone.

"Look, Brooke. This is what I think, okay?"

"Okay. I'm listening." She turned off the hot water and drew her knees up: another cramp.

"Remember what I was saying, in the diner?"

"Yeah. You wanted to go to your parents."

"No, I mean before."

"Look, Alex, could we not talk about that right now? I'm only six and a half months. This is a miscarriage I'm having, okay?"

"Okay. Yeah, I guess okay. But I guess, I'm voting to stay here, you know? Since you've waited all this time and now it's coming out. Only—Only—"

Putting all her weight on her arms, Brooke lifted herself to standing. Her belly sagged between her hips. She grabbed two dinky towels and wrapped them around her waist and swollen breasts.

"Only I don't know what to do," he finished. "To help."

"You can do just one thing," Brooke said. She made him meet her eyes. "Don't get angry with me," she said. "No matter what happens, or what I do. Don't get pissed at me."

"Right," said Alex, as if this were a real order that he could follow. He cupped the back of her head and drew her to his chest. Her arms slipped around his waist. For a moment they stood together in the bathroom, synchronizing their breaths.

Then they stripped the covers off one of the beds. Alex laid the remaining towels on it. Climbing on, Brooke picked up the phone. "It's not working," she said, waving the receiver as if Alex could see a broken part.

"Who cares?"

"Me, who's supposed to be home by four, that's who."

"I think we need to give them a twenty-five-dollar deposit. I saw a sign."

"That's a rip!"

"They're covering their butts. You get back what you don't use."

"Have you got twenty-five bucks?"

"I have thirty left over. We can call at four. If we're still here."

With a clatter, Brooke dropped the receiver. She drew her knees up. Alex hung up the phone. "Breathe," he told Brooke, who was clamping on her lower lip with her teeth. "Don't hold it in."

"I've *got* to hold it in!" she exploded at him. She swung her legs over the side of the bed and sat up. There was a little blood on the towels, not much. "Have you any *idea*," Brooke hissed, "how *loud* I could get?"

"Pretty loud, I figure." Alex reached a hand out to stroke her hair. Brooke's face was white, gaunt like an old woman's. "I don't know what's happening to you," he said. "You have to tell me."

"I don't have to tell you anything."

"I'm the only one here!"

"So go away. Oh fuck." She rolled back and moaned, deep in her throat. Alex wanted to grab her arm, yank her out of there. Stubborn little bitch, just like his sister Charlie, no sense. Then faintly, reading his mind, Brooke said, "You promised. Remember. Not to get pissed."

"I'm not pissed!"

"Rub my back?"

"Okay. Okay." He pulled off his outer shirt—it was too warm in the room—and moved over to the bed where Brooke lay. They'd given each other back rubs, the first couple of months they were going out. It was a way to explore a person's body without screwing or threatening to screw. He used to sit on her ass while she lay with her top off, and he'd move his hands out from her spine under her shoulder blades and around to where her breasts spread sideways beneath her raised arms. He'd rub his thumbs against the delicate white flesh there, and after the first couple of times she lifted for him, so he could slide his hands underneath and catch a feel of her whole breasts.

Propped on her bed, trying to find a spot on her back under her loose white shirt where he could dig his thumbs in and give her some relief, Alex wanted to remind Brooke of that time. The spring before this one, it was. Then she started moaning again, saying, "Not there, Lex, lower. Yes, that's it—no, you're too soft, rub harder—*harder*—"

"Jesus, baby, I'm trying."

"I know, Alex, I know. Listen." The cramp was gone now. She sat up. Her face and arms glowed with sweat. "I don't think—remember, you promised not to be pissed—but I don't think this is a normal miscarriage."

"Yeah, Toto," he said—you had to get funny, what else did you do in an Econo Lodge with your girlfriend opening the oven door?—"and we're not in Kansas anymore, either."

"If you stay here, you'll miss your game."

He shrugged. "Exhibition match. I'll tell them I got a flat tire."

"I'm not going to have a baby, though. You know that, right?" She put her fingers on his face. He turned away.

"If I thought you were going to have a baby," he said slowly, "I'd have taken you to a hospital."

But he hadn't taken her. She hadn't let him, Brooke thought. From the start it had been like that—she had been pigheaded, not listening to Alex Frazier with his facts, with his sensible plans. Now, as the afternoon wore on, as the sun shot through the window, the idea of the hospital drifted further away, to another world. "I feel like I have to go to the bathroom," she said for maybe the twentieth time.

"Okay. I'll help you. Up," Alex said.

She looked at him. He looked like her father, his right temple resting on the fingers of his right hand, his left hand hanging downward in a gesture of defeat. "No," she said. "No, not that way. I've got to do it on the bed. It's the baby, I think. The fetus. I don't know. I've got to push it *out*."

"So push it," he said. He turned, put his hands on her knees. "It's time, that means. Jesus, Brooke, don't hold back."

It was a wave, this pushing, that crashed over her head and then moved down through her, expelling everything in its path. She held her breath as it grabbed what was in her abdomen and tried to pummel it through the opening.

"It's gone, now," she said when it had passed. "I'm not sure anything moved."

But it came again, a matter of seconds later. "Push," Alex was saying now, only there was pain like a thick blanket between her and him so she could hear but without understanding. She clenched her teeth, squeezed her eyes, and bore down. Then it passed again. Then again—the wave, the pressure, the squeeze, oh my God the pain, the pain, the thing down there going nowhere, and then it passed.

Again and again.

At some point—had it been five minutes? two days?—she glanced over at the bedside clock, but the numbers swam.

"What time is it?" she asked. Coming out of a dream.

"Six fifteen. You've been pushing since three."

"Oh Jesus, I forgot to call home. Jesus. Here it comes again." And it did, but she couldn't give it her attention, the wave of pushing and pain.

"You're worn out, Brooke." He had his cap off; his T-shirt was soaked in sweat. Stepping to the bathroom, he filled a plastic cup with water and drank it down; he motioned to her, but she shook her head. Filling it anyway, he brought it to the nightstand. "Worn out," he repeated.

"Don't talk about going to the hospital, Lex. Not now. Get the phone to work. Okay?" she said, and she started to cry. She was just so fucking tired.

"I think I should reach up. That's what they do on *ER*. Reach up and see if you've got enough room, or whatever."

"That's TV, Alex."

"They have doctors consulting."

She didn't move, not even when the next wave hit. She could hear him in the narrow bathroom, washing his hands. Nothing was right. Nothing ever had been right. Then he was back. His hand went up into her, a dull pressure. He kept the other hand on her knee, to steady himself. "I can feel something, up there," he said at last. "It's—like—protruding out of the main place, but it's awful squeezed in here. And there's a bone—your bone, I mean—that's kind of in the way. I can't get a grip on anything."

"We've got to get it out, Alex. I can't push anymore."

"At the hospital—"

"You want the hospital?"

"I'm saying for you," said Alex.

Brooke moaned again. He held her slippery hand. "I've got to rest," she said when it passed. Her eyes were shut. "Let me rest. Go downstairs, okay? Pay for the phone? I'll try again in a little bit."

Alex flew out the door, escaping. He took the stairs down. The lobby was carpeted in deep red, with shrimplike curlicues in royal blue swimming through the plush. Music you couldn't blame for anything piped through the stale air. "Here," he said to the same clerk who'd checked them in. "We'd like to make a couple phone calls."

"We don't tolerate parties," the clerk said. He had an oily mustache and a strange growth behind his left jaw—not a mole, more like scar tissue. He spoke with an accent.

"No, no. We're not calling friends. Just some—some relatives. In the area."

"We can monitor. Go over the limit, we switch you off."

"Local calls," said Alex. He unrolled the money and placed it on the polished counter. There was blood on the back of one hand. "Can I get a receipt for that?"

"What a world." The clerk shook his dark head. "You're an entrepreneur now."

"I just want to make sure—you know, when we check out—"

"Yah, yah, you can have this piece of paper."

While the clerk turned to find a receipt, Alex swiped his hand on his jeans. He gazed out the picture window. Out on Route 6, cars churned by. Upstairs Brooke would be moaning again, thrashing uselessly. It wasn't alive in there; she was right. The thing he'd touched—it had been like a warm, wet rubber ball caught in a chute. You couldn't get it out in one piece. And she couldn't push it out. It was dead matter, that was all. At the hospital, they'd call it a miscarriage—or no, a stillbirth—and there would be Brooke's mother looking at him like he'd raped her daughter, and his own dad lecturing him about whether he was ready to go off to college and run the risk of knocking up strange girls. Right now there was none of that; they knew nothing. Even Isadora, who'd given Brooke the abortion remedy five months ago, could think they'd just taken care of it themselves.

"Never mind about the receipt," he said to the clerk.

"No, you take it! You take it, now you made me run it out!" The lump under the clerk's left ear had gone reddish. He yanked the perforated sheet from the printer and thrust it across the counter at Alex. Alex crumpled it into his pocket, pushed out the glass doors, and sprinted across the parking lot.

A breeze had kicked up, the way it had been doing in late

afternoon—clouds on the horizon threatening, but they never delivered. This was what people on the outside were wondering: Would it rain this time, or would the drought go on forever? What about the reservoir? They hummed along, going home from work or heading for the game Alex was going to miss, and they thought about weather.

Inside, it was different.

Unlocking the car door, Alex paused for just a second. But no one needed him out here, that was the fact of it. He ducked his head inside the car and started rummaging around. He needed a tool. Something long and thin, but blunt. Baseball glove, Charlie's dumb car games, a bunch of old magazines in the back. This was the junk car, his mom said. He moved the front seat, checked underneath. Windshield scraper, hockey puck, half an apple dried to a pucker. Then—under the magazines, when he got desperate and started just shoving stuff around—left over from the potluck she'd gone to a month back, the stainless steel serving spoon his mom had been looking for. It was coated with spinach gunk, a scrap of paper napkin stuck to the back.

"The ticket," Alex said aloud.

He rode the elevator up with his eyes shut. Out into the universe, that was where he'd go if he could. Up and out, and tumbling gently over and over—no pain, no impossible tricks, only silence.

Back in the room, Brooke was already on the phone. "I don't care about dinner," she was saying, her voice high and light. "No, don't keep it warm for me. We'll probably get pizza. Yeah, a bunch of kids. Love you, too, Mom."

Alex watched her hand tremble as she cradled the receiver. He stepped forward. "I got something," he started to say. But Brooke was twisting back into the bed, her bare legs white. "Jesus," Alex said. Below her the towels were dark red, swampy with blood.

"Something gushed."

"Christ, this can't be right. Jesus." When he got near the bed he felt dizzy. He sank down on the other one. He'd heard of men fainting; he wasn't going to do that. Just, there was so much of it. And the smell, like his uncle's farm almost.

He thought of his coach, of that tone of voice he used at the half when they were down by three. "Here," he said. He caught the blood up in the towels—there was a fair amount leaking through and over the sides—and when he'd run with them to the bathroom and thrown them in the tub, he came back with his Polartec jacket. "It washes out, right?" he said.

Brooke didn't answer. Her hands were on her naked belly, pushing at it. Her skin looked glazed; her hair was a wild tangle from all the thrashing about on the pillow, and there was no grace left in her limbs. He'd never seen her so ugly—he'd never seen her ugly at all—and he'd never wanted her the way he did right then. This thing hurting her—he'd get rid of this thing.

"I'm not going away," he said to Brooke. "Just to the bathroom, to get this spoon clean. You hearing me?"

He thought she nodded, though it might have been a tossing of her head. The bathroom was blue-white garish, the ceiling fan like a giant bee. He ran the water scalding; lathered the spoon up; scraped at the sticky bits with his thumbnail. Then the rinse, just as hot. No clean towels; he wiped it on three of the tissues that popped from a box in the wall.

"Now hold still," he told her.

He took the shade off the bedside lamp and placed it on the rug beside the bed, to help him see. From outside came a slow roll of thunder, and a flash of lightning in the uncurtained window.

His right hand went in, as did the spoon held by his left. The spoon pushed and prodded at the blood-slicked rubbery walls.

When his fingers touched the round thing—*the head*, he made himself think it—he slid the bowl of the spoon around, like fitting a shoehorn around a heel. Pressing against the spoon, his fingers managed to grip and pull it. Pull and pull, Brooke screaming now, screaming, "Stop, Alex," and it came, dragging its scrawny body behind it.

And there was—*yes*, Alex would admit it to himself, in the dark before dawn and much later—a moment where the spoon and the hand both squeezed too hard. Where the hard surface between them might have buckled just a little bit. But if it happened, when? On the way through the birth canal perhaps, exuberant that he had the thing now? Or perhaps just after, when he saw what must have been its face, and *yes*, there was a trace of life, not the kind of life he'd ever imagined but just the promise of it that he almost remembered from his own beginnings, before he was Alex or knew that he was anything. Over and over he would try to remember, to freeze the moment, but again it would pass, and only what followed would remain.

Chapter 1

2008

The afternoon of the christening party, the garden sparkled. It had rained the night before. Summer flowers rimmed the wet grass. The brick patio that Brooke had persuaded her boss, Lorenzo, to put in was large enough for the drinks table and a fair amount of milling around. The whole garden, in fact, had been Brooke's project. The regular patrons of Lorenzo's Nursery loved sitting in it. Drinking the iced tea the nursery provided, they would talk plants until they had persuaded themselves to try a new hosta or a wild geranium. The boost in sales since installing the garden was the main reason Brooke could co-opt the space for the christening. She and Sean had nothing like it to offer. Sean's brother and sister-in-law, Gerry and Kate, whose son Derek was the focus of all the attention, lived in a crowded condo with a backyard the size of a shoebox. When Sean's family got together, the event was bound to be boisterous. This time they were two dozen, not counting the children Sean's family seemed to produce in droves. The garden at Lorenzo's, even with soggy grass, was a godsend.

"Poor little bugger's exhausted," Sean said. He nodded at baby Derek, still clad in Irish lace but drooling in his stroller, his big head dropped to his shoulder. "Not like our Meghan, here."

"Don't remind me," said Brooke, spilling more chilled shrimp onto the platter.

"What'd I do?" Meghan, a bundle of six-year-old energy with hearing keen as a bat's, cartwheeled between cousins across the wet grass toward her parents.

"Screamed bloody murder all through the cleansing away of your sin," Sean said. He kissed Meghan's red hair. "You'd have thought it was an exorcism."

"What's that, Mommy?" Meghan asked, taking a shrimp. She always asked Brooke about words, even the words her father used.

Brooke smiled wanly. "Exorcism's taking the devil out of you," she said.

"Doesn't always work," added Sean.

Meghan stuck her tongue out at him and cartwheeled away.

"D'ja see that?" Sean said to his brother Gerald. "Girl gives her father no respect."

It was a joke, but Gerry and Kate exchanged a look. Gerry said, "Our first was like that. Then she got a sister to look after. Set her straight soon enough."

Brooke felt her husband's quick intake of breath. It had to come up. How could it not, at a family christening? Still, she gritted her teeth. Would they never let up? Sean had three brothers and a sister. Every one of them had produced multiple offspring except for the youngest brother, who was gay and lived on the West Coast. Though no one attended church regularly anymore, they all christened their kids and described themselves proudly as Irish Catholic. Once, when the mild allusions and teasing about Brooke and Sean's only child had grown more insistent than usual, Brooke had turned to one of her sisters-in-law and asked if she didn't think ZPG was a good idea. "ZP who?" the sister-in-law had replied, and Brooke couldn't bring herself to press the point. In any case, the population growth of the O'Connor clan was far from zero, and Brooke's in-laws considered that the number one—meaning Meghan— didn't really count.

Sean, Brooke saw as she brushed the back of his palm with her fingers, didn't really count it either. No matter how much he loved his daughter, Meghan alone would never be enough for him. He stiffened and made smart cracks when his siblings teased him. He couldn't defend the choice Brooke had made, and he wouldn't simply remind them all it was none of their business. "So I didn't tell you?" he said now to Gerald. "We're sending Meghan to you for the summer. You can clean up her act, hey?"

Brooke slipped away from the men. She picked up a platter of chicken wings and wove her way through the crowd. Though she stood taller and blonder—WASPier—than the rest of the O'Connors and most of their friends, she managed to glide almost invisibly. She made small talk about the garden and the church ceremony. Though Father Donnell's eyes ranged up and down her slim white pants and silk top, their conversation extended only to the climbing roses and the science of pruning. There might have been a time when Brooke seemed an object of mystery to many in the christening party. But it had been seven years, now, since she had come to Connecticut and married Sean. Her quiet accommodation struck most of those who took a barbecued wing from her platter as a little dull, nothing more.

Everywhere, children darted through legs and cultivated grass stains. Counting Derek, Kate had informed Brooke, there were seventeen kids present under the age of ten. The small plastic climbing structure on a patch of sand in the corner of the garden was swarmed, but Meghan and her favorite cousins preferred the grass and a game of chase among the flowers. "Shouldn't we get them out of there?" Kate asked when Brooke stopped by the bench where she was sitting with Sean and Gerry's mother, Matilda, known to all as Mum. Not yet sixty, Mum sat with her hands folded in her lap, a half pint of whiskey in her bloodstream.

"They're fine," Brooke said. "Wing?" She extended the platter and a fistful of paper napkins. Kate shook her head. Gingerly, with a pale thumb and forefinger, Mum reached forward. The edge of bone she pinched slipped away, shot across the platter, and ended on the grass. Mum bent down to retrieve it.

"No, no, Mum. I'll get you another. Here." Quickly Kate plucked a chicken wing and a napkin and cupped them in her hands, prepared to feed her mother-in-law like a toddler if need be.

"It's a fine party," Mum said to Brooke, ignoring the food. "But you should be giving it for your own, you know."

"Mum!" said Kate. She glanced apologetically at Brooke.

"It's okay," said Brooke.

"Five I had, and look how they all turned out. Good young men."

"Fanny's a sweetheart, too," said Brooke.

"So have you got another in the belly yet, Miss Brooke?"

"Mum, please," said Kate.

"You want to shut me up, get me another drink."

"In a minute. Eat your chicken."

Mum took the wing and nibbled. Watching her, Brooke missed her own mother, who had promised to visit before the end of summer. Not that she was close to her mom—the ties that bound them were, in their own way, as tangled as Sean's to Mum—but at the very least her mom would have no words of advice about family size. The kids were crowding around, begging for chicken wings. Brooke crouched and let them grab, then called after them to toss bones in the garbage cans, wipe hands on napkins. When she glanced up, Kate was looking thoughtfully at her.

"We couldn't have done this without you," Kate said.

"I'm happy to share the space."

"Not just the space. You planned everything." Kate sighed. "I thought I could manage with four. Now I'm not so sure. This fellow's the last, I'll tell you that." She leaned toward Brooke. Narrow-shouldered and snub-nosed, Kate had been a bouncy cheerleader when she married Gerry. Childbearing had widened her hips and burdened her breasts. She colored her hair a deep auburn. "They tied my tubes, when they took Derek out," she confessed in a low voice. "I didn't tell Gerry till after. We can't afford another. We've got to get a house."

"I think you're fine with four. Two of each," Brooke said.

"I wouldn't have had the courage to do it if this one hadn't been a boy. Feminism's a dirty word with this clan."

"I'm not sure it's a word they can pronounce," Brooke said, smiling.

"Still, you know. Mum's got a point." Kate glanced around. Mum had risen and was making her way purposefully toward the drinks table. "If you wait much longer, Meghan'll be halfway through elementary school. Look how mine play together." She gestured toward the climbing structure, where her two oldest—both girls, their ages sandwiching Meghan's—chased each other around the slide. "More than six years apart, you'll never get that pleasure. There'll be other pleasures, of course," she hastened to add. "I don't mean that, if you're having trouble, you should stop—"

"I appreciate your concern, Kate. Really, I do." Brooke had straightened up. She liked Kate, she reminded herself. Kate had helped her learn the ins and outs of the O'Connors; had protected her from them. Her platter almost empty, she was already moving away. "We're just taking our time," she said.

She set the handful of wings down with the rest of the food, which looked fairly scavenged. Two of Sean's cousins were combining platters, tucking the empty ones away. Cumulus clouds crept over the horizon; the air was growing heavy. Several stands of late iris and daylilies had been trampled, Brooke noticed. She'd have to get to work early tomorrow, cut away the ruined blooms, prop up the injured stalks. Sean's younger brother Danny was tossing up chunks of watermelon and catching them in his mouth, to the delight of a gaggle of nieces and nephews who tried the same and were littering the grass with juicy pink blobs that would draw bees. By the begonias sat a human layer cake: Gerry with Meghan on his lap and baby Derek, now awake, on hers. Derek's lacy christening gown trailed over Meghan's knees. With her uncle's arms cupping them both, Meghan was giving the baby a bottle. "Look at me, Mommy!" she cried when she saw Brooke. The bottle immediately dipped; the baby's arms flailed. "I'm nursing!"

"Good girl," Brooke said. "Keep the bottom up high, okay? Don't want Derek to suck air."

"Here you go, Derry. Here you go." Meghan turned her attention back.

"She's a natural," Gerry said.

"She loves your little guy," Brooke said. Though Gerry didn't reply, she heard his remark in her head: *She'd love one of yours better.* They never let up, even when they were silent. Even Neal, the gay one, when he visited from San Francisco, asked what was in Brooke's oven.

"Uh-oh," said Meghan. Derek had twisted away from the bottle and begun to fuss.

"It's okay, honey," Gerry was saying. He tried to lift the baby, get the bottle, and slide Meghan down at the same time. Brooke stepped in and picked up Derek. As she put him to her shoulder, she saw

Gerry's eyes widen, as if her knowing how to burp a baby was a miracle. She turned away so that he couldn't see the aggrieved look on her face. Derek gave a hiccup and a belch.

"Eww!" cried Meghan. "It's all nasty on your shoulder, Mommy!"

"Doesn't matter," Brooke said. "It washes out. *You* feel better, don't you?" she said to the baby—whose face, truth be told, looked like that of a jowly old man contemplating a jar of pickles. She was about to set the baby on her hip when she found Gerry reaching for him. She handed him over and went to find a paper napkin for her shoulder.

The cumulus cloud had risen and darkened; the smell of ozone was in the air. The various components of the baggy family called the O'Connors—though there were Mulligans among them, and Peases and even a set of Wuertenbachers—picked up their toys, their platters, their sticky children. Brooke gracefully and efficiently put away the leftovers and stuffed the trash bins. Sean's cousin Dominick—a source of pride for some in the clan, an irritant to others—stood arguing with Father Donnell about school choice. A civil rights lawyer in Philadelphia, Dominick was rumored to have political ambitions. He was beefy even for an O'Connor, with shoulders that hunched forward and small, keen eyes that missed nothing. "You people use that word *choice* at your convenience," he was telling the red-nosed priest. "If it's a woman wanting an abortion, you reject the word. If it's a Catholic school wanting state funding, you own it."

"So that seems right to you, does it?" said Father Donnell. "That a mother can choose to kill her unborn child, but she can't choose to send her living children to a safe place where they'll learn Catholic values?"

"They can get the Catholic values on Sunday. You make that twelve-year-old rape victim carry to term, she don't get her life back."

"She has her life. She's a mother."

"Okay, look." Dominick pulled a jumbo shrimp off a platter just as Danny's birdlike wife, Nora, swept it away. "I don't mean to push your family-planning buttons. But when you're talking state education coffers that are stretched to the max—when you're talking special-needs kids who can't get the funding for basic skills training—then I'm sorry, Father. I don't see shelling out for week-day Bible class. Hey, Brooke, you packing up the cooler?"

"Rain's coming," said Brooke, nodding at the cloud.

"Brooke has an opinion," Father Donnell said, waving his bottle in her direction. "She's got one, but she'll never share it. Will you, Mrs. O'Connor?" When Brooke didn't answer, he said in a boozy stage whisper, "Calm as a lake. When Sean was a young hellion—"

"Sean," interrupted Kate, "has to sing us a lullaby. One for the baby, anyway." She held Derek against her midriff, facing out. His eyes were glazed with fatigue.

"Oh, now," Sean said. He grazed the baby's silky hair with a rough finger. "Everyone's still talking."

"They're O'Connors, aren't they?" said one of the Wuertenbacher cousins. "Nothing shuts 'em up."

"The rain will, soon enough," said Brooke. "Go on. A lullaby."

She squeezed her husband's arm. Everything Sean did, she knew, he did to perfection. Underappreciated things, like his singing, like the work he did on their home garden, where his thumb was greener than Brooke's—things he advertised to no one but simply carried forward. "He has a kind of grace," she had said once to her mom, back in central Pennsylvania. Her mom had laughed. Brooke hadn't discussed Sean with her after that; she would avoid the subject when her mom came to visit. Father Donnell was right; she kept her opin-ions under wraps. But if she let herself loose, she would resort to a word even more old-fashioned than *grace*. She would say he kept his troth. Like Gareth, she would say, the knight in *King Arthur* who comes disguised as a kitchen boy and takes all the abuse anyone can heave at him before he becomes a hero. But she would lose her mother—rolling her eyes at Sean's freckles, his fading hair, his humdrum job—with the words *kitchen boy.*

Now Sean's mother was pinching Brooke's forearm. "Thinks he can sing," Mum said. Whiskey laced her breath. Brooke tried to step away with her, but Mum's aside had already carried across the lawn. "Asked for lessons, whole time he was growing up. Priest paid for a few, and what good is it?"

"He sings in that chorus, doesn't he?" said Sean's sister-in-law Nora, from the other side of the picnic table. "You know, the one with the symphony."

"Couldn't be bothered with the church choir," said Mum. "Ungrateful."

"Come on, Sean," Dominick said. "Give us a tune."

"I don't know," Sean said. Quickly he glanced toward his mother before his eyes sought out Brooke's. "Had a ragged throat earlier, and this beer—"

"Sing, sweetheart," Brooke said softly. "Before it rains."

Sean set down his plastic cup. He stepped away from the table. A hush fell over the group. Sean's shoulders squared. His arms hung to the elbow, where they crooked, the palms of his hands up as if he held a cloud in his forearms. His torso filled with breath. "Oh Derry boy," he sang. "The pipes, the pipes are callin'. From glen to glen, and round the mountainside." His clear tenor voice filled the warm air. Tears sprang to Brooke's eyes. "The summer's gone, and all the flowers are dyin'. 'Tis you, 'tis you must go and I must bide."

Meghan tugged at her mother's pants. Brooke leaned down. "The flowers *aren't* dying," Meghan said.

"Ssh, honey. I know. It's a song."

"Why are you crying?"

"Because it's so pretty. Ssh."

Sean's voice had begun to soar. It was like spun sugar, Brooke thought, the sweetness of the held high note. She knew little about music—her father had liked Keith Jarrett, and Bach on rainy days—but on the first full weekend she'd spent with Sean, a decade ago, she'd woken to hear him singing Italian in the shower and had wanted him, suddenly and completely, back in bed. Now Kate had tears in her eyes, too; Father Donnell as well. "'Tis I'll be there, in sunshine or in shadow. Oh Derry boy, oh Derry boy, I love you so."

The air held stillness. A few of the children started to clap, but mothers stayed their hands. They motioned to baby Derek, who had dropped off to sleep in Kate's arms and looked for once, as the sunlight slipped behind a cloud, like a lovely baby. Sean's body relaxed. The smile that crossed his face was slightly rueful, as if he had gotten away with something. "Oh, Sean," Nora finally said, and stepped forward to kiss him on the cheek.

"That's my song, there, you stole," Danny said when the other women had finished planting their lips on Brooke's husband.

"It's Derry's now," Sean said. "Passing to the next generation."

People began packing up strollers and coolers. "That," Brooke said, taking Sean's hand in hers, "was a magic moment."

"Tell that to her," Sean said, jerking his head to where Mum was making her way down the gravel walk with Kate.

Mum, Brooke wanted to say, has a tin ear and a pole up her drunken backside. But she knew better than to start. "Why don't you help me with the plates?" she said instead.

Soon the last of the stragglers were driving off, wives at the wheel, with another round of teary thanks from Kate to Brooke before a sleeping Derek was strapped into his seat and the parking lot emptied. Meghan executed another dozen cartwheels on the flattened grass while Brooke and Sean folded tables and tucked them into the nursery shed.

The rain began as they drove home, lightning illuminating the sky and then fat drops fanning dust from the windshield. "So Kate's quit her job, you know, with this one," Sean said as he turned off the interstate into the west end of Hartford.

"Strange. She said they were buying a house. But I guess with four—"

"They can live in our house," said Meghan from the back, kicking at Brooke's seat.

"Be a bit crowded, don't you think?" Brooke said.

"Nuh-uh. Baby Derry in my room. Auntie Kate and Uncle Gerry in the basement. Rosie and Sarah in Mommy's study."

Sean chuckled. "And Jimmy?"

Meghan frowned. "He can go stay with Aunt Fanny."

"I don't think they want to live in our house, honey," Brooke said. "They want a house of their own."

"But we've got lots of room. You could even have twins, Mommy, and they could have their very own room. They could have *my* room. I would go sleep in your study, and—"

"I am not having twins, sweet pea." Brooke twisted in her seat. A flash of lightning lit Meghan's face, pale with excitement and fatigue. "But we'll see lots of baby Derek. When you're a little older, you can babysit him."

"I don't *want* to babysit him." A whine crept into Meghan's voice, and she kicked the back of the seat again. "I want a baby of my *own*."

"You mean of Mommy's own," Sean said. He pulled into their driveway and turned off the ignition. The rain was steady now, the blacktop slick.

"Well?" Meghan glanced from one of her parents to the other.

"Well, that's a grown-up decision, Meghan, and we'll just have to see." Brooke's voice was firm. She did not look at Sean. "Now it's past your bedtime."

By the time they got Meghan to bed, walked the dogs through the rain, and washed the party things, it was past midnight. "And a long day tomorrow," said Brooke.

"I can pick up Meghan if you like."

"Would you? I've got a coffee date."

"Date?" Sean turned from where he was packing away the picnicware.

Brooke flapped her hand dismissively. "Old friend from high school, coming through town. Not the best timing, but I said we could meet."

To her relief, Sean didn't ask more. The two canaries caged above the sink chirped irritably. Pulling off her silk blouse with the spit-up stain, Brooke dropped it into cold water to soak. The dogs—two Lab mutts and an excitable terrier, all rescued from the Hartford pound—milled anxiously before they settled in the mudroom.

Upstairs Brooke sensed her husband's eyes on her as she ran a washcloth over her face and arms. He hadn't asked about her date, she realized, because he was still thinking Meghan's thought, *a baby of my own*. She felt a knot of panic in her chest. But he needed to be up at six for work. Not enough time or energy for a tussle about family size. Pulling off his T-shirt, Sean came to stand behind her in the bathroom. As he wrapped his arms around her waist, their eyes met in the mirror. Sean stood almost an inch shorter than Brooke. Against the small of her back she felt his belly, which was not fat but solid, a "tire" as the O'Connors said. Recently he had grown a neat goatee to camouflage his delicate chin and make up for the hairline working its way back from his forehead. The forearms circling Brooke's rib cage were fleshy but muscled, with stiff reddish arm hair that crept onto the backs of his hands. He rested his chin on his wife's shoulder. Against her backside she felt his penis rise. "They are right, you know," he said softly, holding her gaze in his bright golden eyes. "If not for our sake, for Meghan's. You saw how she was with that baby."

Brooke let her breath out around the panic knot. "She's got lots of cousins."

"Not the same." Sean's hands moved up, began massaging Brooke's breasts under her light robe. "Maybe you should wean off the Pill," he said.

"My boobs'd shrink."

"I don't love you for your boobs. We've got plenty of savings. Gerry says—"

Brooke twisted to face him. "Gerry wasn't put on bed rest for any of his kids," she said. "Neither was Kate."

"I know, I know." Sean studied her collarbone, her jaw, her ears. Sometimes, Brooke thought, her husband was memorizing her. "But it all came out fine. You said it was the most worthwhile eight weeks of your life. And the doctor said it didn't mean a second time—"

"Plus I can't cut back on work," Brooke interrupted him. "Lorenzo's counting on me to set up this landscaping contract with Aetna. We've got the new location in Simsbury. And with Jessica leaving for nursing school—"

"Ssh. Ssh." Sean put a finger to her lips. The plain, solid lines of his face betrayed a sadness he didn't like to indulge. Sean's Irish temper sent its sparks not outward but inward, where they smoldered and built up ash. Worse, Brooke's excuses bewildered him. His love for her harbored no doubts, and he had seen the joy she took in Meghan. Every time they talked about another pregnancy it went this way, but he loved her too much to stop. Sean possessed what Brooke's father—who read and quoted philosophers as if they were his best friends—called the sign of true love, a constant disposition to promote the other's good. "I've heard it all before," he said now, lifting his finger, trying to lighten his voice. "Sometimes I think I'll just have to replace those little pink pills with fakes, what-do-you-call-'ems—"

"Placebos."

"Right. And when you see it's all working out, Lorenzo isn't falling apart without you and resting in bed isn't such an awful thing, you'll be grateful to me. You'll say, 'That Sean, he's not exactly a prize, but he knows how to love me.'"

He kissed her—lightly, playfully, desperately—on the lips. Brooke pulled away. "I can't joke about this," she said. "The way your family puts pressure on—it amounts to harassment. I'm not the only woman in the world choosing to have just one child, you know."

Sean would not let go of her hand. "You're the only one who's married to me," he managed to say.

"Please, honey. We're tired. We'll end up fighting. Let's just go to bed."

Brooke shrugged off her robe and slid between the covers. Sean stood for a minute silhouetted in the bathroom door. Then he flicked off the light and joined her. Lightly she stroked his back. She had good reasons—well, perhaps not good to anyone else, but like bedrock to her. Reasons that were impossible, impossible to spell out. She might as well have twisted Sean's sunlit singing voice into a glass-breaking screech. Silent, stroking his shoulder blades, she felt his pain, his daily uncertainty. The wide bed on which they lay breathing could have been a boat tossed in a storm. Deep inside the cabin, she knew, beat her heart. Its hatches had long since been battened down—not against Sean, but against a mutiny from her own troubled past. When Sean reached around and pulled her arm across his ribs, she felt a pull on those hatches. *Let go*, she thought. But she couldn't, or they would all be out in the storm.

One by one she kissed his vertebrae. At last he turned. Rain lashed the windows, and a pale wash of sheet lightning in which tears gleamed in Sean's eyes. He bent to kiss her breasts. They moved together cautiously, as if their bodies were fragile as reeds. When Brooke moved down on the mattress and gently sucked the soft pouch of her husband's testicles, he gasped in delight. For a fleeting moment Brooke let herself believe it was enough, that he would see she loved him despite her stubbornness. She caressed him with her lips, her tongue, her breasts. Yet even as he came, deep inside her, his hands clutching hers, she felt him battling desire, as if love itself were the storm that would break her, and she him.

Chapter 2

In the gray light just before dawn, Sean slipped from bed. A light breeze stole in at the window; the storm had broken the August heat. Quickly he showered and shaved. He used a safety razor these days. He got a closer shave and there wasn't the hum of the electric to wake Brooke up. Ever since he'd been promoted to floor supervisor at the print shop, he'd had this schedule, six thirty to three. It worked great. Most days he could pick Meghan up from school or summer camp.

He padded downstairs in his socks, let the dogs out into the backyard, poured instant coffee, packed his lunch. He kept the blanket over the birdcage; Brooke would wake her canaries when she was ready. Sipping the coffee, he studied the garden he'd put in five years ago. Theirs wasn't much of a house—a raised ranch in a neighborhood of Victorians and mansard roofs—but he was proud of the place. Twice the size of what he'd grown up in with three brothers and Fanny, and he'd just about paid off the mortgage. Cardinals flitted from apple to oak tree in back. Remembering what

Meghan had suggested last night, Sean chuckled. Kate and Gerry in the basement, that would be rich. Maybe when Gerry got fed up with Kate's putting on ten pounds per kid he'd go after Brooke, see if he could persuade her where Sean hadn't, to spawn another O'Connor. That was what the guy had winked at yesterday. At a christening, for Chrissakes.

Well, they'd put down a few, Gerry and Danny both. It had started as good-natured ribbing, the kind they all fed on, this time about Sean's hair creeping down from his head to his chest and then up over his shoulders. He oughta get a wax job, Danny had said. It had gone from there to Sean's tire and how if Brooke wanted one of those buff guys, they could find Sean a nice bouncy Polish girl who'd breed him a herd of boys. Christ, Sean thought, Gerry with two of each now, he was so puffed up it must hurt to breathe.

But it was Danny who had really pissed Sean off. "Maybe she just got all dried up inside," he had said, waving a beer toward Brooke as she distributed chicken wings. "These blond types do that, you know. Run outta juice."

"Really." Sean had felt a kind of fire behind his eyes. He was ready to take a swing at the guy! They never learned, his brothers, that there was such a thing as a not-funny insult. But he'd kept his fists at his side and said, real slow, "At least she still balls me."

Right away he'd regretted the words. He hated guys who talked that way about their wives, like they were supposed to be sex toys. But what could you do, with brothers on your case every time?

"That so?" Gerry had said, crossing his arms over his chest.

Sean met his eyes. "Twice a week," he said, which was true. Also true was that every time he saw himself in the mirror—the balding pate, the dumb goatee, the heavy hips—he felt that in getting to make love with Brooke he won the lottery twice a week and then some. "Makes no sense," he said. He'd grinned so Gerry could see he was, in fact, getting laid by this gorgeous woman. Jeez, look at Kate, he thought, and how often did she give Gerry any action?

They had shut up for a little while, though they would start again next time with the blonde jokes and the frigid jokes, and Sean would have to throw it back at them. Talking that way left a bad taste in his mouth. Better to take a swing next time, he thought. He wrapped his sandwich in waxed paper, rinsed his mug, and tiptoed upstairs. From the doorway he watched Brooke sleep. Pale light washed her fine cheekbones and the hand she had flung over the edge of the mattress. She slept naked, and the thin sheet undulated over her hip, her shoulder, her surprisingly full breasts. He drank her in. He remembered the sweetness of being inside her last night, the high-pitched cry she always muffled, because of Meghan. She loved their girl so much—why *wouldn't* she have another? Sean remembered talking with her yesterday about Danny and Nora, how they always seemed on the verge of splitting up. "No way," Brooke had said. "They've got the two kids and one coming. They'd have to be a lot more miserable to call it quits now."

So would it be easier to call it quits, since Sean and Brooke had just one? This wasn't exactly what Sean's brothers said when they teased him, but it was the likeliest explanation. Wasn't it? Brooke was so quiet, so hard to read. You knew—Sean knew, anyhow—that she wasn't placid by nature; she wasn't boring. She was keeping her spirit corralled, muffled, under wraps. Maybe there was somewhere else, with someone else, where she let it go. Maybe, resisting the notion of a second child, she was really wrestling with whether she would leave Sean for this other man, for this other version of herself. A coffee date today, she had said. No pronoun used for the high school chum.

Sean shook his head to rid himself of these thoughts. They were crazy. Wasn't he the guy Brooke was with last night? Didn't she whisper in his ear, *Oh you you you?* Did she not say she felt a charge go through her, every time he sang? Only when he was drunk or tired did he get these suspicions, and boy did his brothers pick up on them, like dogs on a scent.

He tiptoed across the hallway to Meghan's room. He leaned down to kiss her forehead, just slightly clammy in the August warmth, and smelling of strawberry shampoo. He knew it wouldn't wake her, as it would Brooke. Still, all the way driving to work, practicing his scales the way he did, each day, in the car, his lips remembered the taste of Brooke's skin, the flush of her neck as she came.

From the window of his small office Sean could see the bright light atop the Travelers Insurance tower, gleaming safety. Otherwise there wasn't much of a view. Central Printing lay in the north end, a low-slung beige box along a strip that once included a glass manufacturer and Sealtest bottling. After dark, gangs used this street as a shortcut to confrontations and drive-bys on Albany Avenue; there had been six killings on or off Albany already that year. Some of Sean's guys carried .22s. He just drove an old car. When he left the shop today he'd keep his head down, and lock the doors before he put the key in the ignition.

Sean thought sometimes he should have gotten into the audio industry, where he could have learned about recording the human voice even if his own was just meant for the shower and the Hartford Chorale, where tenors were outnumbered but still a tiny forest in which to hide. Unless you auditioned for a solo, Brooke would say, but she was just indulging him. He'd tried being a church choir ringer, but he couldn't stand the Masses. And then he'd hear Mum, who never learned to whisper, saying to her friends, "He thinks he's a star." Well, he kept it under control, didn't he? Studied the tapes in the car deck, where he didn't bother anyone, and sang arias when he took the dogs to the wooded paths on Avon Mountain. The few times he'd caught sight of other walkers staring at him, he'd stopped right away.

Learn a trade, his dad had taught him, and you can have all the little hobbies you want. He had gotten into the print business because he wrote a neat hand, trained in it by the sisters at St. Ignatius. It had started as a part-time thing when he was at the state college. Back then people wanted hand-lettered signs. It was cheaper for a place like Central to hire a college kid than to mess with the fonts. One job had led to another, and now here he was with a dozen guys under him, half of them old enough to be his father. From the start the business had been under siege. First it was the cheap inks and paper in Taiwan—anybody not in a hurry could job the stuff out and get it flown back in a month. Then it was desktop publishing, color laser printers, making every Joe and his Mary a catalog designer. And now the economy going bust.

It was past three in the afternoon, time for the shift to change. He stepped out of his office. Already he'd called Brooke to say he'd have to stay late. Meghan had dance class anyhow, she'd said. She could pick her up and drop her at the class before she had coffee with her friend; Sean could get her after. "Bye, sugar," he'd said, and Brooke had said "CD Pyg," the way she always did. *CD Pyg* stood for Constant Disposition to Promote Your Good, which Brooke— or rather Brooke's father, who passed away before Sean really knew him—said was the true sign of love. Sean liked the sentiment; he wasn't sure he liked having it shortened to a code. And he was uneasy. Maybe because of the party yesterday. Maybe from that reference—again—to the no-gender friend. Hell, maybe just because of what he was about to do. But he wished now and then she'd say "honey" or "sugar" or "love."

God, he thought, listen to you whine. He could hear the whoosh and clank of the presses, the shift shutting down. Already the night crew was trickling in, getting coffee in the lounge. Down to about a half dozen now. They had a big museum catalog on the way, but the rest was wedding announcements and some posters. Last month the hospital had pulled its account. They could run their brochures off their own laser printers now; other info went on the hospital website. Sean's boss, Larry Dobson, had hired a new sales guy out of Boston, fresh-faced fellow named McMahon, but nothing had come of it yet.

Sean had the pink slips in his top drawer. Clearing his throat, he moved onto the floor. "Hey, Edson," he greeted the stripper. "Nice work on that fold."

"Yeah, it was a bitch," the stripper said. "We got that Duofold coming in?"

"Delayed. We're repricing. You seen Clyde?"

"He's in the can. Guy spends a lot of time there, know what I mean?"

Sean knew. Clyde was on something, meth maybe, made him hyper, jittery, a little aggressive. He was a good layout artist, but recently he'd gotten sloppy. Still, Sean figured, someone would have had to go. Four in the layout department didn't make sense anymore.

He hung around, waiting for Clyde to emerge, then saw Seymour, the color separator, packing up for the day. What the hell, Sean thought. Do Seymour first. "Hey, Sy," he said, ambling that way.

"Hey, Mr. O'Connor." That was Seymour: refusing to call a boss by his first name, whatever the other men did. All thirty-five years of Seymour's time at Central Printing, he'd called the floor heads "Mister," and he'd seen plenty of them, from two decades his senior to squirts like Sean. "How'd that christening party go?"

"Came off beautifully. That sun dance you did really worked."

"Tell me you gave 'em a song."

"I put the baby to sleep. Better than making him howl, I guess."

"That's a precious gift, that voice, Mr. O'Connor. I heard you folks sing that *Messiah*, three Christmases ago, with the symphony. Pretty stuff."

"Thanks, Sy. Hey, can I see you in my office a moment?"

That was all it took, really. It was like the Mafia, Sean thought, offering to take a guy for a ride. Sy was the only man on the Central team who'd heard Sean sing—along with a hundred other voices—and he never failed to bring it up. Now his face adjusted itself. Carefully he packed his thermos into his lunch box. "Sure, Mr. O'Connor. Give me just a sec."

In his office, Sean paced. He'd never smoked, but times like this, he wished he did. Anything to take the edge off. Sun still poured in the dusty window; the air conditioner hummed, but he was still sweating. At last the tap on the door. "Come on in."

Seymour was in his late sixties, Sean figured. Last year there had been a hip operation, this year cataracts. But he held himself erect, his slight shoulders squared and his sharp chin up, the thin lips pressed together. "Have a seat, Sy," Sean said, gesturing at the padded dinette chair that passed for seating in his office.

"I think I'll stand, Mr. O'Connor," Sy said evenly. He placed his lunch box on the edge of Sean's desk and folded his hands in front of him. "I'm sure what you've got to say won't take long."

His face reddening, hands sweating, Sean went through the drill. The computers were doing all the color separation work these days, Seymour knew that. This catalog coming in was the only fine-art four-color they were likely to get all year. They'd thought and thought about ways to rejigger the thing, but the fact was they had to start phasing some areas out, and Seymour was in one of those areas. Larry Dobson had put together the best package he could manage for valued employees like Seymour. Sean had the details right here.

Reaching for the manila folder he'd prepared, Sean's hands shook. Christ, he hated this. "I ever tell you," Sy finally interrupted, "about the place the wife and I bought, up there on Peaks Island?"

Sean set down the folder. "No, Sy. Didn't know you had a place."

Sy nodded. "Just outside Portland, Maine. Take the ferry there. We've been going up summers for, I don't know, maybe twenty years now. All my kids had their summer vacations there. Wife teaches grade school, you know."

"I did know that. Lucille?"

"That's her name, yes. Good memory, Mr. O'Connor. This past Christmas we decided to spend up there as well. Plenty cold. But the kids all came, and five grandkids. We squeezed in somehow, kept each other warm. And my wife, she said she thought she could get a job, there, in the Portland school system. And I might take to watercolor painting."

"That's a great plan, Seymour."

The separator smiled ruefully. "Tell you the truth, I'm not ready for it yet. I'll be restless. Plus I hoped to get more of a nest egg together. You know, for the grandkids. But you got a job to do, Mr. O'Connor. I don't envy you."

"Thanks, Sy." Handing over his packet of severance papers, Sean felt he was giving Seymour his death warrant. "You make this part easier."

"Yeah." Seymour shook his hand and turned to go. At the door he paused. "That's what guys like me and you do, isn't it?" he said thoughtfully. "Make things easier for the guys doing better than us."

He shut the door with a click. Sean felt socked in the stomach. But there was nothing to be done. He pressed his thumb and forefinger to the bridge of his nose. It was almost four. What had Brooke said about picking up Meghan? His phone buzzed: Larry Dobson. "Coming up," he said. Quickly he locked his office, crossed the half-empty press floor, and mounted the stairs to the small, quiet quarters where the money stuff happened. Larry's office lay at the end of the short hallway, his door open. The secretary and book-keeper were both gone. Sean's shoes made no sound on the tightly woven carpet. He tapped at the open door. "Larry?"

"Can't talk," his boss said, but it was Larry on his cell phone, standing at the window, looking over the parking lot toward Inter-state 84. "I know, I know, I know. Later. Hey, Sean," he said, turn-ing and flipping the phone closed. "I've got to run meet the girlfriend. Window treatments." He rolled his eyes.

"I feel for you."

"I mean, 'Do these blinds make me look fat?' What do they want?"

"I know a place just up the street—"

"Don't get me started." Larry waved away the subject. He was a well-groomed athletic type, almost exactly Sean's age, who'd taken over the business five years ago when his older brother died of can-cer. What he'd been up to before then, Sean didn't know, but he had the feeling Larry had spent most of a fancy education playing varsity golf. Larry was divorced, two kids. He hadn't wanted to hire the sales guy, McMahon. He thought his own strength lay in schmooz-ing the clients; he liked to remind Sean and others that Central Printing's name was on a Little League logo, the donors' wall at the Mark Twain House, and a brick on the new library plaza down-town. But business was falling and the competition gaining, so he'd ordered layoffs on the floor and brought in muscle at the top. "I just wanted to know if—you know." Larry tried to smile. The expression came out crooked on his tanned face. "If the parking lot's safe."

"No more dangerous than usual, boss. I talked to Seymour. He was ready for it. Clyde's probably waiting for me downstairs."

"Okay then." Larry nodded more times than necessary. He might have been considering how safe the parking lot would be for Sean, but if so, he set the concern aside. "You're the best I got, Sean."

"It's tough times."

"Take a day off when you need it, okay? Paid. I've got your back."

"Thanks," Sean said, though he and Larry both knew there was no day off to be taken. Even with less work, presses still broke down; last-minute changes still got called in. Minutes after he returned to the floor, he saw Larry trot down the stairs and out the side door, off to fetch window treatments. Sean moved among the night shift. He greeted Larry's cousin, Ernie, a new pressman who ran the shift with his head down, masticating his words. After checking a cache of inks, Sean returned to his office to find Clyde leaning against the door.

"Thanks for coming in," Sean began, unlocking it. "Sorry to keep you late."

Clyde was Brooke's age, about four years younger than Sean. Sean knew this fact only because when Clyde first came onto the floor, he tried to get to know him a little and found out he grew up in Windermere, the little town in western Pennsylvania where Brooke came from. Yeah, Clyde had said, he knew Brooke, they graduated the same year. But he didn't know her that well. It was a big regional high school, he said, and they didn't run with the same crowd.

The subject had not come up since. Sean thought of it now, as he flicked on the fluorescent light and moved behind his desk, only because Clyde looked so much older than Brooke. Meth, or whatever he was on, had dried and cracked his skin, so even with a full head of shaggy brown hair he looked like a preview of the old man he'd be. "Cut to the chase, man," Clyde said. His gaze darted around the office. "If it's about last Friday, I can explain."

"It's not about Friday."

"Okay. Shit. I'm sitting down. Mind?"

"Please." Sean motioned to the dinette chair. As soon as he sat, Clyde began picking at a bit of loose vinyl. "How are things on the floor?"

Clyde narrowed his eyes. He studied Sean. Though he was a much bigger guy than Sean, he looked thin in the arms. Sean wasn't in the best shape of his life, but he worked out twice a week. What was he thinking? A new shift was coming on. This guy wasn't going to tackle him. "What's this about?" Clyde asked.

Sean sighed. He looked down at the floor. "Can't be news to you," he said, "that business isn't great."

"Oh shit. Shit!" Clyde was on his feet. He kicked the dinette chair into the corner, the hollow metal legs clattering. Sean felt his stomach clench. "I knew it," Clyde said, not looking at him. "I fucking knew I was going to get canned today. I shouldn't of come in. Fuck."

"Clyde, it wouldn't have mattered if you'd called in sick—"

"You planned it, didn't you?" Clyde turned back to the desk, where he planted his fists and leaned on them. "You and stick-up-his-ass Larry."

"Clyde, I'm not in charge of staffing or layoffs. You know that. Larry gets together with the accountants and I get my orders."

"So you're just doing your job."

Sean reminded himself to breathe. "That's right."

"Heil Hitler!" Clyde put an index finger under his nose and shot out the other arm in a Nazi salute. "But the commandant isn't getting rid of *you*, is he?"

"Not yet." Sean had known this would be difficult. Counting

Seymour and now Clyde, he'd had to lay off eight guys in the past nine months. He'd seen one man go down on his knees, and another bolt out the door and disappear, to collect his paperwork by mail. He knew Clyde would be one of the thornier ones. Yet as far as he knew, the guy didn't have a wife or kids, and he was young enough to shift fields. Sean couldn't waste too much pity on a guy who did whatever Clyde did in the bathroom three times a day. "We're all vulnerable," he added.

"Oh yeah, right," Clyde said. He rolled his eyes. "You got your very own blond shield," he went on, "so I guess you can talk for now."

"What's that supposed to mean?" Sean wanted to stand up. Clyde was leaning over him, threatening authority with size. But a confrontation wasn't going to move this along.

Ostentatiously Clyde shrugged. He pushed away from Sean's desk. "You're hitched to a member of the ruling class, man," he said. "Don't forget, I've seen how that works."

"Are you talking about my wife?" Sean did stand now. He went to check through the window. The shift was getting into place. Time to finish up, not get distracted by this loser's insults. "This is not personal, Clyde. Let's not bring in personal stuff."

"I know Brooke, remember?" Clyde said. "Shit, I tried to date her once. Mostly for my old man's sake. Not that she wasn't hot. But when you see what a little influence can do—"

"You're blowing steam. Brooke hasn't even got family in Connecticut."

"When they say the apple doesn't fall far, they don't mean mileage. This guy she used to be with?"

"You mean in Windermere? Long ago and far away, Clyde."

"You should of seen how his dad made out. You know her family ran the quarry, biggest deal in town—"

"Brooke's father is dead. Okay?" Sean returned to his desk.

Holding out the manila folder, his hand shook. *This guy she used to be with.* "And I was part of this outfit before I even met her."

"I'm saying she knows how the system works, right?" Clyde smiled strategically. "Easier to go up the ladder with a boost. This guy Alex, he probably thought the same."

"There's no Alex here. Look, Clyde, take this package. If you have any questions—"

"But you know, she iced him anyhow. They were like the perfect couple. I mean, they were *tight*." Clyde pressed his fists together. "Then boom." The fists flew apart. "After graduation she just breaks up with the guy. Like that. Heart of ice. And Alex was like the soccer star and everything, but he just took off. And his dad—well, you don't want to know."

Larry Dobson was on the interstate by now. Sean could move to the phone and call the local cops, or he could wait Clyde out. Easier to give the guy his hot air for a minute. "What's this got to do with you, Clyde?" he asked mildly, setting the manila folder on the edge of the desk for Clyde to take. "Or with me?"

"I'm just saying." Clyde's eyes prowled back and forth. "If I could of had her, I would of. Fuck the consequences. But you don't want to depend on the influence. She drops people, you know?" He pressed thumb and forefinger together, then released them, as if releasing a tiny, clinging hand. "People kill themselves over shit like that."

He was jacked up, Sean reminded himself. Getting his digs in. Nothing more. "You don't know my family," Sean said. "Now it's time for you to go."

"This guy Alex, I'm telling you. His dad—you know, she looks good, but—"

Sean had opened the door. He pressed his lips together. Clyde's voice trailed off. Sean did not look at him. Finally Clyde picked up his folder and marched out through the shop, flipping the bird as he went, whistling a tune that was quickly lost in the hiss of the presses.

To his surprise, as he shut the door and straightened the dinette chair, Sean found himself in a cold sweat. He sank into his own chair behind the desk; tipped it back; shut his eyes. It was awful, this fucking economy, but he couldn't be sorry Clyde was gone. He couldn't remember hiring the guy, except that he'd had some experience and there was the weird coincidence of his knowing Brooke. Now Clyde had done this sad, sick thing, dredging the muddy hole of his brain for something he could use to hurt Sean on his way out. He was going to have to ask Brooke about this coffee thing; he'd have static electricity in his brain until he did. Christ, he should have opened the door and booted the guy as soon as Brooke's name passed his lips. But there was Larry, always quaking in his wingtips about lawsuits, so Sean tried to ease people out, listen to them, take some of their shit.

He should go. Meghan would be done with her class, waiting for her daddy. He'd take her for ice cream; they'd sit at the picnic table outside the creamery, licking their cones, and she'd tell him all the travails of summer camp. But he stayed in the chair, his eyes shut. He'd never heard about this Alex guy before. He'd met Brooke when he and Gerry and Danny went on a half-assed camping trip in the Adirondacks, nine years ago, the weekend before Gerry got hitched. There was a big nursery right by the first campsite, and he'd gone there to ask about trees—Kate had grown up by an orchard, and Sean had this idea of giving the newlyweds an apple tree for a wedding present. There had been Brooke, an angel in denim and straw hat. She'd talked him out of the apple and into a lemon that they could grow indoors in the condo. She'd ended up coming back to the campsite with a map, to show them all the best trails. The next day he'd let Gerry and Danny tackle Old Man Peak alone and taken Brooke out to lunch. She was so calm, he remembered, not like his family with all their loves and hates bubbling over like water in a pot. Her smile had an edge of sadness that he took for wisdom, especially when he learned that she hadn't gone to some fancy university but only the local community college, so what felt like braininess had to be something else. After the wedding he'd come back for a week, staying in the tent by himself until he talked her into bringing him back to her place, a cheap duplex where she lived alone. There wasn't any guy named Alex then; she'd never mentioned such a guy. They'd talked about old flames. Hers had been in high school mostly. He'd gotten pretty serious about one of the altos in the chorale, but that had ended six months earlier. The only thing that had ever made him suspicious was the simple fact that this elegant, lovely, smart, kind woman could give a shit about a run-of-the-mill guy like him.

They'd gone hiking, just the two of them, that week when he came back. On an overlook, he'd launched into "Lonesome Valley," and she'd said she had never heard such a sweet voice. Later she told him that was the moment she fell in love with him. She said the music lit him like a flame. He believed her. That was how he felt, when he let his voice go—like a flame rose up inside him. But maybe a flame like that flickered out, for a woman like Brooke. Once upon a time she thought this Alex was all lit up, too. Christ, why'd he let a loser like Clyde get inside his head?

Sean's cell phone rang. *Brooke.* Grabbing his keys, he hauled himself out of the chair and left the office. "I'm on my way to get Meghan," he said when he finally answered. He stood in the bright sunshine outside the building. "I got held up at work. I should be there on time."

"I know you will," she said. "I just wanted to say hi."

"Well, hi." He unlocked his car, an old black Beetle the guys at work teased him about. The parking lot was clear, Clyde's car gone. "How's your—your date going?"

"I'm back at work. It was nice to catch up, though. Meghan says she doesn't like ballet anymore." Brooke sighed. As he started the rasping engine, Sean strained for something in his wife's voice that would either put some legs on his uneasy feelings or dispel them. "I told her she has to stick it out."

"Right." Sean kept the phone to his ear as he pulled onto Homestead Avenue. Brooke didn't usually call during the day, especially not during the nursery's high season. Only she'd been with this friend, and was changed.

"When I get home," Brooke said, "let's talk. Okay?"

"CD Pyg," Sean said, knowing she'd like it. He tucked the phone away. His heart was racing. Fear, or hope? Either way, a drink would sure help. But he shook off that desire, along with the day's ugly confrontation, and went to fetch his daughter.

Chapter 3

Everyone at the nursery agreed: Lorenzo had a complete crush on Brooke O'Connor. Given what Brooke had managed, no one blamed him. He never acted on it; he just stood by the window in the flower shop, watching her mulch and prune, water and spritz. Brooke was what you called a treasure. If she hadn't accepted Lorenzo's lousy minimum-wage offer seven years ago, the nursery would have gone under by now. As it was, they had a half dozen commercial accounts. And the ladies from Simsbury couldn't get enough of Brooke's advice, Brooke's landscaping skills, Brooke's garden with the elderflower iced tea she made from the plot of herbs she tended behind the potting shed.

Aside from her gardening skills, the dozen employees at Lorenzo's knew only two things, really, about Brooke, and they were the same things they came to know within days of meeting her. She was pretty, and she was kind. When they asked her if she grew up in Hartford, she shook her head and said, "But I've been here a while." When they asked if she'd studied horticulture, she said, "It's just something I fell into." When talk turned to politics or current events, she used worn phrases like, "It's a shame" or "What can you do?" As Rob, the guy who oversaw the commercial accounts said, you would think her stupid if you hadn't seen what a genius she was. This description was passed on to Brooke by Shanita Brown, who worked in the garden shop and was closer to her than anyone else at Lorenzo's.

"Which is not," Shanita had added just a few days ago, "saying much."

"You know everything about me worth knowing, Shanita," Brooke had said, and flashed her a smile.

"Uh-huh." Shanita was clipping away at the box hedge around the perennials. Tiny and fierce, her dreadlocks pulled back in a scarf and her skin turned dark coffee by midsummer, she had started at Lorenzo's when she came out of rehab and her two kids were in foster care. That was four years ago. After a year, Brooke had persuaded Lorenzo to let the kids play in the garden after day care, and Shanita had come full time. She still had boyfriend problems, but she was on birth control and sticking to it. "One thing you do learn from hustling," Shanita said, her clippers fast as hummingbirds, "is how to read people. The folks that are hiding something? You don't push them. You let them come to you." She dropped her right arm and straightened. She wiped a hand across her sweating brow. "Far as anyone round here knows," she said, gesturing to the five acres of Lorenzo's south Hartford estate, "Brooke O'Connor got no past before she walked in here first time. I know different, and you know I know different. One of these days, when you need to, you going to trust me with it."

"You bet I am. How's Dillon's arm?"

"Oh, he broke it right enough. Damn fool, climbing trees." Shanita went back to clipping. Brooke's muscles relaxed. Shanita had seen most of the underbelly of human nature. Nothing Brooke could tell her would cut the tie forged when Brooke found a way to bring her kids to Lorenzo's. But what was the point of sharing old sins that made no difference now? Sometimes Brooke thought fondly of the woman she might have become—sprightly and funny and smart, oh so smart, with as many kids as she wanted—as if that woman were someone she'd known and hoped wistfully to meet again. Meanwhile the weight of her past kept her steady, moving forward, glad for the light of each day that brought no retribution for what was five years past; then ten; then fifteen. Only recently, with Sean begging incessantly for a second child, had she felt each step like a sinking into quicksand.

Today, though, she thought maybe she'd found a solution. Late in the morning she was cleaning up the last of the damage done to Lorenzo's Garden while Shanita's kids tumbled around the climbing structure. Suddenly there were a couple of new kids, giggling as they swooped down the slide. "Are they okay here for a sec?" a woman asked as Brooke turned away from the dahlias.

"So long as they don't leave this area," Brooke said. She glanced at the children—Asian girls, both of them, looking like twins but also looking nothing like their freckled mother. "Sweet," she said.

"Aren't they? We planned to adopt just one, but these two were inseparable, even as toddlers."

"Aren't they sisters?"

The woman smiled. "Now they are," she said. "I'll be just a sec."

Brooke loved children. She loved Meghan past all reason. When Sean asked if she didn't want a second child, if she didn't want to jump on that merry-go-round again, she felt her capacity for love like an ache. But she dreaded giving birth. She could not explain to Sean why the idea terrified her. Every time she thought of another pregnancy, she felt a tornado moving straight at her, fast and relentless.

Sometimes she had to watch her breathing, to stave off what might be seen as a panic attack. She ought to see someone about it, she counseled herself, and by "someone" she knew she meant a shrink. But she couldn't see a shrink. Shrinks were like the gardeners of history. They delved into your past with words as their spades. So tell me, the shrinks would say—raking, digging—why you're meeting this man today? Alex? Any connection to these thoughts of pregnancy?

Get out of my garden, she would tell them.

Finishing up her task, she kept half an eye on the girls, who were quickly bossing Dillon and his brother, Charles. Shooing away the invisible shrinks, she thought: Adoption. Of *course*. Plenty of people adopted. They didn't even have to look as far as China. There were babies in Central America looking for a home, babies in eastern Europe. Sean's family had its share of bigots, but Sean wasn't among them. It would make sense to anyone who asked. Brooke had had trouble with her first pregnancy; people would understand that she had reason to be concerned.

But this man you're meeting, the shrinks would begin. Shoo, she would tell them.

"The other day," she said to Shanita over lunch, "I was picking up Meghan, right? And this Jewish dad picked up his daughter who looked—I don't know, Mayan or something. Straight hair, black eyes. He scooped her into a bear hug. She was his daughter, plain and simple. Shanita?"

She snapped her fingers in front of her friend's glazed eyes. Shanita's head jerked up. "That's my name."

"What do you think?"

"About what?"

"Adoption."

Shanita gave her a long look. "You mean like Madonna, swooping down on Africa to get her toys?" she said at last. "I think that is disgusting."

"No, I mean normal adoption. Like of a Chinese girl, or—or I don't know, a baby needing a family. You think parents feel the same way toward their adopted kids?"

"Brooke, baby, you asking the wrong person. Fought tooth and nail to *keep* my kids from being adopted. Why you ask?"

"I'm thinking about it. How it might work. For Sean and me."

Shanita packed up her sandwich. Her face had darkened to pitch. She leaned across the table and repeated, "You're thinking about it."

"Sure. Lots of people make a family that way, Shanita."

"You thinking up *here*." Shanita pressed her finger suddenly into Brooke's temple. Brooke's eyes teared up with shock. "But ain't nothing happening *here*." She removed the finger and grabbed at Brooke's rib cage, just under her left breast. Brooke pulled away. A fat tear rolled, uninvited, down her cheek. She felt the imprint of Shanita's hand on her heart.

"What are you doing?" she gasped.

"You got any idea what is involved in bringing up a child that got someone else's genes? Someone else's moodiness or asthma or I don't know what all?"

"I'm sure it's not the same. But it's still wonderful." Brooke dabbed at her eyes. "Or it . . . it can be."

"That decision lies at the top of a *mountain*. I mean, if you are not planning to be like Madonna."

"Who said anything about Madonna? Those girls who were just here—"

Shanita cut her off by grabbing her wrist. Her eyes smoldered. "I owe you a lot, Brooke," she said in a low voice. "And most of all I owe you this little nugget. You cannot solve a problem in here"—she pressed Brooke's trembling hand to her own neatly rounded breast—"with the tools you got up here." She pulled the hand up to her temple.

Then Shanita let her go. She stood and tossed her crumpled bag across the back patio into the wire bin, a perfect swish. Turning back to Brooke, she said, "And I don't care how good those tools are. Might as well try to fix a car engine with a dentist drill." Brushing crumbs from her T-shirt, she walked away, muttering, "*Adoption. Shit.*"

Brooke felt rattled. For the rest of the afternoon, she stayed clear of her friend. At three she checked in with Lorenzo, who was doing inventory on a shipment of baby chrysanthemums. "I'm ducking out in a minute," she said, "to take Meghan to dance class. Then I've got—well, some errands. Back in a couple hours."

"Thought your hubby did all that," said Lorenzo, winking at her. Lorenzo's winks didn't mean anything. They were his way of bridging the divide between boss and employee, of staking a claim to intimacy with Brooke. Lorenzo was close to seventy, by Brooke's estimate—a short, dapper man with a white mustache and a permanent tan, pale only in the spray of crow's feet around his dark eyes. He was a widower of sorts. The year Brooke arrived, his partner Angelo had died of AIDS and he wore a mask of suffering. Customers at the nursery claimed Brooke had brought him back to life, but she brushed such comments off.

"Sean's got some stuff at work," she said now. "And Meghan's angling to quit her lessons. I don't want her twisting him round her finger."

"Tough love, baby," Shanita called from where she was picking at leaves, checking for bugs. "Only way to go."

"You'll be back, though, right?" Lorenzo asked. He stepped over to where Brooke was gathering her pocketbook. "I was thinking we could talk about your hours. Maybe shift you to take charge of the new location this fall. Get it all set up to open early spring."

Brooke's eyes widened. However much responsibility Lorenzo had slowly given her over the years, the Simsbury location was his darling. For the past year he had talked about nothing but how eager he was to lord it over his newly acquired suburban kingdom. He loved putting on his Italian charm whenever one of these country-club women came into the nursery; he wanted nothing more than to dwell among them and hear them laugh at his jokes. "You mean just for a week or two?" she asked.

Lorenzo shrugged. "You understand that clientele," he said, winking again. "You're my best girl. Can't keep you locked up on Park Street. And I am not going to be around forever. "

"Of course you are." Brooke tried winking back, though it felt more like a tic than a wink. Lorenzo's hair, Brooke noticed, looked thinner; the sun shone through the frosty strands onto his leathery scalp. Perhaps he was ill. She wanted to touch his arm, remind him in some corny way of how they were all a family, here at the nursery he'd built. But he held himself apart, in his courtly way. So she didn't ask what was wrong, why he was giving her the new location he'd dreamed of for himself. Instead she pressed him a bit, as if probing for his backbone. "Well, if I set up the Simsbury branch," she said, "I'll need Shanita to help me."

Lorenzo shook his head and waved a hand in the air. "You girls figure it out," he said. "Now go on, run your errands. I need staffing for spring, that's all I know."

Brooke cut through the West End to the grade school near Elizabeth Park. In the semicircle of waiting cars, she found herself paying attention to the complexion and hair of the kids getting picked up. She stepped out of the car into the sunshine. There was another Asian girl, her blond mother waiting with an infant strapped to her back whose features Brooke couldn't make out. Shanita, she thought, could talk all she liked about what she felt and didn't feel. Shanita didn't know what happened when Brooke thought about giving birth again.

She had Meghan, she reminded herself. Nothing bad was going to happen to Meghan. But Sean wanted another. Her family—just hers, no one else's—needed another. And they could have a child without triggering the fears that rose like a tsunami from Brooke's past and washed her away. She studied the children jumping into their mothers' arms, the ones whose features didn't match but whose expressions did. Shanita's case had been different, she told herself. It had been about foster homes, older kids who needed their birth mom. Her advice didn't extend to Brooke's case. It couldn't.

"Looks like you're not sure which one's yours," said the man standing by the Mazda next to her car.

Brooke blushed. "Oh, she'll make herself known when she comes out. I don't worry about that."

The man stepped out of his car and stretched. He was an inch or two taller than Brooke, and not much older; gray hair was just making its appearance at his temples. The shorts he wore revealed the muscled calves of a soccer player. "Quite a rain last night," he said.

"Broke the humidity, I guess."

"True enough. Not so great for my business, though." He squinted at the sky.

"And what business would that be? Air conditioning?"

"Pools." He extended his hand. "Tad Horgan. Jason's dad. I think our kids are in the same group here."

Tad's handshake was warm and firm. Brooke hadn't noticed him before, but her circle of fellow parents was confined to the ones whose daughters played with hers. "If you say so," she said. "Meghan's still at the boys-have-cooties stage."

"And Jason definitely has cooties. Got them from me, I'm afraid."

"I doubt that." He was flirting with her, Brooke thought. She glanced at her watch. She was due at Starbucks in a half hour. "How did you know Meghan's in his group?"

"Jason is not at the girls-have-cooties stage. Causes him some problems with the other boys. But I think he likes your daughter. Your clone, I should say." He winked. "Didn't take rocket science to figure who you were, but I still don't know your name."

"Oh, I'm sorry. Brooke O'Connor." She wanted to steer the subject away from kids before they got to the "How many others?" question. "So, pools," she said. "Backyard pools? Country-club pools?"

"Just those kidney-bean things. I run a little franchise out in Manchester."

"You're not a swimmer, though."

"A shower's about as much water as I need, personally. How'd you know?"

Brooke cracked a smile. "An old boyfriend was a soccer player. He had your legs."

"I'll be damned." Tad looked down at his calves. "Wonder how he's managing without them."

Brooke chuckled. "I'm meeting him for coffee. I'll ask."

"Ah." Tad's eyebrows lifted.

"Not like that. Old times. You know."

"If you say so. Anyhow, you're right. I kick the ball around, most Saturdays. Buncha Jamaican guys and two palefaces. Look, here they come."

From the quartet of bright blue doors at the entrance to the school the kids poured out, bearing their kites and lanyards and still-sticky collages. A towheaded boy in a Spider-Man T-shirt flung himself against Tad's car and got in without a word. "Well, hello to you too," Tad said. He turned to Brooke. "See you here again."

"Not often. My husband's usually the pickup guy."

"Have I—?" Tad paused, his hand on his chin. Then he opened his door. "Of course!" he said. "Sean O'Connor. Don't know why I didn't put it together, Meghan gets into his car. *Duh.*" He pulled a goofy face. "I guess I had a mental image," he said, "and I—"

And you didn't figure I'd be with him, Brooke finished silently. She saw Meghan at the blue door and waved. "So you know Sean."

"He prints our pool brochures. I don't know, maybe I thought you were divorced, I don't know."

"Sean'll be back tomorrow. Hi, Bug," Brooke said to Meghan, who was dragging her bag of artwork. Recently she had been focused on kittens—kitten pictures, collages of kitten photos from magazines, a fluffy kitten resembling a sheep, made of glued cotton balls stuck to cardboard.

Meghan glanced at the boy in Tad's car. "Mommy," she hissed, her eyes darting back and forth.

The adults exchanged smiles. "You got a cute clone there, Mrs. O'Connor," Tad said.

"She gets it all from her dad," Brooke retorted, shutting down the flirtation. When the Mazda had driven off, she tucked herself into the car and nodded at Meghan to do her belt. "You took your time," she said.

"Mommy, that boy Jason is *smelly.*"

"Really? I didn't smell him. How was your day?"

"I don't want to go to dance class. I hate dance class."

"That was your day? Hating dance class?"

"Mommy." Meghan emitted a great, grown-up sigh as they exited the parking lot and headed toward the dance studio. Did Brooke

sigh like that? She glanced sidelong at her daughter. Tad Horgan
had called her Brooke's clone, but Brooke had looked different as a
child—paler, longer in the face, with a bumpy nose she was glad not
to have passed on to Meghan. It wasn't as if, were they to adopt,
there would be one who matched and one who didn't. Would there?

A half hour later she found a parking spot right outside Starbucks.
"Here goes," she said softly to herself. All day, she had been not-
thinking about this encounter. She had not-thought about it while
she set up the chrysanthemum display, she had not-thought about it
while she'd argued with Shanita, she had silenced the shrinks, she
had not-thought during the exchange with Tad Horgan. No, that
wasn't true. On no other day would she have told a man she'd just
met that his legs looked like a soccer player's. Unable to resist, she
pulled down the visor and flipped open the little mirror. Deliberately,
she had left no time to change clothes or put on makeup. If he wanted
to see her, he'd have to see her as she was—grimy, disheveled, no hiding the crow's feet. She pulled away the elastic holding her ponytail,
finger-combed her hair, and shook it loose. There. That would do.

Inside, she blinked in the sudden dimness before she made out
his posture, the familiar tilt of the head, shoulders back, knees
akimbo. "Alex," she said as she wove her way around the espresso
line.

He stood. His hair was shorter, still dark, the same cowlick over
his left eyebrow. As he stepped around the tiny table for a hug, he
seemed both heavier and smaller than she remembered—only a couple of inches over her own height, and heavier not from weight gain
but as if gravity pulled on him more. "You really came," he said. He
put his arms around her in a hug made clumsier by the chair-
cluttered space. Quickly she pulled away, sat.

"Was I late?"

"No! I just—all those years, you wouldn't see me. So I was ready to be stood up. Can I get you something?"

"No, no. Just sit."

"And let you sip at mine?" He grinned slyly at her. Here came the past, trailing anecdotes. She never used to order fries or dessert, but would pick at his shamelessly until it became their joke.

"I see you got a venti," she said lightly, "so I figured you were ready to share."

He sat. What was so different about his face? "Glasses," she said. "You never wore those."

He took off the wire-rims. "Six years now. I have astigmatism. Doctor in Japan nailed it, my first year there."

"And now you're back."

He nodded. "For now, yeah," he said. Brooke felt as if she could hear her own voice, could hear Alex, and all the voices around them in the Starbucks—and he was only two feet from her, this well-dressed, muscular man who held an entire past world inside him, like one of those Christmas globes—but she wanted it all to slow way down, until she understood what was going on. Pay attention, she ordered herself. "They offered a transfer to Boston," Alex was saying, "and I'd gotten divorced, and I thought maybe I heard my own country calling to me for a change."

"Divorced," said Brooke. "Wow." She took a sip of Alex's latte. It was lukewarm; he had been here a little while. "I hadn't known you were married."

"Six years."

Quickly she did the calculation. Like her, Alex was thirty-three. She knew he had gone to the Far East after college; from her mother she'd heard he was back in the States, at Stanford, for an MBA. But after seven years of Brooke's saying, "I don't want to know," her mother had stopped reporting on Alex Frazier's whereabouts. So he must have met his wife in business school and then gone away again, to Japan. And lived there, thinking it would be forever. Alex waved a hand in front of her face. "Sorry," she said. She had been staring at him, her mouth hanging open like the village idiot. "I just—we're getting so old."

"Are we?"

"Feels that way. Sean and I've been married for seven years. We have a daughter."

"Yes, I heard her in the background when I called. Meghan, right?"

"Yeah." She stole another sip of his coffee. She wanted her own cup, now, but she didn't want to stay long, to let the conversation range too far. Then she heard herself say, "Sean wants us to have another."

"And you don't."

"I—can't."

"Hmm." He expelled a breath of surprise. "Can't? Or won't?"

"Won't, can't. You know."

Did he know? She watched him run his hand over his cheeks and chin. He had shaved close, and she recalled his thick stubble. His neck was darkly tanned; soccer, still? "I hadn't thought," he said slowly, "I could bear having even one."

"But then you did?" Surprise struck her like a slap. But why shouldn't he have had a child? Of course.

He nodded. "Dylan," he said. "Had heart problems from the start. He died just after his second birthday."

"Oh, Lex, I am so sorry."

He shrugged. "Apparently a majority of marriages end in divorce after a child dies."

"That's why you're here. In the States, I mean."

"No. Maybe." When he frowned, his mouth looked exactly as it had fifteen years ago. A son, Brooke thought. Like her, he had gone on, and he had fathered a son, and now the son was gone. "Once Tomiko and I broke up," he said, "it felt like I was just running away."

"It didn't feel that way before?"

"No, Brooke. It didn't." There was the old harshness to his voice, the same she'd heard the last time they met face to face, when he came back from Boston University and she'd moved out, had moved to the Adirondacks and was living alone, and she'd come to his dad's funeral and heard his last plea. "Look, I really did have business, here, in Hartford, I mean."

"I guess so. Look at your threads." She indicated the loosened tie, the tailored shirt. How funny the two of them must appear, the gardener and the businessman.

"We've got a small branch office here. HR wants to close it. So much happens over the Internet, now. But I said I'd have a look, see what their foot traffic's like."

"And?"

He scratched his head. "We really ought to close it."

She eyed his watch. Just shy of five. "And I really ought to get back."

"I don't think I'll recommend closing it just yet, though."

"Why not?"

He gazed steadily at her. Heat rose into her face. On the phone Alex had been lighthearted, just passing through, operating on a hunch that she was still at the address her mom had mentioned on an old Christmas card. Surely, she had thought, a decade and a half was long enough. "I'd like to see you from time to time," he said at last. "If that's okay. I'm not going to, you know, invade your life or anything. But you've been in my head since I moved back." He shifted his gaze to the coffee cup, which she had drained. An ironic smile played on his mouth. "I'd like the connection, Brooke."

"Well, that's fine," she said. Her tongue felt dry. "And you could meet Sean at some point. And Meghan."

"Sure," he said, nodding.

Though he wouldn't do that for a while, Brooke thought as she drove back to Lorenzo's. She wouldn't ask him to. Not only that. She wasn't going to tell Sean whom she'd met, or why. Once she started, there would be no stopping, not with Sean so watchful of her these days, so eager to know why she wouldn't go off the Pill, what was up with her.

When she had rolled into the familiar gravel lot at Lorenzo's and turned off the ignition, she fished out her cell phone. Her heart, where Shanita had pressed her hand, felt swollen. Think, she told herself. Whatever Shanita said, it was better to lift away from the heart, into the head, where you could think.

"When I get home," she said to Sean after they'd discussed their mercurial daughter, "let's talk. Okay?"

Chapter 4

The sky over Hartford was the deep blue of summer evening as Alex emerged from Max Oyster Bar. It had been an awkward business dinner. Restructuring, they called it, and Alex knew when he accepted the transfer from Mercator Investments that he would be the fall guy for a number of these closings in the Northeast. The guys who had taken Alex to dinner couched their desperation in grim jokes. A bear market was an eighteen-month period when your wife got no jewelry and you got no sex. Well, no one would lower the boom on the Hartford office right away. They were too close to all the insurance companies the town boasted, with their own financial network. Alex would recommend a half dozen staff cuts and a performance review of the guy who'd downed three vodka tonics. From here he'd go to Albany and repeat the drill. For now he needed to stretch his legs. He left his car in the lot and walked west.

Maybe, he thought as he headed toward the lowering sun, Brooke had married an insurance guy. He should have asked. So much of her life he couldn't know. What did he want from her?

Friendship, he told himself. He'd lost track, after all, of the others they'd known from those days. It wasn't as if they had done each other any wrong, however Brooke had reacted in those years. She seemed fine, now. Maybe, if he made enough trips to Hartford over the months, if they shared more lattes—he smiled as he thought of her sipping at his; old habits die hard—he would find a way to tell her the truth. What he'd done, those years ago. What had happened to the baby, what he had done with his own hands.

That old adage, the truth will set you free. A few well-dressed strangers hurried past him on their way to the train station. Were they free? You couldn't tell. Who would have claimed, two years ago, watching Alex stride into Shinjo Station on his way to the Tokyo office of Mercator Investments, that he was bound up in the chains of a lie? It wasn't as though he had felt the lie pressing on him, year upon year. He had gone on—with his job, with Tomiko, with Dylan. If he hadn't seen Brooke this afternoon, he might not have thought of that long-ago night for months, or years.

Long shadows fell across the street in the slow August twilight. If he walked far enough, Alex thought, and then drove the two hours back to Boston, he might get a night's sleep for a change. With Tomiko's hands massaging him, he used to nod off in less than a minute. But he would never feel those hands again. He had spoken to her the day he left Japan. Good luck, she had said over the phone. He had not seen her for three months. He had not been naked with her for two years. Time got wobbly. How many weeks had it been since he landed at Logan, since he took the apartment, since he first keyed Brooke's number into his cell phone? Insomnia made you lose track.

He fingered the little ring box in his pants pocket. He had brought it to show Brooke, then backed off. He had not come here to bring her pain. She was still sensitive as a tuning fork, he thought.

If not for her mom, he never would have gotten her phone or address. Mrs. Willcox had always liked him, always been perplexed by the breakup, and always wished he would come back and knock some sense into Brooke. That feeling, he inferred, had not changed when Brooke decided to marry this Sean O'Connor from Hartford. Mrs. Willcox had sent Alex's parents the wedding announcement with a handwritten note in the margins to the effect that she'd have liked one name to be different. Alex's mother had sent the announcement to Alex in California. He'd tucked it away with old mementos, and taken the job with Mercator far away, in Tokyo.

He walked by the train station and up the hill past the Hartford Insurance Company. Traffic was thin. Not much of a night scene in Hartford. Lit along the street as he walked westward were stones with plaques bearing lines by the poet Wallace Stevens. Must have been from Hartford, he surmised. Had Brooke read this fellow, back in the day? *I was of three minds / Like a tree / On which there are three blackbirds*, read one plaque. Another: *A man and a woman / Are one. / A man and a woman and a blackbird / Are one.* Alex squatted and read the words; read them again. Brooke would know what these things meant. She would know why the guy was writing about blackbirds, what it meant to say a man and a woman and a blackbird could be one. For the moment, it freaked him out, as if the poet's lines were speaking to him in a code he couldn't decipher. *I was of three minds.* A nervous shudder went through his body.

The city fell away behind him. He realized he was hearing August crickets. Under a streetlamp he consulted his BlackBerry and turned left just before a park to find himself in a neighborhood of shade trees and modest Victorian houses—densely packed, but otherwise not unlike the Windermere neighborhood Brooke had grown up in. As a couple headed his way on the sidewalk, their golden retriever pulling on a leash, he caught his breath. It had not occurred to him that he might bump into her, with her husband, out for a stroll on a summer evening. But no—they were older, the woman shorter, laughing at something the man had just said with a laugh that bore no resemblance to Brooke's. They greeted him and moved on. Still, he began to move more stealthily. He wished he'd worn a baseball cap. If she saw him here, after their innocuous rendezvous, she would never meet him again. But it came to him that this was where he'd been headed since he left the restaurant. To see where Brooke lived, the life she'd made for herself. He would just have a peek, then he would walk back to the car—the August air, still warm but with a hint of fall's tang, was clearing his head already—and drive the hundred miles to Boston.

There it was, number nineteen, just a few houses in from the next main street, where cars still rumbled by. The house was plainer than the others Alex had passed, built probably in the 1950s rather than the 1890s. Lights were on downstairs, the blinds drawn. An ugly chain-link fence surrounded the narrow property, though down the center walkway a riot of late-summer lilies rose into the light cast by the streetlamp, their petals closed against the summer night like demure skirts. As Alex stood at the corner post, a pair of dogs bounded over, while from the back a third sent up a bark. Alex shrank back into the shadow of a large oak tree. His heart hammered. From the back of the house he heard a little girl's voice. "Bitsy! Mocha! Lex!" she trilled. The largest of the dogs, a mutt with a Lab snout and basset ears, gave a last, disgruntled bark and trotted after his companions. Alex heard a screen door slam shut.

His neck was damp with sweat. *Lex.* Ruefully he wondered: Which dog had his name? The big ugly one or the little yappy terrier? He waited a moment, then slipped along the side of the fence, toward the back of the house. The blinds were drawn everywhere except the kitchen, where he saw only the child trotting through, a slight girl with reddish hair. Light from the second floor shone over the backyard. In its center was a small climbing structure and a sandbox. By the back fence, another garden. A trellis at the back porch supported a climbing vine rich with white blooms, open in the night. Moonflower, Alex remembered. Nostalgia muffled his agitation. He knew next to nothing about plants. But there had been a wall of moonflower mixed with morning glory by Brooke's front porch, back in Windermere. He remembered sitting out there with her on August nights, the air already chilling at sunset. He shut his eyes, now, and drew in a deep breath. Yes, it was the same scent, a haunting mix of lemon and musk that made him think of nothing but Brooke, of her hair and her mouth and her breasts, Brooke on the porch in Windermere.

He sank to the ground. He hadn't come looking for this sensation. It came at him on all cylinders, pressing him down. This errand was not about Brooke, he wanted to say to himself, not about Brooke and him. He was only renewing old acquaintance, settling into his new life, his American skin. But the scent of the moonflower plastered his tongue to the floor of his mouth.

The last time he had sat with her on that porch, the sun had been rising—the moonflowers were closing up, the morning glory beginning to unfurl. They had been out all night at a graduation party. She had seemed all right at the party; she had seemed happy and relieved and in love with Alex. There had been that canvas lounge chair, on her porch, and he had leaned back in it with Brooke tucked between his legs, her head on his chest where he could stroke her hair and let his hands wander down to her breasts. They had talked about the party—about his buddy Jake and Jake's girlfriend, Karen, whom neither of them liked. But Jake would marry Karen anyway, Brooke had said, not because Karen had big tits or because Jake was blind to Karen's meanness, but because the world after high school was going to scare Jake too much. Brooke turned out to be right; she was usually right, when it came to their friends. In other things, she was the fanciful dreamer and Alex the hardheaded realist. "Idealist," she used to correct him. Everything for him was black-and-white, while for her it was all shades of gray.

"Shades of pink, more," he would tease her.

"Pink's too ordinary," she would say. "Mauve. Taupe. Dusty rose. Umm-ber."

That night on the porch, though, with shades of dawn lightening the horizon, Brooke told him she had buried her dream. She was not going to Boston, which she and Alex had planned to discover together, he at Boston University and she at Tufts. She was not going to college at all. She was not going anywhere. Her fingers had stroked his thighs gently, he remembered, as she gave him this absurd news.

"Is it because of us?" he asked. "Is it because of what happened?"

She had shrugged. "I just think my days of magical thinking are over. No more witches for me, no more knights in armor, no more grails."

"College isn't a grail."

"It's not anything for me. Not anymore. I already told my parents. I want to work with my hands for a while. See if I can't"—she sat up and clasped her hands together, as if she'd caught a firefly in them—"connect with something."

"You connect with me." He had started to get angry, but already, he could tell, she wasn't there to receive the brunt of it. Physically, yes—she was there in his lap, on the porch, by the moonflowers— but her emotional self had flown off somewhere, out of his reach. "We were going to connect in Boston together, damn it, Brooke! I turned down Bucknell, remember? For BU? Just so we could be in the same city?"

She shook her head. "It's too late, Alex."

"Are you saying you don't want to be with me anymore? Are you breaking up with me?"

"It doesn't feel like that."

"Well, what does it feel like, then?"

She had started to cry. "It feels like I'm in love with you. But I can't—after what we did, after how I botched everything—I can't put it behind me. Not with you. We'll never put it behind us, Lex."

He could have told her then. He could have told her what he'd done, with his hands. He could have lifted her guilt from her with the leverage of his greater guilt. But he felt none of that, then. They had made a mistake—Brooke, in her dreaminess, had misjudged her pregnancy, and he'd let her fantasy go on too long, and then they'd ended it, and it was over. That was how he'd seen things, then. So he hadn't told her, because to him there was nothing to tell. "We are putting it behind us right now," he had said instead. "Look, we graduated, you were salutatorian, we went to the party, we had a great time—"

"It's always there. Always, for me. But I have to go on with my life somehow. And the only way I can think to do it is to make a different future. Not to be always looking in your eyes and seeing . . . seeing it."

"You're not seeing it, you're seeing *me*." He had almost shouted this. A light had gone on in Brooke's house. Rather than stay and confront Mrs. Willcox, he had whispered fiercely, "Honey, we are going to talk about this when we've gotten some sleep. Not sleeping makes us crazy. I'll call you later. Okay? Okay?"

Later, she had not changed her mind. Stubborn, he had called her. You, too, she had said. She had signed up for classes at the community college in Scranton; she showed him the forms. Then Mrs. Willcox had called him. She wanted to know what he had said, what he had done to change her daughter. He liked Brooke's mom better than his own, but he could not come up with an answer to satisfy her. He and Brooke had made love one last time, late that August, before he went off to Boston on a soccer scholarship. It had been in his bedroom, with his parents out at a party and him babysitting his kid sister Charlie, who was seven that year and hooked on Jodie Sweetin; they just had to sit her in front of a *Full House* videotape and her eyes would be glued to the screen for an hour. Brooke had clung to him with the ferocity of a drowning person. She had wanted to use her tongue all over him, not just his penis but his ass, his feet, the back of his neck, as if she were storing the taste of him somewhere in her mouth. When he'd finally come inside her—no diaphragm anymore, she'd insisted to her mother that she needed to be on the Pill—he felt as if his soul had burst. He wept like a baby.

Then he went to Boston, and she stopped returning his phone calls. He told himself she would snap out of it. They would get back on track. They had been through too much together to break up the way a normal high school couple did when college drew them apart. At the same time, he was busy. There were soccer practices and econ classes; there was a whole new world to find his way in, a world he had once thought he would explore with the girl he loved. How they used to lie on the couch in his basement and picture it! He would be on one side of the Charles River, she on the other. They would make new circles of friends; they would bring their circles together. Freedom and commitment at once. Now that dream had drifted away like morning mist.

The first couple of times he drove home, speeding west on the Mass Pike and the interstate, he saw Charlie and his parents, and Jake, who was at the hardware store then. Brooke's mom called the house a couple of times, but he never wanted to talk to her. It was Mrs. Willcox's fault, too—that was how he thought—for not knowing her daughter better, for not guessing what was wrong and doing something to right it. So he avoided Brooke's mom. When he ran into her dad coming out of the town library once, he shook the guy's hand and they stood awkwardly, making useless small talk about Boston until Alex couldn't take it and said he had to run.

Once, visiting home, he went to see Isadora Bassett, the young mother of twins Brooke had babysat all through high school. He was no fan of Isadora, but whatever he thought of her advice, Brooke had relied on it and might have been relying on it still. Isadora had only shaken her head sadly and said that Brooke had left the community college after a few months. She was living far to the north, in the Adirondacks, working with some landscape firm.

Funny, he thought as he sat on damp grass outside the chain-link fence by Brooke's home in Hartford, how thinking of Brooke had become a series of memories within memories, like a series of refracting mirrors. In the tiniest distant mirror, Isadora appeared as a cool, hip young mom, with an open mind and solutions that challenged their own parents' narrow ways. Only in the closer mirrors could you tell that she wasn't the wise mentor Brooke had taken her for, but a lost hungry soul who fed off Brooke's need for easy answers. When he'd asked her, that day in the snow—his sophomore year in college? Junior year? He couldn't be sure—for Brooke's address or phone number, she had looked frightened. She didn't have either of them, she said. She thought Brooke was mad at her. Though she had tried, really she had, to get Brooke to talk to her own parents. As she'd spoken, she'd taken hold of both Alex's hands, as if she were pleading with him. He had thought, *You bitch*, but he had said nothing. What was the point? As he'd left, he'd asked Isadora to let Brooke know he was happy for her to call or write or come to Boston . . . but he knew the message would never reach his girl.

Then he'd come home that last summer, after graduation. Not

because he wanted to be in Windermere, but because his father had inexplicably driven his new Mercedes over a guardrail and into the Susquehanna River. He left no note, only the insurance papers on the kitchen counter. He hadn't been drunk. Only he had increased the insurance payout six months earlier, and Alex's mom reported that he'd gotten more isolated than usual, neglecting his accounting clients, heading out alone to go snowshoeing in the state forest, leaving her and Charlie by themselves.

An accident, Alex's mom told everyone. But Alex soon learned about claims pending against his dad, some kind of sleight of hand with the accounting. The investors poised to buy the quarry from old Albrecht, for instance, had suddenly withdrawn. Alex's father had driven into the river, and two weeks later the quarry was put up at auction, its crew laid off. The last business to disappear from Windermere.

Brooke had come to the funeral. At that point he hadn't seen her in—what?—three years? She'd said she was living in a New York hamlet called Eagle Bay, where she sold flowers and shrubbery to the New Yorkers at their so-called camps. She had looked thinner, tougher, her eyes larger in her smooth face. They had stood in the vestibule of the church, their conversation interrupted every few seconds by one or another neighbor bearing condolences. After the service he had asked her to stay, to go for a walk with him, a beer, anything. She shook her head, her pale hair pulled back tight from her temples. She had smelled like the mountains, like spruce and laurel. "I'm going away," he'd said at last, before she escaped. "I'm going to the other side of the world. If you came with me, you'd be a different person. We'd both be different. If you didn't like it you could come back."

"I like it where I am, Lex," she'd said.

"No, you don't. You're only half yourself. Admit it," he'd said after the next interruption—desperate, now, pulling out his last cards, not believing in his own hand. He leaned so close his lips touched the whorls of her exposed ear. "You haven't wanted anyone the way you want me. And you won't. Ever."

"I know," she had said.

Then she was gone.

And Alex was off, to Japan, where he taught English for a year and interned at Citigroup until he grasped most of the angles on the Asian markets. Then to Stanford for his MBA. Finally back to Asia with Mercator. Then Tomiko, and their home in the Asakusa District, and Dylan, and friends, commitments, the trappings of a life. Visits home became every six months, then once a year at Christmas, with invitations to his mom and Charlie that they never acted on.

A year later, Dylan was born; two years more, and he died. It had been a genetic abnormality, a heart with a hole in it. Try as they might, the doctors could never close the hole, and so the muscle finally gave way in the little body. But the apartment in Tokyo yawned empty. Two pregnancies ended in miscarriage. Tomiko grew thin and gray-faced, and looked at Alex as though he brought death into the room with him. Finally one day he had come home from his spacious office to a note and all her things gone. She was sorry, Tomiko had written. She needed to start her life again. She was going back to her parents.

He had worked and mourned. He had found a certain kind of comfort in women's beds, women kind enough to bring him inside their warm, urgent bodies and either independent or hesitant enough not to pursue him when he stopped returning their calls. But Tokyo had become a noisy, ugly city, a place where things died. He put in for a transfer while the markets were still surging, a lucky bit of timing. Instead of being laid off in the Far East, he had become part of the restructuring team on America's East Coast. In Boston, where he had roots of sorts—college friends, familiarity with Brookline. For almost two months now, he had felt himself looking toward the future and not toward the past. And then old images had crept close enough to start haunting him again. The lofting of a soccer ball on the green field outside Windermere. Brooke with her shining face, her pale hair. The moonflowers. The nights in the low hills, where the stars came at them thick as champagne bubbles. The smell of Charlie's silky hair as she laid her head on his belly and he laid his on Brooke's, the three of them making a U shape on the old quilt they used for picnics. Brooke and her stories, Morgan le Fay and Merlin emerging from a tree. The two of them jumping from the edge of the old quarry through the blue air, into water so cold they came up gasping. Coming into Brooke, the sharp edge of her diaphragm deep inside.

A truck horn sounded. Alex bolted upright. His heart was racing. The sky was pale gray, stars winking out. He had fallen asleep on the knoll of grass by a chain link fence—where? He wiped his eyes. Hartford—he was in Hartford. He was looking through the fence at the house where Brooke lived. Christ. He must have slept four hours, maybe five. He stretched his neck; the vertebrae popped. He felt as though he'd sunk to the bottom of a deep ocean.

In the dark house, a light snapped on. Upstairs—the bathroom. They could not see him, but Alex felt suddenly exposed, ashamed, a trespasser in Brooke's predawn life. Stealthily, his body sore from the hard ground, he rose and slipped through the trees, back to the sidewalk, and quickly eastward toward his car.

Chapter 5

It took twenty-four hours for Brooke's notion really to sink in. That first night, Monday, Sean was beat. Laying off those two guys had knocked the stuffing out of him. Well past dinner he was still unsettled by the things Clyde had said, even though they were stupid and pointless, the kind of crap a cokehead getting fired would let loose. Plus Meghan was cranky. He'd been late fetching her from dance, and she hated Madame Cassat, she said; she hated the girls in the class who'd laughed at her when she got her legs all tangled up in fifth position, and ballet was stupid. Madame Cassat had made her sit on the piano because she slapped Bethany, the girl who laughed at her. She hated the piano, and she didn't like the ice cream Daddy had bought her, it had nuts in it and she hated nuts.

"She's coming down with something," he'd said to Brooke as he came downstairs. Meghan hadn't wanted a story; she'd wanted Daddy to sing to her, and he'd gone through every lullaby in the book and finally sat on the edge of her bed stroking her hair until she snuffled into dreamland.

"That's no excuse for whining," Brooke said.

He'd poured himself two fingers of Jim Beam and collapsed in front of the tube in the back room. *ER* was on, a rerun. "Maybe we should let her quit the dance class."

"It's important for her to stick to it."

"Maybe she's overscheduled," Sean said. He was only half listening, half responding. He felt drained. If it weren't for the risk of keeping Meghan awake, he'd have sat down at the old upright and banged out Beethoven's Pathétique, which always captured his frayed emotions and distilled them. Instead he muted the sound on the TV and turned to his wife.

"Four afternoons of camp and two hours of ballet? I don't think so." Brooke was cleaning the canary cage, scraping the shelf underneath into a plastic bag and changing out the food and water. The birds twittered and tilted their heads, begging for a scratch. Sean helped out with the dogs, and Blackie the cat was splayed across his lap, but he balked at birds. He liked to tell Brooke he could get a CD with pretty sounds, and it wouldn't shit. "She's an only kid with two working parents."

"Who maybe need to listen to her?"

Brooke nodded. A smile crept across her features. "And not spoil her by letting her change her mind every week," she said. "What's she going to do at home, all by herself?" Under the overhead light, her hair shone like polished oak. She twitched the slim line of her nose, with the bump below the bridge that he practically worshipped. The male canary—Dum, she called him, for Tweedledum—hopped onto her hand and she pulled him out of the cage. "This is what I wanted to talk to you about," she said, coming to perch on the edge of the couch. Blackie raised his head, shot a hungry look at the bird, and twitched his tail, but otherwise he lay still. One false move, he knew, and Brooke would knock him across the room. With animals as with plants, Brooke was impressive. "I want to talk," Brooke said, stroking the bird but looking at Sean, "about another child."

His heart, right then, had expanded with hope. As she went on, it shrank. She was talking not about birth but about adoption. About all the babies waiting for them in China, in Peru, in Lithuania. Did he want a Lithuanian kid? He could not picture a Lithuanian kid. Brooke stroked Dum faster as she talked, until he wanted to take the bird from her hand and feed it to the cat, just to get his wife to slow down, to back up. When had she started thinking adoption? Just recently? Because of the bed rest she'd been on with Meghan? Made no sense. The doctors had said there wasn't any further risk of it happening the next time, and anyhow it was Brooke herself who said every second in bed had been worth it for their little girl. Wouldn't it be worth it this time, too?

She explained to him. She stroked the bird. The female, Dee, began scratching with complaint at the sides of the cage. Even the dogs trotted into the room; they smelled the anxiety, the storm brewing. Finally Brooke said, "Sean, I'm answering your questions, but I don't think you're hearing me."

That was when he could have said something, done something. But fatigue clamped his tongue. "Let's talk about this tomorrow," was what he answered instead.

"Okay," Brooke had said. "No rush." She'd finally put the damn bird back in the cage and covered it, and he'd more or less stumbled into bed. He'd fallen into sleep as if he were racing away from thinking—about the guys at work, about Brooke, about Meghan, about the child who didn't exist but he could feel like a ghost inside him. He didn't dream, or at least didn't remember any dreams. Only deep, empty darkness. He'd startled awake at quarter to five and hadn't found a way back to sleep, so he'd gotten up even earlier than on a weekday and tiptoed to the bathroom.

They didn't talk about it on Tuesday, or any day that week. Distractions abounded—a rush print job, Meghan's summer cold, yard work, a neighborhood cookout on Saturday. Throughout, Sean chewed on what Brooke had said. Let me get this straight, he said to her in one of maybe two dozen imagined conversations. You do want a second child. You think it would be good for Meghan. You'd like us to be a bigger family, a family that fills all sides of the kitchen table. But you don't want to get pregnant. Excuse me—you don't want to be pregnant by me.

It's nothing to do with you, she said.

It's everything to do with me! Aren't I your husband? Aren't I Meghan's daddy? Don't I deserve to know why my wife can't stand the thought of carrying my child?

I told you, she said in these conversations. But she never really told him, just hung her head and looked mulish.

Don't tell me it's the bed rest, he thought of saying. Who waited on you hand and foot when you were in bed? We'll go to the doctor together, that's what we'll do. Listen to him tell you you're not at any greater risk than the normal woman. Don't bullshit me about the bed rest.

By the following Monday, he was driving to work with the conversations already in his head. Let's be honest, he'd hear himself saying. Let's be honest. Brooke, honey. All the good stuff, our little girl got from you. The brains, the looks. Even the way she does cartwheels—I could never do a cartwheel. But in the end, okay, she's an O'Connor. You don't want another one. You don't want to give birth to my baby. You'd rather get yourself a little Oriental. They're so smart and you don't think about the looks the way you would with my kid. Go ahead, Brooke honey. I have a constant disposition to promote your good. Do what you want. Just don't lie to me.

This conversation made him feel sorry for himself. Tears of self-pity let loose, right there in his office. When Larry called him in to schedule the art catalog, he had to duck to the men's room and press a wet paper towel to his eyes before he went upstairs, and even then he looked like a blubbering idiot. But the worst came in the conversation he imagined with Brooke after he'd picked Meghan up and was repairing the back fence as she drifted from sandbox to swing. It'll be easier for you to leave me, won't it? he said to Brooke this time around. With just one kid? Get pregnant again and you'll be stuck with us forever. Don't tell me you're not thinking about leaving. What else do you think about, when you get that look in your eyes, that look like you're watching someone a million miles away? Or maybe just five miles, at Starbucks, with your "friend" you refuse to name. You're so smart. You offer me what I've been asking for, another kid. Then you tell me it can't be my kid. If I insist on my kid, I'll put your health in danger. So it's the Chinese kid or nothing. I say nothing. Then you can leave. Just like you left that high school guy, that guy you went with right up to graduation. You can find the guy you've been looking for, all these years with your eyes fixed on the distance, and have his beautiful kids.

That evening was his first chorale rehearsal of the season. They were working on the Bach Christmas Oratorio, with all its complicated fugues. Sean's sight-reading wasn't good enough to let him miss a single rehearsal. Usually he made a casserole for all three of them and ate his first, to be out of the house by six thirty. But tonight, by the time Brooke got home from the nursery, he'd polished off a couple of beers, had cooked nothing, and was wallowing in self-pity. From her, by contrast, came a lively happiness. "What's got you so cheerful?" he said as she hummed in the kitchen. Meghan sat at the table, drawing by numbers.

"I don't know. It was a good day. Meghan's over her sniffles. I'm not so sure about you, though," she said. She put her hand to his forehead, like a mother. It irritated him. She hummed a few more bars. "Remind me how this goes?" she said. "You sing it all the time. 'Oh what care I for my money and land—what care I dum dee dum dee dum.' Remind me? It's so pretty when you sing it."

What care I for my new wedded lord, he thought to himself, *for I'm off with the raggle-taggle gypsies, oh*. But he only said, "Got a bit of a sore throat. That's an ugly song really. About a wife who runs off."

"With the gypsies," said Brooke. She started humming again.

"What's a gypsy?" said Meghan, looking up from her drawing book.

"A lot of nonsense," Sean said.

Brooke glanced sharply at him. "You sure you're not coming down with something? Should you be going to rehearsal?"

"I should, yes. Why? Have you got a date?"

"Don't be silly."

"You had a date last week." She looked puzzled. "Last Monday."

"Oh, that." She stuck her head in the refrigerator, pulled out a bag of baby carrots. "We're all so old."

She hadn't said that it wasn't a date, or wasn't a *he*. "You can't catch up to me," he said. "Unless this fellow was your babysitter."

She was humming again, that goddamn tune. Then she smiled like he'd made a joke. "Oh, no. Alex was in my class in high school. Two months younger than I am, but you know, he's going gray already."

"Must have been nice to see an old flame."

She rolled her eyes at him. "So long ago. He was in Tokyo for years. Now he's in Boston. Next time I see him we'll all be gray."

Alex, he thought. The gypsy tune dinned in his ears. *Tonight you'll sleep in a cold open field along with the raggle-taggle gypsies, oh.*

He glanced at his watch without even registering the time. "I'm running late," he said.

"But you haven't eaten."

He rinsed the beer bottle and kissed Meghan on the head before he left. If Brooke worried about anything besides his being ill, she didn't show it. She was still humming as he headed out the back door. It was nothing, he told himself all through the drive. It was coffee with a fellow she threw over long ago. Lives in Boston. But wouldn't she like to have his babies, oh.

The chorale rehearsed in the community room of a wealthy Episcopal church at the west end of Hartford. Nine years, now, Sean had sung with them. For his audition he'd chosen the tenor solo, "Comfort ye," from Handel's *Messiah*, and had worked on it for weeks before showing up to sing it to Geoffrey, the potbellied bass who directed the group. Geoffrey's eyes had widened as Sean began, and then his face had settled into a beatific smile as Sean got to the part about warfare being accomplished. Sean's sight-reading had been more than rusty at that time, but Geoffrey had let it go; he needed tenors, especially ones with honeyed, pitch-perfect voices.

Early to the rehearsal hall—he had not been running late—Sean helped lay out the folding chairs and bantered with the other guys who'd escaped their households or their lonely apartments to set the hall up for rehearsal. Gradually he pushed the name *Alex* to the back of his mind. Here, he felt at home. It was strange how well acquainted he was with all these people without really knowing them. When rehearsal fell on someone's birthday, they all sang "Happy Birthday" in harmony. When one of the older singers—and there were plenty of those—went into the hospital, a card was passed around. A few members were married to one another, and now and then there was a romance that bloomed and faded.

As Sean unfolded the beige chairs in the alto section, he caught sight of Suzanne, the soft-featured accountant he'd dated the year before he met Brooke. She smiled at him—it had been nine years, after all—and found her seat, arranging her pocketbook and music and water and the knitting she always turned to when the altos weren't singing. She was a few years older than Sean and was settling, he sometimes thought, into a fussy middle age. When they first met she was recently divorced, plain-faced but shapely and friendly in the way of people who expect the world to reciprocate about a third of their generosity. Insecure, in other words, but hopeful. When they made love in her apartment—Sean still lived at home then, with Mum and Danny—Suzanne worked hard to please him, murmuring (when her mouth was not otherwise occupied), "Oh, be happy, be happy, be so happy."

Driving with Suzanne to rehearsal one night, as they chatted about Sean's work, about Gerry's upcoming wedding, he had glanced over her eager, open, needy features, the bones of her face like putty. At once he had felt how her devotion would descend on him, would choke him, and he had known they had to break up. It had taken place gradually, over several weeks, and Suzanne had never protested, had never challenged him to "talk," had never asked why he was drifting away. It amazed him, he told Danny back then, that you could know a woman naked, could be inside a woman one night after the next, and then you could change your mind and gradually become strangers. Danny had shrugged. Thank sweet Jesus for that, he'd said.

Since then, Sean had heard, Suzanne had tried a couple of times, on her own, to get pregnant, and when that hadn't worked out, had begun taking in foster children. Now, as he finished setting up the chairs, she pulled out a sweater she was knitting, in blues and grays. "Christmas present?" he ventured as he passed her row. He nodded at the knit sleeve.

"Hi, Sean," Suzanne said. She smiled, her lips still plump. She held up her handiwork. "For a six-year-old boy," she said. "Do you think it'll do?"

"He'll count himself lucky."

"I don't know. They'd probably rather have sweatshirts. With a Patriots logo or something."

"Nonsense. You're doing a great thing, Suzanne."

She raised and lowered an eyebrow—skeptical, for all her sweetness. She glanced around the room. "So are you," she said.

"Oh, sure. Chairs," Sean said. He chuckled, self-deprecating, and moved on. It wouldn't do to get deep in conversation. But he felt Suzanne's eyes on him, while the rest of the chorus trickled in, and he stood a little taller, sang a little clearer.

As he drove home, his mood had lifted. He pulled into the driveway with his windows open; after he'd shut the engine he sat for a moment. He listened to the August crickets, breathed in Brooke's moonflower. From inside the house came Bitsy's yapping; upstairs, Meghan's bedroom light was on. Bach still played in his head—the opening chorus, *Jauchzet frohlocket*, cheer and glory. And he loved this neighborhood. True, their house lay at the south end of the block, too close to Farmington Avenue with its fast-food stores and gas stations. But he'd come up in the world from the duplex in East Hartford. The neighborhood school would be fine for Meghan through fifth grade, then maybe they'd move farther out, to one of the suburbs. Of course Brooke never noticed how they'd managed to hold their own in the West End. To her, this was just normal.

He entered the house quietly. The dogs milled around him, Bitsy scrabbling at his pants leg, Lex licking his hand. From the front hall he heard Brooke upstairs, telling Meghan one of her endless stories. "The Lady of the Lake was like a gypsy," she was saying as Sean tiptoed upstairs. "She could be good or evil. She lived in the woods and was very mysterious. It was from Merlin that she learned all her magic."

"Merlin," Meghan chimed in, her voice high and thin, "was Arthur's wizard."

"And a great wizard, too. He taught the Lady everything she knew, and she became more powerful than he was. Girls do that, you know."

Meghan giggled. Sean peeked in the door. Just the nightlight was on, but he saw Meghan making finger-shapes in the glow it cast.

"So when the Lady saw that King Arthur had trouble in battle," Brooke was saying, sitting on the edge of the bed, "she determined to give him the sword Excalibur."

"He pulled it from the stone!"

"That was his first sword. Excalibur was his grown-up sword, his magic sword. But it really belonged to the Lady of the Lake, and she had to have it back one day."

Sean drifted away. Downstairs, he felt thirsty. He popped open a beer. These were the things that touched his wife's heart, he thought. An old boyfriend named Alex. Gypsies, and running away, and mysterious deadly women in lakes. Not family. Not an out-of-shape, ordinary printer and an impulsive, freckled daughter. He felt the joy of singing Bach drain out of him. He was back to real life and its discordances. Passing through the kitchen and family room, he covered the canaries, who looked at him quizzically. He let the dogs out to pee. Then he stood at the picture window in the living room, gazing out on the street, until he felt a hand on his back. "Hey," said Brooke.

"She's asleep?"

"Like an angel. And last night she was a devil."

"You really think those help? Those stories of yours?"

"She loves them. Not as much as your singing, but—"

"I think," Sean interrupted, "they get her riled up. Thinking about swords in lakes, people trapped in trees. I don't know why you fill her head with that garbage."

His arms were crossed over his chest. Brooke pressed against his side; she tipped her head, trying for eye contact. "They're old, old stories," she said. "I loved them as a child. They're the only stories I know, really."

"What, you don't know Goldilocks and the Three Bears?"

She chuckled. "Meghan outgrew that one maybe three years ago. Why are you so grumpy? Do you want something to eat?"

"I'm not hungry," Sean said—though, suddenly, his stomach felt like an empty cavern. He drank his beer.

"Well, you should be. How was your rehearsal?"

"It was hard. It's hard music. I'm tired. And now Meghan'll have nightmares, and I'll be up half the night."

"Why would she have nightmares?"

"From that claptrap you tell her. You want her to sleep peacefully, tell her something that ends happily ever after." He shook his head, drained the beer. "You don't know how to go from point A to point B."

"Really." Brooke moved around him, her hands on his torso. She leaned against the picture window. "Like for instance."

"Like we want another child, let's have another child. Is that just too straightforward for you?"

He felt her stiffen. "Sean, I told you. Meghan's birth wasn't exactly straightforward."

"It was straightforward enough." He turned away from her, moved to the couch. "Except for someone who doesn't want to have her own husband's children."

"Sean, don't." Brooke followed him. On the couch, she tucked her legs underneath her. They were sleek and tanned, the calves scratched by thorns but smoothly muscled, the arches of her feet high as a dancer's. She wore a white tank top and beige shorts, her summer uniform. In the light of the streetlamp just outside their house, he could see the outline of her nipples. "I surfed the web a little before I went to work today," she said. "I'm getting info from a bunch of agencies. Some of them are obviously scams, but—"

"I don't want to adopt a kid, Brooke."

She looked down. She picked at an invisible bit of lint on her shorts. "Well, I don't feel safe having one. And it's my body."

"Brooke, that is *bullshit*." He hissed the word. Despite the beer, his mouth felt dry. She looked at him with those wide blue eyes, eyes that were clear as a lake and hard as steel. When he sat forward they blinked, as if she feared he would hit her. "You loved being pregnant," he said, slapping his index finger against his open palm. "You loved nursing." He slapped the middle finger against the palm. "You loved what your body could do." He slapped the ring finger. "Don't give me this feminist crap."

"It's not crap."

"If you don't think my kids are *smart* enough and *beautiful* enough to come out of your *smart* and *beautiful* body"—he was spitting the *b*'s now; a fleck of saliva flew onto Brooke's cheek—"then you should get yourself some gorgeous brilliant seed and have his babies. You can have Alex's babies, how's that?"

He turned to her. Her face had gone chalk white. Like a statue she sat there on the leather couch, before the fireplace that gathered them together in the winter, in the small square living room whose walls she had painted a garnet red and hung with prints of abstract art that Sean couldn't understand but found vaguely pleasing. It was all perfect, the life they'd made full of love and laughter. It was all about to go up in smoke. The blood had drained from Brooke's face because he'd stamped the truth on it. "I will love his kids," he said, soft but fierce. "I will treat them like my own. If, that is, you will let me."

"Sean, this isn't about Alex. It isn't even about you."

"It is *exactly* about me!"

He picked up a small glass figurine of a cat curled into itself, its back rounded and sleek. He'd bought it for Brooke at some stupid outdoor craft show in the Adirondacks, when he used to drive back there to see her. He'd said it reminded him of her, that she was lovely and contented, but mysterious inside, and he loved her not for the beauty but for the mystery. Now he lifted the piece of glass and made as if to hurl it into the corner of the room. Two of the dogs shrank into a corner, their tails curled into frightened commas. Brooke said, "Sean. You'll wake Meghan."

He finished the throw, like a pitcher loosening his arm. He set the cat back onto the coffee table. "I'm going out," he announced.

His steps crunched down the drive. He felt he was being watched. Good, he thought. Let her watch me. For a wild moment he had a thought of taking the car, of driving over to East Hartford where Suzanne lived, if she still lived in that apartment, with her foster kid or three, and plowing himself into her shapeless, willing body, her muddy alto voice. But he'd left his keys on the kitchen counter. At the sidewalk he turned first right, then left, down Farmington, a ten-minute walk to the Half Door on Sisson Street. On Wednesday nights, Paddy O'Rourke performed his fiddle here, and when Sean was younger he used to put down a few and join in the singing.

But tonight was Monday; the place was pretty quiet. A soccer game played behind the bar. Sean took a pint from the barman, Tommy, a stocky guy who knew when and when not to talk. He

watched the game. Bach still played in his head, but only the messy
parts now, the fugue he could never learn. *Alex*, he thought. One of
those names that could be a boy or a girl. Stupid. After a while a
couple of guys came in complaining about their wives. He ordered
everyone pints.

Then, he didn't know. Maybe he joined in the complaining. A
poisonous feeling filled the warm space of the Half Door, and you
had to order more just to douse the poison, so he did. The beams
lining the ceiling of the bar were hung with incongruous
mementos—a couple of miniature harps, dried sprigs of holly, soccer cleats, Paddy's Day lime-green plastic hats. In the corner a couple of slutty-looking girls were downing puke-green apple martinis
that the guys coming in would buy for them. After a while one of
the girls went out with one of the guys, and some minutes later the
other girl shuffled out by herself. Sean noticed these things, but he
couldn't say how much time lapsed between them. Kids, he remembered saying at one point, and one of the other drinkers misunderstood him.

Yah, the guy said, the wife pops 'em and lets her body go to shit.
Best birth control in the world, makes you not want to touch the
bitch again.

No, no, Sean said, that wasn't what I meant. Or maybe he didn't
say it but just got quiet, sipping his pint, light-years away from Bach.
When Tommy said he was closing, he paid up with a credit card,
crumpling the beer-soaked receipt into his back pocket.

Walking home, he almost bumped into a guy on the sidewalk,
right in front of his own house. One of those professional-type guys,
not real tall but muscled, good-looking, in need of a haircut, dressed
in chinos and a polo shirt. Sean felt like throwing up on him but
he only asked what was he doing there, was he coming to bang his
wife?

Sorry, the guy said, just walking. Was that Farmington in front of him? Sean didn't answer. He pushed past the intruder, through his gate, up the walk. Brooke had left the light on, and he got his key in the lock on the third or fourth try. Inside, everything was still, alert. Lex trotted over and sniffed his hand. The other dogs just stood there, wagging their tails slowly like they were fanning themselves. The cat's eyes glowed like coins from the dark corner. Sean pulled himself upstairs by the railing. By the bathroom nightlight he brushed his teeth, then pressed one hand against the wall to steady himself while he took a three-minute piss. He didn't flush. In the bed, only a white sheet pulled up to her bare shoulders, Brooke was pretending to sleep. He let her pretend. He could remember scarcely a note of the Bach; it was all a jangle. Tomorrow, he thought, as he dropped his head on the pillow and the room spun above him. Tomorrow he'd set things straight.

Chapter 6

With summer camp over, Meghan was spending the late August days watching cartoons and chalking the sidewalks and driveways with Jackie and Taisha, the only two neighborhood kids who hadn't left on family vacation. These two weeks before school started were the hardest. Brooke couldn't get away from the nursery at what was still high season. Babysitters were impossible to find. Usually Brooke and Sean handled late August on a day-to-day basis, trading off child care with neighbors and moving their work hours around. But Sean had been acting wounded ever since Brooke brought up the idea of adoption. So she tiptoed around him; she tried to make things work without messing up his day. Today, Meghan would simply have to come with Brooke to the nursery. She got bored there, but too bad. Shanita's kids had played there for hours without complaint.

At nine forty-five, the call came—fifteen minutes later than yesterday. Brooke watched the lit numbers pulse on the phone as the rings sounded, four of them before the machine picked up. "Brooke, it's Alex again. I'm still going to be in Hartford tomorrow. Meeting's been changed to afternoon, so maybe we could do lunch? So much I wish we'd said before. Here's my cell." After he left the number he paused, as if he wanted to go on, maybe just to remind her that this was his third call. Then he hung up. Brooke pressed Repeat on the machine, listened to the message once more, then erased it.

Her coffee drained, she rinsed the mug. "Bitsy!" she called. "Mocha! Lex!" The dogs trotted over. Lex licked her hand; Bitsy panted. She leashed them and banged out the screen door. The girls were in Jackie's wide driveway, across the street, circling their bikes in slow motion like pink moths. "I'm taking the dogs for a walk!" she called to her daughter. "When I come back, we need to go to my work. Okay?"

"No!" Meghan called back. She kept circling her bike, the streamers wafting in the hot air. Brooke sighed. No point in reasoning. She pulled on the leashes and headed up to the park with the dogs.

If only Sean weren't acting so jealous, she would call Alex back. She'd change the plan, invite him for dinner. An old friend, why not? But even as she rehearsed these thoughts, she felt Shanita's hand gripping her heart, telling her she was making this stuff up out of her head, telling her she wasn't feeling the thing she was saying. Just like with the notion of adopting. Well, what was she supposed to do? If she let her heart do the thinking, she'd have gone out of her mind the last time she saw Alex Frazier, a dozen years ago.

His dad's funeral, that had been. Her heart had lodged in her throat, all the way through the service. Afterward they had served sandwiches and coffee, but she couldn't swallow a thing. The sorrow in Alex's eyes—she saw it and wanted to go to it. To wrap her arms around his firm young body and say something, say anything, say *love*. She had drifted close. Stood in a loose circle with Alex's old friend Jake, next to his kid sister, in middle school by then, a firecracker of a girl with coltish legs. Searching his face, she found the same eyes that had looked into hers that afternoon in the motel room, after he came back up and it was gone, emptied out of her. She saw the same dull blue in his eyes and she shut the doors of her heart. She locked them together with a key. She excused herself from the circle, said good-bye to Mrs. Frazier. When Alex caught up to her outside the church, tried to get her to walk with him, said he was going away, she shook herself free.

She wished, walking the dogs, that she hadn't erased the message. She wanted to hear his voice again, camouflaged by age and the answering machine. That voice conjured not the man in his thirties in his business attire, not the grieving son with words strangled in his throat. It conjured the sixteen-year-olds they both had been, back in Windermere. It conjured the hoarse cry of victory after the goal Alex had scored to win the soccer game; the steam that came off his body after. It conjured his swift, tightly packed body as he charged down the field, the feet so nimble, capturing the lofted ball and dancing it past the opposition. And his hands. Corralling the dogs toward the park, she stopped suddenly on the street corner, struck by the memory of Alex's hands.

The fingers were short, stubby, the palms no longer than Brooke's own though Alex topped her by two inches and had feet like a puppy's, too big for his build. She loved to lace her fingers with his, to feel the calluses that developed from the landscaping job he held on weekends. Of course he never touched the soccer ball with his hands—and sometimes, watching him work the ball down the field, she imagined that he was keeping the hands for her. The way he touched her wasn't like other boys. He didn't grope or pinch her. He brushed her skin with the blunt tips of his fingers; when she took her bra off for him, he cupped her breasts in his palms as if they were baby birds he might keep warm until they flew away.

His being her boyfriend, even after they'd gone steady for a year, had still been such an unbelievable thing, an accident due at any moment to be corrected, that she had to perform certain rituals—hold her breath to the count of forty-three, repeat the Nicene Creed, keep her eye on Alex's jersey number rather than his face each time he headed a soccer ball—to keep the spheres of chance in their proper alignment. When she missed her period, she didn't go to him at first. She didn't go to her mom either. She went to Isadora.

She had babysat for Isadora for four years, and Isadora was still the only adult who asked Brooke to call her by her first name. "Please, none of this Mrs. Bassett," she said. "Bad enough that I gave up my name and didn't even take it back when I left him." Isadora was a painter who had lived everywhere—California, Europe, India—and had a house full of exotic fabric, sculptures, boxes filled with mementoes. She always asked Brooke to stay a while when she came back home from parties. She asked Brooke about her life, and Brooke got the feeling Isadora really wanted to know; that she found Brooke's life not silly or wrongheaded but downright fascinating. In return, Brooke learned plenty about Isadora, about the drugs she'd done and the lovers she'd had, about her stint in a rock band in London back in the seventies. She had turned out all right, though. She had a big house in Windermere and a pair of sweet kids. From Isadora Brooke had learned that you could live your life in ways different from your parents. Disaster would not strike.

"Deciding not to have children," Isadora had said when Brooke explained her dilemma, "is as old and natural as deciding to have them."

Isadora gave Brooke a tea that tasted like hot mud. Pennyroyal, she explained. You sprinkle it on baked potatoes sometimes. Plus black cohosh, tansy, mugwort, goldenseal—all of them the leaves and flowers of plants, the recipe as old as humanity.

"How long will it take to work?" Brooke had asked, tucking the little baggies of herbs into her parka pocket.

"That's hard to say. You shouldn't drink it more than ten days. That's all it takes, and any more might start to affect you systemically. It won't necessarily happen right away. A friend of mine took this cure in her fourth month, and miscarried in her seventh. But it wasn't alive; it hadn't been alive for a long while."

"What if it doesn't—you know—work, completely?" Brooke couldn't get herself to say *kill the fetus*, even though that was what she was thinking. "Does it get messed up, somehow? Its brain, I mean."

"It *will* work." They were in Isadora's kitchen, which faced south and caught all the light winter had to offer. Isadora put her cool, slender hands over Brooke's warm ones. "And remember, you're not alone in this." She made Brooke look at her. "Alex is a good boy, Brooke. He can help you in your decisions."

"I know that," said Brooke. But at first she wasn't sure. What had occurred to her, once she knew—rather, once she had proof, because she knew, in spite of having worn her diaphragm, that very night—was that she didn't have a clue about Alex, not really. They knew each other's bodies, sure. They both liked Deep Blue Something and neither of them was a Phishhead like so many kids at school. Brooke knew Alex wanted to travel to exotic places like Cambodia. She knew he worried about Charlie. Alex's parents were both as old as Brooke's dad; when they compared their moms it felt intimate, like something you didn't share with just anyone. But even with the plan to be together next year in Boston, they were still a high school item. Anything could happen, and suddenly they'd break up, and it didn't mean Alex wasn't a good boy but you didn't want to depend on that.

The only thing Alex had ever complained about in their relationship was Brooke's diaphragm. It hurt him, he said. He didn't understand why, if her mom was willing to take her to have a diaphragm fitted, she wouldn't let her go on the Pill.

"She doesn't want me putting chemicals in my body," Brooke had tried explaining. "She wants something I'll take responsibility for." She did not add, as her mom had, *And if boys know you're on the Pill they'll think you're loose.*

"You'd have to take responsibility for one of those tabs every morning," Alex said.

"I know. But she wants me to be conscious of what I'm doing. What we're doing."

Strictly speaking, it had been the parental consent clause that sent her to Isadora. On a scrap of paper, during math class, she had scribbled herself a syllogism—they'd just learned syllogisms, in Humanities—*A. You can't get an ab—without telling your parents; B. If you tell your parents, they'll refuse to sign; C. You can't get an ab—.* But in truth Brooke wasn't sure about B. Her mother would probably sign eventually, vindication curling her lip as she read the clause aloud. Brooke thought less about the prospects of having a baby or giving it up or even marrying Alex (Alex! Whom she hardly knew! Even after two years!) than about how justified her mother would be when she learned that Brooke had neglected to wear the diaphragm.

"But I did wear it!" she had told the nurse at the free clinic in Scranton. Confidential, the ad had said, and the place was tucked away in a seedy office building that made her think of drug dealing. The woman who examined her was dark-skinned but not African; something more exotic. She spoke with a lilt that turned each sentence into a question.

"It was sized too small?" the woman said, moving her fingers around inside Brooke.

"My mother's gynecologist sized it. She's been going to him for twenty-five years."

"But it was sized before you had engaged in intercourse?"

"Well, we'd done it once—"

"And a girl's body stretches? You can feel this shifting around in here?" Brooke nodded, though the woman couldn't see her head. "This may cause pain to your partner, also?"

"He always says it hurts him. I thought it just was like that."

"In any case, not adequate protection? This is the explanation of your pregnancy?"

The woman pulled the diaphragm out; Brooke felt, as always, the queer, damp explosion of the rubber coil. The woman asked if she knew about the parental consent clause; when Brooke nodded, she received a sheet of paper with boxes to check off. "You need only one signature?" the woman pointed out, her varnished finger-nails tapping the paper. "The court may approve a grandparent?" The cost would be four hundred dollars, which Brooke knew she could get from Alex. Only once he had paid it, would he ever want to see her again? She wasn't a safe bet anymore, as a girlfriend. She'd screwed up.

Late at night, drinking Isadora's tea, she told herself it could not be true. She did not screw up. This was not the sort of event that happened to her. The readings were false; this was a trick God was playing, testing her. Brooke often thought of God as a sort of club president, setting up initiation rites and watching from his tree house to see if you passed. Her parents were Presbyterians, who talked mostly about changes in the wording of the service, not about God.

She had trouble taking the proper doses of the tea. You had to drink it on an empty stomach and not eat or drink anything else for at least an hour. "Get an immersing coil at the hardware store," Isadora had instructed her, and that wasn't hard—they cost a dollar sixty-nine and looked like a giant IUD—but even with brewing the stuff in her bedroom over that Christmas break, Brooke was always making excuses for not having a cup of eggnog or for running upstairs in the midst of stringing cranberries. You couldn't even put honey in it, Isadora had cautioned, and if it steeped less than five minutes you didn't get the right mix of reactions.

"I don't think the tea worked," Brooke said in late January.

Isadora looked her up and down, as if there would be a sign. Brooke's pants were just a little tight around the waist, like everyone's after Christmas. "You sure you drank it on an empty stomach?" Brooke nodded. "Three times a day?"

"I set my alarm in the morning. Then I skipped lunch and steeped it in the girls' room by the gym. Then late at night."

"You let it steep—"

"Five minutes." Brooke had started to get annoyed at Isadora's questions. She'd always been a smart girl, good at following directions. She'd followed her mother's directions with the diaphragm. "This isn't getting us anywhere," she said, in a voice that surprised her with its sternness. "I need to know how much longer I should wait."

Isadora had gone to her kitchen window. Thoughtfully she picked brown leaves from one of the many plants she kept on the sill. The low midwinter light and artificial heat weren't doing them any good. In her winter turtleneck, her brown hair combed straight, she looked scarcely older than Brooke. "Not much longer," she said.

"But you said your friend. In her seventh month."

"She was an adult. She was ready to take on the consequences."

"Well, jeez, what consequences are you asking *me* to take? I mean, either my parents disown me or I end up an unwed mother! I thought this was a better *option*, that's why I took it."

"Your parents won't disown you, Brooke."

"You don't know them."

"And maybe Alex would like to be a father. Have you asked him?"

"Alex's got a soccer scholarship to Boston University." Isadora had no answer to this. She was looking out the window, her face pale; she might have been crying. "Will you get me more?" Brooke asked.

"Of the herbs? No."

"I'm willing to wait. But I have to be sure."

Isadora had shrugged; she had turned from the plants and come to stand next to Brooke. "This is an old, old recipe," she had said. "I've never known anyone to take it and bear a child. But I'm not a doctor. I can't make you guarantees. You're scaring me, Brooke."

"Scaring *you*," Brooke had said, with a twist of her mouth.

Now, in the park, she waved at another dog walker, an older fellow she often saw there with a pair of basset hounds. He tipped his hat to her and smiled, pleased at a young woman's attention. She wasn't far, she realized with a start, from the age Isadora Bassett had been when she gave Brooke those herbs. At the thought of handing a seventeen-year-old a recipe to rid herself of a baby, Brooke shuddered. How weak Isadora had been! Wearing the same fashions as the high school girls, talking about drugs as though they were cool. Well, it was a long time ago. Except Alex was back now; she had seen him, the old question still lurking in his eyes.

She had told him only because of the diaphragm. They had been at his house one Friday that February, babysitting his sister Charlie. How old had Charlie been, then? Six, maybe seven. First grade. Alex's mom had tried for years to conceive a second child, and when she had given up, Charlie at last came along. Mrs. Frazier seemed to resent the whole thing, as if Charlie had played a trick on her, like a kid who will hide and hide until the adults are exhausted, and then spring out. But Alex was crazy about her. He was so protective, Charlie called him Alexander the Great. When he and Brooke babysat Charlie, they all played Chutes and Ladders, which Charlie loved, and sometimes Brooke read to Charlie from the edition of King Arthur tales illustrated by Arthur Rackham that Alex's mom kept on a top shelf of their den. At age seven, Charlie had a whole family tree in her head, starting with Uther Pendragon.

Brooke had read to her that night about the birth of Galahad. Charlie had already learned of Lancelot and Guinevere and sat with her pale eyes gleaming as Brooke explained why it was necessary to bewitch Lancelot into becoming Galahad's father. She left Charlie turning the pages of the book, her brow furrowed, determined to read the book for herself.

My God, Brooke thought as she pulled the dogs around the rose garden. The details that came back! Later, in the basement, she and Alex had watched *The Fisher King* on videotape, with Robin Williams playing the medieval history prof who goes mad. Alex had had a cold and sniffled all through the movie. When it was over, she'd made him play out the scene where Robin Williams tells Amanda Plummer he has a hard-on for her the size of Florida but he doesn't want just one night. She'd unzipped Alex's pants. "You'll catch my cold," he whispered huskily as she slid beneath him—her own pants off, her sweater hiked up, the scratchy weave of the basement couch against her back.

"Colds don't get communicated down there." She giggled, though it hadn't been a funny movie. When he still didn't reach for her she said, "It'll make you better. Blow your nose."

That got a laugh out of him. He shoved his jeans to his knees. He was plenty hard. They had to be very quiet; his house was new construction, thin walls. Suddenly he turned her over, so she was kneeling on the scratchy cushions. His knees shoved between hers, pushing hers apart. She spoke his name, but he didn't answer; he was in her, at once and deep. He thrust, and in her head she heard

the violins from the movie, then the drums. Then he brought his
hand around her hip. He kept moving in her, but his hand, his
hand— "Oh!" she cried. The tingle rushed to her lips.

"*Ssh*. You'll wake Charlie up. What is it?"

"I . . . I *came*."

"You sure?"

"Yeah, I think. I must have. God, Lex." Tears started unbidden
to her eyes. She swallowed; she reached back to touch his naked hip,
to keep him moving. "It was so sudden."

"I'm proud of you, you fox."

"Oh, Alex. I *liked* it."

"I thought you *always* liked it."

"I did, but—you know—I didn't, like that. Oh, Lex, I love you."

"Brookey, Brooke."

He was moving faster already. Then it was over, his belt buckle
slapping the back of her thigh. The tears wouldn't stop leaking from
her eyes. They sank to the couch. He brushed her cheek with the
back of his index finger. Then his eyes widened. "It didn't hurt," he
said.

"What didn't hurt?"

"Your diaphragm."

"I didn't wear it."

His eyes widened further. "But my God, Brooke, that's—"

She put her finger to his lips. They were full pursed lips, a rose-
bud of a boy's mouth. "I've been pregnant," she confessed. Her heart
thudded in her chest.

"What d'you mean, you've been . . . are you pregnant now?
Brooke, this is the first time—" His head pulled back. His hand
hovered over the tiny curve of her belly, as if measuring it. For a
moment, his face filled with a soft wonder.

"I don't think I am, anymore. I'm waiting."

It all spilled out then. She told him about the bad fitting of the diaphragm, the parental consent clause, her visit to Isadora, the tea. "That's why I didn't have anything to eat at your parents' holiday party. I felt so rude, but—"

"You're saying you're going to miscarry?"

She nodded. She felt his muscles tensing. The wonder was gone from his face, and his stare frightened her. "That's what Isadora promised."

"Isadora's a dreaming hippie." He rose. He pulled on his T-shirt, his shorts. When he sat in the chair opposite her, fully clothed in front of her nakedness, his face had rearranged itself into hard, practical lines. "You can't be ridiculous, Brooke," he said. "You have to get an abortion."

The dogs were whining. Brooke looked down. Lex's leash was tangled with Bitsy's, and Mocha's rear leg was trapped in her leash so she limped. Lex had just laid a poop in a bed of black-eyed Susans. Quickly Brooke glanced at her watch. Eleven o'clock already. "Christ," she muttered. She disentangled the dogs, swept up the mess in a bag, and jogged back through the park's rose garden to the tree-lined street. She would be late for work, even if Meghan cooperated. What, oh, what did Alex want with her?

Chapter 7

It was funny, Alex's sister Charlotte said to him over coffee at Lalla Rookh, how people looked at them and thought she was dating this cute older guy.

"Do girls at Tufts do that?" he asked her. "Date their professors?"

"I don't know." Charlie picked at her pilaf. "I think it's against the rules these days. There's this one psych professor you hear about. But I think he's gross."

"Well, you tell him hands off you. Big brother's back in town."

"You sure about that?" Gingerly she lifted her wine. She was twenty-two now, legal, but on both the occasions when Alex had taken her out, she had studied the clear glass globe and its rich red elixir as if the wine had magic tricks to perform. Yesterday had been her birthday; she'd gone out with friends from Tufts. Today, Alex's turn; he'd picked this restaurant, a bejeweled little Persian place, because it was named after some nineteenth-century poem by Byron or one of those guys. Charlotte was majoring in literature. "I mean, are you really going to settle here? Seems so boring, after Tokyo."

Alex's mouth twisted. "Every big city's basically the same, Charlie."

"Nuh-uh. Those kids we saw out in the Ginza District? You'd never find them here. That was like sci-fi. *Blade Runner.* Haruki Murakami."

Alex knew better than to ask her who Haruki Murakami was. He loved listening to his kid sister show off. When she had come to visit him and Tomiko, the summer before her senior year in high school, she had learned enough Japanese to get around on the subway, and she insisted on going off by herself and then meeting them hours later, exactly on time, draping her parcels over her forearm exactly as she'd seen the Tokyo girls do. Tomiko, eight months pregnant then, had loved her. A half dozen times, during the week she visited, he'd found his sister and his wife bending their heads together, whispering and then giggling about something. When he'd asked what the joke was, they had both wiped their hands across their smiling lips— like sisters—and said it was nothing very funny.

"So?" Charlie insisted. "Don't you think you'll move back there?"

"That chapter's over, Charlie. I can't keep living somewhere just because you like to visit."

"Well, I did. But it's not that. It's . . . you know. Tomiko."

He met her gaze. She'd always been a robust kid, loaded with baby-of-the-family pranks. While he was away at school or later in Japan, he would get e-mails from his parents wringing their hands over Charlie's suddenly purple hair, her high school crush on another girl (who was, true to form, a Very Bad Influence), the popcorn balls that set the kitchen on fire. If she hadn't been so smart, so alert—he could swear her ears pricked up, like a fox's, at a new idea—she might have spun off into real trouble. As it was she studied Milton and wrote biting satires. Before she left Windermere, she had founded a children's theater program and directed a Christmas farce that scandalized the town. Any guilt Alex had felt for being absent so much of his sister's life was assuaged when he saw how completely she threw herself into that life. "You can visit Tomiko anytime you want," he said. "She really likes you."

"I never even met Dylan." She took a large bit of lamb stew and talked around the meat. "I wish you guys could have gotten over it. Had another. Pushed on. I mean, it was awful. But shit happens."

"Not that simple, Charlie."

"You sent two Christmas cards with his picture. I saw what kind of kid he was. He would have wanted you to stay together."

"You're right about that." He drained his glass and refilled them both from the bottle he'd bought. He didn't want to talk about Tomiko anymore. "But then I wouldn't be here, taking you out for birthday dinner."

"It's weird having you in town."

"I love you, too, Charlie."

"No, I mean . . . I'm used to e-mailing you, Facebooking you."

He looked around. "And now we come here and some stranger thinks you've got a sugar daddy," he whispered conspiratorially. "What's with your own boyfriend?"

"What boyfriend?"

"My point."

She wrinkled her nose. She was not, he thought, a conventionally pretty girl. Her features were too strong—a prominent chin, heavy eyebrows—and she had cut her dark hair into ragged locks that she finger-combed back from her face. She would look great astride a horse, and in fact he remembered tales of her brief adolescent obsession with riding, though he was gone from Windermere by then.

"There was a guy," she admitted, "last year. But he graduated, and you could tell it wasn't going to work. He wanted, you know, something more domestic."

"You mean he wanted you to move in."

"More than that. He was going to want a wife. He'd started talking about kids!"

"You don't want kids?"

"Alex, I'm only twenty-two." She met his eyes and then focused on her wineglass. How grown-up she was, Alex thought, and still the same scamp who had gobbled up all his devotion two decades ago. "But no, I don't think I'll want children. I hope that's not horrible." She drained the glass. "I'm ambitious," she said bluntly. "And I don't care what those old feminists claim; a kid is like a ball and chain for a woman trying to make it."

"Make it as what?"

"Anything. I don't know yet. As a lawyer, maybe. Maybe a playwright. Let me get through my Chaucer seminar first."

"Okay."

"But you. You should still have them."

"Have what?"

"Kids, silly."

Alex regarded his sister fondly. He felt the temptation, after more than three decades, to unburden himself to a sibling—to someone who could absorb all his pain, all his mistakes, like a sponge, and who would still be, after it was all told, his sister, his brother. Charlie had that, because she had him, and he . . . but no. She was still a kid, with that bounce in her step. He wasn't going to filch it from her. "Not a lucky part of my life so far," he said.

"I always thought you and Brooke should have a kid."

His wineglass halfway to his lips, Alex felt his throat close up. He set the glass down.

"The unmentionable Brooke," Charlie continued. "We never talked about how attached I was to her, you know. That was long before Tomiko. We never talked about what happened with you guys."

"Is this your psych professor talking? Early childhood trauma."

"Don't be sarcastic, big brother. That's *my* job."

Alex shifted in his chair. In her teen years, Charlie had become an expert at annoying their mom this way—desanctifying every sacred cow, no adult subject off-limits to her callow wit. Over long-distance calls, after hearing his mother ignite into rage, he'd made her pass the phone and ordered Charlie to cool it. Now he was the one with a tinderbox sparking. "Brooke and I were children," he said now, his lips tightening. "Younger than you. We did stupid stuff."

"I hear she's in Hartford now. You should go see her. Rescue her from her life. That was what happened in all those stories she used to read me."

"What stories?"

"Blond maiden locked in tower, handsome knight with magic lance."

"That's phallic imagery, Charlie."

"Good boy." Alex's kid sister grinned at him, her mouth stained pink with the wine. "You're not just a bean counter, after all."

It was easy to stay busy. The Mercator office in Boston controlled staffing in five dozen branches around the world. Alex spent days huddled with the IT guys, debating how to drive corporate traffic onto the web without diminishing service. Evenings went to predictive flowcharts, the imagined shape of corporate finance after the crash. A note on the bulletin board by the coffee machine advertised a soccer team—*See Fabrice in Accounting*. He jotted down the name for when he had more time. As summer mellowed into fall, he took a couple of Sunday hikes. In the leafy hills west of the city, he felt the loss of the high peaks in Japan where he'd summited with Tomiko, before sorrow piled on thick enough to force him down into the foothills of the past. He took calls from old buddies he'd last seen at his dad's funeral—Brian, practicing law now in Rhode Island; Jake, still in Windermere. Sure, he said smoothly, I'm in the States for good now. We'll catch up. Sure, sure. Balding, energetic Francisco, one of the IT guys at Mercator, threw a Labor Day picnic, and Alex woke the next morning from a vivid dream of Tomiko to a strangely white apartment and the sweetly curved hip of a disheveled market researcher next to him in the bed. He gave her a nostalgic kiss, as if she had already receded into a hazy past, and exited into the dry, windy day, his eyes blinking tears.

The previous week, after a second meeting in Hartford, he had paced up and down Brooke's street until some drunk accosted him and he walked rapidly away. She wasn't returning his calls. On the cracked streets of that city—a tumbledown version of Boston, a jacked-up version of Scranton—he couldn't get her out of his head. And not just Brooke but Windermere, the flat-roofed high school, the sloping soccer field, the cheap diners and motels strung out along Route 6. Two weeks later, leaving Mercator's brick-front Hartford office, he thought he glimpsed another familiar face, wolf eyes in a gaunt frame that stared at him before turning and trotting swiftly to a low-slung Mazda. Someone from Windermere. Not a friend. Reece? Clyde? Clyde, that was it. Quickly he took a second look. Sure enough, it was the same guy. Of all people to turn up here. Clyde had been a thug in high school. He'd had a big-breasted, slow-witted girl—sophomore year? junior year?—whom he beat up; rumor was he pushed her down a flight of stairs so she would miscarry. By senior year he was gone from school, working in the coal mines to the west. Thinking of that sad, humiliated girl, Alex felt ready to turn back and take a swing at Clyde, for old times' sake. But when he wheeled around, the bum had vanished.

Hiking through the Massachusetts hills, he had mourned his

marriage and his lovely lost son. Driving east from Hartford, he mourned further back—to Brooke, to the newborn whose eyes he had glimpsed only the one time. His fault, all his fault and always his fault. And for what? How did he ever find himself in that motel room, doing the things he did? It hadn't been that uncommon, knocking up your girlfriend. For a couple like Alex and Brooke, it shouldn't have been a disaster. If only Brooke hadn't started on that stuff, that "tea," that creepy brew mashed up by Isadora Bassett.

March, he thought as he drove east. The month of March had tipped the scales. Over that spring break, Brooke had been supposed to come to Florida with Alex's family, but she wouldn't. Because nobody knew yet, she'd said. Not that Alex had wanted anyone to know—Christ, he hadn't wanted it to go on that long, had wanted to go down to Planned Parenthood right away, but there was the consent clause. She had been stuck on it, the consent clause. The bit about her mom, who'd had Brooke when she was eighteen and was always thanking God for her little girl—she would never sign. "You can't be positive of that," he'd said, taking Brooke's hands in the cold car, the night before he left with his family. "She could surprise you. Remember how she surprised you when she let us go camping alone last summer?"

"That didn't really surprise me, Lex. I just didn't want you counting on it."

"How about when she pierced a second hole in her ear? Hmm? Didn't that freak you, just a little?"

"That was fashion."

"So, abortion is fashion, these days."

Their breath had come steaming out of their mouths. For a second, while she hesitated, looking out of the cloudy windshield, he'd wanted to kiss her mouth, the way he used to, lips barely open and the cold teeth between. He remembered how they'd acted out that stupid scene from *The Fisher King*. *I don't want just one night.* They were parked on the hill just above her house, where the subdivision was going up. "I can't tell my mom you feel fat in a bathing suit," Alex said. "She'll just want you to come more. Plus she'll want you to keep Charlotte company."

"Spunky little Charlotte," said Brooke. Three days before, Charlie had broken both her arms trying to fly from midway up the huge spruce in the park. Who were the guys? Alex had kept asking her while she sat sniffling, her egg-shaped eyes staring guiltily at him, waiting for the plaster on her arms to dry. Who were the guys who said they'd catch you? They tried, Charlie had said. She'd been seven that year, a wild child.

"You think Clyde and those assholes did it?" he asked Brooke.

"Jeez, Alex, I don't know."

Brooke ran her tongue across her upper teeth, under her lip. Moonlight caught the curve of her cheek—a little fuller by then, nothing noticeable. Under her big sweaters and leggings, the difference was invisible. Still, by that point, he didn't like to have sex with her unless she pushed for it. Not that he didn't want her—in fact, it was weird how much he liked doing it with her body changing, blooming—but she kept telling him not to think about the pregnancy, and it was hard not to think about a thing when it was under your hand.

"I'm going to tell my parents," he said, shifting in the cold car seat.

"No, you're not." There was a new tone to Brooke's voice, as if she knew the future. You couldn't argue with her. Sometimes he thought she was making fun of him.

"They're different from your parents. They don't have an anti-abortion thing. My mom could talk to your mom, Brooke."

"Lex, Lex." She moved the back of a finger up and down his jacket sleeve; for an instant, he hated her. "You keep talking about an operation that I'm not going to have. I don't *need* an abortion, Alex."

"Dead babies don't keep getting bigger!"

"Sure they do. It's just a vegetable I'm growing in there, Lex. It hasn't got a brain. When it comes out, you'll see."

"Well, if that's true, then let's just get it out. Let's see *now*."

Brooke shook her head. He'd never imagined she could be so stubborn. Surely it was the hormones working. Her brain and the baby's, they were both turned to mush by that stuff Isadora made her drink.

Down in Florida, he managed mostly to forget about it. His parents had decided he and Brooke were breaking up. They couldn't avoid talking about Brooke's grandfather, old Albrecht; Alex's dad's accounting business had just picked up a notch with the Albrecht account. But they avoided Brooke's name. Disney World had a huge soccer expo. Pulling Charlotte in, one day, Alex played Virtual Foosball against Romário and won five rematches. He was still high as an escaped balloon when they got back to the condo.

"I can't *wait* to get on college varsity," he said, knocking a Hacky Sack around the sand-colored living room. "Blast those guys from Tufts off the field. That guy at the interview, Tom Hays? He was telling me Tufts got five out of the last six."

"Who says you'll make varsity?" his father asked from the card table, where he was letting Charlotte win at checkers.

"I've got a freaking scholarship, Dad."

"Don't say 'freaking,' " his mother called from the kitchen.

"You'll be a freshman nonetheless. There's a junior varsity, you know."

"Huh," said Alex.

"He'll make whatever he makes," said his mom. She was old for a mother, Alex thought as she came into the living room, wiping her hands on a cloth. She'd waited a long time to have him. Brooke's mom was young. His gut locked; he let the Hacky Sack drop from his foot. "He's happy, that's the point," his mother said with a glance toward the card table. His dad pursed his lips. Charlotte, oblivious, was trying to reach a finger inside her cast. "Stop that, honey," Alex's mom said. Her voice changed abruptly, and when Charlotte didn't stop, she stepped over and gave her hand a quick, hard slap.

"Your mother said stop," Alex's dad put in when Charlie's eyes filled.

"Why don't you go out to the beach, Alex," his mother said, her voice honeyed again. "There's an hour of light left."

"Pretty girls," said his dad.

"Jesus, can't you people hear the difference!" Flicking the Hacky Sack from the rug to his hand, Alex shook it at his parents. From the kitchen drifted radio music, something from the sixties but orchestrated. They looked at him as if he'd just shaken them from sleep for no reason. "The way—" he started, but he didn't go on; he'd pointed it out before, how they barked at Charlotte. But they never took it in. "Never mind," he said. "I'm going out."

On the beach a group of flat-chested preteen girls jumped in the crawling waves and giggled. Beyond them, various human shapes spread over the sand. *Barbecuing*, Brooke called it. Lifeguarding all summer, she still kept her creamy skin; she disdained people with nothing better to do than splay themselves out under the sun. He ached, right then, with missing her. When he heard footsteps behind him, he turned, imagining for a split second that it was Brooke, not pregnant anymore and come to find him down in Florida. But it was his sister, in her T-shirt and cutoffs, her arms hanging heavy from her thin shoulders. "Charlie," he said, and his heart swelled and sank. At least his kid sister did his bidding, scamp though she was.

He couldn't account, now, for how so much time had passed between that trip to Florida and the last week of high school. All he remembered was graduation looming around the corner and Brooke staying clear of him. Those had been her actual words—"I want to stay clear of you for a while"—but they hadn't broken up, because she wasn't returning anything to him or seeing anyone else. See anyone else—how could she, the way she was? It wasn't until the last day of school that he had determined to cut through her fog. Then as now, he liked things to be resolved. Either Brooke was his girlfriend or she wasn't; either she was going to have a baby or she wasn't.

He had waited for her after school. Coming out of the double doors, she didn't look that different—a tall willowy girl in a loose dress. They had a few hours till he was due at an exhibition game, varsity versus alumni, the Old Guard weekend. He couldn't believe how happy he was to have her in the car with him again. He kept risking an accident because he wanted so much to turn and look at her. The cool planes of her cheeks; the tiny wave in the bone of her nose; her small ears, the wires she threaded through the lobes. "I have to say something," he said. It was the first line he'd delivered since *Come on* at the parking lot.

"Okay. Say something."

"If it comes out okay—I mean, grant me this, there's a *possibility*—if it's alive and well and all that, then we'll just get married and live with my parents, and I'll go to Penn State."

"None of that is going to happen, Alex."

"I'm just saying. And if it's—you know, dead—then I'll help when it comes out. And if it's alive but not okay . . ." He slid his eyes up to meet hers. She was almost smiling, like he was amusing. "If it's alive but not okay—if that stuff, you know, fucked up its brain or whatever . . ."

"Who've you been talking to, Alex?"

"Nobody! *Nobody*. That's just the problem. The days go by, and you're still—you know—and we don't talk to *anybody* about it."

This was not completely true. The week before he'd gone to his best friend, Jake. He had lied about the details, said Brooke was just barely knocked up and they'd probably get the abortion before graduation. Jake said that all the chicks in Windermere ought to either get abortions or move away. That would send a message to the assholes in the health department. You know, Jake had said, what they do in China? They just put them down a well. Newborns. They don't feel anything, right at that point. That way society doesn't got to pay for 'em, and you don't get a life of suffering. It's like throwing a pot and it won't fire up right, you junk it. You start a new pot.

"I talked to Isadora," Brooke was saying.

"And she said, what, 'Oops, sorry for the bad advice'?"

"She took a look, if you must know. She pressed around. She put her ear to my belly."

"What, she's a nurse now?"

"Said something seemed off in our calculations. It ought to have kicked by now, if I was more than six months."

"So, fine. You just missed for a few months, and then we really knocked you up, and now you can have the operation."

"No, Alex. I told her I was sure."

"What the fuck does either of you know!" Alex banged the steering wheel, which gave out a halfhearted honk. "We live in a town crawling with doctors—"

"She picked up the phone to call my parents."

"Yeah? Okay," said Alex. His foot pushed the pedal a little harder. He was ready to forgive Isadora Bassett, if only.

"And I just looked at her while she started to dial. So she put it down. I'm not the only one afraid of my mom, Lex."

"I'm not afraid of your mom! That bitch," Alex said, and he meant Isadora, but he didn't care how Brooke took it.

The diner had a bright yellow sign, Daisy's Kitchen, and one pickup parked outside. The lot was dusty. There had been a drought all that spring; the farmers around Windermere were worried. Alex steered Brooke in, the way he'd seen kidnappers do in movies, just enough pressure to be sure the person doesn't bolt. "If it's not okay," he started again when they were in the booth, "I think we ought to be prepared—"

"God, Alex." She rolled her eyes. "You think the weirdest thoughts."

"Are they so weird? Huh? Aren't those the three possibilities? No baby. Baby. Monster-baby." He sat back in the booth, arms over his chest. The waitress came over, her face like a scared bird's, to ask if they were ready to order. He got a Coke and fries for himself; Brooke ordered a slice of blueberry pie, which he would probably eat most of. They'd taken the last booth. Reaching across, Brooke touched her hand to the yellow bruise above Alex's left eye, where he'd taken a header at the last soccer game.

"I want," she said, after she had caressed the spot for a few seconds, her cool fingers lifting the pain out, "to be your girl."

Panic seized his vocal cords. His lips could hardly move. "You are my girl."

"I mean I don't want to be a weight on you. Not ever. I've seen that happen."

"You're not a weight on me. But this—this thing is. This pregnancy thing."

There, it was out. He'd named his stake in what Brooke did. The food came. He poured ketchup over the fries. As she always did, Brooke sneaked one long ketchup-free fry out from the rest and nibbled it, like a carrot. She showed no interest in her triangle of pie. She was blinking a lot, and it took Alex too long to figure out that what she was blinking away were tears.

"I've never made a mistake before," she said abruptly. She had to say it twice for Alex to understand; the French fry got in the way.

"No pain, no gain," he said, stupidly. He was trying to unscramble the tears. Why did girls decide to cry when they did? Why'd they decide to do anything when they did?

"But it's not fair to have to take the consequences of someone else's screwup."

"The doctor who fitted you, you mean." She nodded. "Well, you wouldn't've had to, four months ago."

"Don't start on me with that, Lex. I'm trying to say something to you."

"Okay. Okay, baby." *Don't fuck it up*, he'd ordered himself, waiting at the school exit. He couldn't bring himself even to think the word *love*. "I'm listening. I'm not talking, I'm just listening."

"Because . . . because I've never made any mistakes—any real mistakes, I mean—I don't know how to ask for help. Do you follow me? Asking for help—well, in my family, that means you're in the ooze, or go back three spaces."

"You lost me there, babe."

"Candy Land," she said, as if he should have known.

He smiled in spite of himself. "Charlie likes Chutes and Ladders."

"Well, I used to cheat at Candy Land."

"What?" He almost spat out his fries. "You never cheat. You can't even lie."

"What do you mean? I've been lying to my parents for six months."

"That's not lying. It's just keeping quiet."

"It's lying when you buy Tampax and flush it down the toilet without using it."

"But Candy Land? Who cheats at Candy Land?"

"I told you. I did. I played my cousin Kurt when he was five and I was eight. He was used to me winning things. He thought I was better at things than he was. He didn't understand that Candy Land's just a game of luck."

Alex pushed her pie at her. "Eat," he said.

"Not hungry."

"Look, you want to hear what I used to do to my sister? When she was like four, and I was fourteen, I stole all her Halloween candy. I dumped the wrappers on the floor and told her the dog had gotten it. I stole candy from a *baby*."

"When'd you stop?"

"Lemme see. How long ago was November?"

That got a grin out of her. He loved to see that, her big white teeth—made her look like a kid, choppers too big for her mouth. "We're bad people," she said.

"Sinners," he said, and took a forkful of her pie.

"Hey. Did I tell you I got a summer job?"

"You haven't told me anything. You've been steering clear of me, remember?"

"Well, I did. Lifeguarding at Hammond Lake. Bring on the SPF fifty." She took a sip of his Coke, swishing the ice in her mouth. He let his fork dangle over the pie. "Aren't you going to congratulate me?"

"I don't get it. You wouldn't come to Florida. How you gonna look in a swimsuit *now*?"

"The job doesn't start till the Fourth. If I haven't lost it by then, I'll wear a T-shirt."

"Brooke—honey—people look fat *afterward*. Jesus, I thought girls *noticed* stuff like that."

"Well, my dad came home with the offer from a buddy of his, okay? Now how am I going to turn it down? 'Sorry, Dad, I don't feel like taking the cushiest job in central Pennsylvania this summer, thanks anyhow'?"

"I'm trying to get you to think, Brooke."

"I can't think when I'm with you. That's why I wanted to steer clear."

"Seems to me you can't think *without* me. A job in a bikini!"

"Not a *bikini*. Lifeguard suit. I'll wear a T-shirt."

"You know what we are going to do now, Brooke Willcox? I am going to pay for this food, and then we're going to drive back to Windermere. We'll go to my house, sit my parents down, and tell them what's happening."

"You go. I'm not going."

"Then you'll sit here, and I'll come back and fetch you."

"I won't be here when you get back."

"What, you'll run away?" She shrugged. He felt in charge, suddenly. This was all she had been waiting for, he was sure of it—for him to announce what they were doing about the problem, and then to do it. He pulled eight dollars out of his pocket and set it under the damp Coke glass. He stood up. "You're coming with me."

"Don't boss me!"

"I said, you're coming." Reaching across the booth, he took hold of her upper arm. It was smoothly muscled—he had just time to notice, and to remember it was because she swam—and it worked hard to jerk away from him. But the hands he never used in his sport were strong anyhow, and he pulled her across the red vinyl seat to a standing position.

As she strode ahead of him out of the diner, he touched the back of her neck. Like a horse, she flicked him off. And then, after he'd unlocked his side of the car and slid in while she waited, and unlocked the door on her side, he saw a new expression on her face, a look of pure amazement. He pushed the passenger door open to follow her gaze down to the dusty parking lot, to the pool of water big as a plate between her feet.

Chapter 8

The trailer complex lay five miles outside the upstate village of Windermere, a good hour west of Scranton. The state highway that rushed by it made a constant whooshing sound, not unlike the river by the Polish village where Josef Zukowsky had grown up, where he had married and seen two of his three daughters born. The third daughter, Luisa, had emerged here in Pennsylvania, and she was the slow one. So much, Josef used to joke bitterly with his Polish companions, for all the great advances in America. But in truth, he knew, Luisa would have been slow no matter where she had been born. In truth, the way she had remained like a child all her life had kept her dear to his heart.

No one called him Josef anymore. His wife, Marika, had passed on almost two decades ago. His eldest daughter had moved to San Francisco. He was Ziadek—Grandpa—to his remaining daughters and his son-in-law; Ziadek to the other struggling souls who lived in the trailer park; Ziadek, he supposed, to himself. Ten years ago, when he lost half a lung, he had finally stopped working at the quarry. He stayed home. Across a garden and a walkway in the trailer park lived his second daughter, his husky Katarina with her hair dyed deep red and determination etched into her strong-boned face. She had a husband, Chet, whose English was even worse than Ziadek's and who was gone most weeks, driving his rig as far as Nebraska. Back when Ziadek first retired, he kept an eye on Katarina's two sons after school—but they were gone now, off raising hell in Binghamton or Brooklyn, he couldn't keep track. Still, he had his Luisa for company. And he had Luisa's beloved girl, Najda. To all of them, he was Ziadek.

These days, he was on oxygen, and with Katarina breathing down his neck about it, he had finally given up smoking. He spent his days crouched in the pocket garden between his house and Katarina's, or making the rich soups they all loved, or playing chess with Najda. Except for the bawling truck horns that ruined the delusion of a river running nearby, and except for the wind that whistled through the trailer in the frigid upstate winters, it was not a bad life.

Najda, though—that was the problem. "Foundling," her name meant, because Luisa had found her, in the pouring rain, that day Luisa tried to run from home. How long ago was it, now? They'd celebrated Najda's fifteenth birthday in June. Fifteen years, then. Ziadek couldn't remember why Luisa had run away that time, so long ago. She ran off a lot, after Marika died. Ziadek couldn't blame her. Marika had cuddled her, protected her. Marika had blamed herself for Luisa's being slow—she'd been too old when she gave birth to the girl; the doctors had warned her such a thing could happen. When Marika died, the others teased and tortured Luisa, and Ziadek—well, he was still at the quarry then, what could he do?

And then he had come home from the grocery one night, in the rain, one of those deluges that break a long drought, and there was Luisa in the tiny sitting room of the trailer, with a tiny infant sucking at her nipple.

Ziadek had screamed at the sight. It shamed him now, to think back, but he had screamed, and dropped his bag, and the cans had rolled over the floor. It all flashed through his head. Someone had raped his Luisa, his poor simple slow Luisa, a child really though she had all her women's parts, and now this infant had come out of her with no one around to help, and surely, surely the girl would lose what little mind she had in the first place. Luisa had jumped, at the scream, and the baby had made a gargling noise and fallen away from the nipple. That was when Ziadek had seen the truth. Luisa's nipple was wet with the baby's spit, but not with milk. It was not plump, the way a woman's breasts are when they nurse. Luisa stood up, quick with fury, and he saw her blouse was soaked from the rain, but she was not tired in the least, and her legs and hips moved as they always did. This was not a girl who had just given birth to a child while her father was off at the grocery.

"You scared her!" Luisa had said, clutching the infant tight.

Ziadek saw then that the baby was wrapped in bloody towels, and its flesh was dark, almost purple. He stepped close, and his daughter stepped away. "Ssh, ssh," Ziadek said. "She scared me. I won't hurt her, darling. Let me have a look. Let me see what you found."

Slowly, suspiciously, Luisa tipped her arms and showed him. Ziadek gasped. The baby was tiny, wrinkled, its eyes still shut, its little mouth working. Its skin was covered in blood and the cream of birth. It breathed in tiny gasps, its throat clotted. From its belly ran the still-blue stump of an umbilical cord. This was a newborn.

Swiftly Ziadek lifted the little thing from Luisa's arms, held it up by its wormy legs, and slapped its back. Mucus gushed from the tiny mouth. The baby gave a cry—not a lusty cry, more like the peep of a bird, but a cry nonetheless—and when he cradled its head and flipped it up, it took in a great yawn of air. "Papa!" Luisa cried, and tried to get the infant back from him, but he was too quick for her. He stepped to the galley kitchen, pulled two dish towels from the hooks, and quickly wrapped the little thing in them. The color was better now; it seemed to be breathing normally. Tiny, though—it was too small, really, to be born. He frowned and looked at Luisa again.

"Did this come from you?" he said.

Luisa looked confused. She twisted her hands in front of her. They were bloody from the towels, which now lay in a heap on the floor.

"Did this thing come," Ziadek repeated, "from your body, daughter?"

Biting her lower lip, Luisa shook her head. She had the small round head and small chin that others like her shared—*mongoloid*, the ones who teased called her—and her face bent toward her half-exposed chest. "Found her," she answered. "In the trash."

"Where? What trash?"

Luisa pointed toward the door. He knew where she meant. Across the road from the trailer park, the motel run by Pakistanis. Luisa had a bad habit of rummaging in their trash, coming home with stuff the transients had left in their rooms: broken Barbies and packs of cigarettes and once a hypodermic that got her a good tongue-lashing from Ziadek. She knew she was not to go over there, not to climb up to the Dumpster or rummage around.

"Come with me," he ordered her.

"No." Luisa hung her head. She began blubbering. "'S mine," she said at last. "I found her."

Ziadek was panicked. He was a citizen of this country, though he had forgotten most of the English he'd learned to pass the test. But Katarina had never married her husband in a church. Chet was a hard worker without ambition; he got by from one work visa to the next. Ziadek was not sure if his grandchildren were even legal. He was in no position to draw attention.

Still. A baby was a baby, however shriveled and looking to die. "You can hold her," he told Luisa. Then he marched Luisa out the door, carrying the barely breathing thing, through the pouring rain to the car.

The Pakistanis wanted nothing to do with it. Someone must have driven by, they swore. You never knew what people would toss in a Dumpster. Ziadek saw the older one shoot his brother a glance, and soon after the brother glided out of the office and up the stairs. When he came back, his brown face was overlaid with a chalky look. Still the one at the reception insisted: They would not phone the police. The girl was lying to Ziadek; if he examined her he would see. She had given birth on her own and needed to admit it. But the towels, Ziadek said, the towels were motel towels. Plenty of motels in the area, the man said—did he think he could get them on the towels?

Luisa was tugging at Ziadek's shirt by then. He glanced down. The tiny one's mouth was working again. It was hungry. Already its little life was fading away. "We'll be back," he said to the Pakistanis, and drove away in the rain, to the supermarket a mile down the road, to fetch formula.

They never went back. That first night, Ziadek faced down Katarina and her brawny, tattooed husband Chet. "Yes," he had said to them, "we can report the baby. We can give the baby to the state, and the state will find a place for her. And we know where she will grow up, what kind of place she will grow up in if she grows up at all. And our Luisa here—your sister Luisa, look at her—she will go on sucking her thumb and being lonely as a tree in a desert. Or we can let them care for each other."

"But they both need care! Look at this dying thing! And *she*"—
Katarina pointed at Luisa—"needs her own babysitter!"

"Did I not buy your home?" Ziadek asked her. "Did your mother
not watch your children until she drew her last breath? Are we not
with this one already"—he nodded at Luisa—"from the moment
she gets off from the bus until the moment she boards it the next
day? Do you talk to me about babysitting? Look at your sister!"

They had looked. They had seen the glow on Luisa's face. "But
what if someone comes to find—" Katarina began.

"They won't come," Chet said. He loosened the lock of his tattooed arms. "They left her for dead. Ziadek is right. She's ours or
no one's."

And so, that night, Katarina had prepared Luisa. As luck would
have it, she was having her monthly time. Katarina had gently penetrated her, had broken her hymen. Next day they took the baby to
the crowded emergency room. Katarina, who spoke perfect English,
explained that it was Luisa's child. She did not know who had made
her sister pregnant, no. Luisa had gone off, Katarina said, and
returned carrying the child. The doctor looked from Luisa—her
round face, her almond-shaped eyes, her blank forehead—to Ziadek.
These things happened, the doctor said. It was tragic. He did not
want to bring infant neglect charges against Luisa. He sent Luisa
away—for dilation and curettage, he said, to be sure everything was
out. He sent the infant to the ICU. Ziadek and Katarina sat in the
waiting room, looking at each other, breathing. When they were
allowed into the recovery room, they found Luisa sitting up, her face
pale as plaster.

Had the hospital been less crowded, Ziadek thought sometimes,
or had they produced better insurance, someone might have looked
more carefully, might have suspected Luisa's story. As it was, the
doctor came back with a pediatrician, a stern man with heavy black

glasses, who had examined Najda. The pediatrician said they could tie Luisa's tubes. No, no, Katarina said; that would not be necessary. But about neglect, the first doctor said. The baby was more than twenty-four hours old already, a four-and-a-half-pound preemie with no medical care. She would need at least a week in the ICU, probably more.

The doctors were good men. They looked sadly at the little family sitting around Luisa's cot. He would have to contact child services, the pediatrician said. Luisa must never be left alone with the child. If she would get her tubes tied, he said, nodding at Luisa, it would go easier for them all. Luisa was not much at comprehending; when others began talking above her head, she usually went off somewhere, into whatever dreamland slow people inhabited. This time, though, she had not gone off. She met the doctors' eyes. She nodded.

Every night, that first month, Ziadek watched the local news. He waited to hear about a lost babe, a premature infant someone had impulsively abandoned and now missed. Or a pregnant woman found dead somewhere, the child inside her gone. All that came was the usual violence down in Scranton—rapes, drive-by shootings, arson. Luisa devoted herself to the baby. Katarina named her Najda. Before work in the early morning, Ziadek drove Luisa to the hospital, where she sat for an hour by the respirator. She no longer tried to run away, no longer descended into tantrums. When Najda came home from the ICU, Katarina instructed her sister on infant care, and Luisa did everything to the letter. She sang the baby to sleep, she sat up when the baby had colic, she minded her diaper rash. While the baby slept—and the tiny one slept long and profoundly, gathering its little bit of strength to live—Luisa knitted sweaters and booties, more than they could ever use, and soon Katarina began taking the extra ones to the summer craft fairs, and they sold, and Luisa was proud to think she was earning Najda's way.

But the doctors had been right, about damage. That became clear early on, as little Najda sucked her bottles and slept and woke and cried her peeping cry. She moved only her left arm and left leg. When she first rolled over, it was only from left to right; she did not have the strength to roll back. After a few months they brought the child to Dr. Walczek, who had cared for Luisa as a child. Hypoxia, Dr. Walczek said. Lack of air to the brain, to the left side of the brain, could cause this kind of defect. That side, he said, controls the muscles of the right side. It also controls speech. The baby would never walk properly, said Dr. Walczek, and she might not talk. But she could see fine, he said, and hear. For a preemie—he smiled, and the baby smiled crookedly back—little Najda seemed alert.

That was fifteen years ago. Since then they had managed well enough. Katarina worked from home, phoning marketing surveys, until Ziadek retired. Now he was the one who watched his Luisa with her knitting, helped Najda on and off the special bus, met with the social worker. These days Katarina worked at the Wal-Mart. Chet's long truck hauls kept him away weeks at a time. Even on oxygen, Ziadek was the man of the house; "Alpha Ziadek," Katarina called him, whatever that meant. The doctor's prediction had come true. Najda could do little with the right side of her body. Her speech was slow, halting. She did better in Polish than in English, but even in Ziadek's tongue she skipped over words, like an old record with scratches. "Bishop queen four," she could say when they played chess. But questions like "Why does the moon always wane on the left side?" came out "Moon . . . shrinks . . . left, why?" And then she would fix Ziadek with those keen blue eyes of hers, challenging him to know just what she meant and to give her a straight answer. Much as Ziadek understood English, Najda understood what everyone said; she just couldn't give it back except in translated pieces.

Najda was still small—no taller than Luisa, who had stopped growing at thirteen, and much thinner than Luisa, who couldn't keep herself from the chips and sodas her sister brought home when Wal-Mart had specials. Once a week, the Medicaid paid for Najda to go to the special gym in Scranton where sleek, muscled trainers helped her take halting steps with a metal walker and watched her exercise in the warm pool. Before he had the lung operation, Ziadek drove Najda and Luisa, who liked to watch, to Scranton. Now, with the oxygen, Katarina had forbidden him to get behind the wheel except in emergencies, and so they had to wait until she was off work and could take everyone down the long highway. Being so restricted, so unable to take charge, annoyed Ziadek beyond measure. He had always been of use in his life.

Luisa had left the special school program—she was learning nothing there anyway except to make change and read prices, as if they were all being trained to work the grocery checkout—and made Najda her life. For Najda when she was ready for school, it was different. Every day, the same blue van picked her up as used to pick up Luisa. They rolled the wheelchair onto the lift, and Ziadek put his arm around Luisa's shoulders as the hoist operated, moving Najda up and away with the rest of the students, to be gone for seven hours. In the van rode the same sort of students as had ridden with Luisa: students with cerebral palsy, with autism, with what the administrators called cognitive deficits. At first glance Najda looked like the rest of them. The right side of her face had little expression. Her right arm and leg, even with all the water exercising, were withered. Now and then little tics assaulted her—she jerked and twitched and drooled a little, and sometimes she hummed to keep from emitting the growls and barks that wanted to come out. But where Luisa had gone placidly through the days learning to count the coins and solve the brightly colored puzzles, Najda finished all the puzzles and rolled her blue eyes when she had to do the coins for the dozenth time. By the time she was eight she was reciting—without the humming, with barely a hint of a stutter—poetry.

"We mainstream them three times a week," the teacher had told Katarina when Ziadek made her call. "She has all the opportunities available in the system."

The social worker, too, said Najda needed to stay where she was. "She is doing remarkably well," this person said, pulling Najda's charts from her file folder. She always looked at the charts when she visited them, Ziadek noticed; she never looked at Najda or Luisa, and at Ziadek only when he raised his voice. "Stability is the most important factor in her development."

But Najda was not interested in stability. She wanted to learn, and she wanted to do it in her own way. "Not . . . power," she said the other day, her voice breathless with frustration. "Not . . . point power. Point. PowerPoint." She nodded vigorously when she'd managed the phrase. "Fun," she said. "Laugh." But Ziadek and Luisa both knew she was not talking about having fun. Najda held her left hand up, as if it were a sign or screen held next to her face. "Chistory of Hess," she said clearly. Ziadek nodded. He knew what she meant—knew it as easily as if she had said the syllables in their proper order, "History of Chess." "Words," she went on, nodding at her hand-screen. "Pictures. Teacher . . . teacher make speak Najda." She flung a hand toward Ziadek, as if he were in the audience for her PowerPoint presentation. "Laugh," she commanded him.

"Well, fuck the PowerPoint," Ziadek said in Polish. "Write him an essay, honey. Show him all you know about the history of chess. Show the bastard. He can't let kids laugh at you like that."

But Najda had dissolved in tears, and Luisa was dabbing her face with tissues. "Hush, Ziadek, hush," Luisa said to her father.

Najda went to the new county library, two miles down Route 6, where she waited for her half hour turn on the computer and struggled to master this PowerPoint, which Ziadek understood was like a slide show only with words and decorations along with the pictures. Sequencing was the problem; also speaking. At night, Ziadek heard Najda repeating the names of games from Persia and China, the names of chess masters from the royal courts. The teacher gave them only five minutes for the presentation, and she had enough knowledge for an hour's talk. Pages and pages of clumsy pictures she drew on lined paper, trying to squeeze it all into squares that could flash onto the computer screen with a little pointer to highlight. When the moment came and her words dissolved into a hum anyway, the class laughed just as Najda had predicted. She stopped halfway through. "Checkmate!" the kids called out now, when they saw her in the school corridor. Maybe they mean it in a friendly way, Katarina tried telling Najda, but Najda only shook her head miserably.

Such things kept happening. The more Najda understood of what was expected in the mainstream classes, the more she couldn't bear how little anyone expected of her. Where Luisa had been a sweet, docile calf who learned all she needed and stopped, Najda was like a fettered eagle, meant to soar to the clouds but held down by the holes in her speech and the muffled laughter of the other students. For three days now, when the blue bus stopped by the entrance to the trailer park, Najda sat in the room she shared with Luisa and refused to get out of bed and into the motorized wheelchair the Medicaid had bought for her last year. Before his surgery, Ziadek would have lifted her bodily, stripped the nightgown from her, wrestled her into clothes, and dropped her into the chair. Now he was too weak. Next week the social worker would come, and she would learn that Najda was not going to school.

"Do you understand what that means?" Ziadek said to Luisa as she helped Najda into the chair, an hour after the school bus had gone. "It means they will find you incompetent to be her mother. It means they will take her away. Do you understand that?" he repeated, this second time directly to Najda. The girl gave him a piercing, agonized look. She was growing, he realized, into a beautiful young woman, confined as she was and with half her body useless.

"It's okay," Luisa said, stroking Najda's blond hair. "He's not mad at you, really. We'll get ice cream later. It's okay."

"I am not giving you money for ice cream," said Ziadek.

But as they left, Luisa pushing Najda through the yellow leaves that had begun drifting from the poplars around the trailer park, he relented. Calling Luisa back, he gave her a crumpled five-dollar bill. Luisa would push her girl the two miles to the flat-roofed library, where Najda would read books and spend hours on the computer, clicking keys to find out all the things she hungered to know. She was dyslexic, the social worker had said, as well as aphasic. Learning of any kind would take her longer than others. But she was not stupid. Listening to the social worker, Ziadek had worked not to laugh. Stupid! No fifteen-year-old who could outplay him in chess could be called stupid. That much he knew.

Katarina came over, the third night after Najda started refusing to attend school, to confront her sister. Luisa and Najda were playing Candy Land, Luisa's favorite game. Behind Luisa, the television played Najda's favorite series, one of those medical dramas where all the nurses looked like movie stars and the doctors made smart-ass remarks. While Luisa studied her next move, Najda sneaked peeks at the TV. When had she first outrun her mother?

Ziadek could not say. It was so easy for outsiders to take the teen-aged girl to be as slow as the woman who watched after her, simply because Najda got her words mixed up and made curious sounds. But he guessed that for five years at least, Najda had been indulging her mother. If Luisa wanted to play Candy Land, they played and Najda satisfied her restless mind by watching the medical show. If Luisa wanted to watch cartoons, they watched while Najda did Sudoku. The rest of the family did the same, one way or another.

All, that is, except Katarina when she was angry, which she was that evening. She banged into Ziadek's home like a tornado. She was a big, handsome woman, Katarina—forty-one years old now, her two boys grown and gone already. She had mothered Luisa from the moment their own mother took sick twenty years back. She was still wearing her Wal-Mart vest; her hair, dyed red to disguise the early gray, fluffed out from her head and curled against her neck like a mushroom cap. Out in the back, Chet was shouting into his cell phone. He'd come over to Ziadek's place with her, but he didn't want much to do with family matters. "Am I to understand," Katarina said in Polish, "that you're just letting her play hooky?"

Luisa looked at her older sister, a frightened smile on her pump-kin face. "She might go tomorrow," she said.

"No," said Najda in English. She moved her blue plastic child-piece to a yellow square. "Library school me." Her head began to jerk toward the right side, always a sign that she was agitated. "Your move," she said to Luisa.

"Don't be ridiculous." Katarina marched around the two players and flicked off the TV. She turned directly to Najda. "We all had to put up with it," she said, leaning on the table where the game was set up. "I put up with it when I couldn't even speak English. Chet, too. Luisa put up with it when kids called her names. You can put up with a little boredom and teasing. In a year you can leave school.".

"I'm here," came a voice from outside. Chet appeared in the doorway. His muscles going to fat from the years in the truck cab, he still presented a formidable challenge. "And I'm sick of my wife having to worry about this shit."

"If you want them to take you out of here and give you to a bunch of strangers, missy—" Katarina was saying to Najda.

"Talk to *me*," said Luisa. She looked regretfully at her Candy Land marker, then turned resolutely toward her sister. "She's mine. You should talk to me. Shouldn't Katarina talk to me, Ziadek?"

Ziadek drew on his oxygen. It came into his nostrils by way of two clear plastic nibs connected to tubes that pinched his mustache, circled his head, and snaked down to the tank they kept on a special dolly. The oxygen was always cool. It left a slightly metallic taste at the back of his throat. He wondered sometimes if they put drugs into the gas in the tank; when he breathed deep, he seemed to pull back from the world around him and view it as if it were one of the girls' television shows. He turned to Luisa. "You must decide, then," he said gently. "Will you make her go to school? Or will you take this risk?"

"Make her go?" said Luisa. Confused, she looked Najda up and down. Najda gave a little giggle. She knew what her mother was thinking—that Najda was too big for her to carry or force.

"You punish her," said Katarina. "She'll go to school right enough when you take away her chess. When you won't push her to that tin-can library."

Najda stuck out her tongue at her aunt. She started to speak for herself, but came out with what usually emerged, when she was overwrought—a kind of "muh-myeh-gah-dyeh" nonsense that grew slowly louder as she tried to shape it into words.

Chet stepped into the trailer with his big hands on his thick hips. "What do you want her doing?" he said—first to Luisa, then to

Ziadek. "Spending her days with a moron and an old man? She needs to be with young people! Look at her. If she won't go to school—"

"She *likes* the library." Luisa had begun to cry. "She likes me. You can't call me a moron. Ziadek, tell them."

"You. You." Najda pinched her lips together until she could get the words right inside her mouth. Then she burst out, "Robby smokes pot!" Ziadek smiled. Robby was Katarina's older boy, a pile of trouble whom Chet had thrown out only a month before. Najda was cutting the legs out from under Katarina's argument by shifting the focus to her own kid. A smart girl, he thought. A strategist.

"Robby"—Katarina leaned over the table and forced Najda to meet her eyes—"is not the point. My sister"—she pointed to the weeping Luisa—"has loved you since you were born. Is your pride so important that you'd risk her losing you? Hmm? And where do you think they would take you, Miss Najda? To the library?"

With her good arm, Najda swept the Candy Land pieces and cards from the table. Luisa doubled her wails. "Christ!" shouted Chet, who had moved to Ziadek's side. "Will she ever be grateful?"

"Were *you* ever grateful?" Ziadek asked him.

"I didn't get plucked out of a Dumpster by a family that had enough to take care of without rescuing some—some slut's . . ." *Abortion*, Chet wanted to say. He had said it before. But Ziadek's look forbade the word. "Somebody else's mistake," he said.

Ziadek cut a sharp glance at Najda. She had found the remote, turned her TV show on again, and was increasing the volume. Luisa had taken heavily to her hands and knees, picking up pieces of the game. "Stop it," Katarina ordered her. "You didn't spill it. You shouldn't clean it."

"She *can't*," Luisa spat out. She looked pleadingly at Ziadek. She meant that Najda could not get around on hands and knees, he understood; but she meant more. She meant that Najda couldn't be any way except what she was. Everything her older sister did, from rushing to Luisa's side when she thought Najda took advantage of her, to turning her head away in embarrassment when Najda struggled with words, said that Katarina considered the girl still, after fifteen years, a refugee, one who should be grateful each day for the garbage hound who had rescued her and the family who lied to keep her out of the hands of the state. But Najda was not grateful. She was determined, ambitious, and frustrated. She played Candy Land with Luisa because she loved Luisa. But she did not consider that she owed any of them a damned thing.

"Najda," Ziadek said. Oh, how he missed Marika! She had been a frail woman while the quarry had built up his arms and legs, made his belly a rock. But she was the stronger one when it came to the girls. "We will find a new school for you. There are other schools besides the high school in Windermere."

"Private school?" said Katarina.

Ziadek shrugged. "There are places. They can understand what Najda needs. This is America."

"But, Ziadek, the money—" Katarina began.

He held up a warning hand, cutting her off. "We will find the way to pay for it. A scholarship."

"Charity," Chet spat.

Ziadek ignored him. He spoke to Najda. "But you must search it out. At your library. At the computers there. You find what will make you happy. You bring it home. We are a family. Do you understand me? Turn that thing off."

A handsome doctor on the television was staring, bewildered, at a patient's chart. Najda flicked the remote and wheeled her chair to face Ziadek. Her eyes were wet. She looked from one member of her family to the next. Single words were her specialty, and she uttered just one of them.

"College," she said.

Chapter 9

School started, with Meghan in first grade. Sean took pictures of her in her new clothes with her bright pink backpack and sparkly sneakers. By October, Brooke's schedule would loosen up, and she could take Meghan to and from West Elementary. Until then, Sean stayed on pickup duty. He didn't want Meghan riding the bus. He'd ridden the Hartford school bus and knew what kind of bullies were on it. Not that getting away from work was easy, with almost a third of the staff laid off and Larry eyeing production levels. But Sean punched in a quarter hour before he was due and kept his men moving. Each day that first week, he left at two forty-five, loaded Bach's Christmas Oratorio into the car player, and sang his way to the school. In the car, his voice soared. He held the high A neck and neck with the soloist. He rejoiced in the news of birth and miracles, and he left the print shop far behind.

Then he pulled into the parking lot and shut off the engine. The arias looped through his head as he stepped out, but the only music on the lot was Top 40 and hip-hop from the waiting cars. The waiting moms looked at him sad-eyed. He didn't care. So they thought he was unemployed, so what? All the babies gurgling in their car seats, on the other hand, bothered him; the toddlers on the grass rankled. What had started as a point of pride—O'Connors didn't pop just one offspring—had become a hunger. The arias faded in his throat, and silence descended.

Sometimes Sean dreamed about the kid they didn't have, with his fat cheeks or her chunky growing muscles. He woke up bereft. Brooke, meanwhile, had kept talking adoption. Subtly and not so subtly she left brochures on the coffee table, flyers on the mail table, numbers by the phone. As if to demonstrate the process, she'd taken in another cat, a stray with health problems who got more attention than Sean. Adoption, he wanted to shout at her, is not the point. How dumb, he wanted to ask her, do you think I am?

Then Brooke's mom came to visit and put a lid on the adoption talk.

"I've got something to say to you both," she said when they had finished their first meal together. Brooke had prepared it, lamb chops and arugula salad, but her mom—Stacey, Sean was supposed to call her, not *Mother* the way you would in his tribe—would shop and fix the rest of the week's meals. They would come straight out of the cookbooks she brought and would leave behind, fancy hardcovers with pictures of shrimp tails arching up like ballerina legs out of some delicate mush. For weeks after, a slightly rotten spice odor would linger in the kitchen. Nothing would arrive on Sean's plate by itself. They had taught Meghan not to wrinkle her nose and to say "I don't care for any" rather than "I hate that icky stuff."

"Can I be excused?" Meghan asked, and Sean nodded at her. She skipped out to the back with the dogs. Evenings were still warm, though dying into that blue twilight that Sean remembered from childhood, when he and his brothers would go out looking for their dad.

"My daughter," Stacey continued, leveling her gaze at Sean, "has always lived in her imagination."

In Brooke's mother Sean could spot the square jaw and wide mouth of his wife, and Stacey's way of tilting her head while she listened was also familiar. From her dad, he supposed, Brooke had her distinctive nose and pale hair—Stacey's was tinted, now, but clearly she had always been brunette—as well as her height. Over her firm, compact body Stacey had complete control. She wasn't exactly graceful, but she could have been one of those tai chi instructors you heard about. Every movement was intentional, nothing wasted.

"And so," she went on, "when she told me you two were thinking of adoption, I knew she was making up another story."

"Mom, please," Brooke said. Her forearms lay on the table, as if she would reach for Sean's hand, but of course he was at the other end, Stacey in between.

"The story of a foundling, or some such nonsense," Stacey went on. "And the problem with stories is, they are not life."

"And your story," Brooke put in, "is I'm still twelve years old."

"If we have another child," Sean said firmly, "Brooke and I will decide together what the best road is. Same as we did for Meghan. Right, honey?"

Brooke nodded. His tone of voice brooked no disagreement, and she certainly wasn't going to argue in front of her mother. From the start, Stacey had treated Sean as a paltry stand-in for the husband Brooke was meant to have. No need to throw gas on coals that still glowed, a little, with disapproval. Quickly, Stacey glanced from one of them to the other. She had barely nipped at her chop—which, Sean assumed, she would judge as too well done. He wanted to pick his up by the bone, but he'd wait until he was in the kitchen, cleaning up.

"Margaret Mead said one or three," Stacey said, pointing her fork at Brooke.

"One or three what?"

"Kids. She thought odd numbers were better. With two, you just get butting heads all the time."

"Margaret Mead faked her research," said Brooke. Cutting a glance at Sean, she mouthed *CD Pyg*. They were, for a moment, on the same team.

"Five in my family," said Sean, "and there was plenty of head-butting."

"Well, that's a full litter," said Stacey.

Meaning, Sean knew, that his mother had spawned children without thought; that he came from a class that didn't know any better. Best to leave the room before his own stoked coals fanned into flames. He began clearing plates. When Brooke rose, he motioned her to sit. In the kitchen, he cracked another beer and drained half of it at one pull, like a teenager boozing on the sly. As he rinsed pots, he heard the women in the other room. Two of Brooke's old friends in Windermere had new babies. One had just gotten divorced.

"Then there's Alex, you know, back in the country," Stacey said. Sean turned down the hot water he was running. "So sad," she went on. "He lost that little boy they had, and then I guess his marriage just dissolved."

"I know, Mom," Brooke said. "Alex caught up with me the other day."

"*Did* he now."

"Don't look like that, Mom."

How did she look? Eyebrows lifted by a breeze of hope? That her daughter could leave this shanty Irish and go back to the high school dreamboat? Sean's heartbeat thrummed in his ears. He didn't catch Stacey's words, but Brooke went on. "His company's got a branch in Hartford. We acted like, you know, old friends." Then, after Sean had creaked open the dishwasher door, she said, "I wouldn't say never, Mom. I'd say unlikely. I'm not going to drive to Boston to have a drink with my high school boyfriend. Sure, yeah, it's sad. But I'm just saying."

He couldn't stand it. He peeled the rubber gloves from his hands and stuck his head back into the dining room. "Say, love," he interjected, putting a bubble of brightness into his voice. "Why don't we have this old boyfriend of yours over for dinner? Sounds like a lonely guy."

If there was nothing to it, she would say sure; she'd ask Alex; didn't know when he'd be back in town but why not; how good of Sean to think of it.

She wrinkled her nose, from below the bridge to its tip. "It'd be awkward," she said. "Too much water under the bridge."

He couldn't give up. "I'd like to meet this mysterious guy."

"He's busy getting settled in Boston. I don't see him coming to Hartford anytime soon."

Sensitive as a tuning fork, Stacey picked up the jangling music in the room. "I don't imagine *you* bring your old flames around," she said to Sean.

"I don't meet them for coffee, either."

"It was just the once," Brooke said—too quickly, and as she blinked her eyes rapidly at him, Sean knew she was lying. "We'll save the rest for our high school reunions. Right, honey?"

Sean retreated to the kitchen, where he finished the beer. For the rest of Stacey's visit, the name *Alex* and the word *adoption* went off limits. Still, over the next three days, every time he stepped onto the back porch where Brooke and her mom were talking and they stopped, he felt a secret hovering in the air. At night, Brooke stretched out against him and sighed. It was so exhausting to have her mom there, she said. Her mom never met a daughterly decision she couldn't criticize. Her mom had started this new job with the schools back in Pennsylvania, and now she had opinions on schools. Her mom needed a boyfriend, someone to listen to her. Then Brooke kissed him and stroked his body lightly, and thanked him for being patient with Stacey, and they counted the days until Stacey left.

Still, the next morning, as he came into the kitchen, mother and daughter exchanged a glance, like a plot hatching. They were the team, now. And last night, after Stacey had finally left—with a grand-motherly hug for Meghan and promises all around to spend one of the holidays in Windermere—Brooke went off on a walk. A long walk, hours after Meghan was in bed. She didn't ask if Sean wanted to go. She didn't even take the dogs, who whined and moped till she came home. "Where'd you go?" he asked when she slipped past midnight into bed.

"Around the park," she said. "Through the neighborhood." Her voice was too nervous, too tired for him to press for more.

Waiting for Meghan to come out of the school, he remembered how he had loved the enigma of Brooke. That Mona Lisa smile of hers—well, she showed her Chiclets teeth, but you could practically hear the stories murmuring behind those curved lips—had been seductive once. Now he could do with a little less mystery and a lot more straight talk.

He was keeping one secret of his own. Not to do with their family; he would never do that. It was about the Bach. Last Monday, at the chorale rehearsal, during the break, Geoffrey had sidled up to him. How was he liking the music? Magnificent, Sean had said, pausing over one of the brownies the sopranos always brought. That Bach, he knew a thing or two. And did he feel comfortable with the German? Geoffrey asked. Well, sure—he thought he did. Years ago Sean had picked up one of those courses on tape, real Germans after whom you repeated: *Wieviel Uhr ist es? Wieviel. Uhr. Ist es. Danke schön. Bitte schön.* He thought he'd gotten pretty good; when they went over diction in the chorale, he usually had it dead to rights.

But Geoffrey, as it turned out, wasn't asking in order to criticize Sean's German. The symphony, as everyone knew, had been cutting costs. The oratorio required four soloists, among whom the tenor—the Evangelist—carried most of the weight. The best the symphony could do was to bring professionals in for the three performances and the dress rehearsal. To prepare the thing right, they needed someone internal to sing the parts at the tech rehearsal. "To tell the truth," Geoff said, leaning close to Sean, "it's something I've been pushing with our board for a while. You know, we should have understudies ready. And ringers for this group." He glanced around the big square church kitchen where they served snacks. "To keep some of the oldsters on the beat."

"Good idea," Sean agreed, not wanting to report Ed, who always sat to his left, a retired chemistry teacher with a tendency to scoop notes.

"How much training have you got, Sean?"

"Training? You mean music?"

"No, I mean for the long jump. Of course I mean music. You ever get your master's?"

"Geoff, I went to Central. Majored in graphics technology."

"But you trained your voice."

"In the shower."

Geoffrey looked nonplussed. "Well," he said hesitantly, "I'd still like you to do this—"

"Do what?"

"Learn the part. The Evangelist. We couldn't pay anything this year, but when people see what a big help it is, having a soloist for those last rehearsals . . ." He shook his head. "The problem is your authority with the membership. I hadn't realized. I've approached Betty in the sopranos, Chuck in the bass section—"

Sean felt his face flush. He knew what Geoffrey meant. Betty taught at the Hartt School, a prestigious conservatory. Chuck had sung opera professionally when he was younger. And the Evangelist! The one who stood forth and announced the decree from Caesar, the shepherds in the fields, the angels, the birth. "You could ask that new guy," he said. "I forget his name—the skinny guy from New Haven? I think he went to Yale for music."

"He doesn't have your voice." Geoffrey clapped Sean on the shoulder. "Let me think how we can swing this," he said. "Meanwhile, d'you mind studying the part?"

"No. No, not at all. I love the part."

And so he had put away his CDs of *Bohème* and *Turandot* and spent his commuting time mastering the tricky intervals and precise cadenzas of the Bach. But if Geoffrey decided not to use him—if they thought he'd be an imposter, singing up there in front of the group—he did not want his family, especially not Mum, to hear how he'd gotten his hopes up. *Thinks he can sing, that one.*

Finally there was Meghan, pushing through the double glass doors of West Elementary, leggy and distracted, carrying yet another art project too big for her. "Hey, Bug," Sean said as she found the car.

"Daddy. Don't call me that."

"No one's listening."

"Granny heard you call me that, and then she called me that. Is she gone?"

"Left yesterday, don't you remember?" She nodded as he opened the back door for the unwieldy cardboard. "What you got there?"

Meghan sighed. "Arithmetic project," she said. "We had to make up a game."

"Sounds like fun. Do we get to play it when we're home?"

"No." She climbed into the passenger seat and strapped herself in. "It's a bad game," she said. "Taisha made fun of it."

They pulled out of the lot. He glanced over at his daughter. She wasn't quite holding back tears, but her face looked burdened, for a six-year-old. *Tröstet uns*, he sang to himself, *comfort us and make us free*. "I bet Mrs. McIlvoy liked it, though."

"She said she did. But she always says that."

"Aw, just you wait. Some boy will act up, and she won't like that."

Meghan's eyes widened. "Some boy *did*," she said, as if her dad had ESP. She twisted in her seat to face him. "This boy Christopher?" she said. "He's got really funny teeth—like this?" Sean glanced quickly to see his daughter clamp her upper teeth over her lower lip. He managed not to laugh. "And he asked this girl Ellen how come she had Chinese and her parents had American knees!" Meghan put her hand over her mouth and giggled.

"And the teacher didn't think that was funny?"

Meghan bounced in her seat. "She made him go to the principal. And he had to write *I am sorry, Ellen*. He put just one *r* in *sorry*. I saw."

"Did *you* think it was funny?"

"Da-ad."

"I'm just asking." He turned down their street. Fall was in the air, yellow leaves piled against the curb, but the air was still warm. If he met Gerry at the Half Door later they could sit in the back garden. Gerry was having his problems, too, with the baby colicky and Kate still not losing the pregnancy weight. She didn't want to have sex with him and Gerry was starting to think that was fine; he had to picture other women anyhow—thin women, happy women—to perform. That problem, Sean thought, he didn't have. He always wanted Brooke—even when she put up her *everything's fine* front, even when she was lying to him.

He parked the car. Meghan was starting ahead, frowning. "What is it, Bug?"

"What are shy knees, Daddy?"

"Shy what? Oh. Chinese."

"But it's about *knees*."

"It isn't really. It's about being mean to people who look different. We used to tell it this way." He turned to her in the car. Her summer freckles were fading. At least she had Brooke's mouth and jawline; she wasn't all O'Connor. Sean took off his sunglasses and put his fingers at the edges of his eyes. "Chinese, Japanese," he said, pulling them up then down. "American knees." He put his hands on his knees. His daughter still looked confused. He felt both silly and embarrassed. "It's because Chinese people have narrow eyes," he said, "and Ellen's parents aren't Chinese."

"Because she's adopted."

"That's right." He grabbed her art project as they stepped out of the car. From inside the house they could hear Bitsy yapping, the canaries singing. The new cat would need its medications. Meghan jumped down onto the gravel and slammed her door. "You know what adopted is, right?"

"Da-ad."

"Just checking." They started toward the house. He put his hand on her shoulder; she was up to his rib cage now. "You learned about it from Mommy."

"I don't know."

"You and Mommy getting along better now? Now that she let you quit ballet?"

Meghan shrugged. "I think I want to do ballet again."

"But you're getting along okay."

Meghan twisted her head to look up at him, obviously confused. He stopped at the front door and leaned the artwork against the siding. All the dogs were barking now. He knelt in front of his little girl. He took both her hands. "I'm worried about Mommy," he said.

Meghan's face went grave, then slowly lit up. "Is she—is she gonna have a baby?"

He chuckled ruefully. "I wish, Bug. I think she's . . ." He didn't know how to go on. Guilt caught in his throat. He was using Meghan. But he pressed on. "I wonder if you can keep a secret. Not a big one. Just to be nice to Mommy." Meghan nodded, her mouth pursed and sober. "Don't tell her I'm asking you, okay?"

"What are you asking me?"

"Where did she—" he started to ask. Then he realized Meghan couldn't know where Brooke had gone last night; she'd taken the walk after Meghan was in bed. "Does Mommy have any new friends?" he asked instead.

"I don't think so." Putting her finger to her chin, Meghan affected a thoughtful expression. "Mommy," she said, "is not that friendly a person. Jackie's mommy has lots of friends over. They play Scrabble."

"Does she talk on the phone a lot? When I'm not home?"

"I don't know." She twisted the second hand free of his and started for the door. As he straightened up she said, not looking at him, "Sometimes the phone rings and she won't answer it. I tell her it's ringing. She says it's a junk call. Yesterday I went to answer it and she wouldn't let me. She pulled my hand away, Daddy!"

Meghan's voice had gone quivery and melodramatic. She was a little girl who liked attention, Sean thought. He shouldn't push this anymore. "Well, Mommy is under a lot of pressure at work," he said as he pulled out his keys. "You should do what she says and not give her grief. If you think she's upset about something, you just come tell me. Okay?"

"Is she ever gonna have a baby, Daddy?"

"Course she is," he said without thinking. "So long as we don't bother her about it. Now let's play that arithmetic game you made up."

Chapter 10

Brooke shouldn't have been surprised, she supposed, when Alex came by the Simsbury location of Lorenzo's Nursery. "You always were persistent," she told him as he helped her lug a spruce into place.

"Tell me to get lost," he said, shaking clumps of dirt from his raincoat, "and I'll be a disappearing act."

"I thought I did tell you. Fifteen years ago."

"That was different. I'm not trying to sleep with you now."

"You're not, huh?" Brooke grunted as she ripped open a sack of peat moss. She straightened and brushed her hair from her eyes. It had been two weeks since her mom's visit. Though Sean's testiness had not abated, their lives had returned to the rhythms of autumn in Hartford. He rose before dawn and minded the animals; she got Meghan up an hour later and took her to school—real school now, first grade. Then to the nursery, the only change being this new location and Lorenzo's handing her, every day, more responsibility. A fat raise, he'd hinted, was on its way. Her life's roots were in the soil here, now. Still, she had not completely shaken the ghosts that seemed to haunt her whenever she connected the wires that led her back to Windermere. She eyed Alex. "What are you trying to do, then?"

He grinned and looked out over the river that ran by the nursery site. "Renew old acquaintance?"

"I live a hundred miles from you."

"Near one of our branches."

"Alex." She straightened the tree, her glove sticky with sap. "We don't qualify as acquaintances."

He pulled off his glasses and wiped mist from the lenses. All day the fog had been trying to lift. "I've been seeing a lot of my sister, did I tell you?"

"Charlie?"

He nodded. "She's really great, you know? Scary great, though. She hasn't got any internal filter. My parents were so old when she came along. And the second she became a teenager, I disappeared on her." He shook his head. "She never wants kids. She wishes you and I had had a baby. She thinks I should beg Tomiko to come to Boston. What the hell am I supposed to do with that?"

"Charlie thinks we should have had a baby? Really?"

He shot a glance at her before replacing the glasses. "I'd say she was fishing, but she's not that clairvoyant."

"She's in college now?"

"Graduating this year. She wants me to take her to Windermere over her fall break."

"When's that?"

"In three weeks, I think. She's at Tufts."

Tufts. A strange, skittering electrical charge went through Brooke. It had been just this time of year when she visited Tufts with her father. She'd chosen it for the medieval studies professor she'd met. She could still picture him, a slender man who had probably looked too young for a professor until he was past forty and then was suddenly wearing wire-rimmed bifocals and walking with the suggestion of a stoop. "Must be great for her, to have you nearby."

"Everything she talks about feels coded, to me," Alex said. He crouched next to Brooke. "Here, let me help with that."

Together they packed peat and soil around the newly planted tree. When the rest were in, they would make an elegant hedge along the road and give the grounds privacy. On the other side of the lot Shanita was working with the two landscape guys Lorenzo had taken on for the project. Around them, the fog was coalescing into mist, a few droplets here and there. Nervously Brooke imagined Sean coming by and finding Alex here. Not that Sean ever stopped in unannounced, much less that he would know she was up in Simsbury. But the jealousy that steamed off him made her feel guilty. When she'd gone on long walks at night, trying to shake off the unease that had settled like lint on her marriage, her mind followed twisting byways to truths she could never share with her husband, and that did no good. And Alex was one of those byways. "What do you mean, coded?" she asked.

"Well, take abortion."

Brooke straightened up. "Take it where, exactly?"

"Charlie's in this moral philosophy class, right? And she wants to talk it out with her big brother. So she jabbers about the slippery slope of the argument—how the only difference between infanticide and an IUD is the passage of time. She wants me to help her sort this out. Me!" He flung up his hands.

"So be—what is it called? Socratic. Just hold the argument out here." Brooke thrust out her arm, her mud-caked gloves.

"Is that what you do?"

"I don't have a sister. And Meghan's not at the stage yet."

While she fetched the wheelbarrow, Alex's cell phone rang. Holding up a finger, he stepped away. With half an ear she heard him talk about streamlining, about market pressures. She slipped the next spruce into the hole they'd dug, and poured in more peat.

Tufts, she thought again. Of all places. With a boy's smile, that professor—what was his name?—had listened to her describe how she'd loved *The Mists of Avalon*. Then he'd drawn out a sheet of ruled paper and in small, spiky handwriting had made up a list for her, filled with authors she had never heard of. "I want you," he had said, "to start thinking of the Middle Ages as a *problem*." She hadn't understood him, and she never went to the library to find any of the books. Still, she couldn't wait to sit in his classes, where he would turn to her as if they were very old acquaintances and ask her what she thought of this problem.

It was mostly the knights she had cared about. Not the ladies with their high pointed hats, their pasty faces and tight unsmiling lips, but Galahad with his flowing blond hair, his helmet cradled in his arm and his boyish neck looking so vulnerable. Or William Wallace on the crag, the sword on which he was leaning backlit by the setting sun, a cross of gold. He would endure a horrible death; they all would—the black knight's sword in their throat, or bleeding to death like Arthur, or disemboweled like Percival. What did they want with those pencil-hatted ladies? She would endure with them—would stand the trials of pain and fearful visions, would drink the poisoned mead.

As she straightened from her planting, the ghost of a smile crossed her face. Alex was still on the phone. Glancing at him, she remembered the letter. She had sat down to write it a week after receiving her acceptance from Tufts. Longhand, of course, and on new stationery she had bought at the store in the village where no one shopped except for graduation gifts. The sheets had been beige, with an almost invisible print under the surface of gold and lavender flowers exploding into one another, like a crowded tapestry. The same print, in full color, lined the envelope and made her think of the heavy curtains that hid the dying Gawain in *Mists of Avalon*.

Dear Dr. James, she wrote—that had been his name, James, she could see it now on the stationery. *I am looking forward to being in your Chaucer class next year, if I can get through Freshman Comp. I want you to know something before we meet again. I am with child. I have taken a potion—potion*, she remembered, took a long time to arrive at—*but my face will surely bear the mark of my sorrow. I trust you to treat my fragile self, not with pity, but with honor.*

She did not mail this absurd letter, but sealed it in the square envelope and took it from her drawer, now and then, to study the address and imagine the high stone walls of the university and the soft, Virginia-inflected accent of her favorite professor. Finally, one day, she had burned it, the flame rising like a lady's pointed hat.

Even more keenly than the letter, she remembered the last Saturday of May that year, how it dawned cold and overcast. Like today, she thought. She'd had the keen sensation, as she woke in her narrow bed, of crossing a bridge, a long narrow span that dissolved behind her. She had touched between her legs, but the skin there was dry. Damn, she had thought, damn. She shut her eyes. It was like vertigo, the feeling of the bridge, like one of those swaying rope bridges over chasms that they showed in movies. Had the thing kicked? That was one possibility that terrified her—it would kick, to announce it was alive, and everything she had claimed would shatter. In medieval times, they had called it quickening. She put her hand to her belly; pressed. She felt nothing but the usual hard, growing sphere. Then she hit on it. Third trimester. She was six months. Sitting up in bed, she calculated. The tail end of November, all of December, January, February, March when she'd missed out on Florida, April, most of

May. The operation wasn't legal at this point. Or maybe it was, but only in special circumstances. They said you had a baby now. The bridge lay between the first two-thirds, when she didn't have to believe in it, and the last third, when she did. On the other side of the bridge she could have gotten help if she had asked the right people. Now there was no one to help her, except Alex.

"Hey," he said behind her.

Brooke almost jumped. She looked up from the fresh mound where she'd planted the spruce. A truck was pulling into the dirt drive, its back loaded with more plantings. Absently she waved at the driver.

"Sorry about that," Alex was saying, waving his cell phone. "I have to get back to the branch office. These guys are desperadoes. You all right?"

With the back of his finger he brushed dirt from her cheek. She felt lightheaded. Not meeting his gaze, she sat on a stump. "I was thinking about that time," she admitted. "About how the days went by. It seems so impossible now, the way I let time slip through my fingers."

Alex crouched, his forearms on his knees. Still she would not look at him. They were silent for a long moment. When he spoke, she felt as if she had known this was coming; that he had traveled, not only from Boston, but from Tokyo, from across the silent years, to tell her this one thing. "It was my fault," he said.

Brooke examined her nails: dirty, cracked. "Don't be stupid," she said. "It was a long time ago."

"You don't understand. I mean really my fault. I mean I did something. To the baby."

"It wasn't a baby, Alex. It died before it became a baby."

"That's what I'm trying to tell you. He didn't die, like that. I killed him."

A gust of wind knocked down one of the unplanted spruces, and a chill ran down Brooke's spine. "Nonsense," she said.

"I've been thinking," he went on, "since seeing Charlie, how I want to back up. Face consequences."

Abruptly, Brooke stood. "Consequences?" she said, and she heard the ragged edge of her voice. "Don't talk to me about consequences. My whole life is a consequence."

He frowned at her. The mist was intensifying, the breeze blowing in tiny needles of rain. "Brooke, you thought it was a miscarriage. You've got your husband, your little girl—"

She shook her head. "It's never over," she said. "I caused it and I—" Her voice trailed into the mist. She looked at Alex, this man she had not seen in more than a decade. What possible concern of his could her life be now? But she went on. "With my husband," she said. "He wants a second child."

"And you don't, right? That's what you told me."

"It's not that." She drew in a deep breath and exhaled. "If I hadn't, I don't know, denied ours, yours and mine, its chance to be born, I would give him—give us—a second one. A third one. Whatever could make us happy."

"I don't understand," Alex said. "Did you not want your daughter?"

"Oh, there was no question with Meghan."

He stood. He took her dirty, clammy hand. "If what happened, with us," he said cautiously. "If it made you not want to have children at all, that would make sense. But to have one—and she's okay, right?"

She couldn't meet his eyes. "She's beautiful."

"To have her, and then refuse another—"

"It's not rational, okay? I stopped pretending I had an argument about this a long time back. Any guilt you've got isn't rational either."

"Oh, yes, it is."

She swiped at a tear, feeling the grit smear across her cheek. From across the yard, Shanita was calling—it was raining now, they should go in, finish later. She held up a hand, then stepped back and faced Alex. He looked the same to her now, even with his glasses misting over. The boy she had known. "It's deeper than reason," she said. "You remember how I went to Isadora?"

"Don't remind me."

"She talked—maybe she was just making me feel better—but she talked about the spirit children. Who were waiting to be born. She used to tell me I should talk to this spirit child, tell it that this really wasn't its time. She said the child would understand, that the spirit children were all very understanding." She wiped her hand off on her jeans, then placed it flat against Alex's chest. "When I had Meghan," she went on, "I felt like the spirit child I was meant to have had cut me just a ton of slack, and now it was emerging as my daughter. I felt incredibly lucky. But I get suspicious of luck. If I push that luck, if I try for a child beyond the one I needed to have—" She broke off. Meeting his eyes, she suddenly remembered. "Christ," she said, "what am I saying? My kid is alive. Oh, Alex, I'm sorry, I didn't think."

A corner of his mouth twisted painfully. "If the spirit children are seeking revenge," he said, "they got theirs with me."

"I didn't mean that." She wanted to reach her arms around his lean torso, but he held himself rigid as a tree. "Look, we shouldn't talk about this. I'm so sorry about Dylan."

"I wish you'd met him. Maybe I can meet yours."

From behind Brooke came the bleat of the truck horn—Shanita, ready to leave. "I've got to go," said Brooke.

"Have a drink with me. Next week."

She shook her head. "We'll dredge up more useless memories."

"It's time for us to talk. You haven't heard my side of it."

"Yes, I have. You feel guilty. Join the crowd."

"You haven't heard my side, Brooke."

She stepped away. "I don't want to hear your side."

"Yes, you do."

It was too much for her. With a quick step, she reached his damp, stubbled cheek and gave it a fleeting kiss. Then she turned and hurried across the muddy lot, the rain now coming steady and Shanita glaring from the cab of the truck.

Chapter 11

Najda

When it comes to the way I act around people, I make an exception for Mrs. Kendrick at the library. Sure, she acts the way the rest of the world does, like I'm retarded and half deaf. She talks slowly and points to her own mouth. She smiles at me the way people smile at babies, so the babies will imitate them and smile back, even when the babies don't know what happiness even is. Mostly with people like that I go way deep inside, to where I'm smarter and quicker and funnier and better than all of them. I picture them in a swamped boat, or maybe even drowning, or hanging by a thread over a canyon. I smile and leave them behind to die and I go about my business.

But Mrs. Kendrick's face lights up when she sees me. It's not like she pities me. So I stay right up at the surface with her. When I thank her I mean it. Pretty soon I'll have plenty to thank her for.

Today—like the past five days—I'm at the library with Luisa. Luisa's my mom. To her face I call her Mom. I'm expected to, plus I love her. I don't want to hurt her. But to myself I call her Luisa.

Somewhere, I know, I've got another mother, a mother who didn't want me because I was too fucked up, even as a baby. Sometimes I hate that mother. I put her in the swamped boat, far far out at sea, where she calls and weeps and apologizes while she drowns. Other times, I find her deep inside me, where we talk and laugh together like normal people, and she knows how to love me, she knows what I'm capable of. It's for those moments that I'm reserving the name *Mother*. A tiny, hopeful part of me believes there'll come a day—there has to come a day—when I'll use it.

Today I got sneaky. Before I let my mom bring me here to the library—before I would listen to those Jonas Brothers songs she sings all the way down the road—I dawdled and messed around until it got late. That way I knew Luisa would miss *That '70s Show*, which is her very favorite, if she stayed at the library more than a half hour. "Go on," I told her when she kept glancing at the library clock. "Go home. Your show."

"But how will you get home, Najda?"

I demonstrated my wheelchair for her. "Self," I managed to say.

"It's not safe. That's two miles, and remember when your wheels caught?" She looked at the clock again. "I'll come back," she said. "Right after the show. Okay? Okay, Najda?"

"Dokey okey," I said. That's one mix-up I can correct, but it brings a smile to my mom's face so I never do. Luisa kissed me on the forehead—I hate that—and left. Now it's just Mrs. Kendrick here to help me.

I get a half hour on the Internet before the next patron gets a turn. If no one's waiting, I can stay. Today, two people are waiting. I click the keys fast as I can. Google search. *School*, I start to type, *Pennsylvania*. No, *Pennsylvania New York Ohio New Jersey*. Anywhere I can take a bus to. But that's too many words; no matter how hard I concentrate, I won't get them all right. Stick with *Pennsylvania*; add

Disabled. If I type too fast, the letters all scramble themselves on the screen. Even Google can't sort out *sochol Pensnylnavia.*

When a hand falls on my shoulder, I know it's Mrs. K. "Can I help you, dear?"

I look up and smile. Mrs. K is tall, kind of mannish. I can tell she plucks the hair from her chin and eyebrows. She wears clothes that hide her figure. She wears a wedding ring, but she's got no pictures of kids or husband on her desk. I wonder what she ever wanted in her life, why she didn't get it. I need a new school, I want to tell her, one that will teach me something I don't already know. "School," I manage to get out. "Things. I don't know."

"If you don't know what you're looking for, honey, you should give Mr. Gustavson a chance." Mrs. K nods at the man sleeping in the metal chair by the radiator.

"Please." Shit. There comes a tear, dripping onto my cheek. I hate crying. But it happens when I think too hard about this. Ziadek says there must be a place for someone like me, a place that can help me get to college. I pull out one of the scraps of paper they keep by the computer, for taking notes. I do better writing in cursive. When the letters link to each other, I don't have to track them down and keep their order straight. I manage to scrawl *new school Najda.* I nod toward the keyboard.

Mrs. Kendrick takes the seat next to mine. She bends her head so I can see her lips move—yes, I get it, Mrs. K, I'm deaf—and says slowly, "Is this something your family wants for you, dear?"

"Ziadek, yes," I manage to say.

"Your grandfather."

My throat hums a little. Words get blocked up. Finally I say, "Please," and I nod again at the keyboard.

Mrs. Kendrick purses her lips. Then she says, as if to herself, "I think there's a lot going on in that noggin of yours." She types something quickly on the keyboard. A list of sites appears on the screen. "Let's see," she says, scrolling down. "I don't know your diagnosis, you see, that's the problem." She turns to me again. She speaks more slowly. "You are not autistic."

The man waiting by the radiator raises his head. My face goes hot. I remind myself that I'm fond of Mrs. K. Carefully I put the words together in my head, so I won't be misunderstood. "I look myself," I say.

"If you need help," Mrs. Kendrick says. Her fingers touch my palm, like she's going to start speaking in fingered Braille, like Annie Sullivan for Helen Keller. I nod quickly. Mrs. K glances at the clock. "You have twenty minutes," she says. "Twenty." She flashes all her fingers twice.

When Mrs. Kendrick's gone back to the gray desk, I scroll through the sites. A lot of places are aimed at autistic children. Also a lot at teenagers with behavior problems. I may have behavior problems soon, if I have to stay in this backwater, with these stupid people in that idiot school. But there, on the second page: *Alternative schools for multiply disabled*. I boot up the site. It's a national list. There's the Center for Fulfillment in Michigan, the Goodwin Center in Florida, the Teasdale Academy in Nebraska, the Crosby School in Pennsylvania. By "multiply disabled," several of them seem to mean retarded. But it takes a long time to read through all these pages, more time than I've got, and the library doesn't let you save bookmarks on its browser. So I click Print again and again. I can take the pages home and study them with Ziadek. On a handful of them—the Crosby School especially, I like the picture of their campus, and there's a link to their pre-college curriculum—you can enter a postal address for a brochure. My hands have started sweating. Ziadek's right. There really are such places. The sidebars on the sites list all kinds of stuff about money, about school referrals, but I don't care. I enter the address to have the brochures sent. I put Ziadek's name as my guardian. By the time Luisa finds out that the school I'm going to isn't just a bus ride away . . . Well, it'll be too late by then, won't it?

With five minutes left, I open a Word document. I type my home address again at the top; that comes easy. Then I paste the address—copied from one of the tabs for Further Information—of the Pennsylvania Commissioner for Special Education. Then I concentrate as hard as I can. I type:

```
Mr. Commissioner:


I would like to receive ifornmation on funding
pobissilities for a neurologically damaged girl with
good cognitive fuictoning whose needs are not met
by local system.


Yours truly,
Najda Zukowsky
```

I can't get the word *school* right, so I leave it out. Funny how the easiest words come hard. Last week when I was here, I read up on Freud. He'd have something to say about why I can't type *school*, but I don't know what it'd be.

"Time's up," comes a voice at my shoulder—the Gustavson guy, who seemed asleep but here he is at the top of the hour, ready to surf his horse-racing sites. I nod. I sign off. I buzz over to Mrs. K's desk and put my name down for the session in an hour. I go to the printer and count my copies. I fish coins out of my pocket. Back at the desk, I lay the copies and the payment down.

"My goodness," said Mrs. Kendrick. "You've made a lot of copies. Are you going to *read* all this?"

Is this a library? I want to say. Are these books? Do you promote literacy? But I work not to be irritated with Mrs. Kendrick. I pluck a ballpoint pen from the tall cup on the desk. I sign my name to the letter. Then I push two more quarters across. "Stamp?" I ask.

When Mrs. K frowns, her eyebrows draw together like a pair of beetles. With her index finger she draws the letter toward her. "We're not a post office," she says, "but I might have a spare stamp for you. Do you need . . ." Her eyes stray to the writing in the letter. I know she's not supposed to be reading it; she's not supposed to interfere with the patrons' private concerns. But I don't say anything. "Do you need an envelope, too?" When I nod again, Mrs. K makes a few gestures across the surface of the letter. She does it so quick I can't read the difference, but I know what she's up to. She's fixing the words I got scrambled up. Then she opens her drawer and pulls out an envelope already embossed in the top right corner.

"Address, me," I manage to say. My throat feels dry.

"Of course," Mrs. K says. She passes the envelope to me. I quiet my shaking hand just enough to copy the address I've pasted onto the letter. Then, carefully, using my lousy right hand to steady the paper, I fold it into thirds, the way I've seen people do, and tuck it into the envelope. This takes a long time, but Mrs. Kendrick turns her attention to something on the computer while I work. When I'm done, she says, "Now a stamp's just forty-four cents. You'll need change."

"No," I say, a little louder than I should. "Envelope."

"Right." The eyebrows go up, then down. "Absolutely right. And you'll mail this yourself, then? Or would you like me to put it in our Out box?"

"Please," I say.

I really do like Mrs. Kendrick.

Forty minutes until I can get back onto the computer. I tuck the printed information into my side bag. I wheel over to the stacks. There isn't much here in the county library. The building is mostly to manage all the real libraries in the towns and also the Bookmobile. But there's a little poetry section, and in the middle of it I pick out the new book I found last week, with the jacket photo of the pretty, pale woman—she looks kind of like the mother I keep imagining—who died from leaving the gas on. While I wait for my next turn, I move my lips. The words are wicked harsh. They describe a place full of stone and blank faces. *Mother, mother,* she writes, and she says her mother brought her here, to a cold kingdom. I don't understand these verses. And they're really hard to memorize. But there's something about their fierceness that yanks at me. This girl says what she feels, whether it's fair or not.

When the guy after Gustavson gets off the computer, I'll log back on. I don't have much time left for the things I need to do. I'll leave the lists of schools alone for now. I want to read up more on the nature and causes of hypoxia in infants, what can be hoped for. That's going to be the subject of my college essay, when I get that far. I want to be prepared. The other thing I'll do before Luisa comes back will be to check MyBirthMom.com, where I registered a month ago. Yes, crazy people lurk on a website like that. Yes, I've wasted a lot of time already, writing back to women who say they gave birth near Windermere fifteen years ago. Yes, each one of them so far has been either lying—why do they lie? Do they imagine I wouldn't know if I'd actually been born in Louisiana?—or African American. But somewhere out there lives the person who let me slip from her body into the world. Someday, maybe, that person will get a second thought, will want me back.

I read once that memory begins when language begins. Ziadek's told me they thought I was retarded at first, because I didn't speak until I was four years old. But I know I had language before then, because I remember. I even remember all the work I had to do to shape the words inside my head into sounds that Ziadek and Luisa and Katarina could understand. Still, I don't remember as far back as that other mom, the one I call *Mother* in my head. The earliest memories I have are of Jude and Robby, Katarina's kids, putting me up in a tree. I remember they challenged me to climb down. Look at her, Jude said, she looks like a bird with a wing broke. And he poked at me with a stick. And Robby said, Well, jump then! We'll catch you! But I didn't jump because I knew he wouldn't. I sat there on the branch looking down at them while they went farther and farther away, and then I wet my pants because I couldn't hold it.

Does my real mother have other kids? Kids that would have been mean to me like Robby and Jude? Kids she loves more, so she got rid of me? These are stupid questions, the kind of questions a person like Luisa would ask. But I can't help it, they run through my head over and over.

You do not do, you do not do, I read in this book of poems by the blond mother, *Any more, black shoe*. But that's about a girl who hates her father. I don't even have a father; I never think about a father.

A throat clears a gob of phlegm. The second guy's off the computer. Quickly I tuck the book back onto the shelf. I wheel myself over to the station and log back on. Out of the corner of my eye I spot Mrs. Kendrick, smiling at me. For safety's sake, I open a window on the computer next to the windows I'm really investigating. *THE MATHPAGE*, this extra window reads in bright letters; *TOPICS IN PRECALCULUS*. I've already studied this site, but Luisa won't know that. If she comes in without warning, I just have to click on this math page. I glance at the clock. I need to pee. My throat's parched. But I've only got a half hour. I set to work.

Chapter 12

Danny was the only one free to meet Sean for a beer. Gerry, he maintained in the garden at the Half Door, was getting henpecked. "Pussy-whipped," said Danny.

"That's ugly," countered Sean. "I don't care what you think about Kate, that kind of talk is ugly."

It was after seven, the sun below the horizon already. Sean had left for the bar as soon as Brooke got home. She'd had her walk, he maintained to himself; he could have his happy hour. His brother fidgeted, across from him. Danny was losing his hair, not from the forehead like Sean, but balding from the back of the crown, like a monk's tonsure, so his face still looked like the mischievous kid he'd been in high school. "Call 'em as I see 'em," he said. "You know she got her tubes tied, after Derek?"

"Pretty good idea." Sean sucked on his beer. "They've got four. The economy's not helping anyone."

"But she didn't tell Gerry, man. No consultation. That is fucked up."

"You don't think Nora would do that, if she didn't want any more?"

"No way. It's a decision you make together." Danny smacked his lips. He looked around the bar. Danny was in sales, and he was always hoping to make a contact at the Half Door. He turned back to Sean. "Brooke?" he said.

Sean felt a knot in his lungs. He coughed. "We've got a little disagreement," he confessed, "about family size. But she hasn't tied the tubes."

"You so sure? She hides something, that one. With that little smile of hers." Danny attempted a poor imitation of Brooke's sly smile. He was on his fourth beer, Sean on his third. Sean had known his brother long enough to detect when Danny was spoiling for a fight. That was how they'd grown up, after all—the four of them teasing and prodding each other, looking to hit a nerve, while Fanny wrung her hands and Mum egged them on. But Sean didn't want a fight. He wanted someone to help him figure out his life.

"I think," he said, signaling Tommy for another, "she's seeing someone."

He hadn't meant to say that; didn't know he thought it until the words were out of his mouth. But Danny only grunted. "Bitch," he said. "You think she married you just to get the one kid?"

"I think she married me"—images of the early days, the curve of Brooke's hip and the warm light in her eyes, flooded Sean's head—"because she loved me."

"They get over that."

"Speak for yourself, Danny! You're over Nora. You keep her around because you couldn't get along without her. But you don't love the woman."

"Hey, I am not the cuckold here. You want a detective on it? I know a guy."

"I do not want a detective!" Sean slammed the new beer onto the counter. Foam sprayed. "It's this guy," he said, tamping down his voice, "she knew in high school. Lives in Boston. Seems he can't get enough of the Mass Pike. I check the phone and see his caller ID on it. I don't know what the fuck's going on."

"You ask her?"

"Sure! She says he's divorced, he lost a kid, he's lonely, it's old times. She doesn't invite him to meet her husband and kid, though."

"And she's hedging on having another kid." Danny nodded sagely. "Makes sense. She is still a good-looking woman."

"You're not helping me."

"So talk to the priest."

"Consult a celibate about my wife. That makes plenty of sense."

"None of it makes sense if you're talking females. Either they get fat on you or they screw around on you. Those are the choices."

"I love my wife, Danny, can't you get that?"

He'd taken the bait. He saw that with Danny's satisfied grimace. "I'm just trying to help, brother," Danny said casually. "Look, are things okay at the print shop? Because I can get you a commission job. Territory as far as Springfield, you'd meet some new people, you're still a young guy—"

"Fuck you, Danny. All right? Next time I want your help I'll put a hole in my head instead." Sean slapped a twenty and a ten on the counter and turned to leave. Before he'd slid from the stool, his brother was already looking around the room, eyeing business prospects.

A storm cloud seemed to build right behind Sean's eyes as he walked home in the autumn twilight.

Work, he said to himself, that was all it was—they were still in the hole at the print shop, and Larry not meeting his eyes, it made him anxious, snappish. No, that wasn't it. It was Brooke. Twice, now, she had admitted seeing this Alex character. Both times she had gone on long walks after. When he talked to her at night, she was half listening. When they made love, he felt her half absent. They said only human females had orgasms, but hers seemed to come from some blunt animal part of her, while the human Brooke was spinning a thread somewhere else. He almost wished she would bring up adoption again; at least that would mean she wanted to keep building a family with him.

Talk to the priest, that was all Danny could offer. But Christ, he hated the Catholic church. Only the choir had kept him going, when he was younger, until he realized how out of tune all the voices were. Now he sang on the symphony stage, with people who hardly knew one another. Bach was a genius, but he gave no advice. All Sean wanted were two simple answers. Why wouldn't his wife bear him another child? And what gave with this Alex character?

She's having an affair with him. That was one answer, and it fit both. What did Brooke call it? Occam's razor. Simplest answer probably the right one. What it had to do with a razor he never understood. Felt the edge of a razor right now, cutting at him, slicing him into ribbons.

Brooke had dinner on the table, chicken in some kind of lemon sauce. "You're in fine shape," she said, glancing at her watch. It was almost eight. "I fed Meghan already."

"So we don't have family dinner now?" He felt it like a contagion caught from Danny: a compulsion to pick a fight.

"Sure we do. At seven. When people use their cell phones, I even remind them." She poured herself a glass of red wine. "This is like the fifth time in two weeks, Sean."

"Eat with Meghan then. If you're so uptight about mealtime." He popped open another beer and set it on a coaster. He watched Brooke move fluidly between stove and table. She had cut her hair a week ago, and bought a couple of new tops on sale. She looked younger, more sprightly. Through her cotton sweater he could make out the shape of her nipples. Who was she looking so sexy for? Alex? "Be like Mum if you like," he said. "Feed my supper to the dogs."

Their eyes met. This was Brooke's chance to call his bluff—to say, "All right," pick up his plate of chicken and rice, and dump it into the blue plastic bowl by the fridge. And then to take him to bed, where he wouldn't perform but would thrill to the touch of her fingers on his skin. Instead, she sipped her wine. She said abruptly, "I am not your mum. I don't know what's gotten into you. Meghan wanted to play her arithmetic game with you. She made it up—"

"I know she made it up," he interrupted. "I fetch her from school, remember? While you're hawking weed killer."

"What is going *on* with you? Is it work? Are there more layoffs?"

He looked from her to the glazed carrots on his plate. He'd tended those carrots in their backyard—St. Valery, the brightest, sweetest kind. He had a momentary impulse to fling the whole pretty thing in her face. His head hurt. What would it take to shake the truth out of her? Why had she never trusted him with the truth? "I'm not hungry," he said. He pushed the plate away and picked up his bottle. "I'm going to find my daughter."

"Sean, she's in bed."

"Don't you keep me from her." He turned. He felt his legs sway a little under him. "Meghan wants to take ballet," he said.

Brooke sighed audibly. She had taken the seat across from him at the table and lit a pair of candles; soft light fell across the plane of her cheek. "We talked about that last month. She made a choice, now she should stick to it. She's got soccer this fall—"

"I will pay," he said, "for the lessons. I will not have her mother hold her back."

"Listen to you talk," she said. But he was already out of the room. All the dogs got up and started to follow him—but when they saw he wasn't going outside, they returned to Brooke. They were her dogs, after all. From their cage, Dum and Dee twittered mindlessly. He finished the beer in one swig and set the empty bottle on a bookshelf. Holding on to the railing, he pulled himself up the steps. Meghan was in her room, her bedside light on. On her bed, the cardboard she had brought home lay open. Humming tunelessly, she moved plastic toys around the board.

"Hey, Bug," he said. He lifted the chair from the hallway and set it beside her bed.

She looked at him and made a face. "Ew, Daddy. You stink."

"Grown-up smell, honey. You winning your game?"

"It's not a winning game." She took her playing piece—some pink princess figure from a Happy Meal box—and moved it over the crooked squares. The squares had stickers pasted into them with sums: 2 + 3, 5 + 9, 3 + 7. Around the board Meghan had drawn kitten faces in little clusters of three and four and eight. She held her piece over the square with 6 + 7 glued down.

"Thirteen," Sean said. Meghan frowned. She had not drawn thirteen more squares. "Walk it backward," he said, sweeping a hand over the board. "Who cares?"

"I care." Meghan's voice trembled.

"The phone ring for Mommy today? While I was gone?"

"I don't know, Daddy." Suddenly she picked up the pink princess and flung it across the room, hitting the cat Blackie, who yowled and ran out. "I hate arithmetic! I hate Taisha!"

"Everything okay up there?" Brooke called from below.

"What's not to be okay?" he called back.

"Meghan should be in bed!"

"Is that a fact?"

A short pause followed, then the inevitable. "I'm going for a walk. Night night, Meghan!"

Meghan had pushed out her lower lip. She looked tired. "Night, Mommy," she said, but not loud enough for her mother to hear. Sean did not say anything. He looked out from Meghan's window to watch Brooke turn down the sidewalk, her shoulders hunched, hugging herself.

Chapter 13

It was awful, this agitation. Leaves began drifting down from the trees; in the nursery, they were cutting back hours, putting everything to bed for the winter. Yet Brooke felt her heart like March, when the ground thaws and streams begin running everywhere, when last year's living things rise out of the mud, stinking and fertile.

For years she had told herself she could not have loved Alex. They had been too young for love. Her own carelessness had hurt them too much. In any case, she had reasoned, he would not have loved her for long. He was better looking than she, more at ease; girls flocked to him. She, by contrast, was a little odd—pretty enough in a gawky, artless way, but easily flustered, her very passions making her ill at ease with carefree young people.

And it was all so long ago! Fifteen years! Unprompted, she would not have recognized Alex in the pained face, with its hollow cheeks and dress-up eyeglasses, that had stood with her in the mist. Six years ago, in a last bit of wistful news, her mother had told her Alex was married and living in Japan, half a world away. Now, each time she thought of him in a Boston apartment, back within her range, she ordered her heart to slow, her lungs to expel the breath they held so tight.

Almost two weeks after he came to find her at the nursery, she drove the truck back from Simsbury to the main site in Hartford to find her boss waiting for her. Shanita had gone home early for a sick kid. Lorenzo sat on one of the benches by the greenhouse, a crisp straw hat shielding his face from the lowering sun and his hands on the knees of the jeans that he always kept mysteriously pressed to a sharp crease. He looked old, Brooke thought, and frail, like an old Italian winemaker who should be napping away the afternoons on a terrace outside Naples. "Don't you trust me to lock up?" she said as she stepped down from the cab.

Lorenzo smiled, his lips thin. "I was waiting for you," he said. "It is time for us to talk."

"Funny," said Brooke—though it was not funny, nothing these days was funny—"you're the second guy this month to tell me that."

He stood, pressing hands to knees, to help himself up. Lorenzo wasn't seventy yet, and he had always been vigorous. Dreading and denying, Brooke knew what was coming. "Have a glass of wine with me," he said.

"Second one to ask that, too."

The invitation itself wasn't unusual. How many times had they finished a busy day in Lorenzo's small air-conditioned office, clinking glasses of Chianti? Of all people in Hartford, Lorenzo was the one to whom Brooke had come closest to revealing her past. Just last spring, when they had finished setting up for Easter and had retired to the office to toast the holiday and talk about Lorenzo's baroque faith in the whole Christ-child story, she had blurted out, "You know, I gave birth once. Once before Meghan, I mean. A stillbirth."

And Lorenzo had put his dry, warm hand over hers and squeezed the back of the palm. "Not with your husband," he had guessed.

"No," she had said. Then she had wept, quietly but for what had felt like a long time, while her boss just kept his hand on hers and now and then patted it, saying, "Go on. Go on, dear. Go on."

Now she looked at her watch. "I can't, Lorenzo," she said. "I've got to pick Meghan up."

"I thought your husband did that."

"Not this week." She met his brown eyes. She had told no one, not even Shanita, of the unsettled weather at home. Ever since her mother visited—and that was the easiest, to blame her mom, who trailed anxiety behind her like perfume. But her mom wasn't at fault, she was. She had to focus on her life now, to push the past back into its box and seal it up tight. The effects jangled all around her. Sean was drinking one more beer after dinner, then two, now three. Meghan had started acting out. This morning she had refused to dress herself; and when Brooke caved and played along, pulling Meghan's Cinderella underpants over her long legs and bunching a Hello Kitty T-shirt to pop over her head, Meghan waited until the whole exercise was through before she stripped everything off and demanded an outfit with no pictures on it. Only a call to Sean at work had gotten Meghan to knock it off.

And yet just this morning, clutching her bottom lip in her teeth, she had answered Alex's persistent calls with a text message. They could have a drink, she wrote, on Monday night. She didn't mention that was Sean's night at choral practice. She had felt, pressing Send, like a sneak. She would invite Alex over, she had told herself many times; once he met Sean and Meghan, everything would fit back into its place. Only that wasn't so. Because if Sean were to meet Alex, he would have to learn what Brooke had done with Alex, what she had kept hidden all these years.

Funny, she thought now, standing in the nursery parking lot, how she could tell Lorenzo about a lost child, and not her husband whom she loved.

Lorenzo had removed his straw hat. A cool breeze lifted his hair. "You run along then," he said. "Next week we can—well, actually, next week I'm going into the hospital."

Blood drained from Brooke's face. She had sensed this, sensed he was terribly ill. But she did not want to hear it. She searched his tanned face. "Can you tell me?"

"They think I've got a year. Maybe a bit more, if I do all the nonsense they've got lined up for me."

"My God, Lorenzo. No."

"I'm afraid yes, my dear. It's not something you can quarrel with."

"Cancer?"

He nodded. "Pancreas. They never catch it in time. That's what they told me. So I have to make some plans, Brooke. And they are going to involve you. Like it or not."

"I don't know what to say." She looked at her watch again, as if the hands would have moved backward. "I've got to go. Can I take you to the hospital? Can we talk tomorrow? Over the weekend?"

"No, no." He took her arm. Gently he steered her toward her car. "Weekend's for your family. They're keeping me overnight, I think. You can come see me."

"St. Francis Hospital?"

He nodded. He opened the door of Brooke's car for her. Then he took hold of Brooke's temples, bent her down, and kissed her forehead. His lips were barely moist. "Sneak me in a glass of wine," he said. "They will claim it will kill me, but they will be wrong about that."

Awful, she thought, awful. She loved Lorenzo like a father, her own having died a year after she came to Hartford. Once home, she wanted to tell Sean, but he spent the evening practicing his music, letting the distance between them grow, and she said nothing. She put six beer bottles into the recycle bin.

That night her dream came back, for the first time in years. She called it the Warehouse Dream. In the predawn she woke unsettled. Beside her, Sean breathed noisily from the beer. She remembered the first time she'd had the dream, when she still lived safe in her parents' home, no one suspecting what had gone on in a motel room five miles from town. In it, she was roaming a large warehouse, or an underground catacomb. She was both looking for someone and fleeing someone. They were strangers, both the one she sought and the one she fled, but she had killed one of them and the other was seeking her out. She used to wake with her heart banging in her chest. When she would go out in the daylight, following a night with one of these dreams, she had felt the sting of accusation from everyone she saw. It was the Warehouse Dream that had first made her feel she could not bear to look at Alex. He had said he loved her. Only love could have led him to tolerate her murderous foolishness, to stay with her, to spare her. But the day would come when he, too, turned and accused her.

This time the Warehouse Dream was set not in a warehouse, but in the new nursery in Simsbury, with its arbors and hanging roses and a greenhouse filled with shards of glass. She kept thinking Lorenzo would come take charge, set things to rights, but he never came; and then she was running, running to find what she had killed, to flee what would kill her. She woke sweating, in darkness. She lay breathing while light gradually filtered through the Venetian blinds, bringing Saturday with it.

Always, she thought as Sean turned and she fit herself around the bend of his strong back, she had known her past would catch up to her. For months and even years, she had thought someone would find the remains of the fetus. They would charge her with a crime, though she didn't know what crime. Had she miscarried? Aborted? Or had she, in her young and dreamy foolishness, killed a child? She had said only, "It's dead, isn't it?" and Alex had nodded, and she had turned her face away. She had been weak with loss of blood, dizzy, her vision blurred. She could not say, now, why she was so certain it had been a girl. Need for her baby had flooded her like the need to breathe. But she could not have her baby; there was no baby. Alex had left the motel room with the bloody bundle under his jacket. When he returned there was no bundle, and she had asked no questions.

When she had moved away from Windermere, the Warehouse Dream had followed her. For a time she thought no one would touch her again. She would spend her caresses on animals, on lame and discarded and flawed creatures. She would bend her passions to plants. Flowers and dogs, bushes and birds, she thought, had no moral code. They never, even silently, accused.

Then she had met Sean. She had never known anyone— anything—like him. He seemed made, almost literally, of honey— his sandy hair, the sun-kissed skin, amber eyes. His voice pulled on the cords of her heart. And he did not frighten her, the way everything else human had since that wretched night in the motel. In his arms, she almost believed she could emerge from the cocoon she'd spun around herself. The dream didn't stop, but it came less frequently; she woke with her nerves intact. If she could be careful, she told herself, and steady, if she kept her head down, if she made no more hideous mistakes, there might still be a life for her.

Seven years ago, when Sean lay beside her and talked about having a kid, Brooke felt she had found her redemption. Until then, she had been a girl who, blessed with a baby, had poisoned it and let her boyfriend dispose of its tiny human remains. With Sean she was being given a window of grace, a chance to do something right. Bringing Meghan into the world concluded that strange pact she had made with the ghost of the stillborn child. *I will love you this time*, she found herself whispering to the baby.

Two weeks ago, with Alex, was the first time she had ever told anyone about this crazy idea of the spirit children. And even then, she hadn't admitted how they still scared her. Every time Sean pushed for a second child, she pictured the soul of the one she had destroyed. Out of pity, it had allowed her to have Meghan. If she indulged herself in a second child, if she acted, truly, as if nothing in her past could cripple her, it would have its way. It would show her different. And so she had retreated to lame excuses to postpone a second pregnancy: the bed rest for Meghan, her work. Sean hadn't bought the excuses. He had come to hate her for her stubbornness. And so, on her long walks alone through the park, Brooke had chipped away at her own shell. When she pictured a second child and the nightmare images began—it would be deformed, she would stumble and drop it in the street, they would all perish in a car crash, Meghan would fall ill and die—she shut her eyes, even as she walked, and let her breath out, and breathed in slow. The past was the past, she told herself. Her risk was no greater than any other woman's. Wasn't Meghan proof enough? She had done her penance. *No, you have not*, a little voice said when she strayed off the asphalt path onto the grass and her eyes snapped open. *You have not told Sean.*

I can't, she said to this voice. And the shell closed over her again.

Now Sean was drinking, and she was fleeing—not the booze itself, but the truths that the booze would eventually get to. She couldn't bear the look of pure horror she imagined in Sean's golden eyes.

He shifted in the bed; turned to her. His breath had the sour
tinge of last night's beer. "Hey," he said. "You're awake."

"Can't sleep."

"Turn over."

She obeyed and felt his warm hands on her shoulder muscles.
One thumb pressed into a knot of muscle; as she felt it give way, a
tide of well-being seemed to lap at the shores of her body. "Don't you
have to get up?" she asked.

"Ssh. Relax."

She knew she wouldn't fall back to sleep, but his hands felt good.
She shut her eyes. "Lorenzo's sick," she said at last.

"Sick like a cold?"

"Sick like cancer. I think he wants me to start taking over."

"That's a big job." His hands were straying, now, over her shoulder blades and around to her breasts. She started to tense again. If
he brought up the idea of a second kid . . . "You want to run a
nursery?"

"I think I would. I don't want to think about Lorenzo, you
know."

"But he's telling you to."

She turned over. It was too dark to make out his features. "What
do you want?" she said; and before he could answer "Another baby,"
she added, "Do you want to keep working for Larry at the print
shop?"

His finger pushed aside her bangs. They had not made love for
more than a week. By evening he was testy, and she was distracted
by the presence—in her head, even if she didn't see him or return
his calls—of Alex. Now she felt more than she saw his wistful smile.
"I want to do music," he said. His voice sounded a little dreamy, as
if he weren't awake enough yet to make sense. "I want to sing it.
Teach it. Be better at it."

"Then you should."

"You know the Bach we're doing."

"You've been humming it."

"Yeah, well." He bent to kiss her neck, then her right nipple. From outside the door Brooke heard scratching—the dogs, their hearing too keen. Sean lifted up his head. He was hesitating. "Geoff—you know, the director—he's wanting me . . ."

"What? Wanting you what? Sean, you've got to tell me."

"Do I?" He was propped on his elbow now, his free hand cupping the back of her neck. An edge crept into his voice. "Because you don't tell me a thing."

The scratching at the door exploded. Behind it, Meghan's piping voice. "Mo-o-m-m-y. You awake? Daddy?"

Before Brooke could answer, the handle turned. The dogs poured in. Bitsy jumped on the bed, a mass controlled by a wagging tail. Lex put his paws up, his wet nose at her shoulder. Meghan stood in the doorway, her blue pajamas ghostly in morning light.

"I had a bad dream," she said.

His back to Brooke, Sean swung his legs free of the bed. The moment bled back into the night, and the day began.

Chapter 14

Riding the escalator to the bowels of the Boston MBTA, Alex felt himself in a farce. What was he doing, all dressed up like a banker? Floating downward in a phalanx of men and women in summer wool, into the hot, rubbery air of the Kenmore T station. As if his life, which ought to have been spent in a jail cell, had some connection to corporate portfolios or the Asian markets. As if there were some point to this daily exercise—the shave, the shoe polish, the brisk walk to the T, the crowded ride, the glass-walled building on Water Street. Days when he felt this way, his small office on the fifteenth floor, with its sliver of a harbor view, felt like a jail cell itself. And yet he got there every day on time, opened his briefcase, checked his BlackBerry for meetings.

The subway train felt primitive, squealing and bumping over the tracks. For six years Alex had taken the Yamanote Line from Ueno station down to Mercator's charcoal slab of a building across from Tokyo's Imperial Palace. Now he leaned against the cracked vinyl of his seat, shut his eyes, and tried to put himself back in the crowded

Tokyo car, with the departing melody from Ueno like a child's finger exercise. Back to the house he and Tomiko had found in Asakusa, the old part of the city, near Tomiko's parents and walking distance from the primary school where they dreamed of sending their children. No, not dreamed of; planned on. And Tomiko—she was so smart, with her Ph.D. from Stanford, her dissertation on multinationals, her postdoc at Hitsubashi—had begun cutting back her hours. She wanted time with Dylan; she wanted to write. A blog, she said, for women executives in Japan, and maybe it would be a book or maybe not, she didn't know, she was experimenting. Three days a week they brought Dylan to the *hoikuen*, a day care place so spotless and calm Alex felt he was leaving his baby boy to be painted into a still life. Then they would ride the Yamanote Line together. As the commuters packed in, Tomiko's body pressed against his. At the stop before his she got off for the America-Japan Society, the only place willing to give her flexible hours. Sometimes Alex got off with her. He walked by the shuttered bookstores in Kanda before submitting himself to the skyscrapers and the murmur of investment opportunities that it was his job to capture before they became shouts.

How long had that golden season lasted? Three months—Alex counted them now on the Boston T, October November December, the fall Dylan turned two—before Dylan's health and Tomiko's job collided and she threw herself into caring for him full time. By December they knew there would be no kindergarten for their son. No more *hoikuen*, no more romps in Ueno Park with Tomiko's dogged father chasing the laughing boy under cherry blossoms.

Still Alex had ridden the train, into the heart of the city at eight, back by nine P.M. if he was lucky. Had jogged home from the station; wrapped his slender, brittle, indomitable wife in his arms; sat by the bed of the sleeping child, sipping red wine and listening to Dylan breathe.

You don't feel it like I do, Tomiko had said, after it was over.

What do you mean? I feel like I've died myself.

Not like I do. I watched him every minute. I saw it take a piece of him every minute. Like sand through an hourglass, and you can't tip it back up. You didn't feel him fighting, like I did, and your insides torn out bit by bit. You didn't feel that.

All right, have it your way. I didn't.

The T squealed into Copley Square. Loud commuters boarded, swinging their briefcases and cracking jokes. Alex gave up his seat. That life was gone, he reminded himself. Gone no matter what. Dylan's fight had been fixed from the start. Here in this corner, ladies and gents, we have a dark-eyed mischievous toddler with a crooked smile and his mother's heart-shaped face. And here, in this corner, we have Death.

But there had been another fight, like a shadow behind Dylan's. And in it, Alex himself had been Death, and his opponent had not yet uttered his first cry. That truth had frozen him. While Dylan struggled and Tomiko suffered, Alex had ridden the train, back and forth, and sat in his son's room and lain next to his wife and listened to her weep, and the horror of it all had pinned him down so that Tomiko thought his heart was stone. Now he had lost both of them, Dylan to a tiny coffin in the ground and Tomiko to a set of suitcases by the door. All because he could not own up to what he had done fifteen years ago.

As they pulled out of Boylston, others rose and crowded by the exit doors. In Tokyo, they would have been standing already, the seats folded up for the commuter rush, the odor of sweat and men's cologne thick in the air. When the doors opened at Tokyo Central, a swarm of dark suits would explode from the train like contents under pressure. Now Alex reclaimed his seat, his hands clasped over his briefcase. He tried to shake his mind into clarity. He had no wife anymore, he reminded himself, no child to be responsible to. The time had come to address the great, squatting monster of his guilt, to do penance.

Downtown Crossing, and Alex chose the stairs over the escalator. He climbed into the dry crisp air of early fall. Around him, men who looked like him checked their cell phones. He pulled out his BlackBerry, then tucked it back. He felt a cold sweat on his belly. What if Brooke said no? What if she said, simply, "Don't go back to Windermere"? What if she said, "Don't go. I love you"? If she said, "If you don't go, I love you. If you go, I love you not." If she said any of these things, would he still take next week off, drive to central Pennsylvania, and find someone to whom he could confess a fifteen-year-old crime? The last time he went to Hartford, he had told himself it would not matter what Brooke said; she had only to know his resolution, and then he would be on his way to the authorities, whoever they were. But as soon as he saw her, he felt a pull on his resolve. And so he had brought it up—had said *I did something. I killed him*—but when she dismissed his guilt as just that, the phantom guilt people feel when something bad has happened, he hadn't pressed on.

Brooke would hold him responsible eventually. Of that he felt sure. She hadn't escaped the past, after all, any more than he. Like a kaleidoscope her face had changed while he'd taken that phone call—from a colorless loveliness that betrayed no feelings to a collage of set-aside ambitions, sparks of intelligence, fierce passions. Everything she had chosen—*everything*, he realized with a strange quickness at his heart—had stemmed from the fear and shame brought on by what happened to her when she was a girl of seventeen. Her botched solution to an accidental pregnancy had led her to give up college, to take a job tending mute plants, to harbor dumb animals, to marry a man she thought she could never disappoint—in short, to bury in some remote place everything that had made Brooke Brooke. There was the daughter—but even when it came to children, Brooke wouldn't let herself off some invisible hook. Spirit children, she'd called them, the ghosts haunting her.

He would take her blame onto himself, he thought as he swung through the revolving doors into the Mercator building. He could at least do that. Doing what he needed to do, he would make at least one person whole.

Meetings all day. The markets were tanking. Alex's boss, Peter Lloyd, had a world map on his wall, with colored pushpins for the Mercator offices that offered diversified investments, the branches that handled only corporate accounts, the storefronts that presented a quirky alternative to Schwab or Fidelity. In Japan, Alex had calibrated capital and cash flow so as to package mutual funds that would rise in the Morningstar ratings. Here, he looked at the patterns on the map and calibrated strategy. Which colors meant survival, which would bring destruction? "At least," Peter said as they wrapped up, "we stayed out of the mortgage mess."

"Not in Asia, we didn't," admitted Alex.

"That's why the Asian offices have gone"—Peter gestured toward the map—"from green to blue. And why you're here."

He was supposed to feel grateful, Alex knew. He had salvaged what he could of the Tokyo base. But business success, right now, tasted like chalk. "I've got Hartford again on Monday," he said.

Peter Lloyd regarded him from under flaring white eyebrows. "And I expect a report on my desk," he said, "by Wednesday."

"Springfield as well," Alex said—though Wednesday was a lifetime away, and Springfield just another pushpin on a map—"That'll be Tuesday, though. Separate trip."

"Going to the Sox game tonight?"

"Buddy of mine's got a couple of box tickets," Alex said.

Peter whistled. "Well, aren't you the lucky youngster."

The buddy was Brian Whiting, his old high school classmate, who had been calling Alex ever since he landed in Boston. Alex hadn't planned to get in touch with anyone from Windermere— well, Brooke, though that had been less a plan than an instinct— but Brian had heard from his family, who had heard from Alex's mom, and there had finally been no avoiding him. The Sox, fresh off last year's Series, were up against the Yankees, and Brian had made it clear he was offering Alex pure gold. He should be grateful, Alex thought as he packed up for the weekend. Along with Jake, who was still back in Windermere, Brian was his oldest friend. He was an attorney now in Providence, private practice, criminal defense, a success story. He wanted to get Alex settled in Beantown, find him a girlfriend, a new life.

He dropped his briefcase at the flat he'd rented on Bay State and changed to jeans. The night was cool, breezy, leaves beginning to drift from the trees. As he exited the building, his phone rang: Charlie. "Hey, big brother," she said.

"Hey, kiddo. You having fun this weekend?"

"Maybe. There's this new guy, Pablo, he's having a party. Or we could take off for Windermere."

"So soon? I thought you were talking fall break."

"Mom says the leaves are changing already. You want to go?"

His stomach clenched. "Not yet," he said.

"Why not? Do you have to, like, *prepare* for a trip to Windermere?"

She laughed, and he tried to join in. "No, I mean I've got stuff to do this weekend. Fall break'll be fine. I'll take a few days."

"Good, because I want to do research there. For my moral phil paper."

He chuckled. "What, on the moral qualities of autumn leaves?"

"Funny man. There's one of those big Christian groups out there, picketing Planned Parenthood. I thought I'd interview them. Hear their side. Look at their cute photos of unborn babies. I am a college student. My mind is open."

He had to stop. He leaned against an iron railing at the corner. Choking, he kept his voice light. "Well, just be sure it's not so open that your brains fall out," he said.

Charlie, Charlie, he thought when he could let himself breathe again. He had been the upstanding one, she the pile of mischief. Yet by the time he was her age, he had already been marked, branded, guilty. What would she think of him, when she came to know? *If*, he tried correcting himself, but the word came back, *when*.

Brian was waiting at the Cask'n Flagon, right across from Fenway. "Christ," Alex said when he had woven his way past the Sox fans to the lean guy waving his hand. "You're bald."

"Shaved," Brian explained, running his hand over the smooth crown of his head. "I was getting this pattern baldness thing, so I figured, take it all off. But look at you." He nicked his chin toward Alex's full head of hair. "You're still the dude."

Brian had tanned too deeply over the summer, so that his strong-boned face seemed sheathed in smooth leather. He was divorced, Alex learned in the din of the pub; no kids. Brian pushed an image of himself as a playboy, talking about summer in the Hamptons, one girl and then another. He was talking to Alex, but he could have been talking to any one of the professionals unwinding before the game. It suited Alex fine. They managed beers and hamburgers, then walked over to the stadium, the lights already gleaming. Around them the fans—Sox, mostly, but a fair contingent of New Yorkers chanting *Jeter! Jeter!*—bottlenecked through the doors. From a distance, in the stadium, they could hear a soprano belting out the national anthem. Brian asked Alex if he'd seen the Sox open in Tokyo, at the beginning of summer, and Alex said he had. Normally, he had little interest in baseball. Soccer was his sport because it moved, all the time. He had no patience for a sport that operated without a clock, that wasted endless minutes in discussions on the mound. But the Sox opener in Tokyo—a first for the major leagues—had been one of his last nights out with the small contingent left at the Tokyo office. He had felt a bizarre, suffocating nostalgia as the Boston team strode out under the Japanese floodlights. "I knew I was coming back, then," he said, shaking his head. "I missed everything all at once. Tokyo, I mean, and the States, too."

Brian nodded and said, "Powerful," but Alex saw he wasn't listening—just eyeballing the crowd, navigating toward their seats.

By the time they settled in the box, behind first base, the anthem was over and the Yankees were at bat. They talked about Brian's work—trial cases, mostly corporate malfeasance but a few ordinary criminals, a couple of crime families. "You know they're guilty, right?" Alex said when they'd ordered beers.

"What are you talking about? I presume innocence." Brian grinned raffishly. Already in high school he had been a politician, deploying the First Amendment against the ban on tattoos and stoking rumors about an unpopular physics teacher. Alex had liked him but had never trusted him.

"Innocence," Alex repeated, as if trying out the word. Bottom of the first, and the Sox had struck out; the Yankees went up again. Charlie might be on her way to Windermere right now, going to ask Christian picketers why they were opposed to killing unborn babies. He could feel his guilt like a stray dog, rubbing up against his shins, refusing to leave his side. Its stink rose to his nostrils. "What if you get somebody off, and then they go murder a child or something? Doesn't that kind of haunt your sleep?"

"Ssh," Brian said. He leaned forward and pointed. Derek Jeter stepped to the plate. Alex tried to pay attention. They watched Jeter line-drive a single. "The system needs to work," Brian said when the boos and applause died down. "The system needs me to do my best. If it lets the guy off, there's a failure somewhere else. That's what ought to haunt someone's sleep."

The beer vendor came around; Alex signaled for another. "Ever had a client volunteer his own guilt?" he said.

Brian shrugged. "Sure. He still needs an advocate. I can try to get temporary insanity, reduced sentence, immunity if there's more than one guy involved." He cracked a peanut with his teeth. "You do what you can."

They watched the game for a while. Between at bats, Brian reminded Alex how often he'd e-mailed him, since Tomiko left, to persuade him back to the States. No way were the women of Tokyo more beautiful than the ones in Boston or New York. Now, Brian said, Alex was seeing what he'd meant. This—this box, this game, the women in crop tops waving their little pennants—was the life. For all his shaven-head cool, Brian seemed to Alex to be lonely, an upstate Pennsylvania boy putting on urban chic. "What if a guy came to you," Alex said as the fourth inning ended, "with a tale of some crime he'd committed, only there was no record of it on the books?"

"He wouldn't come to me," Brian said. "He'd go to the cops, or the DA."

"But they'd assign him an attorney."

"Hey, not this attorney." Brian held up his hands. "I'll never do that public defender shit. Those guys are so exploited, you would not believe."

"Okay, but just say."

"Say what?"

"You're doing the public defender thing. Or someone else is. And there's this guy confessing to some crime. Let's say . . . let's say a murder of some homeless person who's never been missed. And he can show you, I don't know, the gravesite where he buried the bones or something. He can prove his own guilt. Society hasn't given a shit about this crime before, because they didn't know it happened. But now it's the criminal himself. Bringing the case to life."

Brian shook his tanned head. "Never happen," he said. "With a cold case, maybe. You give up on some burglary or other—"

"Stick with murder. No statute of limitations on murder, right?"

"Fine, murder. The case goes cold, then years later someone's guilty conscience gets to them and they come forward, and they have to basically convince the jury that they did this thing, because usually by then there's been a whole parade of crazies making the same claim."

Alex felt jumpy. Before them, the Sox were at bat, probably winning, but he couldn't focus on the score, the runs. He drained his beer. "Yeah, but I don't mean like that," he said.

"Why would you care, man?" Brian looked at him. They'd both been half listening to each other, making the sort of connection that feels temporarily good, like a back rub. "If nobody missed the dead person, it probably wasn't somebody needing to be kept alive. If this hypothetical killer hasn't done anyone else . . . I don't know. We got our hands pretty full with the shit we already know about."

"I guess." Alex felt Brian's eyes still on him, neither of them watching the ball game. "Something like that happened in Japan, just before I left," he lied. "In my neighborhood. The guy who turned himself in lived down my block. I've been wondering what's happened to him."

"What'd he claim to do?"

Alex felt himself too deep to stop. "Killed a baby, he said. Right when it was born, so no one ever knew."

"Man, that's weird. His own kid?"

Alex nodded. His stomach was an iron weight. "He said so."

"He proved it? Dug the little corpse up or whatever? Brought the wifey in to testify against him?"

"I don't know, man. I came over here."

"Well, that's just sick. You got to feel sorry for someone like that. I mean, look at you. You lost your kid to disease. Must piss you off, a guy like that. Aah, stop thinking about it." He slapped Alex's cheek with the back of his hand. "You can't get morbid. You're young, man. Start a whole new family, now you're stateside."

"But what if—"

"I would defend him, okay? I would defend the slick little baby killer. And with any luck, the system would put him away and he'd get what he deserved from those badass punks in the prison system. Now watch the game."

They watched. When Brian went to take a leak, he came back with a pair of young women, who stayed and joked for two innings before they left the box. "That was an opportunity, there," Brian said as they retreated. "The short one, Caroline? She works in my office. If you'd said something I might've been able to hook you up."

Alex smiled. "I said something."

"Yeah. 'Hello.' How long since you and Tomiko split?"

"Eighteen months. But I've got a lot on my plate right now, Brian."

"No, you don't. You're just a slow mover. I remember you in high school. It was Brooke or nobody." One of the Sox popped a fly. They watched the ball arc high in the stadium lights and land foul, in the crowd behind third base. "When she disappeared on you, I don't think you dated all through college." He cut a glance at Alex. "Did you?"

"I don't remember, man. It was a long time ago."

"You knocked her up, didn't you?"

Alex's breath froze in his lungs. "Who told you that?"

"Jake, I think."

Jake, of course. Alex's mouth twisted knowingly. Jake had been his best friend, closer even than Brian because Jake played soccer. Unlike Alex or even Brian, Jake had never been much for school, and his ambitions never extended beyond finishing a six-pack and jumping off the highest rock in the flooded quarry. But he loved Alex like the brother neither of them had, while Brian was always pushing rivalries. Jake had stayed in Windermere, become a cop, risen to detective. Do you realize how cool it will be, Jake had asked Alex back at his dad's funeral, to say I know Alex Frazier? To say I connect to a guy who's working on the other side of the fucking world? More than once, Alex had imagined Jake's face when he came to learn what Alex had done all those years ago; he saw how the bright expression would fall, how disappointment would veil Jake's eyes.

He drained his beer, considered another, rejected the idea. He wondered what Brooke was doing. Her daughter would be asleep. Brooke wasn't much for TV. Maybe she was reading some historical romance. No. That was the old Brooke. She was drinking a cup of tea now, or a glass of wine, looking out the window, deciding to send him a text and call off that drink. The way she had touched her hand to his jacket, at her nursery . . . there had been more than nostalgia, more than pity in how it rested there, the long fingers almost stroking his chest before she pulled away.

God knew it was not love he had come to the States looking for. Not with Brooke. Not after all these years. But he was surprised at the nub of her presence, when the space between them shrank to inches, as if she were the fulcrum on which he might finally turn.

"So? Alex? It's been years now, you can come clean. She didn't go off somewhere and have your love child, did she? Not that it was easy to take care of that kind of thing, in that backwater."

"No." Alex stood up. He couldn't sit still. He would say he needed the men's room. "No. Brooke had—" He couldn't lie that way, couldn't say *an abortion*. He lied a different way instead. "It was a scare, that's all," he said. "I told Jake about it. Son of a bitch couldn't keep his mouth shut, I guess."

"Yeah, he's still like that. Hey, if you ever go back to Windermere again, you can ask him your question."

"What question?"

"About your Japanese baby killer. He's on the police force."

"Yeah, he told me."

"So you'd think he'd have to learn to keep a few confidences, in that job."

Alex's laugh was hollow. How many lies had he told in the course of a baseball game? How was he ever going to step forward with the truth when the lies came so easily?

Chapter 15

The weekend felt to Brooke like the point on a seesaw, suspended in the middle, before one side or the other answers the pull of gravity. On Saturday, she and Sean left Meghan across the street at Taisha's house and went together to the Simsbury location, where they laid in the rest of the spruces and oversaw the construction of a winding walkway up to the old house that would become the garden center. Sean hummed and sweated and got a sunburn on his head for his trouble, and that night they took Meghan to a Disney Snow White remake called *Enchanted*. Leaving the theater, they held hands. Though Brooke would never have called her husband handsome, she had seen other women drawn to him the same way she was, not just by his voice but by his warm, slow-spreading smile and the golden eyes that flicked over her before he started up the car. But the charm of the day dwindled with the light. Sean stayed up after Brooke had gone to bed, listening to the Bach on his headphones and polishing off the six-pack Brooke found, next morning, in the recycle bin. He was still sleeping when she took Meghan to a birthday party. Meghan bounced in the car seat.

"Mine," she declared for the third time as they turned onto the birthday girl's street, "is the best present for Jackie."

"It's a nice present, honey," Brooke said. They could go back to Simsbury today, she was thinking; they were happy there. But today Sean could resent being free labor. And she would mention the six-pack, or not mention it and he would hear her anyway. When did it start, this anxiety? "And the lady wrapped it so nicely."

"It's the *best*." Meghan bounced. On her lap was a colorfully wrapped box of American Girl accessories that had cost more than what Brooke had paid for her own clothes. "No one else knows her mom got Josefina for her. And we're giving a whole *outfit*. I want Jackie to open mine first."

"Maybe she will."

Meghan flung her arms around her mother's neck before she left to join the other giggling, dressed-up girls. Brooke smiled, her heart easing a notch. When she returned home, Sean was up, shaved, sitting on the back patio with his coffee and the paper. The dogs settled at their feet; Blackie rubbed against Brooke's shin. The new cat hovered by the flower bed, looking spooked. Protected by the hedges on three sides of the yard, Brooke felt the elusive warmth of the October sun on her face. Sean cradled a cup of coffee. He nodded at the flowers. "I won't be weeding those," he said.

"Doesn't matter," said Brooke. "They grow back no matter what we do."

"I've got a cold coming on. I'm drinking too much."

"You're upset with me. With us."

"That's no excuse." Sean set his coffee down on a wrought-iron table, marred already with bird droppings. She could hear the congestion in his voice. "Mum ought to have left my dad, when he first got out of hand. She let it get to her instead. Didn't do anyone any good."

Brooke felt stung. "Your mother is a nasty drunk," she said. "I'm nothing like her."

"I didn't mean you were. I didn't mean that, Brooke. I have— you know."

"CD Pyg."

He reached for her hand, and she gave it to him. His palms were broad, little tufts of reddish hair on the backs of the knuckles. But he let go of her quickly. "All I want," he said, "is our life. Our little girl. All I want is to understand my wife."

Brooke's face flushed. She nodded. She bent down and kissed the back of his palm. If he only could know her! But he could not— could not know what she had done, and still love her. Sitting in the quiet backyard, all the familiar materials of her life around her, Brooke felt her marriage was impossible. Stroking Blackie, she released fur that coated her clammy palms and got on her tan shorts. Sean wasn't denying drinking; wasn't even saying he would try to stop. How often they had talked about drinking, about his parents. She pushed Blackie from her lap. "We should get rid of these stupid cats," she said.

"I thought you loved them."

"I don't—" she began, but couldn't finish. *Love anybody*: Was that how the sentence ended? She rose. She went to the patch of zinnias and began pulling weeds. Lex and Mocha followed her, sniffing among the flowers. "You've got rehearsal tomorrow, right?"

"I'm going early. Geoffrey's got me learning the Evangelist." Turning, Brooke frowned. "Solo," Sean explained. "Just for rehearsal, to help out the group."

"Oh, honey. That's terrific." She stopped herself. *Honey*. It had slipped out. Well, why shouldn't it? Her heart surged with pride.

"He's lucky to have you," she said, turning back to the flowers, "and he knows it."

"Not lucky when he has to shove me past the trained musicians." He shook his head. "Showing up with a cold won't help."

"Anyone can catch a cold." She brushed dirt from her hand and came back to the patio. Leaning over his chair, she kissed him on the lips, coffee tinged with beer.

Her blood surged, then. Because she was proud of Sean? she wondered the next evening. Or because she had confirmed the evening was free? Innocent, she told herself; this drink with Alex was innocent, however guilty their past. After Sean left for rehearsal, she simply put away the dishes and combed her hair. A quiet, pudgy twelve-year-old, Emma, walked over from around the corner at seven and took instructions to get Meghan ready for bed.

"I'll be back to tuck her in," Brooke said. She caught a last glance in the hall mirror before she headed into the twilight. She wore jeans and a knit top with a loose vest that hid her figure, but she had threaded garnet earrings through her lobes that reflected light and caught the deep embroidery of the vest. Quickly she pushed her fine hair one way and another, seeing what best drew the eye away from the harsh lines around her mouth and toward her arched brows and high, clear forehead. "Damn it," she whispered at last, and stuck a clip in her hair.

They met on the south side, in an Afghani place where they were unlikely to run into any O'Connors, especially on a Monday night. Alex's posture, Brooke noticed, was almost frozen, his arms close to his side, not the loose-jointed familiar figure she'd first greeted at Starbucks ten weeks ago.

"I have to come clean," he said after he'd ordered a bottle of wine.

"Clean about what?"

"What I did. To the baby."

The bottle came. Brooke frowned. Would they drink all that? Did they need all that? "Is that what you came here for in the first place?"

"No. I wasn't thinking about it. But now I can't help myself. It's all connected." He poured wine for each of them, then took a slow sip. "I want to back up. Face consequences." He reached into his jacket pocket. Drawing out a black ring box, he snapped it open. "I clipped this," he said. "From his head. With my nail clippers. Don't ask me why."

Brooke looked at the tiny lock of hair with horror. "Put it away," she said. "Please."

"I should toss it out. But I can't."

He snapped the box shut and tucked it into his pocket. Still trembling from the sight of that hair—dark, curled like a *C*—Brooke searched Alex's face in the dim light.

"Lex," she said. She had expected banter, idle bits of news, his life in Boston. But from the sleepless glaze of his eyes, she saw he had no energy for niceties. "I should have gone to my mom, the way you told me. You've got nothing to come clean about."

The scent of cardamom and nutmeg came through the bead curtain partitioning the dining room. A votive candle sat in a red base between them. The dimple in Alex's right cheek looked sardonic one moment, nostalgic the next. Under his unruly hair his eyebrows, thicker than before, rose toward the center as if in a question. His blue eyes flitted around the room, then settled on her, taking aim. "You don't really know what I did, Brooke," he said.

"Of course I know. I was there. You wanted to go to the hospital. I wouldn't. And you know, maybe it was alive in there. I never felt it kick, but still. Maybe I killed it, suffocated it or something, because I wouldn't go. But all you did, Lex—"

"He was alive."

"That's what I'm saying, Alex. Maybe I could have brought that pregnancy to term. We'll never know."

"When he came out, he was alive. I saw his eyes. I squeezed him too hard."

"Alex, you're not remembering anything right." Panic built in Brooke's chest. "It was not a he. It was a she. And it—she—never breathed air. Never cried. My God, Alex, I would remember that."

"You'd practically passed out."

"I wanted to hold her. I remember that."

From the corner of her eye Brooke saw the waiter, hovering. She and Alex were speaking in low tones, but the air crackled between them. "Is everything all right?" the waiter asked hesitantly. He was young, maybe nineteen. He wore a fez with tiny mirrors on the sides. "Would you like to see menus?"

"Maybe some water," Brooke said. She turned back to Alex. "I wanted to hold her," she repeated, "but I knew she wasn't alive. And whether it was worse, what we did, or whether some pro-lifer would say an abortion would've been the same thing . . ." She held up her empty palms. "We can't go back, either way."

"I looked at him," Alex insisted. "I saw his eyes move. Then they stopped. And the head—the skull's not completely hard, you know. You can hurt it. And I think I did. My hands squeezed, and I—" He extended his hands, as if they cradled a baby's skull between them. Brooke reached out and held them. He had to stop talking, she thought. She had to make him stop. "If I'd been a doctor," he finished, looking at her through the wreath of their hands, "I might have saved him."

"Her."

"I might have done some emergency procedure. Got him breathing and then seen what damage I'd done. But I was so glad to have the thing out of you. I wanted it to be over."

"We both did. And if by 'over,' you mean dead, she was, no matter what we wanted. Okay, Lex? Imagining anything else is crazy. Completely crazy." The young waiter brought two glasses of ice water. Brooke let go of Alex's hands and drank hers.

"Crazy, maybe," Alex said. "But I want to go back to Windermere."

Brooke signaled for more water. She felt she had never been so thirsty, her throat so dry and hot. "There's nothing there to help."

"I'm going to turn myself in."

The water came. With the glass halfway to her lips, Brooke blanched. "Turn yourself in? To who? For what?"

"To the police. For killing that child."

"What possible good would that do?"

"I don't know. Maybe not any. Or maybe . . . I'm starting to think like you, here." A rueful grin crossed his face.

"Think like me how?"

"Magically." Finishing the wine in his glass, he refilled it. "I feel like I didn't just come back to the States because my marriage tanked. I came because I needed to rip the cover off. To be honest for a change. And I mean honest about a crime, my crime."

"But if I don't believe—"

"I'm not asking your permission," Alex said. "I'm telling you, so you'll be ready."

"For what?" Brooke said—though she knew the answer before he gave it.

"For when they come," he said, "asking you."

A t the break, Sean approached Geoff and asked for the rest of the night off. "Don't want to infect anyone else," he said. Geoff told him he looked like hell and shooed him out the door. Driving home, he felt his ears ringing, the soreness descending his eustachian tubes to his throat. This cold was going to be a doozy, he thought. He'd crawl right into bed, ask Brooke to fix him a whiskey toddy. But when he pulled into the drive and saw her car gone, he knew. He pressed his heavy head against the steering wheel for a minute, then hauled himself out of the car and into the house. Gave little Emma ten bucks; she could walk herself home. Meghan was already in bed. He poured his own whiskey, neat, and nursed it in the kitchen.

By the time Brooke's car crunched on the gravel, he'd played out the fight in his head a dozen times, and left himself bloody and bruised at each round. "Eight years," he said when she'd come into the kitchen, startled as a doe, those red earrings glinting in her hair. "And you haven't been honest with me for a single day."

The whiskey bottle stood on the breakfast table. Christ, he was hammered. Hammered and horny and sick as a dog and wanting his wife, and what had Danny called her? A cold bitch.

"You're drunk," she said softly.

"And you are a whore."

"What. The fuck. Are you talking about?" She went over to the sink, drew a glass of water, and chugged it.

"Ah. Now, there's the stuff. Never heard you say 'fuck' before. Is that amazing or what? Too much the lady. Now you meet your boyfriend, and you come back saying 'fuck.' What do you think of that, guys? Huh?" He nudged Lex with his toe. "She doesn't take you along, either. Little miss lover of all things dependent but she leaves you behind for the old flame. Why d'you suppose that is?"

"Because I needed to talk to him."

"To Alex. You can say his name, Brooke. I know his name now."

"Yes, to Alex. We needed to work out some stuff. From long ago."

"Without telling your husband. Where I come from they call that sneaking around. Not working stuff out."

"I knew you'd be jealous, Sean. I'm sorry."

"Hear that?" He nudged Lex again, harder. The Labrador growled. "The adulteress is sorry."

"I'm not sleeping with him."

She said that quickly, too quickly. His head stampeded. His throat was sandpaper, coated in phlegm. " 'I am not having sex,' " he quoted, " 'with that man.' Which means you did. Or you will. And I don't fucking care which it is."

"I did sleep with him, Sean. In *high school*."

God, he loved her. He knew he loved her more than his life, even as he knocked back the last shot and went to take a piss, his muscles weak. In his stuffed head now he heard the chorus they'd been singing before he left rehearsal—the chorus coming in as the Wise Men, saying, *"Wo? Wo? Wo?" Where is the king of the Jews*, they wanted to know, but all Sean could hear in the tiny room was the voices piling in on top of one another, *woe woe woe, woe woe woe*.

This was the third time in less than a month that he'd picked a fight. All he'd accomplished was to make Brooke lower her head and push forward with whatever she was doing—letting the phone ring unanswered, taking her night walks, drifting a million miles away whenever he tried to have a serious talk with her. And now, pouncing on his Monday night absence to sneak out for a date. She was fucking the guy, how could she not be fucking the guy? He heard his brothers Danny and Gerry in his head, somewhere mixed in with the insistent chorus. They went from asking what such a babe saw in him to promising they could get him a sparky Catholic girl who'd give him all the kids he wanted. He heard Mum, calling him a dreamer. He blew his nose on the toilet tissue, felt the pressure behind his eyes.

He shook himself dry and went back out to the kitchen. The microwave dinged; Brooke pulled out a mug of chamomile tea.

When she turned to him, her eyes were frightened, and not just frightened: guilty. He walked right up to her. He was barefoot, so she stood even taller over him than usual. He put his arm around her waist and yanked her to him. Quickly she set the hot mug on the counter. "Kiss me," he said.

"Sean, you're drunk. It's a problem, you're—"

"You're my goddamn wife." He put his free hand to her crotch. "Kiss your husband."

"Don't talk to me that way, Sean."

"You're coming fresh from him. Don't lie to me. And if you put something in the oven, it'll be his little bread loaf. Won't it? C'mon, Brooke. Tell us the truth." He grabbed her crotch. Brooke gave a soft cry. He felt himself getting hard. "I'm going to get it out of you. Somehow or other I—"

She twisted free of him. He lunged for her hand and caught her forearm. "Ouch!" she cried. "Sean, you're hurting me!"

"Come to bed, we'll get the truth out."

"You're *drunk*." She grabbed her fettered hand with her other and pulled it free. When he lunged at her next he caught only an inch of T-shirt as she moved away. "Let go," she ordered, and he wouldn't, he couldn't, and that was when she kneed him in the groin.

He sank to the cold tile, the old, sharp, sickening pain climbing from his balls through his belly. He twisted. With a grunt, he vomited into the dogs' bowl. Immediately Mocha came trotting over to taste it, and he smacked her nose away. Then he didn't care. "What the hell," he said. "Eat it." He tried but couldn't stand. Knees up, back against the lower cupboard doors, he dropped his face into his hands. Brooke had left the kitchen. She wasn't going to comfort him, help him, make things better with him. He'd muscled her and she'd fought back. He heard her tread on the stairs, and then sounds from above. He needed to stop her. Fine, he would say. We'll just have Meghan. Meghan is great. Or adoption, he'd say. He could love a kid with shy knees, sure he could. Only don't go. Wait, don't go. Whatever else is wrong, whoever he is, don't go. Woe woe woe.

He couldn't get his ass off the cold floor. Brooke walked right past him, a breeze brushing him as she opened the back door. She left it open; he heard her car door open and shut. Then she was back. "Don't go," he murmured.

She crouched next to him. With the tips of her fingers she combed what was left of his hair back from his sweating forehead. He couldn't look up, but he could tell from the rhythm of her breathing that she was crying. "You'll have to look after Meghan," she said. "For a few days."

"You can't leave her. You can't leave us."

"You'll have to stay away from booze. For her. For Meghan."

"I know. Really. I know. Don't go."

"I'm not leaving. Just giving you—giving us—some space."

"You're not telling me the truth."

She didn't answer this. She stroked his thin hair. She ran her hand over his head and squeezed the back of his neck very gently. He felt sick, but he wasn't going to vomit again, not yet. The dogs were panting around them both, Bitsy whining. Would she take them, too, and the cats and the birds? Would she take the flowers?

By the time she came back, holding the birdcage like a lamp, Sean had managed to look up. Under their cloth, the birds were silent. Brooke looked ghostly. Was she Mum, he wondered, and he his father, discord and drink smashing love to pieces before their eyes?

But no. She was not Mum. She was Brooke, and she was gone. The car tires crunched again over the gravel. Lex settled on the tile, his ugly snout on Sean's thigh. The new cat tiptoed over. It was a tiny thing, dirty white, its tail queerly crooked and a hitch in its stride. It rubbed against Sean's side. He shut his eyes. Rage and regret tumbled over one another. What came to mind was clothes in a dryer, the colors and the whites ballooning and falling back against the glass. He thought how he used to snatch out Brooke's delicates, before the heat scorched them. That was what he wanted to do, reach back into the warm moist past and snatch out whatever delicate thing they needed.

He chuckled. God, the kitchen was quiet. No more voices in his head, no chorus. A distant siren on Farmington Avenue. "Ever see a loser like me?" he said to Lex. The dog flicked open his eyes but did not raise his head. "Wife walks out and I get Laundromats on the brain. What the fuck."

He made it up the stairs eventually. He managed a mouthful of Listerine, three Tylenol, a pair of cold tablets that were supposed to make you drowsy. But he lay awake all night, waiting for the car to return. All night he felt the skin of his wife, like a missing limb.

Throughout the long drive back to Boston, Alex replayed the encounter with Brooke. The way she had stared at him, once she understood what he was saying. The candle's gleam in her eyes. The crack in her voice: *I wanted to hold her.* Turn himself in, what a screwy idea. And yet he hungered for it, that wash of horror over her face. If everyone would just look at him, once, with that horror in their eyes, then he would know. He would stand judged. He could begin, bit by bit, to atone. That was what he wanted.

His apartment yawned empty, the new furniture like a display model. Five minutes to midnight. Slowly he undressed. He could call Charlie; she'd be up still. Or even Brian. To tell them? No. Just to talk, to murmur himself into sleep. The bright, thin charge of insomnia lit up his brain in patches. Don't watch movies, the doctor in Japan had advised. Read books. But he had no books here.

Undressed, sprawled on the bed that felt strange to him, a stranger's bed, he flicked the television on mute and saw young beautiful white people arguing in a parking lot. He could not restrain himself. Sliding his BlackBerry off the side table, he punched in Brooke's cell number. He might wake her, yes. Wake her husband. But he had to hear her voice one more time. Had to hear her say the words—*You bastard, you murderer, leave me alone, go die.* As the phone pipped, he exhaled what felt like the first breath since he left the restaurant.

"Lex," she said.

"I thought you would screen my call." The TV had switched to a mute commercial, an SUV on top of a mountain. He couldn't help himself. He smiled at her voice. "Sorry to wake you."

"I was awake. I've been thinking about you."

"Wishing I'd never shown up?"

"I've been thinking," she said—and she sounded very far away, her voice small—"how you did everything right. Whatever you say about long ago, you did. Right school. Right career. Right way to have a family. And life hasn't been all that kind to you." She chuckled drily. "Starting with me, I guess."

Alex flicked off the TV. Rising, he went to his picture window and looked over Storrow Drive, the Charles, the lines of lights. "Where are you?"

"Driving. I have one of those earpiece things."

"Is something wrong? Your daughter?"

"No, no. Meghan's with her dad."

"I'd like to meet them."

"I don't know actually, Lex." Her voice went tight. With his free hand Alex found he was touching himself. He didn't mean to. Brooke's voice brought back the memory of her, not as a girl, but as the woman who had kissed him as they left the Afghani place. Her breast had just barely touched his chest, a more womanly breast than he'd remembered, and it had rubbed—had it, really?—against his thin shirt before she'd pulled away. He shut his eyes, imagined her hand, plain and strong. "It's not just that you want to do—what you want to do," Brooke was saying now. "Seeing you brings back feelings that I . . . that I really do better without. Don't you think?"

"Think what?"

"That this is kind of dangerous. This contact."

"It's not contact with me that's dangerous, Brooke. It's contact with yourself." His hand was moving now. The very word, *contact*, brought her plush skin to mind, the smell of her shampoo.

"I've got to go."

"Don't go."

"No, really. I have to. Don't do anything yet, okay? I mean about what you think you did."

"I know what I did."

"Don't talk to anyone about it yet. Please? For me? I won't stop you later, I promise. I just . . . I've got to get used to some things."

"Okay. Okay, Brooke." He left off touching himself. He pressed his palm against the window, as if she stood on the other side of the glass. "Are you crying?"

"No. Course not. I've got to go now."

She rang off. Alex tossed his phone onto the pile of clothes flung over a chair. "Christ," he said aloud.

This wasn't what he wanted, this bit of hope. He didn't want to get aroused by Brooke, to start dreaming of Brooke. He dropped onto the bed. Here came sleeplessness. So tired, and he would not sleep, not tonight. Jacking off wasn't going to help. The blue pills in his medicine chest would only grind out a headache. Sinking into the bed, staring at the mottled ceiling, he saw Brooke. Not as she was tonight, with her loose vest and groomed hair. But her clammy milk-white face as he pulled the blue infant away, as he found his pocketknife and cut the cord. He heard her sigh, a long *Oh* after holding her breath the whole time his hand and the spoon were inside her, pulling the thing out. And the blood had gushed, and the stringy tissue with it, right through his jacket and onto the bleached sheets of the motel bed.

It's not alive, is it, she had said, and it wasn't a question.

The eyes moved. Didn't they? Alone in his new life in Boston, he heard her again, the rush of words following the rush of blood. Give it to me, she'd said. Let me see. Oh, Lex. I'm going to change my mind. If it's my baby I don't care. Oh, Lex. Let me hold him.

On she babbled. He hadn't heard her, then, the way he heard her now. He passed the baby onto her belly, the white shirt soaked with red. She said something about its heart. She put its chest to her ear, a girl playing at doctors and nurses. But neither of them moved to get the phone that was connected now, neither of them called the people who knew about hearts and how to get them beating.

What had he said to her then? What? *I think you were right, Brooke. It wasn't alive in you.* Was that what he'd said? Was that how he'd lied? He'd felt the lie in him, starting right then, like the hiccups of a penny you swallowed as a kid, a thing that would work its way out.

He saw his hands, lifting the tiny body off Brooke's belly. He saw himself wrap it in a couple of the bathroom towels. They were red with blood, but wasn't the little thing past caring anyway? He had carried it out of the room and down the hall toward the back of the motel. With the thunderclap he'd heard in the room, the long drought had finally broken. Rain came down warm, glazing the asphalt and the green metal of the Dumpster in back of the building. Before he stepped out of the building, he fished in his jeans pocket. There they were, the nail clippers he carried everywhere. Crouching, he lifted the edge of the towel. The infant's eyes were closed—had he closed them?—and its color wasn't so blue, almost pink even. He tugged at a wet lock of hair, clipped it, tucked it into the pocket of his shirt, under the jacket. He touched his lips to the head. Still so warm!

Outside, next to the Dumpster, sat a couple of wooden crates. Holding his bundle, he climbed them. A vomitous smell rose from the boxes and plastic bags in the big metal tomb. He started to drop the body in, but he couldn't. He could not lay it down in that stink. He told himself it would be found in there; he had nothing to throw on top, to cover it up. He stepped back down. He went to the edge of the parking lot, to a back field, high in dry grass, and tried to lay it down there. As rain pelted the little face, the eyelids seemed to flutter with the drops. He covered the head, started to walk away. Then he fetched one of the crates. He tucked the baby inside and set the other crate on top, so the rain wouldn't pound on the body or the mud swamp the bloodstained towels. He set both crates behind a pair of lilac bushes, where no one would see them. As he hurried back, rain fell into his eyes.

Upstairs, she had left the bed. Sound of water running—she was showering, standing on the bloody towels, rinsing herself clean. He didn't go in. He pulled the sheets off the bed; pulled off the mattress pad; flipped the bed over so you couldn't see the bloody stain. The water stopped running, in the bathroom. Are you okay? he called through the door. She said, Yes, but in a tight, hard voice like a ball of tin foil, and then she asked did he have any money. When he said five dollars, she sent him out again, to pick up heavy-duty pads at a drugstore.

God, how he remembered that night! The air stood thick, heavy with cicadas. The cars flew over the road as if they would all circle around and descend on the Econo Lodge. He looked for stars, but even the full moon was blanketed. Fat drops of rain hit the windshield as he turned onto Route 6. A woman was crossing the road, her head hooded, hunched; he swerved and honked. By the time he reached the CVS parking lot, people outside the stores were stomping in puddles, shouting. In the bright pharmacy, the pretty cashier smirked as she rang up the pads. Driving back, wipers at top speed, he steered with his elbows. He could not have explained this peculiarity to anyone, not even Brooke.

But she had it all straightened up, the sheets wet but spotless on the bed, his Polartec dripping, a towel slung between her legs as she lay like a corpse on the bathroom floor—her hair wet-combed, her belly soft now like one of those old paintings, her head turned and resting on her arm, the other shoulder awkwardly lifted. Oh, baby, she said, as he held her there on the cold tile, oh baby, oh my baby, you are my life.

That was what she had said. He sat up, in the plush chair. *You are my life*, Brooke had said, half a lifetime ago, and then she had slid away from him, drawn her whole self tight as crushed tinfoil. And just now, on the phone? She was driving. He looked at the clock. Twelve thirty. Christ, what was she doing out at that hour? Before he could reflect, Alex found his phone among the rumpled clothes. He pressed the green button twice. "Lex?" she said. He could hear it now, the sound of the road.

"Where are you, Brooke?"

"I'm driving. I'm sorry. Can we talk tomorrow?"

"I thought you had an earpiece."

"I took it out. I didn't think anyone would call."

"Where are you driving after midnight? Don't you—"

"I'm sorry, Lex. I've got to go. We'll talk, okay? Get some sleep."

The phone went dead. He stared at it, then out again, over the bright bustling city. A strange panic lodged in his chest, and sleep lay on another continent, a long migration away.

Chapter 16

Brochures. So many brochures spread out, now, on the wooden coffee table that Ziadek could hardly find a place to put his coffee down. Until late at night Najda sat up, thumbing through them with her good hand, frowning at all the words. Being dyslexic, the teachers had said, meant she read very slowly but took everything in, like a deep sponge. Somewhere in America was a place with knowledge for her to soak up, a place where rich people sent their children in wheelchairs and where a few very rich Americans, their consciences pricked, left sums of money for enterprising families like Ziadek's. That was how Najda had explained what she had been doing at the library, filling out forms online and sending away for these brochures.

They needed to apply soon. In a week, the social worker—what was her name, this one? Darcy? Daisy? Delores, yes, Delores—would be coming by. Delores would have heard, by then, from the public school. Whoever was in charge of such things there would have alerted Delores to Najda's continued absence. Katarina had warned that the social worker would never swallow this story of a new school, a scholarship. For once Ziadek feared his older daughter was right. This social worker Delores—they came and went, a new one every eighteen months—had little patience and even less understanding. A heavyset black woman, she felt sorry for families like Ziadek's but she saw them as hopeless and also as foreign, using up resources that bright young black children deserved. Ziadek knew this though Delores never said anything directly to him, just asked Luisa questions in a loud voice and made scratches in her little book.

But on a heaven-sent day like this one—Indian summer, Americans called it, as if the Indians used to enjoy weather like this until the white man came—Ziadek could not beat his brow with anxieties. He wheeled his oxygen onto the narrow deck in back of the trailer, where the gas grill was set up. The warm dry sun, in a sky like a robin's egg, penetrated his leathery skin. He loosed the top two buttons of his shirt and settled in the plastic-weave chair with his book of Sudoku. From around the trailer park, he could hear the low chatter of televisions. Above, the trees that dotted the park lifted their dry canopies, splashed now with rust and gold; not a leaf moved. In his head Ziadek was hearing that old tune that Marika used to sing, "By the Lake." Only as he finished the first puzzle did he realize that his memory of the song was blending with a humming sound, Najda's humming. She and Luisa were back from the library.

"Lunchtime, Ziadek!" Luisa called from inside the trailer. "Hello! Ziadek! Lunchtime!"

He turned to the next Sudoku. It was not good for him to shout, Dr. Sanford had said. They would find him soon enough.

"Ziadek! Ziadek!"

He heard the screen door being pushed aside. He turned to see Najda, her face tight with determination, wheel herself onto the deck. She was still humming low, almost a growl. The sun struck her hair, which Luisa always brushed in the morning until it crackled. The hair shone like a spring daffodil. For the first time Ziadek saw that the foundling, for all her defects, was maturing into a lovely young woman. Her sweater hugged her young breasts; her waist nipped in.

"Ziadek!" Luisa called. She was in his bedroom now. "We're hungry!"

Najda shot Ziadek the glance of a conspirator. But he would not tolerate disrespect in his house. "Tell your mother," he instructed the girl, "where we are."

Wheeling over, she craned her neck to see the Sudoku. It was tempting to ask her; this puzzle was one of the harder ones. She was quicker with numbers than with words and could spit them out without hesitation. Reluctantly Ziadek closed the book. "Go tell her now," he said sternly.

Najda's lower lip pushed out, but she turned the wheelchair back to the open door. "Mo-om," she called in English, petulantly and barely loud enough. Ziadek shook his head. Two weeks ago, Luisa had started her first job outside the home, helping the Guatemalans who ran the Quik Mart by the gas station. But if this stay-at-home situation kept on, Luisa would quit her job, come home, and take orders from her daughter. The girl needed to be back in school, and soon.

"*There* you are," said Luisa. "Ziadek, we need lunch."

"You know how to fix lunch," he replied evenly. "I am not hungry."

"But, Ziadek." He turned. His daughter was twisting her hands in front of her. It wasn't food she was talking about. Something had happened.

"Bring me my ginger ale," he told her, "and come sit."

As Luisa disappeared into the trailer, Najda made as if to wheel herself down the ramp from the porch, onto the flagstone path that led around the clearing, to Katarina's place. "Oh, no you don't," he said to her. "You stay here a moment, grandchild."

Luisa clutched the can of ginger ale with her elbow while she carried a fistful of red licorice in one hand and an apple in the other. As she stepped onto the porch, the apple went down. Ziadek scooped it up. When he handed it to her, her eyes welled with tears. "It'll bruise," she said.

"It will be fine. What are you two fighting about?"

Luisa and Najda exchanged glances. Finally Luisa said, the tears starting to fall, "She wants to go *away*."

Ah. So it had come out. "Some of these schools," Ziadek said gently, "are not so close."

"Nobody *told* me that."

"And nothing has been decided yet. Najda must get a scholarship, or she goes back to the public school."

"I don't want her to get a scholarship."

"Luisa, we talked about this."

"Don't do the forms, Ziadek." Luisa bit off a chunk of licorice and chewed it angrily. She was curled into herself on the other plastic chair, a damp lump of sorrow. "She just wants you to do the forms," she said around the candy, "because she hates me."

"She does not hate you." Ziadek held up a hand to shush Najda, who sat glowering at the top of the ramp. She had started to emit gurgling sounds, and he feared they would form themselves into the words, into *Yes, yes, I hate you.* And what would he do then? Marika would know what to do, but he couldn't think the way she did. He inhaled the oxygen, pure and cool, and still he felt short of breath. "All parents let go of their children," he said, taking Luisa's free hand in his.

She shook her head. "Not true, not true."

Of course it was not true. He had not let go of Luisa. How could he? Someday, in fact, he would have to, or she would not survive his death. Maybe, Ziadek thought as he held his daughter's hand in the October sun, this was the first step, which Najda was taking, to letting Luisa herself go.

"And then they come back," he said, "and love you just as much
as ever. You don't want to lock your daughter up, do you?"

Najda wheeled closer. The sounds in her throat were working
their way out. "That," she said. They both looked at her. "That," she
repeated, "that school." She made a fist of her good hand and shook
it at Luisa. "Kill myself," she hissed. Her mouth contorted in an
awful grimace.

"Ziadek!" Luisa cried.

"You will do no such thing," Ziadek said to Najda.

"Kill myself. Kill myself."

"But you see, my Luisa. You must let her do what she can."
Reaching out, Ziadek ran his thumb under Luisa's crying eyes, first
one, then the other. "Now we will talk no more about this. We will
have some lunch. Najda, you let your mother take you to the park
after we eat. You say nothing more of killing. Luisa, you have work
later, remember? At the Quik Mart? If we have not so many days
together"—here he looked directly at Najda, who he knew understood him so much better than her poor mother—"we must enjoy
every one of them. While your mother is at work, my stubborn one,
we will look at your schools. There is no time to waste."

Najda went obediently inside, her head held high, feeling she had
won. Ziadek sat with Luisa while she wept. Would her foundling
child, he wondered, develop a heart, once she was free to pursue all
the things she hungered to learn? Would she, in her own crippled
way, care for Luisa when Ziadek was gone? There were such people,
he knew. He had seen one or two of them featured on TV—Stephen
Hawking, Christy Brown, people whose minds soared even as their
bodies trapped them. If Najda could become one of those people,
she could find the resources to maintain her mother, who was all
heart and no head, and Ziadek could die in peace.

Chapter 17

The stars chased Brooke's Subaru west from the Pennsylvania border. She wasn't the least bit tired. Her head seemed to have a big open space in it, where the future lay, and her mission was to fill the space, arrange it, make it different from before. Sleep was out of the question. As one radio station fizzed into static, she scanned for another. Country rock; Willie Nelson. Whatever. The white beams of tractor trailers roared past her on the downslope, chugged behind uphill.

Meghan, she told herself, would be fine. "She'll be fine," she repeated aloud every now and then, whenever the picture of her daughter rising from her bed at home filled her mind. This was just for a few days, until Brooke learned whatever she needed. Would Sean drink? Maybe. She had to take the chance.

The sky changed from ink to dull charcoal. At Scranton Brooke took I-380 north through Clarks Summit, then Route 6 until she crossed the Susquehanna and followed the back roads to Windermere. She had left Hartford just before midnight; she should reach the village by five. Speeding west under the stars, Brooke had a clear image, like a blueprint, of how her actions might look to someone who had come into the story seven years ago. She had driven a good but vulnerable man to drink. He had become—no, threatened to become—no, had a moment in which he became violent. Now she was fleeing her marriage. But that wasn't it at all. She was hurtling less away from Sean than toward Windermere, and whatever she might find there. Alex had come to her with a terrible story. On its truth or falsehood rested anything and everything she might do next. She had to find out, if she could, what had really happened. If she could prove to Alex that he had killed nothing and no one—if she could put the liability back where it belonged, with her own young self—then she could face not just Alex but Sean, too, with a clean heart. She could keep her guilt, like the bars of a cage whose clear, smooth design she claimed as her own, gleaming around her. She could go back to what she had become, or let come what might.

Brooke's mom lived in a new condo complex behind the high school in Windermere. She had moved in there five years ago, after Brooke's father died. Brooke and Sean had helped her move, Sean lifting and carrying and Meghan just beginning to toddle around the unopened boxes and disarranged furniture. Now Brooke pulled out the key her mom had given her and opened the door noiselessly. She had left the birds in the car. In the kitchen, lit by a dim light above the stove, she wrote her mom a note. Then she tiptoed to the guest room, stripped off her clothes, and slept dreamlessly. When her mom's radio alarm woke her, she needed a minute to remember where she was, and why.

She emerged from the room rubbing her eyes. The condo was done in buttercream and a color Brooke's mom called peanut, and its temperature felt the same as its colors, pale without being white, not quite cool enough to be labeled cold. Stacey Willcox's hair was in the same family, a muted wheat. "A surprise visit," she said, placing a mug of coffee in front of Brooke. "For my birthday?"

Brooke smiled sheepishly. "Sure," she said. She took a stool next to her mother. "Let's call it that. Happy birthday, Mom."

"Fifty-two," Stacey said. She pulled a tray of mini-muffins from the oven. "Not that I need you to come hold my hand for it," she said, turning them onto a plate. She winked at Brooke. Stacey Willcox would have been a beautiful woman except for the hard lines around her mouth. She had more curves to her figure than Brooke. A strict exercise routine—tennis three times a week, two hours a week in the fitness room—kept her calves hard and her biceps smooth. Her posture was erect without being rigid, and she moved fluidly from the hips, like a much younger woman. Walking down the sidewalk with Brooke in Hartford, last month, she had been mistaken for Brooke's older sister, the one joke they both laughed at.

"That's not what I came for," said Brooke. "But I hope you're celebrating."

"I'm considering the alternative." Stacey knifed the muffins from the tin and placed one on a plate for Brooke. She stood across the breakfast counter from her daughter. "So are you going to tell me?"

Brooke shrugged. She broke open the muffin, cranberry and walnut, steam rising from the center. "Sean and I are going through some stuff," she said.

"Have you got money problems? Why didn't you bring my granddaughter with you?"

Brooke tried not to wince. It was always *your husband* but *my granddaughter*; the questions always followed in a sort of relay, not so much an interrogation as a rehearsal of the questions Stacey had been posing to herself, ending with whichever question she hadn't managed to answer for herself without Brooke's help. "I needed to come alone," Brooke said guardedly. "I thought it would be good for me to revisit some old haunts. Might help me make some decisions," she said—playing into her mom's hopes, but she couldn't invent everything, and there were decisions to be made—"about what I want to do now."

"About divorcing your husband."

"I'm not talking divorce, Mom."

"Really? And your seeing Alex again. That's just a coincidence?"

"I am not *seeing* Alex. I *saw* Alex. He's back in the States. That's normal. And it's not why I'm here."

"Hmm." Stacey's quick nod was like a prosecutor's satisfaction at a polygraph. "Well, stay as long as you like. I've got to get to work. Don't you have work?"

"I'm calling in."

"Hmm. Well. Take a key if you go out. I'll be here tonight if you want to talk."

Stacey glanced at the clock, which read nine twenty-five. She was due, no doubt, at the school superintendent's office, where she single-handedly ran a program that tried gamely to procure state and federal grants for the county's shoestring schools. The job, Brooke suspected, paid little; Stacey's income still came from the interest on the quarry left her when her own father died. But it allowed her to attend regional planning meetings in Scranton and Harrisburg and to carry a torch for culture in the wilderness. Brooke smiled wanly at the girlishly sweet perfume as her mom pecked her softly on the cheek; and then Stacey was out the door.

Brooke missed her dad. Jim Willcox had just turned forty at her birth, a handsome but painfully shy newlywed, a stutterer, a book collector. It was on his shelves that Brooke first discovered the medieval tales that captured her imagination. When her mom was still Stacey Albrecht, a privileged teenager working after high school graduation at the library, she had met Jim Willcox while he roamed the stacks and considered graduate work in history. He never got to grad school, of course; Stacey's pregnancy derailed that. He got his insurance license and provided for his family, and read history books only as a hobby. But he loved his daughter and accepted his lot.

Brooke unpacked. She went out to the Subaru and brought in Dum and Dee; unveiled the cage and set it in a sunny window; refilled their water. As she roamed the living room, the birds' cheerful chirps behind her, she ran a finger over the shelf of her father's books. Decoration, now. She wrinkled her forehead. Where had her dad been, what had he known, that spring of her last year in high school? Always, she had trusted him. He had taken her hiking every summer. He had taught her the names of plants, of constellations. When she began dreaming of a future in medieval studies, he had listened to her ideas; he had nodded at what she saw in those strange and elliptical stories. What was there to trust, if not him? Yet she had not told him. She could not say, today, if he had suspected his only child was carrying a child that year. They had fallen back, both of them, on old habits and ways of relating. She had not crossed the threshold to say, *Dad, help me*. He had not crossed it to say, *Brooke, let me help you*.

Her sharpest memory of her dad was from the days after Alex brought her home from the Econo Lodge well after midnight, thick pads stuffed into her book bag. Between her legs lay a raw wound. Her breasts felt heavy as grain sacks. Her mom had stayed up that night, watching David Letterman in the old family room, and said only, "You've been drinking, haven't you," and it wasn't a question.

"Sorry," Brooke had mumbled. Her mother turned away, back to Letterman. Brooke had made her way upstairs. She'd wanted to shower again but hadn't. Five times that night she changed pads. She kept the bloody ones tightly wrapped in a plastic bag under the bed. She found an Ace bandage and wrapped it around her breasts so they felt less pendulous and needy. Finally, sometime before dawn, she fell into a sleep so deep that she leaked through the sixth pad and into the sheets before her dad's voice woke her. "Brooke, honey," he was saying. He tapped three times very softly on the bedroom door. "Brooke honey." Tap tap tap. "Brooke honey, are you ok-k- . . .ok-k-kay?" Her eyes snapped open to the red numerals on the clock: 12:48. Between her legs she felt the sore tissue and the sticky mess. Horror eclipsed relief.

"I don't feel all that great," she called back.

"Can I . . . c-c-c-can I enter?"

"Gimme sec." She was wide awake, her heart racing, but she made her voice sound sleepy. Swiftly, silently, she threw off the covers. Hand between her legs, she tiptoed to the little bathroom she had all to herself, where she whipped off her nightgown and the drenched pad. With a damp washcloth she wiped off her legs before she found a new pad, new panties to secure it, a fresh nightie in the drawer. With no time to worry about sheets, she brought her biggest, fluffiest white towel back to the bed and laid it over the stain. She managed that much before her knees buckled. She eased herself onto the bed, pulled the thin coverlet over. Her father had started tapping again. "Brooke?"

"Yeah, Dad. Come on in."

Only as he sat by the side of the bed, running his fingers through her hair, did she realize how clammy her skin was with sweat, how thirsty she felt. "Ice water," she said when he asked what he could get her. "From the fridge." While he was gone she stuffed the nightie, the panties, the pad she'd thrown in the bathroom sink, all into the plastic bag under the bed. She loosed her breasts, which ached but less than before and smelled of sweat and salt. Then her dad was back, worry wrinkling his brow.

He said nothing about her supposed drinking, though she knew her mom had reported to him. He was all set to take Brooke to Cowanesque Lake, the big father-daughter outing before graduation. "Oh, Dad," she said when he reminded her.

"Ssh. It's okay. You've got a b-b-bug, Brook Trout." He stroked her hair. That was his pet name for her, from when they used to go fishing. "Too much p-p-partying," he said. "Those germs just fly around."

"I feel like crap," she said, which was at least true.

"You've been stressed all spring. Haven't you?"

"I don't know. Maybe."

"Our ambitious girl." He reached his hand around to the back of her sweaty neck, and kneaded it. Behind his wire-rimmed glasses, his pale eyes drank her in. She could have told him, right then. But it was over, over, and his caring touch eased her muscles. As always when they were together for a while, his stutter vanished. "You've looked pale and puffy," he said—not critically, the way her mom would have, but like someone who would love a pale, puffy Brooke if that was what Brooke wanted for herself. She could have told him, but she didn't have to tell him. He would not make her tell him. What was there to tell now, anyway? "I wonder if we should get you to Dr. Harris."

Panic knotted her gut. "I'm fine, Dad."

"Not fine enough to go to the beach."

"No."

"Well, I'm staying home. I'll fetch you some chicken soup. Your mom's out for the day. We'll just hang around in our slippers. Sleep and loaf."

"Okay." She had shut her eyes. The knot loosened. She felt her-self drifting back to sleep. She heard her father take in a breath, as if to say something; then reconsider; then come out with it after all.

"Alex c-c-c- . . . phoned. Twice."

She frowned. Alex had saved her. Alex was her life. Alex was, suddenly, impossible. "I don't want to talk to him."

Her mom would have asked, Did you break up with him again? Did you kids quarrel? What did Alex do?—as if, whatever Alex had done, Stacey Willcox was prepared to defend him against her daugh-ter who was so lucky to have him as her steady guy. Brooke *was* lucky. For two years, the luckiest girl on the planet, never deserving Alex and certainly not now. No, she could not have Alex, or anyone. She was too stupid and foolish, she would only make a mess of it all again. But her dad didn't say anything more about Alex. He said only, "Let's get a fan in here. Move the air around a little."

Later he said, "I'm just downstairs, okay? Or in the back garden. Just puttering around. You just shout and I'm here."

She slept. Changed the pad again. Slept. While her dad was weeding the ivy by the back fence, she stole downstairs with the nightie and the sheets and mattress pad and threw them into the washing machine on cold. By evening she was running a fever, and when she woke at night there was her dad with more ice water and a couple of aspirin. His skin was dry and freckled from too much sun at the quarry; his lips were thin, the skin of his neck and eyelids already gone to rice paper. But for those two days, he tended Brooke with energy that never flagged and care that refused curiosity. Later that summer—after Brooke had turned down Tufts, while her mom raged and stormed about wasted years, wasted talent—he took her deep into the Alleghenies, where they camped overnight and cooked the fish they caught from the shore of a deep, cold lake.

Now, in her mom's pale condo, she wondered again, as she had wondered that summer. Had he guessed? Her dad's trademark forbearance had grown increasingly resigned, even defeatist, as Brooke matured. He would never have said he regretted the one summer's dalliance with the bright, coquettish junior librarian that had resulted in his marriage and his child, because he loved the child and he could stand the marriage. He would not regret it, because a truly happy life was never his to live. Increasingly, Brooke's dad seemed to know ahead of time what happened to hope or ambition: It died, either quietly or noisily. For himself, he preferred quietly. Hadn't he hoped to finish his doctorate, to travel in the intertwined groves of academe that stretched around the world, to write books that would work in those groves like roots, setting forth new ideas to blossom? Of course he had, and of course he never did those things, because Stacey got pregnant and a part-time stint at Scranton Community College wouldn't cut it and Lester Albrecht had connections in the local insurance agency. He hoped just as strongly—Brooke came to realize this only after she left home, when she could look back and see everything so much more clearly—that the unlikely romance, the accidental pregnancy, the sudden marriage would lead to happiness. Surely it had seemed to him, in his optimistic forties, that with all the love he had to give and all the determination he could muster, happiness had at least a fighting chance.

But by the time Brooke was getting ready to leave Windermere, her dad understood that he would never make his wife happy. He would never enjoy selling insurance. He would never write anything. He would find joy in his book collection, in the mountains, and most of all in Brooke. That Brooke's own dreams would turn to dust he seemed regretfully certain, even as he told her over and over how pleased he was by the little successes that made her happy—the school prizes, the high SAT marks, having and keeping a boyfriend.

So yes, he might have guessed that Brooke was pregnant. He might even have guessed that she had miscarried, or aborted. Guessing, he would have felt huge anxiety, even pain, for his daughter and at the same time despaired of affecting the turn of events. Waiting, tending, being patient—these things he could do. Take her fishing. When Brooke announced, a week after graduation, that she had turned down the offer from Tufts, her dad put every ounce of his energy into diverting her mom's furious disappointment. Never once did he speak to Brooke directly about what she was choosing, or why. He only looked at her with the deep sadness of his pale eyes behind his glasses, the sadness that said it was tragic for her to turn away college, but that college would have brought its own tragedy. Not because it was college, but because life itself, in the end, was a tragic journey.

In the hills, though—there, they were happy. Tucked into the ledges of a great granite boulder in the sun, overlooking a pine-rich valley, both of them with their noses stuck in books; or standing knee-deep in waders, casting their flies through a fine-needled rain. There and then, with her dad, Brooke felt more than at any other time that life would turn out all right, somehow. Now she ran a finger across the spines of his books and smiled at the irony of it. How she missed him! The sun he loved had gotten him, in the end: Melanoma, the doctors said, metastasized to the brain. He had been gone in six months, putting up what everyone knew was only a token fight. His last words to Brooke, when she took a week off to stay with him in hospice, were "Now don't *you* give up before you start." He had gripped her hand as he said it, a grip stronger than any she remembered from her childhood, though his face had sunk into its bones and his eyes had focused on nothing.

Her cell phone chimed, a message. Sean. Guilt scored her heart. *Meghan off to school*, he had written. *Very sad very sorry. Do what you need come home when your ready. CDPYG.* She smiled through an ache of ready tears at the acronym. Constant Disposition to Promote Your Good. If she had no good for him to promote, what then?

A scraping sound—Dum was attacking the bars of the cage, always a sign that he was anxious. "Poor buddy, poor buddy," she said. She reached her finger in for him to pinch. Time to get moving. First stop, Isadora Bassett. As she dressed, she considered calling her. She knew Isadora lived in the same house, the faded Victorian farmhouse overtaken by the town, on a side road just past the cluster of stores labeled the Mall. But a phone call meant niceties, evasions. Brooke wanted to get to the point. As a girl, she had grabbed at Isadora's solution and asked few questions. Now she could remember the names of only a couple of the herbs that had gone into that ghastly tea. Tansy, for instance. They sold a little tansy back at Lorenzo's Nursery. People liked its prim, cheerful yellow blooms; one customer used snippets of the leaves in salad. They sold pennyroyal, too, for ground cover and insect repellent. Up to now she had managed to look at the herb labels and not remember the tea, or not often.

After last night's long drive, the thought of getting back into the car nauseated her. She locked up her mom's condo and set out on foot. Whether the tansy and the pennyroyal—and what were the other herbs? Cohosh? Black or blue cohosh?—would really have terminated her pregnancy: That was the question. If the answer was yes, she could take it back to Alex. So there, she would tell him. We're no more guilty than we ever were. If the answer was no—well, then it had been her fault anyway, hadn't it? For believing Isadora? She thought of Alex's hands, so blunt and strong, pressing on a tiny head. Then she made herself think of something else.

Already, in this part of the state, the air was brisk, the leaves fluttering in golden waves from the poplars lining the drive of the high school. Brooke hugged her thin jacket around her. The route she took went by her old house, which lay past the two-block village center and the green with its old-fashioned bandstand. The sidewalks and storefronts were as familiar to Brooke as the contours of her own body. People always claimed that an old neighborhood seemed smaller, that the change coming over everything familiar was a shock. For Brooke, it was not the change from Foster's Drugstore to CVS or the new glass-front building in place of the old dentist's office that astonished, but the fact that her feet still knew where the cracks lay in the sidewalk; that the October sun struck the brick side of the post office with the same heartbreakingly frail heat she recalled from childhood autumns. As if her childhood had been a dream from which she had awakened, washed by blood, in a cheap motel, she marveled at how brave the little village seemed, its tattered kiosk brightened with mums and its unemployed citizens waving affably from their smoking circle as she passed the bandstand.

She had returned before, since her dad's death. But always with Sean and Meghan in tow, and never on a mission to dig up the past; quite the opposite. Meghan was happy seeing her Grandma in the neat little condo, happy in the new playground behind the elementary school; she wasn't old enough to ask about Mommy's past. This trip was different. Brooke meant to prove Alex wrong and so head off his useless confession. Then, maybe, they could both put the past behind; they could both heal.

She smiled incongruously at that word in her head, *both*. She was not picturing herself with Alex; not yet. But such words and phrases kept rising to her tongue. *Both. We. Together.* She felt again the blunt tips of his fingers, in the bar. She shoved her bare hands into her pockets; the air was brisk.

Past the town soccer field and the gas station, she turned down the little street that must once have been a drive leading up to Isadora's farmhouse. The house was painted light blue; had it been blue, before? She remembered white, with green shutters. In the drive now sat a bright red Jeep. Surely someone else had bought the house. Isadora had an allowance from an ex-husband somewhere, but she was always driving a battered VW or an ancient Saab. Brooke should have checked the phone book. But here she was. She took the newly laid flagstone path to the door.

"Aren't you a sight for sore eyes!" The door opened before Brooke could press the familiar bell. The sun shone on Isadora's white track suit and wide expectant face. She had gained weight since Brooke saw her last. Her hair was dyed a streaky strawberry blond. In a crowd, Brooke might have recognized the round, inquiring eyes and the jaunty slouch—weight resting on right leg, hip tilted out—but she would not have pegged her immediately as Isadora. Isadora had been a free spirit, a disciple of organic foods and nubby earth-colored cotton skirts that flowed from her narrow waist. Now she looked like an advertisement for Slim Fast. "Why, Brooke Willcox. Come in from the cold," Isadora, said, pushing open the storm door. "It's been a hundred years!"

Brooke smiled, or tried to. "We don't get back much since Dad died." Had Isadora been at her father's funeral? She couldn't remember. Her memory seemed to sponge away so much, even the most innocuous markers, anything that might lead her thoughts back to the motel, the stillbirth.

Isadora offered her coffee—"I'm supposed to be at aerobics, but let's forget that"—and they sat in the renovated kitchen, on high black metal chairs at a freestanding granite countertop. Brooke asked after the kids. Ethan and Josie, she remembered their names just in time. Isadora rolled her eyes. Kids, what a mess. "Josie's in college now, can you believe it?" she said. "Premed at Penn State. Where she got those genes, I'll never know."

"And Ethan?"

Isadora looked into her coffee cup. Her mood darkened for an instant. "He's figuring some stuff out," she said. She tightened her mouth into a smile. "Boys are funny creatures. I think he's in California these days. But I can't be sure. His dad sends him money."

"I'm sorry."

"Hey, it's fine. Nobody's perfect, right?"

Whether Isadora meant her son wasn't perfect or her parenting skills hadn't been perfect, Brooke couldn't tell. She tried to stick to the purpose of her visit. "I was pretty stupid when I was a kid," she said. She hooked her ankles around the rung on the stool, as if to anchor herself. "As you may recall."

"You were foolish, not stupid," Isadora said quickly. "And you got lucky."

"Did I?" Brooke held herself still, her fingers clutching the mug handle, as Isadora slid down from her stool and began filling a watering can at the kitchen sink. Plants filled the open kitchen and breakfast room—cyclamen and begonia in the window, a big pot of dracaena on the floor, hanging baskets of callisia and wax plants, an orchid in the center of the table, small pots of herbs slowly fading. They all looked overwatered to Brooke's trained eye, but now was not the time to instruct. She watched Isadora move around the space. Gone were any signs of children—the drawings, the bulletin board with clippings, even photos of Josie and Ethan. The walls, once hung with Isadora's weaving projects and soft-focus posters of Buddhist monks or nude women, now sported bright abstracts that coordinated with the curtains and upholstery. "That's what I wanted to talk to you about, actually," Brooke said.

"Your luck?" Isadora stepped on a stool to water a hanging plant. "How's that daughter I've heard about? She with you?"

"Meghan's with her dad in Hartford. I came by myself."

"Everything okay?"

"I suppose." Brooke felt fatigue at the back of her neck. But she had to do this. "You know Alex moved back to the States. From Japan."

"I hadn't heard." One of the baskets began dripping—overwatered—and Isadora pulled off a half dozen paper towels to wipe it up. If Brooke hadn't been so tired, she would have chuckled. The old Isadora had never let her hands touch paper towel, any more than her lips touched refined sugar. "So you're in touch with your old flame?"

"Sort of. I've been doing a lot of thinking about that time."

Isadora set down the watering can and returned to the counter. She leaned her elbows on the granite. She was wearing makeup, Brooke noticed—a thin film of foundation, careful application of blush, whisper-thin liner accenting her eyelids. "Not a good idea, Brooke," Isadora said firmly. For the first time she met Brooke's eyes. "You had an accident. You took a big risk. It worked. If you knew how I worried about you back then—"

"Did you? Is that why you gave me a bunch of herbs instead of talking sense into me?"

"You were a determined young woman. I tried to help you."

An unlicensed fury welled up in Brooke's throat. She swallowed it down. No point in raging at Isadora. She put her question squarely. "How much faith do you have," she said, going to rinse her mug, "in that little recipe you gave me?"

"Good Lord, Brooke. I'm not an expert. You're the only person I know—"

"You said you had friends who'd used it. You said you'd known those herbs to work. You said it took a while, for one friend. I remember distinctly."

"Well, people I'd heard about. Sure." The smile on Isadora's face seemed made of crayon. Brooke pushed the anger back down, to the pit of her stomach.

"And did you only hear about miscarriages?"

"I don't know what you mean."

"I mean did you ever hear about people who took the herbs and delivered early? I don't mean a premature stillbirth. I mean a preemie, a baby."

"It . . . It could have happened. To someone. Herbs are a lot more potent, you know, than people realize. I used to swear by them, but when you've got an unregulated industry—"

"You did swear by them," Brooke said. She leaned against the sink. *It could have happened.* A preemie could have happened. For the first time it seemed possible that Alex had been speaking the truth. "I reported back to you the week after I miscarried, don't you remember?"

"Not really, no."

"More than five months after you gave me those herbs. And you were like, *I told you it would work.* You did swear."

"But Brooke, I wasn't God."

"No, you weren't. You were an adult. I wasn't. I was seventeen. I believed everything you told me."

"Do we have to go back to this?" Isadora no longer met her eyes. She drained her coffee.

"No. We don't. I just wanted to know how sure you were that those herbs caused a miscarriage for me."

"Well, I'm not sure." Her movements jerky, Isadora returned the milk to the fridge. "I don't think it's my job to be sure. I didn't hurt anyone."

"Did you ever hear of people having trouble later?"

"What do you mean later?"

Brooke's mouth was dry. She filled her coffee mug with water from the tap, drank it down. "With other pregnancies. I was on bed rest for Meghan. Three months."

Isadora's eyes darted around the room. "There could be a connection," she said evasively. "I don't know."

Yes, you do, Brooke thought. But the toned, conventionally pretty middle-aged woman in front of her was not going to come to grips with the past. She was as smooth and tightly knit as the track suit she wore. "Well, thanks for the coffee," Brooke said.

Isadora followed her to the door. "What are you doing now?" she asked. "What are you after, back here?"

Brooke turned. She might tell Isadora she was headed to the police station, to search their archives of unsolved crimes. Or to the Scranton *Times-Tribune*, to see if the discovery of a baby's corpse had been buried in the back pages. Or to the Econo Lodge to confront the Pakistanis if they were still there. Instead she said, "I'm not sure anymore." She smiled diffidently. "Maybe myself. You know, I haven't been myself since that night."

"What night?"

"The night I gave birth."

"Brooke, it wasn't birth—"

"It felt like birth. And it felt like death. And I buried myself along with whatever came out of me. And I don't want to be buried anymore."

It wasn't what she had meant to say, to Isadora or to anyone. It wasn't a thought she had ever had. But Brooke left the blue Victorian with a new quickness to her step, as if she had to get to her destination without losing a second, though she had no idea where that destination lay.

Chapter 18

As he lifted the metal latch on the gate to approach the O'Connor house, Alex heard music. Not just music; a human voice. From inside the house came a clear, lilting strain, haunted with longing. He could make out no words. As he stepped closer, he realized the song was in another language—German, that had to be it, something baroque, Bach maybe. Strange. He hadn't figured Brooke's husband for a classical music buff. Jazz was the only genre Alex knew, and even there he was a tenderfoot. Halfway down the walk, the song stopped abruptly. Alex halted. Then he heard a note on a pitch pipe. A moment later, the song began again. This was no CD, but an actual singer—a nimble and muscular voice, in Brooke's house. It had to be the husband himself, singing. Alex's eyes widened. She had said nothing about the guy's voice. However much he needed to find Brooke and get on with his plan, he would not break the magic of the aria. He turned to go. But then the dogs spotted him from inside the house, and set to barking.

The song stopped. Ten seconds later the door opened. A heavyset man of middling height, a few years older than Alex, stood framed. "You must be Alex Frazier," he said.

"Sorry. I didn't mean to interrupt."

"What do you mean? You called ahead, you're on time. I was just practicing."

"Pretty damn good, for practice."

Brooke's husband didn't respond to this. He held the door open. Alex stepped in around the panting dogs. "Sean," the husband said. Alex shook his extended hand. Neither man smiled. "So you're looking for my wife. Can I get you a beer? Wait, scratch that. Can I get you a Coke?"

"Thanks, no." The house was not particularly warm, but Alex felt himself starting to sweat. He unbuttoned his jacket. "I was a friend of Brooke's," he said, "growing up."

"Her high school sweetheart, I think." Sean led him into the living room, where Alex noticed an old piano, a music stand, the pitch pipe on the coffee table. Motioning to Alex to take a chair, Sean settled on the couch. The Labrador licked his hand as he sat down. "And now you're back."

"I live in Boston now." Alex tried to keep his heart from dropping a beat. "I looked Brooke up, sure. Lots to chew over. Decade and a half, you know."

"I don't know." Brooke's husband smiled mysteriously. He rubbed the stubble on his chin. He assessed Alex. "Brooke never mentioned you until last month. A guy I fired, not too long ago, said she ditched you way back when."

"She did." The beat went missing; he couldn't help it. "Probably the best decision she ever made. But I—well, I was just sort of renewing acquaintance and then she—she called me. No, I called her. Late at night, and she was on the road somewhere. She hasn't returned my calls since. So I thought, you know, I'd stop by."

He heard himself stammer, felt the blood rise through his neck. He had worn out the buttons on his BlackBerry calling Brooke over and over, to no avail since that moment she told him she was driving. Driving where, and why? Twice he had almost called Charlie, but when he thought of the crazy tale he had for his sister, he set the BlackBerry back on the side table. He had made it to his appointment in Springfield, his head spinning not with the profit-loss spread, but with questions about Brooke. Where had she been, where was she going, what judgment had she passed on him? At the end of the Springfield sessions, he had swallowed hard and called Brooke's home. Sean's voice on the phone had been tight as a snare drum. Yes, he had said, Alex could come by tomorrow. He had taken the day off, he said.

Brooke's husband, Alex noticed, had a face that seemed molded from clay, the tawny eyes thumbed deep and the cheeks plumped into rough fullness. Now that he was seated next to the man, Alex could begin imagining Brooke with him. Downcast as Sean O'Connor seemed to be—and here he was in the middle of a weekday, shuffling around his house in a stained T-shirt and pair of jeans, with two mugs of cold, half-consumed coffee lined up on the coffee table—he carried himself with a tensile strength and sense of dignity that acted like a magnet.

"So I thought you might be willing to tell me"—Alex found himself glancing around the warm-tinted living room, its burnished floor and deep-cushioned chairs—"where Brooke's gone. If she's okay. I don't know if your daughter—"

"Meghan's with me."

"I see." Heat rose to Alex's face. In fact, he did not see at all; he did not know what Sean O'Connor meant when he said his daughter was with him. That she wasn't with Brooke? That he wasn't? Sean was looking at him. "Meghan's at school?" he tried.

"Out since three. She's at a friend's house." Sean leaned forward, his elbows on his knees. "I'm not trying to keep you in the dark, Mr.—"

"Just Alex."

"You know, Alex, I get the feeling you could tell me more about my own wife than I could tell you."

"If you mean—"

"I don't know what I mean. Sometimes, to be honest with you, I don't know why Brooke married me. It's not something she wants now. Maybe she wants you."

Alex's face cracked into a smile, not what he was feeling, but nerves had gotten the better of him. "If she wanted me," he said, "she'd have answered at least one of the five hundred phone messages I've left."

From the back of the house came an insistent whining. "Got to let the dogs out," Sean said.

When he left the room, Alex rose. The shelves lining either side of the fireplace held a motley assortment of books, a hefty strand of musical scores, and a couple dozen framed photos. Quickly he glanced at the photo of a young Brooke, her hair a curtain across her face, nursing a baby. The family on a boat in Long Island Sound. A big group photo, a marriage; he leaned close to see that the slender, surprised-looking bride was indeed Brooke, and the beaming guy to her left, his red hair lifted by a breeze, was Sean. In another, two dogs and a cat waited attendance on a comical baby. Had the photos been food and Alex a starving man, he would have salivated. As it was, he heard Sean's steps in the hallway from the kitchen and sprang back from the shelves as if he had been caught red-handed.

"So," said Sean. Deliberately, he sat in a ladderback chair. Alex returned to the couch. A small black cat perched on the opposite arm, blinking at him. Sean looked him up and down. Alex knew his eyes had the hollow, bloodshot mark of insomnia. His shoulders curled forward, tension locking the joints. Compared to Sean, he was dressed for a business day, but to no greater purpose. "Tell me something," Sean said slowly.

"Sure."

"Why'd Brooke dump you?"

The couch felt uncomfortable. Alex shifted; swung his left shin onto his right knee; cleared his throat. Why answer such a question? Why not? "We were kids," he said. "Things change quickly, when you're young."

"Brooke doesn't change quickly. I may not know her as well as I'd like, but I know that much." Sean lifted one of the cold coffees off the table and sniffed at it. From the kitchen, an insistent scratching. Sean rose from his chair and went to let the dogs back in. Alex didn't leave the couch. When they returned, the Lab licked his land. Sean stayed standing, leaning against the ladderback.

"I didn't really come here," Alex said, hearing the tightness in his voice, "to talk about the distant past."

"Didn't you?" Sean's limpid voice had an edge of hostility. "You want my help finding my wife for your purposes, Mr. Frazier, you need to clue me in."

Alex pressed his palms together, miserable. He needed this guy on his team, and he couldn't recruit him. "I don't think it's my place to do that, man."

"So something is going on. You sleeping with my wife?"

"No."

"Okay. Okay, I believe you." Sean whipped out a ragged handkerchief and wiped his brow, all the way over the bald crown of his head. His voice grew louder; the cat jumped off the arm of the couch, and the smaller dog trotted over to him and whined. "But something did happen," he went on. "To Brooke, I mean. And you had something to do with it. And it's wrong, damn it. I'm her husband. I have a disposition to promote her good. I ought to know what's—what's—"

"Been hurting her?" Alex finished for him.

"You could put it that way."

I've been hurting her, Alex wanted to tell him. Her and everyone else. "You are her husband," he agreed. "And maybe she ought to have shared some stuff with you. But her choices aren't mine to make."

He lifted his eyes to Sean. The guy, he could tell, wanted to lift him by his wrinkled white collar. He wanted to shake the truth out of him. But Sean controlled himself. He bit down on the next words: "You're on your own, then."

At a sound on the porch, the dogs jumped up and rushed together, whining, toward the front door. It flew open, and a small ginger-haired girl tumbled in. A pink backpack bounced against her shoulders. "Daddy, Daddy!" she called. Then she turned and saw the men in the living room.

"Well, hi, Bug. Done playing already?" said Sean.

It was the first time Alex had seen Brooke's daughter up close. How pale she looked! Her eyes had a bruised cast, as if she were coming down with something. She had Brooke's long limbs, her wide jaw and mouth.

"Who's that man?"

"Don't point, honey." Sean stepped over to his daughter—she looked like him, too, the russet hair and close-set, tawny eyes—to lower her accusing arm. Alex stood as well, and put out his hand.

"I'm a friend of your mom's," he said. "My name's Alex. You must be Meghan."

Meghan fixed him with a withering stare, but with a glance from her father, she let Alex take hold of her fingers for an instant before she snatched them away. "I need to make a diorama for tomorrow," she said to Sean. "I forgot. Taisha's mom helped her with hers already."

Sean crouched until he was at the girl's eye level. "Well, I'll help you then."

Meghan's eyes flicked to Alex, then back to her dad. "We need to do it *now*," she half whispered. "You're not so fast as Mommy."

"I'm pretty fast, though." Sean stood. He seemed to stand taller, with his little girl next to him. "I got a job to do," he told Alex.

"I can see that." Alex tried smiling at Meghan, but she'd stuck her pinky finger in her nose and would not look at him. Reluctantly he moved toward the door. "It would be good for all of us, I think," he said to Sean, "if you could let me know what you hear. Here's my card." He held the thing out, and waited several awkward seconds while Sean just looked at it, before he placed it on the mail table in the hallway. "It's got my cell phone," he added, stupidly. "Call anytime."

"*Da-ad*," Meghan said.

She pulled on her father's arm. Alex was ready to avert his eyes and make a clean exit. But then Sean caught his sleeve. For a moment, the wall he'd kept up seemed to crumble, just a little. "If you manage to track her down—" he began.

"I'll be in touch." Alex gripped the guy's hand and shook it. "Absolutely. You've got a beautiful daughter." He smiled nervously at Meghan, who was tugging her father toward the kitchen. He waited for Sean to agree that he, too, would share news of Brooke. But Sean only pressed his palm and returned a sad smile.

Alex made his way out as father and daughter retreated to the kitchen. The dogs followed him to the front porch but trotted around to the back. He was left alone in the cool, bright day. He had come up empty. Whatever world of hurt Brooke's husband found himself in, nothing would persuade him to join forces with some man from Brooke's past. Not unless . . . but no. There was a time when Alex should have betrayed Brooke's secret—to her parents, his parents, anyone who cared about her. That time had been more than fifteen years ago, when she'd believed in a potion. That time had passed and left all its consequences.

He would get a night's sleep, he thought, or whatever passed for such a thing. Today was Wednesday. He would finish the work-week. And then, whether he had heard from Brooke or not, he would return to his resolution. Brooke's silence, in the end, he would take as her consent. When detectives came to question her—well, she could be silent with them, too. He shut the gate behind him. Sean's voice—not his suspicious and resentful words, but the aria he'd been practicing, its buoyant rise and heartbreaking fall—played again in his head, as he drove away down the shady street through autumn leaves.

Chapter 19

Brooke was heading out on Route 6, toward the old Econo Lodge. Funny, she hadn't noticed the sign on her way to Windermere. But she had been beat, by then. Now she recognized her impetus as the compulsion people often attributed to criminals, to revisit the scene of the crime. She knew she would find nothing there. Never had she even asked Alex what he did with the tiny limp body. Maybe he had buried it, back of the motel. Maybe he was planning to dig up its tiny bones and present such grisly remains as proof of his guilt.

It had been a mistake to stay with her mom. Stacey assumed Brooke was leaving Sean. Last night, after Brooke had spent the day uselessly scrolling through newspaper microfilms at the Scranton library, her mom had come home early. Stacey had spent the day in Scranton with a bunch of children's-rights advocates; after four weeks of bickering, she reported, they had managed to draw up a new mission statement and knock off early. She had fixed an elegant dinner of salmon and endives. Her manner had softened. Brooke had been such a trooper, she insisted; had devoted herself to her family; had tried every option. Every time Brooke protested that she was not leaving Sean, that they were simply in a rough patch, her mother's lips had pressed together. "Hmm," she had said. "A rough patch." And when Brooke had stepped outside to call home and talk to Meghan, she still felt as though Stacey were eavesdropping.

"Where *are* you?" Meghan insisted.

"I had to visit a friend," Brooke said. "She's sick, and she's having a birthday." She lied not because the truth would rouse any suspicion—it was natural, if she was upset, to visit her mom—but because she didn't want to picture Sean and Meghan knowing where she was as she dug into the past. Later she would tell them; later, when her search turned up nothing and everything went back to the way it had been.

"I want you to come home," Meghan said flatly. "Daddy burned the toast."

But she couldn't come home just yet. One more day, she had told Sean, who sounded sober and sad. Maybe two. By the weekend, she said.

This road out of Windermere had always been a strip, littered with used-car lots, diners, gas stations with rusted pumps, and quick marts. Brooke remembered a few dairy farms, swallowed up now by fast-food joints. She tried and failed to locate Daisy's Kitchen, where she'd had that long-ago fight with Alex. But fifteen minutes from the town limits she thought she spotted the motel, across from a trailer park that was still an eyesore. Only as she drew close did she see it wasn't an Econo Lodge anymore. *PAINTBALL* was splattered in garish letters across a plywood sign at the entrance. She pulled off into the parking lot, asphalt pitted with craters and strewn with yellowing weeds. She got out of the car. A breeze had kicked up. Hugging her jacket around her waist, she moved to the back of the building, where she leaned against a sand-filled metal barrel and took in the desultory view.

Last night she had slept deeply, as if plummeting to the bottom of an ocean. Her mom's place had only a pull-out in the tiny guest room; she woke with the metal bar digging into her back. But for the first time in weeks she had slept through the night, with no dreams that she could remember. Her mom had tried, really she had, to make Brooke feel safe and welcomed and not badgered by questions. Stacey Willcox loved her daughter, however accidentally she had been conceived. "You don't have to tell me what's wrong," Stacey had said at dinner. She had placed her hand on Brooke's, and Brooke had been surprised at how light and dry it was, the anxious hand of a middle-aged widow. "But if you still want to do great things, you know you've got the support."

"I never wanted to do great things, Mom," Brooke had said.

Though now she wondered if she was telling the truth. On the backseat of the car sat the locked wooden box her father had given her in high school. It had moved to her mom's condo at the bottom of a desk drawer filled with volleyball trophies and photo albums. Though the key to the box still dangled from the same chain on which Brooke kept her house keys, she had forgotten its existence until Stacey mentioned that Brooke could do her a favor by emptying the drawers so she could give away the old desk. Brooke had been reluctant to open the box in the condo. Inside, she knew, sat her old diaries, where she had recorded the dreams she used to spin. Dreams, she thought now, that a few hours at this very motel had erased.

She surveyed the back lot—a Dumpster, an array of poisonous paint sprayers, plastic beer cups, and cigarette butts. From inside the paintball arcade came the shouts and screams of kids, the thudding of blobs and bodies. At the edge of the lot, a fallow field waited for a developer. Fifteen years, she thought. Almost half her life ago. She and Alex had both had to leave it behind. Now she would finish this pilgrimage along Route 6. Next, she would spend a day in the funny little Windermere Library, once a church, where all the old *Gazettes* were stored. She would read through every one, for that year and the following year, in case there had been a police report she'd missed. If she screwed up her courage, she might approach Alex's old friend Jake, whom she had spotted in the center of the village as she drove through. He was just getting into his police cruiser, and she had smiled wryly. Jake the prankster, a cop. She wasn't sure she could ask him to check old files without explaining why—but if there was nothing to be found, she could at least return to Alex with the news that the world bore no trace of the crime he claimed. And would that stop his claiming it? She shook her head. "What do you want, Alex?" Brooke said softly to herself—feeling, as she said it, that she wasn't asking the question just of him.

She wandered a short ways into the field. She kicked over a few rotting wooden crates, filled with mud and mouse droppings. Turning to look across the road, she noticed the trailer park. It was indeed the same one that had been there long ago, its *Trails End Estates* sign reduced to *rail End state*. Rising next to it was a pile of land that Brooke didn't remember. She frowned. She walked to the end of the paintball driveway and peered across Route 6. Yes, there it was—a huge sort of mesa just behind the gas station, with a long curving drive leading to its top and spindly trees holding down the earth. One of those landfill projects, probably, erecting a park over a mound of trash. The sun had come out and shone gently on the trees and manicured sod. Brooke tucked herself back into her car and maneuvered her way across the road.

The breeze blew cooler, up so high. Still, Brooke took a park bench facing away from the soccer game being played by a dozen

West Indians. From the swings came the shouts of a few children. For a moment Brooke shut her eyes and pictured Meghan on the swings, Sean with his muscled arms pushing her. That would have been August, in Lorenzo's Garden, after the christening. How sweetly Sean had sung, that day. Then that night, his arms around her, the tang of his sweat.

Lorenzo would be going into the hospital now. She had offered to drive him; she had promised to visit him this week. She couldn't let guilt over her past keep her from doing right by a friend right now. She would send him flowers, she thought, and then she laughed at herself. Flowers to a nursery owner! No. She would find what she could here and then go back. It was possible, she would tell Alex, that there had been life, possible that his panic had snuffed it. He needed to forgive himself, she would tell him. And then she would not go to him, or to Sean, but to her boss in the hospital. She would bring a bottle of good Italian wine, and every time Lorenzo mentioned death she would change the subject. There. That was enough of a plan.

Below, the traffic of Route 6 rumbled by—trucks, mostly, delivering to the weather-beaten towns that lay north of Interstate 80, angling up toward Elmira. Away to the west, the land rolled in slow waves. Brooke felt a kind of vertigo, up on this rise, as if time and space were both tilting beneath her. How strange to think that she had been happy here, had felt at home here, had felt her world complete. She fitted the key into the lock and opened the box.

There wasn't much inside. A couple of old diaries, discarded letters, photos. She thumbed through the diaries. They were filled with earnest reflections on the impossibility of ever being beautiful; on the mediocrity of her English teachers; on whether she should throw her energy into becoming a great scholar or a great poet. There were poems that made her cringe. There were some surprisingly wise observations of her parents—*Dad was young emotionally when he met Mom. He'd lived more places but those places never changed him. Then he met Mom and he was ready, just like she was. Except he was twenty years older. Lacey says she thinks it's creepy, a 40 yr old guy with a girl just out of HS. I tell her it wasn't like that but she thinks I'm being defensive. I don't want to be naïve like Dad but I don't want to act all wise beyond my years either. Not that Mom did that. I don't know what she did really. She must have liked him back then, for a little while. Then I came along.*

The photos surprised her—she'd forgotten about Alex's taking them, with his new camera, one Saturday that first summer when they drove to a remote lake and went skinny-dipping. Shading her eyes in the bright sun, she studied the faded prints. There she stood, a tall, smooth-muscled girl with sun-kissed hair falling over her shoulders and onto the tops of her high, plump breasts. Her waist tucked in effortlessly and fanned out to broad, bony hips and thighs built up from volleyball and swimming. Her belly was flat as a board. Most of all, as the camera came in for close-ups, Brooke saw her own trusting eyes, the unguarded smile directed at the photographer. Her nose already had that pronounced bump in it—her father's nose, looking almost as if it had been broken once and failed to heal properly—that had embarrassed her until Alex ran his finger down its ridge and pronounced it distinctive. She had no shame, being naked before him. He had been naked, too, those sturdy legs and lean torso, the nest of hair between his pectorals. Behind the naked girl—herself—lay a red checkered tablecloth spread on the sand, a picnic hamper, a broad cloth hat about to blow away in the wind. She remembered, suddenly, its blowing away; she had turned and run after it. Sure enough, when she picked up the next photo, there she was, long legs flying, buttocks white in the sun. When she had come back they had made love, there under the midday sun on the tiny, deserted beach.

Tears streamed down her cheeks. Here in these images, their color fading, was the love of her life. She couldn't go on denying it, couldn't go back to a union with a nice man whose frustration with her drove him to drink. Whatever the end of her marriage might bring, these photos told her to end it. She wiped her tears with the rough sleeve of her jacket and put the photos back. About to close the box, her hands touched a torn edge of paper—a letter, ripped in half. As she pulled it out, a hiccup of embarrassed laughter interrupted her weeping. Here it was, the letter to Dr. James, at Tufts University. She thought she had burned it. But something in her had wanted its fantasy preserved.

She pieced the letter together. Funny. She could almost remember flicking the Bic lighter, catching the corner of the envelope, seeing her own reflection in the window at night as the thing burned, the shadow pointing above her head, her face lit gold. But she had torn the thing and saved it. *I am with child*, she read on one of the scraps. *I have taken a potion*—here the page was torn. The next scrap held the end of the sentence—*but my face will surely bear the mark of my sorrow. I trust you to treat my fragile self, not with pity, but*—here it was torn again. She looked through the wooden box. The rest was missing. The envelope lay there, though, with the address she had neatly composed.

Shutting her eyes in the October sun, Brooke remembered the stone buildings of the university, the accent of the professor. She and her dad had eaten lunch in the campus bistro; he had smiled gently, patiently, as she told him how she would learn Middle English, Old English, how she would study *Beowulf.* They had stayed over in Boston and driven home early the next day for her volleyball practice.

Volleyball. Brooke placed a hand on her belly, remembering. The season had been mostly winter, but in spring they practiced outside, to finish out the season. They wore loose T-shirts over spandex shorts. Even that May, no one had noticed her belly. Not that there had been much to notice—not compared to years later, when she'd been carrying Meghan and put on thirty pounds in the first five months. That was one bit of evidence she clung to, even now: Only eighteen pounds she'd gained that time, slight enough that you could have called it a lazy waist. If someone had noticed, things might have gone differently. But the fact that there was too little gain to be noticed kept her thinking there had been nothing in there, or nothing that could be called a baby.

That was the last time she'd played volleyball, that spring. She remembered the sand court behind the high school, the sun high overhead but the air still cool. She'd worked on her serve that season. She was never a power server, like her friend Lacey, but she was tall and a good spiker; she'd call, "Outside!" and someone would set it up for her, and she'd leap to meet the ball and punch it deep into the other team's court. But everyone had to serve. That last day of her volleyball life, the coach had had her in position and was barking at her. "Don't toss it, Willcox! Set it up and catch it on the heel of your palm!"

Her serves had kept going deep that day, or low into the net. Her balance had been off. She couldn't seem to set the ball up straight. The sun bore down on her bare head—had the others been wearing baseball caps? Probably—and made her dizzy. "I've got to take a break," she told the coach after she'd lost her third round at service.

"Period, huh?" said the coach. What had been her name? McQuilken, that was it, a wiry bleached blonde who chewed her nails through every game they played.

"Yeah," Brooke had said without thinking. And then she had not been able to sit there, on the cool bench, with the heaviness lower in her pelvis than before, forcing her legs slightly apart. "I'm fine," she had said after a minute, and McQuilken pulled a girl out of the net line on the other side and let her back in.

That was when she had seen Alex, muscular in his soccer gear, heading out with the others from the side door of the gym. Had seen him pause to watch her as she took the position she was more comfortable with, not serving but up front and to the right. He had waved his buddies on as the serve went over, then came back deep to Brooke's side, and one of the Bowmans saved it to a sophomore in the center, and Brooke was screaming, "Outside! Outside!" and the ball arced high up, descending straight down toward her. *Baby*, she had thought, and she was wicked, wicked; she jumped high and slammed the thing sharply down, so that sand flew up where it hit.

That had been the night, yes, when she tore the letter up. Not burned it; tore it and put it away. It hadn't happened after the night at the motel, but before. She had known her future could no longer go where she had been aiming, at mystical texts and romantic debates with consumptive professors. Her job was to get rid of the mistake inside her and then trudge on.

She crumpled the pieces of the old letter, rose, and went to pitch them into a metal trash bin on the path behind the bench. As she crossed the limestone path, she stepped around a short woman pushing a girl in a wheelchair up the slope. "Excuse me," she started to say. The girl's blond hair caught her eye. "Wait," Brooke said. The crumpled paper in her hand, she stepped back. The tilt of the girl's head drew her attention.

"We're walking," said the woman. But Brooke, ignoring her, was leaning down, to see the girl's face straight on. The teenager's eyes met hers. Her nose was narrow, with a pronounced bump just below the bridge, the same bump that used to make Brooke self-conscious as a teenager. Brooke gasped. She was looking into a mirror—not a mirror of herself, but a mirror of the girl she had just seen in the photos in the box, a mirror of the girl she had been.

"Do I know you?" she said to the girl in the wheelchair.

Something was wrong with the girl, with this breathing image of Brooke herself. Her head jerked up from where it had been lolling slightly to the right. Her bright blue eyes fixed on Brooke with the intensity of an eagle. Her mouth began to work, a series of quick hums and clicks. "I," she managed to get out. "You. Where . . . have . . . you . . ."

Brooke reached out to touch her. She had to touch her, this girl. But the woman behind the chair barked, "Go away!" Her voice was high and sharp. Before Brooke's fingers could touch the girl's face, the woman had whipped the wheelchair around and was running down the hill, pushing the heavy thing, bumping over the lumps in the path. A moan floated from the girl. Brooke stood stunned.

Automatically she stepped to the waste bin and dropped in the crumpled letter. She stood as the wheelchair rattled down the path to the gas station below and disappeared. Then, seized with a realization of the impossible—impossible!—made possible, she started after it. She left the box, from which the breeze scooped out photos and scattered them over the meager lawn. She stretched her legs and flew down the hill.

Walk, the doctor had said. Exercise the lungs. Lower your stress level. After lunch, Ziadek put the dishes away. He set his baseball cap on his head and tied on his shoes. Gripping his oxygen cart like a stroller he maneuvered one-handed, he headed out the door. The day was still glorious. He stepped clear away from Katarina's house—encounters with his older daughter did not lower his stress—and toward the Quik Mart. The asphalt of the narrow road was crumbling; the wheels of the oxygen cart bumped and caught in the crevices. Ziadek stopped every hundred paces and waved to a neighbor or took in the look of the neighborhood, fêted with bright leaves. Next month the leaf blowers would be out making their racket. For a moment, though, the place did not look like a skewed collection of cattle cars into which human beings had crawled for their last refuge. From the bright plastic bouquets washed clean by yesterday's rain to the real-life pots of mums planted next to some of the white gravel walkways, the trailer park felt more like one of those doll villages the girls had played with when they were little, with miniature picket fences and houses with shutters and tiny vegetable gardens. It seemed, in other words, a community.

The Quik Mart was new—well, five years old—built as they finished turning the huge mound of landfill abutting the trailer park into a recreational park. People driving from Windermere to Scranton stopped there to pump gas, as did families bringing their kids to the new swings and baseball fields on the high plateau of the park. Ziadek couldn't drive anymore or smoke anymore, so he had no use for the gas or the cigarettes, but he liked the Guatemalan couple who ran the place. They let him refill his coffee free and they told crazy stories of the drunks who drove through at night, and when he walked home from the Quik Mart he generally felt like a happy and fortunate man. Plus, they had taken on Luisa, hiring her to take out the trash and clean the place up, two hours every day at minimum wage. She could walk there by herself and walk home, and she had not yet begun complaining of anyone's meanness.

On his way across the parking lot, Ziadek paused to exchange greetings with a handsome heavyset woman who was pulling a shopping cart with one hand and managing a wiry little dog with the other. Her name was Olga. She was a busybody, but she had been Marika's friend, and for that Ziadek always stopped.

"Saw your girls go by, poor things," Olga said in cheerful Polish. She always called them his *girls* and *poor things*.

"To the park," he said. "Such a beautiful day."

"Hard for the slow one to find work these days, I guess."

"Haven't you seen her here? She keeps the place shining for the rest of us," Ziadek said evenly, as if twelve hours a week made for a salary. He forced a smile to his lips. Smiling, the doctor had said, would reduce his stress. Sure enough, as he curled his mouth, the oxygen seemed to flow more freely; his lungs expanded.

"Shouldn't that younger one be in the special school? I see the bus coming."

"She should, yes." Ziadek nodded. Better to agree with Olga, not to argue or give her a story. The story would spread around the trailer park like a vine. "We are working on that."

"Josef, it's none of my business. But if the authorities find that poor girl wandering about—"

"It will be a problem, yes. Good to see you, Olga." Ziadek tipped his baseball cap. He skirted the wiry little dog, who growled. He rounded a pair of trucks parked in back of the Quik Mart. From here he could see across the highway to the motel the Pakistanis used to run, where Luisa had first found Najda. It had changed its name many times and now was not even a motel any longer but some sort of amusement place for boys with money burning their pockets. Paintball, they called it. Seeing the façade nonetheless brought a wave of nostalgia—for those early, dangerous days with the infant; for the renewed life Ziadek had found, then, after losing his Marika. From here, too, he could see up the winding road to the plateau of the new park, with its spindly trees and scruffy grass. And from there, racing down the incline as if pursued by demons, came his daughter Luisa pushing the wheelchair, Najda's pale hair flying in the breeze.

Ziadek unhooked his nose from the oxygen. Leaving the canister in the lot, he hurried toward his girls. Behind him he heard the wiry dog yapping. On the highway, trucks honked as they zoomed past the Quik Mart. What could his child be thinking, racing the incline, when the wheels of the chair could suddenly catch and Najda tumble? Had they fought again? "Stop!" he cried as he ran. "Luisa, stop!"

She did not stop. He caught up at the bottom of the hill, where a light and a crosswalk protected them from the traffic coming off the busy road for the park or the gas pumps. Ziadek was out of breath, his head light. But Luisa scarcely paused for him even as he grabbed her arm. Her round face was white as powder, her lips drained. "She'll find us! She'll find us!" she cried as she hurried across the walk and the parking lot of the Quik Mart.

Ziadek stumbled after. "Who will find you?" he managed to gasp. "Is Delores up there? We will talk to her. You cannot run from her, child."

"Not her. Not her. I gotta go," Luisa called over her shoulder.

Ziadek made it as far as his oxygen, and there he had to stop or he would faint. Fitting the plastic back into his nostrils, he watched as Luisa jerked the wheelchair over the crumbling asphalt back toward their house. Najda, he noticed, had not uttered a sound. Her face had looked even stranger than Luisa's—not so terrified, but more in awe, as if she had seen a spirit. When he had gathered his strength, he turned toward the house. To Olga, who stood by the side of the road open-mouthed, he nodded in a dark way that he knew would put a lid on anything the meddling woman might be tempted to say. Fittingly, a small cloud had drifted in from nowhere and blocked the sun, chilling the air as he made his way carefully home. He was an old man, he thought to himself. He could not keep up with this drama forever.

"So," he said as he entered the trailer, blinking in its sudden darkness. "What bogeyman has frightened the two of you?"

Najda had gone to the window, where she sat like a statue, looking out. Luisa hung over the kitchen table, her head in her arms. Ziadek drew himself a glass of water at the sink. He would rather have had the Quik Mart's coffee, but he was in no mood to brew it for himself.

"So?" he repeated.

"She *saw* us," Luisa said into her arms.

"Who, that fat cow, that Delores? What of it? What is the worst that can happen?"

Luisa was shaking her head, but it was Najda who answered. "No," she said. Then, as if the word had broken a spell, she began to jerk her mouth the way she did when she had too many words in her head and no way to let them out.

"Who then?" Ziadek sat heavily at the table. Gently he shook his daughter's shoulder. Luisa would not look up. "Najda, come to me," he ordered.

The girl buzzed her wheelchair around. Her blue eyes were fierce, penetrating, the eyes of a lovely young hawk. To Ziadek's surprise, when she came close, she leaned forward. She reached out with her good hand and stroked her mother's shuddering head, stroked the short full hair down to the nape of the plump neck. She made cooing noises deep in her throat. Then she turned to Ziadek.

"Who approached you in the park, child?" he said.

"Me," she said simply.

"Yes, you. Who spoke to you? Who frightened your mother?"

"Me," she repeated. She licked her lips; she swallowed. "*Like* me," she said. She held her hand out, the palm vertical and facing her, like a mirror. "She, like me," she said, as clearly as Ziadek had ever heard her speak. She picked up a lock of her hair, pointed to her features one by one. "Hair. Eyes. Chose. Neeks." She shook her head. "Nose," she corrected. "Cheeks. This person"—she reached out again to stroke Luisa, who had stopped shaking with tears and lay buried on the table, but she spoke directly to Ziadek—"This person . . . is . . . Najda . . . sister."

Sister, Ziadek thought. He let his breath out. Then a new realization swept over him. Just a short time ago he had looked over the highway toward the place that had been the motel. Fifteen years ago, guessing at the identity of the woman who had left an infant there for dead, he had pictured her as very young, too young to understand that there were places to leave such babies. Young enough to be mistaken, as Luisa sometimes was, for Najda's sister. Fifteen years ago, Ziadek had thought this present moment possible, even likely. Over the years the likelihood had faded, grown impossible. But it was never impossible. Both Najda and Luisa could be making a complete and silly mistake. They could also be right. And if they were right, it was not her sister Najda had seen.

"Oh, my darlings," he said. And he drew on his oxygen, needing all his strength.

Chapter 20

Brooke could have caught up to them. As she rounded the gas station, panting for breath, she had seen woman and wheelchair turn a corner between rows of trailer homes. But the panic etched on the woman's face dissuaded her. If by some miracle—but it surely wasn't—if an infant could have survived not only Isadora's poison tea but also whatever Alex thought he had done, then Brooke had no right to interfere with whatever saint had rescued that child. But it wasn't possible. Her eyes, after looking at those photos of herself as a kid, were deceiving her.

She had retreated up the hill, gathered the papers and photos from the overturned box, and driven back to her mother's condo. The rest of the day, she revisited the search of the day before. She drove to Scranton and slid reels of microfilmed issues of the *Times-Tribune* through the reader. No dead babies reported. No live babies found. She stopped at the police station to ask for Jake, but he was off duty. She returned to her mom's condo, where she managed to navigate the conversation around the shoals of her foundering marriage and her lost potential. She kept her cell phone on silent, so she could check it and see the six missed calls from Alex without letting on. She called Sean and was grateful when he didn't pick up. The weekend, she said to voice mail. She needed the weekend. She would bring home a present for Meghan, to make up for all the nights with no stories.

"You imagined it," she said aloud to herself, more than once during the day. "You imagine things. You imagined it."

Through the night, in her mother's small spare room, she lay on her back, staring at the ceiling. She couldn't shake the image of the girl's face, those probing eyes, the bump in the bone of the nose. But what was she going to do? Barge in on a strange family in their sad trailer home? Say, "Let me have another look at you. Where were you born? When were you born? Is this woman your mother? Look at me. Am I your mother? Aren't I your mother?"

Next day, instead of seeing Jake, she drove out to Trails End Estates. She stopped at the Quik Mart. A cup of coffee—that would help. Clear her head. Put her back on the track she was aiming for: to prove that her distant miscarriage could not have been helped. To steer Alex away from his mission of confession and toward . . . well, toward a future. That was it. A future unburdened by the guilt that was Brooke's alone.

"Are you not the lady flying by," the fellow behind the Quik Mart counter asked her, "yesterday noontime?"

Brooke kept her eyes averted. The place was brightly lit and smelled of disinfectant. Two rickety round tables were set up by the ice cream freezer, filled by a quartet of oldsters. Though the place was a chain store with no sign of hominess, it seemed to have taken the place of a neighborhood gathering spot. The old people whispered among themselves and glanced at Brooke. "That was a misunderstanding," she said softly.

"You the new social worker?"

Brooke risked a direct look at the fellow. He was dark-skinned, Indian looking—South American, she thought. "Social worker for—" she began.

"Our leetle Najda. I tell old Zukowsky, I tell him, 'They will find out.' But you cannot tell that girl a thing. She don' want go to school, she don' go." Leaning across the counter, he beckoned Brooke. She bent toward him, her coffee steaming. "That girl?" he said. His breath smelled of tobacco and spearmint. She nodded. "She ees one fucking *genius*."

"How do you—" Brooke began.

"She come in here, yes? By herself, in that chair. Bzz, bzz." He gestured with his hands, to show a wheelchair rolling around. "She peek up the *New York Times*. She don' buy the thing. Okay. She jus' flip open, yes? To the crossword puzzle. And she seets there, making the words with her mouth. Like thees." He mimed what looked to Brooke like the onset of an asthmatic attack, his lips curling and twisting. "So one day I tell her, okay, I buy thees paper for you. You give me the words, I write them in."

"'Cept I had to spell 'em for you, Martín!" called one of the old-sters from the table.

Martín shot them a look, but kept talking in an undertone, as if he and Brooke were having a secret conversation. "She finish the fucking thing," he said, tapping the glass counter with a scarred finger, "in twenty minutes. And eet was the Sunday paper!"

Brooke was having trouble processing what this man was telling her. *Najda*, she repeated to herself. *Zukowsky*. "That's impressive," she said.

"So I tell you, Mrs. Social Worker," he said, standing straight. "Whatever you do, you don' put that creepled beauty in with retards."

"Thank you for the tip," Brooke said. She paid for the coffee. She wanted to ask how old the girl was, how long the family had lived at Trails End. But a social worker would know such facts. "I'll try to do right by her," she said.

In the parking lot, she called up information on her cell phone and got the address. Zukowsky, 561 Trails End Court. Anticipation squeezed her heart. Slowly she drove around the complex, noting the faded plastic flowers and crooked awnings, the busted pickups strewn like a giant's neglected toys in the back lots. Before long she found it, the number 561 in brass numerals nailed into a post on the porch. The trailer itself was yellow with green shutters, well maintained. Its shades were drawn. She sat with the engine idling, just looking at the place. Then a stocky red-haired woman banged out the back of the next trailer and crossed the yard to number 561. She stared at Brooke, her brows knit together. Quickly Brooke put the car in gear and drove away. What was she thinking? In their eyes she would be a nutcase, this woman arriving out of nowhere, wanting another look at their disabled daughter.

"I'll be home after the weekend," she told Meghan when they talked that evening on the phone. "Did you go to school with Taisha today? Is that working okay?"

"Unh-uh," said Meghan. "Daddy took me. Daddy's on vacation."

"Can I talk to Daddy?"

When Sean took the line, his voice was low and almost intimate, the way he used to sound when they lay in bed together after a long day apart. "I took some days," he said. "Business is slow."

"Really."

"Brooke, I haven't touched the stuff. Not that I'm not tempted."

She softened. He sounded so tired, and so careful. "I'll be home soon."

"Where are you?"

"Just—checking some stuff out."

"He came by."

"Who?" Brooke asked, though she knew.

"Your old friend."

"He's not—"

"I told him I didn't know where you were. I said I'd let him know if I found out. But I won't if you don't want me to."

"Just give me a couple more days, Sean."

"Meghan misses you."

"I miss her, too." *And you*, she almost added, but she didn't know if that was true. All her heart had room for right now, it seemed, was the face she had glimpsed in the park, before the girl and the woman took off. *Zukowsky. Najda Zukowsky.*

It took another day to screw up her courage. First she had to have lunch and a beer with Jake, Alex's best buddy from high school, who frowned when she told him she wanted access to the police department's cold-case file. "You don't want to tell me why," he said—leaning across the table, his chin resting on his knuckles. Jake looked the same as in high school but with padding—fuller face, thicker neck, broader chest, bigger gut. He had married Karen, his childhood sweetheart. Three kids already. Already Jake had asked if Brooke wouldn't come for supper, and Brooke had concocted excuses—her mom's health, family stuff, she only had a day or two before heading back to Connecticut.

"I can't tell you yet," she said, meeting his small, round eyes.

"Hmm." His jaw tightened. They had talked about Alex, how Alex had come to see his mother for just one day, before settling into his new place in Boston. He hadn't called Jake, hadn't stopped to catch up with anyone. That boy was flying too high, Jake had said, and Brooke had hastily agreed. "Well," he said now, "cold cases are in the public record, down in Scranton. All on the computer these days, I think. Show ID and you can have at them."

Thus she had burned Friday afternoon, scrolling through pictures of missing waitresses, victims of drive-by shootings. The cold facts were depressing. One six-year-old girl had been fished out of the Susquehanna River. Three dead infants had been found, but none of them near Windermere, and all in years other than 1993. Still, Brooke found herself squinting at the smudged photos on the screen, trying to remember what she had felt a decade and a half ago, whether a tiny heart had beat against her chest before Alex took it away.

Finally, late in the day, she went back to the trailer park. A cold wind had blown up, the way she remembered from Octobers of her childhood, the advance guard of winter. With trepidation she approached the yellow trailer. Before she could knock on the door, it opened. A slope-shouldered elderly man stood there, a pair of slender transparent tubes running from his hooked nose to an oxygen tank parked at his side. His gaze flitted to Brooke's face and then dropped. "Leave us alone," he said before she could speak.

"Are you Mr. Zukowsky?"

"Not interested. Go away." He spoke with an accent—*Go avey.* But he had opened the door, Brooke noted; he must have been waiting for her, watching for her. He did not shut it. He stood there, withered from the bulk he might once have presented, the cool oxygen snaking into his nostrils.

Brooke gathered her courage. "I'm Brooke O'Connor," she began. "May I come in?"

"What you want?"

"I—I'm not sure." She twisted her hands together. In a matter of seconds, he would shut the door. "I'd like to talk to you, Mr. Zukowsky," she said. "About—about your daughter, I think."

"My daughter is okay."

"Please. Just five minutes."

He let her in. She followed into the small living room, blinking in the dimness. The TV was on with no sound, cartoons playing. A pass-through to the galley kitchen was piled high with brochures. A corner set of shelves held photographs and painted vases. "Coffee?" Mr. Zukowsky said.

So he was not going to dismiss her, to toss her out. "That would be lovely."

She followed him to the kitchen doorway. He poured two mugs from a cold pot and put them into the microwave. He kept his broad back to her while they heated. He had been a strong man once, she thought. A worker with a worker's disease—lung cancer, or asbestosis. A widower, probably, and with daughters, at least one disabled. Did he think she was the new social worker? No. He would not have asked what she wanted; he would have known. The microwave dinged. He reached into a small fridge and held up a quart of milk. "Just black," she said. "Thanks."

He motioned her back to the living room, and they sat. Light poured in the dusty window, motes caught in the rays. Surreptitiously Brooke glanced at the photos on the shelves. There was Zukowsky, decades younger, with a wife and three daughters, one of them clearly the woman from the park. Her flat features and teardrop eyes, Brooke suddenly realized, spelled Down syndrome. There the woman was again, as a plump teenager, holding a baby. And there—Brooke dared not let her eyes linger—was the girl in the wheelchair. Najda Zukowsky. She was still a child. She sat outside the trailer in the wheelchair, beaming. Her hair shone like flax. The chair looked brand new, almost too big for her. Brooke pulled her eyes away. On the coffee table next to the brochures sat a chess set with gleaming ivory pieces. On the tired beige rug, grooves worn by wheels.

Noisily, Najda's father sipped his coffee. "What you want, Miss O'Connor?" he asked.

Her throat was dry, the brew bitter. She pulled her gaze away from the objects in the room to the man. "I have no right," she said, "to ask anything of you. So I should say at the very start that I put myself in your hands. If what I suspect is true, you could bring charges against me. You probably should."

The old man searched her face, taking in the bone structure, the eyebrows, the nose. "What charges?"

"Charges of—I don't know." So many times she had accused herself, blamed herself, failed to forgive herself. But not to a stranger, and not for this particular crime. "Of—of abandonment, I guess."

"What abandonment?"

"Let me back up. Mr. Zukowsky—"

"Please." He waved his hand. "Call me Josef."

"Josef, you don't know me. I have no right to ask you any questions at all. But if you will not give me answers"—where else could she go? How could she rest?—"I think I will never know another night's sleep."

"Cut to chase," Josef Zukowsky said. "You speak of my granddaughter."

She straightened, startled. "I don't—I don't think I do . . ."

"In chair. My Najda. My Luisa's Najda. Our Najda." He licked spittle from his dry lips. Rising, he stepped over to the shelves, plucked a framed photo that Brooke had not noticed, and laid it on the table in front of Brooke. In the picture he stood, perhaps ten years younger, in front of a spindly Christmas tree, with two adult women and a man, two teenaged boys, and a small child in a chair. He did not need to point to Najda. Brooke nodded. Tears started to her eyes. "You come," Josef Zukowsky said in a tight voice, "for her."

Brooke pulled out a tissue. Slowly she wiped both her cheeks. It was true. This man was telling her it was true. Only it had not been his wife who found the baby Alex had left for dead; it had been his daughter. His daughter with Down syndrome. *Our Najda.* She blew her nose, sipped from her mug. The coffee tasted like poison, like the brew she had once cooked up to rid herself of this very child. "Will you tell me," she asked Josef, "how you saved her?"

He told her. Luisa, he explained in his halting English, had been rooting through the Dumpster across the state highway when a man had come out the back of the motel. As soon as he left the tiny infant, she snatched it up and it gave a weak cry. At first, he thought his poor child had given birth. So many things were wrong with the baby. Problems breathing, problems moving, problems feeding. So tiny. On a respirator at the hospital for two weeks. To the doctors they had lied about Luisa, because who else would love this baby? Not the ones who left it in the rain. And Josef had seen the people from Social Services; he knew where they would put the baby. How the heart of his Luisa, who had lost her mother only the year before, would break into pieces. And so the whole family had learned what to do. How to help the girl move her limbs. How to unscramble her sentences. How to find the money the state set aside for disabled children, for new wheelchairs and physical therapy. "We call her Najda," he explained, "because it means, in Polish—I don't know the English word—the one you find like this, with no mother, no father."

"A foundling," Brooke said. Her voice rasped with tears.

"And we say God bring her to us so we can love her. But what God? Not a smart God. A smart God bring us Najda before her brain lose oxygen." He waggled one of the tubes running from his nose. "A smart God don't make my Luisa suffer so much for this child."

Brooke kept a fist to her mouth. Tears rained inside her chest. "Is Najda," she tried asking, "is her brain . . ."

"Very, very intelligent." For the first time, a sly smile crept across the old man's face. "A genius, this girl. You play chess?" Brooke shook her head. "She beats me!" he said, swinging his fist in triumph. "Nine times from ten!"

"Can she—can she move the pieces herself?"

"What you think? She moves from her left side, okay! She has trouble talking, yes. But then she recites. You understand what I mean, recite?"

"Like poetry."

"Yes! Shakespeare. Emily Dickinson. I don't know all. When these things she recites, the words come easy."

"I love poetry," Brooke said. It pained her to smile but she couldn't help it. Not when this man was bragging on his grandchild.

"At library, she goes on this computer. She knows all of it, all about this computer, what it can do."

"But about school—"

"School," Ziadek repeated. Then again, as if tasting the bitterness in his mouth, "*School.* That I cannot speak about." Pushing himself up by the arms of his chair, he rose and stepped to the counter by the kitchen. He lifted the stack of colorful brochures and spread them in a fan over the coffee table. "These places," he explained, still standing, "I will let her go. Not this school here, what they say she must. This school *kill* Najda."

The word *kill* was like a dagger to Brooke's heart. She let go the glossy brochure she had been about to open. Josef sat heavily. The joyful pride had fled; his face had gone cloudy with anger. She bit her lip. Shame drained the blood from her face. The old man laid his big hands flat on the table between them, like a cat about to spring. "Now you tell me," he said, soft and low, "why you try that, yourself."

"Try what?"

"To kill her. To kill our Najda."

"I didn't know." She spoke around her hand. Her tears had started to fall again. He did not offer her a tissue. "I thought she was dead already. Dead in me."

"What about doctor?"

"I was in the motel. It's not a motel anymore, it's—"

"Yes, yes." His voice had gone testy, impatient. Brooke felt naked in front of him. Nothing she could offer about what she had done would make any sense. "But the baby," he went on, his voice steady and pitiless. "It is breathing. No? It has heartbeat."

"No, it didn't. Or—I don't know. It looked all blue. I didn't feel it breathing. As for a heartbeat—Jesus. I don't remember. I must've held her for a few seconds, that was all."

"But you throw her out in rain—"

"I didn't throw her out! My boyfriend was there! He said she was dead. We *both* thought she was dead. Instead we crippled her. Put her in this wheelchair"—she picked up the photo—"and did God knows what to her poor brain."

"I tell you. Najda is genius." He snatched the photo from her. He waved his hand at the photo. "Not enough oxygen to little brain. Speech is hard. Movement is hard. Thinking is fine."

Brooke pinched the bridge of her nose. She could not bear to speak to him. She had no right. "All our fault," she said aloud. "It's worse than what Alex thought."

Suddenly Josef gripped her arm at the wrist. For all his weak state, his grip made her gasp. "You would prefer," he said, and he squeezed the arm brutally, "she is dead? That you have killed her?"

"No. No. I don't mean that, I . . ." She left her arm limply in his, as if he were arresting her. "We were very young," she pleaded.

He tossed the forearm away, as if it were useless. He gathered up the brochures on the table. "You were young," he echoed her bitterly, "and now you know. Najda is safe. She is healthy. You go now. You be happy."

She looked up, startled. "I can't just go," she said. "Najda is my daughter."

"She is Luisa's daughter."

"But I can help her. I can help all of you. I have to help you."

"No. Is nothing you have to do."

She bent to the stack of brochures and lifted one. *CROSBY*, it said in spaced white capitals across the top of the cover. Below shone a photo of a white frame building against a backdrop of rolling hills, with teachers and students—two in wheelchairs, the others not—gathered on a lawn. "You don't understand," she said, not looking up. "I ask nothing of you."

"You ask," Josef said bluntly, "for our Najda."

Chapter 21

Najda

I know as soon as I see the car, with its Connecticut license plate. All day my mood's been black. Last night that fat witch social worker, Delores, barged into the house. She claimed I had to go back to school or face the truant officer. I rolled into my room and shut the door. Let them scream themselves stupid was what I thought. But this morning it was Ziadek, not Luisa, who switched on my light and ordered me—in Polish, which you know is serious—to move my skinny fanny before he paddled it. So I went to music class, practical skills class, that god-awful regular history class with Mr. Monroe the sadist, and math—my only saving grace—where Mrs. Grenier let me work differential equations while the rest studied slope. No one talked to me.

Now I'm off the short bus and back on the trailer farm. Luisa took me for an ice cream when she saw my face, but I didn't want ice cream. "What's that car?" she asks as we draw near the house.

I don't answer. No one expects me to answer. On the rare occasions when I do, my mom seems more annoyed than pleased. Sometimes I think Luisa would rather have a mute buddy than a breathing, quarreling daughter. Like a dog, maybe, or a robot. I roll up the ramp while she takes the steps, and I reach for the door ahead of her. Right then my black mood slips off, like a heavy blanket falling to the floor. Here, in the familiar trailer, waits my past, or maybe my future.

I roll through and into the living room. I catch my breath. Sure enough, there she sits, the woman from the park day before yesterday, on the couch opposite Ziadek. She's come—at last—for me. But everything feels wrong. First there's Ziadek. His face is white; his big nostrils pull at his oxygen. He looks ready to lay hands on the woman. And the woman herself is puffy with weeping. Photographs of our family on the table, on top of the school brochures. There's no joy here. It all feels sad and angry. "Ziadek," I manage to say.

Then my mom pushes in. I've never seen her like this. She doesn't wheedle. She doesn't stonewall. She doesn't even sing out "Ziadek!" like she always does. She just goes after them. "Why's she here?" she asks—and before Ziadek can answer, "Get her out. Get her out, Ziadek! You! Get out! We don't want you! Fucking bitch!"

"Luisa, calm down," Ziadek says in Polish.

"I won't! Make her leave! It's not fair, Ziadek!" This in Polish, too. Then Luisa switches back to English. "You! Get out of here!"

"That is no way to treat a visitor," Ziadek says, still in Polish. Heavily he rises. He starts toward us. I keep my eyes on the woman on the couch. Her bright hair, barely touched with gray. The small bones of her wrist. Her trembling mouth.

"Cunt," my mom's saying. "Bitch. Whore." She grabs hold of the back of my wheelchair. Quickly I lock the wheels. "Go," she says. "Go, Najda. Let's go."

But I won't let the wheelchair move. The woman's stood up. She's got her pocketbook over her shoulder. Luisa lets go of the wheel-chair. "Oh, I hate you, hate you, hate you!" she sputters in Polish—to all of us, to no one. Before Ziadek can reach her, she lowers her head, like a small bull, and butts it into the woman's belly.

"Oof," says the woman. She falls onto the couch. Ziadek reaches for Luisa, but she darts around back of the couch. Then Luisa says it again, this time to me and in English: "I *hate* you." She flings herself from the room into the kitchen. I see her grab a plate from the open shelf—the china plate, the one with grape leaves, that's the last of the set my grandmother brought from the old country—and pitches it across the living room at the couch. The woman's still get-ting back her breath, but she doesn't flinch. The plate misses, hits the bookshelf, and shatters. A large shard flies onto the coffee table, knocks over Ziadek's mug. Then my mom stomps down the hallway and slams the door to her room. Everything's silent. Then muffled sobs, the sound of shoes against the door.

I let the brake off my chair. I wheel over to the woman on the couch. My heart is beating faster than when I have to speak in school, so hard that you'd think it would block out all the words. But the word I've kept inside leaps like a fish from a lake. "Mother," I say in English.

The woman on the couch nods. She pushes herself from the couch and crouches before my wheelchair. She searches my eyes, as if there's something inside them she's been looking for. "I am . . . so happy . . . to see you," she whispers. "To see you"—her voice breaks, but she pushes the word through—"alive."

Now my words get blocked. Only by shutting my lips can I open my throat. "Mmm," I manage. I want to say it again, to say *Mother*. "Mmm. Hmm."

"Najda," Ziadek's saying behind me.

The woman swallows hard. She touches my hand, on the arm of

the wheelchair. "I haven't been . . . any kind . . . of mother. To you," she says. She jerks her head toward the bedroom. "She is your real mother."

Oh, she doesn't understand! How can she? I've left all that behind, that whole pretense that I am the child and Luisa is the adult and that I have anything, *anything*, to learn from my mom— how can this woman understand? She doesn't know how I've waited for her, prayed for her. How I've readied myself to prove I'm not some retard that you throw away, but that I can do things, that I deserve a real mother. She doesn't understand any of it. "You," I manage to say. "You."

"Why don't you just call me Brooke? That's my name. And I'll call you Najda. Such a pretty name, Najda."

Brooke, I think. I reach out with my good hand. Like a blind person I stroke Brooke's hair, like mine only coarser. I tip Brooke's chin up with my index finger. I run my thumb over the broad cheeks, the jawbone. I pull gently at an ear. My index finger trails up and across her pale eyebrows. My thumb traces the eyes, which she closes so I can feel the lids and the shape of the eyeball. Finally I run my finger down her nose, pausing at the bone, like my own funny bump. Brooke remains silent and still, a statue waiting. Suddenly I remember how to unblock the words. I can use the other words, whole sentences that wait in my head. " 'The gentlest mother,' " I begin. It works best not looking at her. I look into the middle distance, somewhere between the couch and the sliding door to the deck. " 'Impatient of no child, the feeblest or the waywardest, her admonition mild.' "

"Dickinson," says Brooke.

I fix her with my eyes. "Now," I say. Then my words fail again. I manage only this much. "You . . . hmm . . . hmm . . . *help* me."

And she nods.

Chapter 22

Was she asking for this girl? Brooke felt the urge not to ask but to beg, to prostrate herself like an ancient sinner. Surely the only sane person in the little trailer was the mother, Luisa, who would have killed Brooke if she could. Look at the evidence! This warped and mangled child, flesh of Brooke's flesh. How could she ever claim her, how could she say, "You are mine. I made you this way"? She couldn't. At the same time she could not run, could not tear herself away. As if her eyes had been starved until now, she looked and looked. Her daughter, hers.

And then, after the humming, after touching her like a blind person, all at once the girl dropped her hands, and spoke poetry. Poetry!

Brooke slipped back onto the couch. She glanced at old Zukowsky. He had collapsed into an armchair, exhausted. His head dropped to one side. Then she realized. "Josef," she said, "you've lost your oxygen." She stepped to the tank, wheeled it close, reattached the two little spigots of air. His eyes were shut. "Can you hear me?" she asked.

She glanced at Najda. "Ziadek?" the girl said, and leaned to where she could place her left hand on the old man's knee. "Ziadek?" she repeated, and then she said something in Polish.

Josef lifted his head. He waved his hands slowly, as if dismissing them. "Are you all right?" Brooke asked him.

"Fine," he croaked. "Fine."

They sat quiet for a moment, watching and listening to him breathe. "I should go," Brooke said.

"No," said Najda. The word came out like an explosion. Brooke picked up shards of the pretty, broken plate. She wiped up the spilled coffee with Kleenex. Then she gathered her pocketbook, waited. She felt she would wait forever. "I want," Najda said after a series of hums, "I want . . . college."

"Okay," said Brooke. "We can get you there. I'll help any way I can."

"M-m-mmm. Money," said Najda.

No one spoke. Brooke glanced at Josef. His eyes had opened and were watching her. She swallowed. She saw an opening here, something for her to do besides grovel. "It's one of these schools"—she put her hand on the stack of brochures—"you want to go to?"

"Scoarding bool," said Najda. She shook her head, as if to clear it. "Boarding," she said.

Brooke smoothed the cover of the brochure. "And you need money."

"Crosby School," said Najda quickly. "Ask Ziadek."

Brooke turned to him—to Josef, whom they called Ziadek. His eyes were on her, as if already conspiring with her. Brooke felt out of her depth. She rose. "I'll work on the money," she said. She reached a hand out, wanting to touch Najda's head, her silky hair. But that would be too much, more than any of them were ready for. "I'll work on it," she repeated. "Najda, you should make things up with . . . with your . . ."

"With her mother," Josef said.

"Right," Brooke said. She managed to brush Najda's stiff shoulder before the girl flinched away. "With your mom. She loves you so much."

When she shook Josef's hand, she placed both her palms around his fingers. They had gone cold. She held him like that for a long moment. Josef focused past her face, on his granddaughter. Then Brooke was out the door, into the startlingly cool air. She fished out her cell phone. As she made her way down the stone path, she tapped out the number. "You're right, Alex," she said when he picked up on the first ring. "We do have to talk."

A lex stared at the phone after he ended the call. His sister Charlie, leaning out his French windows into the cool breeze of the Back Bay, cocked her head back at him. She was dressed in warm fall colors, a deep green jersey with a loose russet vest belted at her waist. On her head she sported a floppy beret in crushed gold velvet. "Don't tell me," she called over to him. "The trip's off."

"I don't know." He felt suddenly light-headed, cold at the lips. He sat on the arm of his couch.

"You don't need to hang with us the whole time," Charlie said. "We can take the bus back. Or Pablo might drive up."

"Who's Pablo?"

"Guy I like. He gave that party, last weekend?" She peered into the small mirror by his bookshelf and adjusted her beret. "He doesn't give a shit about me, though. So that's a fantasy. But there's the bus."

Alex held up a hand. "Just give me a sec," he said.

It was impossible, of course, what Brooke had told him. That the dead could be brought back to life. Aside from that lost night at the motel, Brooke had not seen a person go from life to death. When

Dylan died, he had been in the room. He had felt the blood stop its coursing, the lungs flatten. How quickly the meat of the small arms cooled. The skin went rubbery. Wake up, you wanted to shout, stop this and wake up. But as soon as the body was cold you knew. Life was not a thing that left and might be retrieved. It was an event, and the event was over. You could no more fill the lungs with breath than journey across time.

But Brooke, Brooke. She couldn't bear the truth of what he'd done, and now she had gone to Windermere and found some crazy story she was bent on telling.

When Charlie touched his shoulder, the muscles gave a myoclonic jerk, as if he were on the brink of a dream. "Who died?" his sister asked.

"No one," he said. He tried to focus on her. They were supposed to be leaving his apartment, driving up to Tufts to pick up two of Charlie's offbeat friends, then out to Windermere. They'd stay overnight at home—the second major reason Charlie had asked him to come along, after his provision of a car, was that he would keep their mom calm about having a house full of college kids—and then drive into the Appalachians tomorrow, for the leaves. "At least," he said, his mouth twisting painfully as he made the bitter joke, "no one who wasn't dead already."

"Are you cool to come with us? Because I could borrow your car, and whatever that call was about—"

"No, no. It's fine. We should get going." He rose from the arm of the couch. He glanced at his watch. Five P.M. Dinner on the road; they'd pull into Windermere late. Charlie planted herself in front of him. She tipped her head. Lightly she rested her index fingers on his shoulders. "What?" he said.

"Your traps are way tight, Alexander the Great. You should be doing yoga."

"I should, huh? Will it make me rich and happy?"

"It might," she said. She was half serious. Such a puppy, Alex thought when he looked at her puckered face, all dressed in her leaf-peeping clothes. But she wasn't a puppy. She was a young woman who needed him to be calm, solid, the big brother. Pablo—there was some guy named Pablo; maybe he could hand her off. For now he went to get his fleece, his hiking boots. The traffic would catch them, but no matter; it would give him time to think.

He should have known. Brooke wasn't going to hear the truth from him and just ponder it in her heart, like the Virgin Mary. She was going to strap on her armor and ride out. Now she had found a story tailor-made for her romantic ideas. A poor immigrant family, a grown childless daughter like the princess who rescued Moses, a rescue in the nick of time. Not only had Alex not killed the fetus, so long ago; there had been no death for the fetus, who was more than a fetus, who was a brave living baby disguised as a dead fetus, and so they had made this simple error. They had left it out in the rain. Now all would be well. Only all, in Alex's experience, was rarely well, just as surprises were rarely pleasant.

Charlie's friends were loud, funny, and, by the time they flew past Scranton, fairly stoned. One was a big square girl in overalls and a leather jacket who brayed at every witticism. The other, boasting multiple piercings that glowed in the refracted lights of the highway, ran out of breath as she talked, as if her lungs could hold about a tablespoon of oxygen. One was named Amber, the other Ashley. Happy misfits, like Charlie. Pablo's name kept coming up, and beside him, his pug-nosed sister blushed.

"You going to get that?" Charlie asked at one point as the Black-Berry buzzed and glowed from Alex's shirt pocket. They were winding around the Susquehanna by then, the sky inky, full moon to the west. He pulled out the BlackBerry. Brooke's number.

"No," he said. "Don't want to get arrested."

"I can steer. You put in your Bluetooth."

"It's nothing important."

"You liar."

He reached across the gearshift and pretended to swipe Charlie's nose. Tucking the phone back into his pocket, he remembered his promise to Brooke's husband. If he heard anything from Brooke, he would let Sean know. Now he had heard. But he was letting no one know. He was going to Windermere with his sister, to marvel at the leaves. If he saw Brooke—*if*, he repeated to himself—he would talk sense into her. Then he could let Sean know where his wife had gone. Though by then, perhaps, there would be no reason to let him know anything.

Or every reason. But that thought he left on the road, tossed behind the car like a crushed can, a quick clatter and then it was gone.

Chapter 23

Was it the fall leaves that were already—before her call—bringing him to Windermere? Brooke posed the question to Alex when they met on the village green. Or had he planned to come turn himself in for a crime he hadn't committed?

Tired though he was, Alex felt his blood quicken at the sight of her. She sat disheveled and windblown by the old gazebo, on one of the benches they used to crowd when some garage band from Wilkes-Barre would perform on a summer night. Mums bloomed at her feet. Her hair was pulled roughly back by a barrette, the collar of her thin jacket turned up. There hovered in her movements, and in her eyes, the oddly frantic dreaminess he used to detect when she would get excited about one of her medieval books. "I must have called you a dozen times," he said, perching on the edge of the bench. "I didn't know you were here. I figured you had rendered a guilty verdict."

"So who have you confessed to, then?" Brooke asked. She tipped her head. "Your mother? Charlie? You called, Lex, but you didn't leave a message. You didn't warn me."

He looked down at his nails, the jagged cuticles. Charlie and her sweet, feckless friends were in the mountains now. She had lost her temper at him—really lost it, not just in jest—when he wouldn't come along. Yes, she was dramatic, maybe spoiled as well. But her father was dead and her mother well past sixty, and she had spent most of her adolescence hankering after her absent brother. Now he was here and yet not here. Go on back to Tokyo, then, she'd said with a caustic laugh as she pulled her velvet beret over her bangs and swaggered out the door. "I can't tell Charlie," he said to Brooke. "It's stopped me in my tracks. They could throw me in jail for forty years, fine, I don't care. But you know Charlie. Everything's black-and-white, to her. If I tell her, I'll lose her. If I lose her—well, she might be lost."

"Lex, I know you don't believe this," Brooke said, "but you have to come with me. You'll see Najda for yourself. Then you'll know."

He shook his head. "I won't know anything I don't already. Listen." He reached for one of her hands, which she had shoved deep into the jacket's pockets. He rubbed his thumb across the back of her palm. "If there is one memory I will carry with me to my grave," he said, "it is of that little face and that warm body. I know what I did— Brooke, honey. Don't shrug me off. It's hard to face it. It was a terrible thing. But it happened. You seeing some blond girl in a wheelchair—"

"She wasn't just some blond girl! Lex, she could have been my *clone*. And they found her—they told me where. And when."

"Oh, come on. Did they give you a date? Did they say June tenth?"

"Well, it's not like we got out a calendar—"

"Did they describe exactly where they found this breathing infant?"

Brooke had to hesitate. Her hand fidgeted between his palms. "In a wooden crate."

Doubt, like a black crow's wing, sliced across the clear sky of Alex's mind. Then it was gone. He had told her about the crate, surely. He let go of her hand. "Let's get some lunch," he said. "I'm starving."

"Your mom didn't feed you this morning?"

His grin felt lopsided. "She fed Charlie and her pals. I was too edgy."

"All that girl-noise must've overwhelmed your mom."

"She likes calm these days, that's for sure. And there might be some guy arriving, if Charlie gets her wish. Anyhow, she didn't notice whether I ate. I told her I was seeing Jake for lunch." He stood. "You've got a car?"

They drove east of the village, to a Ponderosa Steakhouse along the highway. Alex glanced around the restaurant and felt relieved to see strangers, leaf-peepers. What he intended to do would soon enough slap his name onto the front page of the *Times-Tribune*. And yet, until he could step into Windermere's sleepy police station and make his report, he dreaded running into anyone who might know him.

To his surprise, over hanger steak and a flabby Merlot, he found himself talking to Brooke as if they had everything else in common—her daughter Meghan, her husband Sean with his astonishing voice, the Red Sox, his bereaved mother—except a botched stillbirth fifteen years ago. Brooke's eyes shone when they got onto the subject of Meghan. "She's the toughest kid," she said. "She's got this cousin who's a big bully, likes to boss the other cousins around. So at this wedding two years ago—Meghan's maybe four then?—her cousin's going around collecting all the favors the kids got, snatching these little plastic bags out of their hands. Well, Meghan not only won't hand hers over but she blocks his access to a two-year-old. Tells the big bully to get lost or she'll kick his shins to pieces. Then she started kicking."

"She looked like she could be determined," Alex said.

"You saw her? When?"

He told her about going to the house, about the awkward meeting with Sean. "I promised him I'd let him know if I tracked you down."

"But you haven't."

"Not yet."

He didn't tell her about Sean's unshaven face, or Sean's cold certainty that Brooke was leaving him for Alex. "I think your daughter's confused," he said gently. "She seemed suspicious of me."

He caught her eye for a moment, but she wouldn't hold his gaze. "Up to now," she said slowly, picking at her salad, "everyone would tell you I've been a great mother to Meghan. I love her. I've kept her safe. I've listened to her. But in the end, you know what? She scares me."

"Scares you how?"

"She's dreamy, like me. Stubborn like me. And I think, can I let her be like that? And what if I can't stop her from being like that? I'm all thumbs, emotionally."

"Brooke, she's just a kid."

"Who needs me. I know. And she doesn't scare Sean. He doesn't have a thing in the world to hide from her."

"He seems like a good man."

"Sean? He's made of gold."

"His voice is, at least."

"Ah. You heard him sing." She grinned. "Now there's a calling for you."

"He ever try it professionally?"

"I wish! But it would never occur to him. Where he comes from? You'd have to be a fruitcake. They talk that way, his family. Really," she insisted, when she saw Alex's face knot up.

"Sorry." He polished off the steak. She had been pushing her food around her plate. "Look," he said, tiptoeing into the question of Brooke's marriage, "I know we couldn't—or anyhow, we didn't—end up together. But I was surprised to meet a guy like Sean."

Brooke's eyebrows went up, challenging him. He pressed on. "For me, Tomiko made sense. You'd have thought the same. You'd have found her . . . captivating."

"Is there any chance that—"

"No." He signaled for the check. The waitress stood pale and forlorn by the door to the kitchen. "Everything died, after Dylan. We even moved into a new house, figuring our old house was dead. We furnished it differently. We bought a new bed!" He chuckled. He twirled his wineglass, in the dim light. "Took just a few months for it to feel dead, too. Tomiko said she was looking for joy. I wished her luck finding it. She remarried last spring. Japanese guy with two kids."

"I'm sorry."

"Just so you know." He gave the waitress his credit card without glancing at the bill. "I'm not doing this lightly. I'm not crazy. Something radical's got to happen, or my life . . ." He didn't know how to finish. His hands made a waving motion in the air, like a tide ebbing away.

Brooke regarded him with her chin on her knuckles. Then she glanced at her watch. "It's two thirty," she said. "If we head for the park now, we should catch them there."

"What park?" he said. "Catch who?" But he knew already. She was not leaving him a choice.

The day was bright but cool, the afternoon sun at a weak angle. The park was deserted. Brooke strode ahead of Alex, a red scarf tied around her neck, its fringed end flapping in the breeze. A wild-goose chase, Alex kept telling himself as he turned up his collar. Still, he felt happy to be with her. The trees were half stripped of their bright leaves already, branches tangled against the sky. He looked down over the blighted landscape. He remembered—

misremembered, probably—some line from *The Great Gatsby*, which he'd read in the required lit class at BU. A guy said to Gatsby that you couldn't return to the past, and Gatsby looked astonished and said something like "My dear boy! Of course you can!" You were supposed to think he was an idiot, of course, a charming idiot. But Alex wondered if you weren't basically fated to return to the past, one way or another. Either you turned around and walked deliberately back into it, with all its small-town gossip and strip malls and mistakes, or it dragged you back by the short hairs.

"Come on," Brooke said, reversing her path and hooking her arm through his elbow. "They must be home. Too cold for them to be up here."

"'They' being this girl . . ." Alex said as they tucked back into Brooke's car.

"And Luisa. Her mother. The one who found her, after we—" Brooke shot a look at Alex. "You'll recognize Luisa," she said.

"What do you mean? Have I met these people?"

"I don't mean you'll recognize her particularly. You'll recognize what she is."

Alex did not pursue this. The more hints, the more answers, and the more this fantasy gained its bearings. They swooped down the hill, around a gas station, and onto the rutted roads of a trailer park. "This is insane," Alex muttered under his breath.

"You want to get out, get out," Brooke said.

"I love you," Alex said.

Silence.

Brooke's smile was indeterminate, as if he had done nothing but consent to whatever she said or did. She drove on. The trailer park meshed its way behind the gas station, a sad labyrinth of human containers. Alex had just begun to catch his breath, to work his way back from the declaration that had slipped through his lips like an escaping bird, when the car slowed. In front of them stood a small knot of people, one in a wheelchair, next to a police car. "Oh dear," Brooke said. Before Alex could stop her, she had put the car into park and rushed out, slamming the door behind her. Alex followed.

Three things he managed to gather right away: that the red-haired woman with the cigarette voice wanted him and Brooke to get lost; that the overweight black woman was a social worker; and that the woman Luisa, whom Brooke had mentioned, had gone missing. The blond girl in the wheelchair—she had to be the one Brooke was fixated on—kept gesturing, sort of humming and grunting at once, trying to say stuff. Alex hovered at the edge. While the cop wrote down whatever he could decipher, the red-haired woman came around the circle to Alex. She wore chinos and a loud sweater knit with pictures of autumn leaves, gold and orange. Her hair, yanked angrily back from her temples and clipped with a pair of barrettes, flared from her head.

"And what do you have to do with this?" she asked.

"Nothing," said Alex. He had been leaning against the door of the squad car, one foot up on a slat of a broken wood fence that attempted to frame a front yard. He held up his hands, presumption of innocence. "I'm with her," he said, "and she knows your—your family."

"Holy shit," said the cop. He dropped his notepad and lifted the brim of his cap. "Alex? Alex Frazier?"

Immediately Alex wanted to flee. How in hell had he let Brooke bring him here? "Jake," he said. There it was under the police cap, the meaty frame and square face of his high school buddy. *Keep it cool,* he thought. "Didn't recognize you in the uniform."

"Jesus, Brooke. You didn't tell me he was coming. What're you doing here, man? Hold on, let me finish getting this report. We were just talking about you the other day."

Brooke and Alex exchanged a quick glance. "I do know the family," Brooke said.

"Do you now?" said the redhead. "Then maybe you can tell us where Luisa's gone."

The black woman had come around the squad car to shake Alex's hand. Her grip was firm and moist. She nicked a glance at the vinyl-sided trailer, with its loose plastic shutters, then turned back to Alex. "I'm Delores," she said. "I'm the social worker for these folks. Hauled out here on a Saturday. It's one thing after another."

"I have nothing to do with it," Alex said. He felt himself—as Brooke shot a look at him, then turned back to the foursome on the uneven brick walk—to be like Pontius Pilate, washing his hands of the very thing for which he professed responsibility. But his claim was true. The misshapen blond girl in the wheelchair—he had no connection to her. She looked like any pretty blond teenager, not especially like Brooke, whose features at seventeen were still seared into his memory. Her handicap was tragic. The left side of her body seemed strong, animate, the face pretty; the right side atrophied and lifeless, like an unfinished sculpture. He turned from Delores to hear the girl trying to form sentences that Jake would listen to, would understand.

"Bus stop," the girl said. She choked the words out as if her vocal cords seized up at every sound. "Good-bye kiss. Money. Hmmm. Ziadek money. Luisa bus." She jerked her head sideways to address the red-haired woman. "Luisa," she said after a series of attempts, "not . . . not . . . baby." At the word *baby*, Alex's gut seemed to seize. She meant that this Luisa wasn't a baby, he told himself; nothing more.

"Gimme sec," Jake called over to Alex. "I got to figure this little mystery out. Want to catch up with you, man."

"Don't worry about it," said Alex.

"Ziadek," Jake said, turning back to the women. "Who's that?"

"Her grandfather," Brooke said quickly. The red-haired woman stared at her, but she kept her eyes on Jake. "Luisa must have taken Ziadek's stash of money," she said, "and left on the bus."

"How in Jesus' name you know that?" said Delores. Taking a step back, she planted herself between Brooke and the rest of the group. Her glare swept from Jake to Brooke. Brooke nodded toward the girl in the wheelchair.

"Najda just said so," she said.

"Who is Ziadek?" repeated Jake.

"You'll leave my father out of this," said the red-haired woman stepping up to him. "He's not well."

"And you are—" Jake looked up from his scribbling. He looked every bit the cop: sober, jowly, his midriff straining at his belt. At the same time, he bore the familiar mystified look Alex remembered from high school, when Jake always seemed behind the curve.

"Katarina." The woman crossed her brawny arms. "Her aunt." She nodded at the wheelchair behind her. "Luisa's sister."

"And where is"—Jake checked his notes—"Ziadek?"

"My husband's taken him to the lung doctor. I want these people cleared out before he gets back. I won't let you give him a heart attack."

"Does he keep cash in the house?"

"Chess set, chess set," said the blond girl. She barked the words, like a command. "Ha. Ha. Ha." She gave up for a moment, then licked her lips and tried again. "Hollow."

"Najda," said Brooke. Stepping forward, she knelt beside the wheelchair. She put her gloved hands over the girl's bare ones, on the armrests. The sun pierced the thin trees of the trailer park and lit them both, their pale hair and skin. The girl's nose had that protuberance, like

Brooke's. But her jaw was narrower, her eyes set deeper. Nothing, Alex thought, that added up to family resemblance. Not in his book. "Do you think Luisa's run off? Is it because of what happened yesterday?"

"Look, lady," said Katarina. She had pivoted from the squad car and loomed over them. "I don't know who you are or what you've got to do with my niece. But you're not helping here. Can you make her leave?" she asked Jake.

"In a minute," said Jake. He winked at Alex. *Winked,* as if they were back in high school, pulling a prank together. Jesus, Alex thought. "Have you got a photo of your missing sister?" Jake asked Katarina.

"Right here," she said. "In my pocketbook. I think you'll find," she said as she fished around, "that this little troublemaker had something to do with her running off." She nodded at the wheelchair as she produced the photograph. She addressed Delores. "She's trying to play hooky from school," she said. "Wants to go to a fancy-ass place. It's driven poor Luisa nuts."

Alex approached the group almost on tiptoe, invisible. As Katarina handed the photo over to Jake, he caught a glimpse. He drew in a sharp breath. "Down's," he heard himself murmur. So this was the missing Luisa—the one, according to Brooke, who had discovered an infant nearly dead behind the Econo Lodge fifteen years ago and had brought it up as her own.

No. Nothing would make him believe it. Either the child Brooke had been carrying was alive or it was dead. For years, he believed it had been born dead. Then the past had somehow come scratching at him like a dog at the door, demanding to be let in, and he had had to revisit the events in the motel room and see them for what they were: a live child pushing its way out of Brooke, his hand on the spoon, his hands squeezing, the eyes staring, lifeless. Nothing could bring that child back to life now, least of all the moon-faced woman in the picture.

"Well, this girl cannot take care of herself," Jake was saying, tipping the photo toward Alex. "Isn't that right, my friend?" He started to hand the photo off, but Alex shook his head.

"I wouldn't know," he said. He met the challenge in Katarina's eyes. He could feel the girl's eyes, Najda's eyes, on him as well, but it was no good giving the poor kid hope. Brooke might have said crazy things to her, might have told her she had a father coming to claim her. But Alex was not playing. "We have no business here," he said to Brooke. "I'm leaving."

"Yes, we do," she said, still crouched in front of the wheelchair, "and I'm not."

"Then I'll call a cab."

"Hey, Alex, catch me later. Traffic control, big water main project in Scranton. I'll be in front of the old station most of the weekend," Jake said.

Alex turned on his heel. Behind him, he heard Katarina's voice. "You want to know where I think she's gone?" she was saying. "I think she's gone to New York City. We took a trip there when she was ten. She couldn't stop talking about Lady Liberty, how you could bring her your poor and your homeless, all that."

"She got enough money for a trip like that?"

"Hey, I don't want to talk about my family's private stuff anymore with her here. You got me, Little Miss I'm-a-Mother all of a sudden?"

"All I know's this girl needs to be in school," came Delores's loud voice. "And if her guardian's took off—"

A steady high-pitched cry rose. Alex had reached the intersection of one pitted asphalt road with another when he glanced back. The girl in the wheelchair had tipped back her head and was emitting sound—a pure wail, steady as a car alarm. He smiled despite himself. Whoever's kid she was, she had a stubborn streak in her and no patience for fools.

He kept walking. He pulled out his BlackBerry. Just as he was getting a taxi number, he heard tires crunch behind him. Brooke pulled alongside, buzzing the window down.

"You may think I'm crazy," she said, "but I'm sane enough to leave when I'm not wanted." She nodded at the passenger door. "Get in, won't you?"

"Am I wanted?" he said.

"I wouldn't stop if you weren't."

He shut his phone and slipped in beside her, his heart slamming in his chest.

The colorful trees whipped by. He heard again all about Isadora, about how the herbs had never been effective. "That's what I've been saying," he repeated, his hand worrying the latch on the glove box. "You delivered a child alive and I did something, I killed it." He heard how Brooke had lain awake the past two nights in her mom's condo, remembering and remembering until she remembered a naked baby breathing on her belly. She was sure it had been breathing. "Not then," he said. "Or, I don't know. Maybe a last breath. We weren't doctors. Memory's slippery, Brooke."

"Then tell me," she said vehemently as they turned into the driveway of a condo complex, the other side of the high school in the village, "why you trust yours so goddamn much. In the face of a girl who looks just like me. Who was found outside that Econo Lodge. In the face of *my* memory."

"Because I know what I'm talking about! You weren't even thinking about this before I showed up in Hartford last month. I'd been thinking about it for months. For years. I had a ton of time to get my memory straight."

She shut off the ignition and stared out the windshield. "You don't have to think about something," she said, "to have it be there. It's the things you don't think about that do it."

"Do what?" He felt driven crazy with her now in the old way, the way she'd driven him crazy when they were young and she got off on one of her tangents. He knew what he had seen, in front of that sad mobile home. A girl who looked no more like Brooke than thousands of other fair-haired girls with irregular noses. A girl who looked more Polish than English, with her blunt cheekbones and the neck that widened to broad shoulders, not like Brooke's delicate English collarbone in the least. Brooke had always loved to believe in miracles, in the coincidences that made for legends. Not Alex. "Do what?" he repeated.

"Change you. The things you don't think about change your whole life. I told myself I was taking herbs to cause a miscarriage, and I had a miscarriage. End of story. So why didn't I go to college? Why didn't I become a scholar? Why didn't I marry you and be happy?"

Her face was wet with tears, but Alex refused to feel sorry for her. "Where are we?" he asked, gesturing toward the condos.

"My mom's place. She sold the house."

"She believe in this—in your idea, here?"

"She doesn't know about it yet. She's not home. She was going to the gym."

"She have any Scotch?"

Brooke slammed the car door. She moved by jerks, her arms tight to her side. In the condo, she rifled through the cupboards of the high-ceilinged sitting room until she found a bottle and a pair of tumblers. She sat on the edge of the couch, clutching the cushions, as if she were perched on a ledge and keeping her balance. She drained half the glass of Scotch and grimaced. Alex sat next to her, his leg crooked so that he faced her profile. "You didn't marry me," he began, "and you aren't happy. And now you think this girl—"

"I didn't do those things," Brooke interrupted, "because I knew something was wrong with the story we told ourselves. I didn't know what was wrong. I couldn't look at it. But now I am looking at it. I'm owning it, whatever that means."

"No!" Alex almost shouted. His hand gripped her thigh just above the knee. "*I'm* the one who's owning it, Brooke! You're right. It was no miscarriage. But my hands, what my hands did"—he set his Scotch on the coffee table and gripped her other thigh—"*that* is the thing that's fucked everything up. Not some miracle rescue."

"What is so miraculous about a damaged child?" Brooke turned to look at him, her eyes red-rimmed. Her hands let go of the cushions and cupped Alex's jaw. He felt her cool fingers. "Maybe you squeezed too hard," she said softly. "Or maybe we just didn't do enough to get her breathing. What's wrong with Najda—it has to do with not getting enough oxygen to the brain. I looked it up." Her voice had gone hoarse. Her lips as she spoke were swollen. "There's no way out of this," she said, "without damage."

"Of course there is!" He leaned forward and kissed her, quickly, as if to stop more such words from forming. "For you, there is," he said. His face was close to hers; he could smell the salt of her tears. He seemed to swim in her eyes. "You believed you had a miscarriage. You never did anything wrong. I did a wrong thing, and I'm paying for it. The damage is done, long ago done. And none of it was your fault. You're whole."

"That's the last thing I am."

Her lips moved toward him then. A great wave of familiarity washed over him, as if he had moved among strangers for fifteen years and only now, in this instant, was seeing—was touching—one who knew him at the core. They kissed for a long while. Her tears kept running down, flowing between both their lips, so they both tasted salt and Scotch at once. His hands went under her knit top. They pushed up her bra, held her breasts, round and more lovely for being heavier since childbirth. "I want to go back," he heard himself say. "Back to you. To what happened. Make it right."

"And I don't." She fought with him still, even as she pulled him onto the stubbled fabric of the couch. "I want to do what we can to help her."

"Help who?"

"Najda! You don't believe me, do you? You don't believe she's our—oh, Christ."

Her hand had slipped under his jeans. He felt her fingers against the skin of his buttocks. He went hard. With a groan, he pushed her top up, over her breasts; he unhooked the bra. "This is what you want," he said. "It's what you've been wanting."

"Is it?" she said, wonderingly.

Her mouth had gone slack. Her body gave off a ripe, passive heat. He took off his glasses and set them on the coffee table. He leaned down and took her breasts into his mouth, felt the nipple harden against his tongue.

"I have loved you," he murmured as he moved from one warm breast to the next. "I love you now."

"Help me then," Brooke said above him. Her hands feathered his back. "Help me help her."

"Brooke"—he moved up to her neck, his hand against the stiff seam of her blue jeans—"I don't believe in her."

But she didn't hear him. She went on, "They need money. Najda needs a better school. My mother is sitting on a trust fund from my grandfather. I've never wanted a share before, but I'm going after it now. And you have money—Oh." She sucked in her breath as he bit softly at the thin, damp skin of her neck. "Kiss me," she said.

And when he had, she pressed him down on the couch cushions. In the dying light, she studied him. Her gaze went through his clothes, through his skin. Were they going to make love? Could the world turn inside out, just like that? She stayed silent too long. Her hand lingered at his belt. "I'm facing my past," he heard himself say— guessing, groping—"so I can live. You don't have to face anything."

Brooke's index finger traced a line from his belt buckle to his throat. "Keeping all the guilt to yourself," she said thoughtfully. "It's selfish."

The accusation hit him in the gut. "What are you talking about?"

"It's all about you, this guilt. Forgive yourself, and suddenly you're not so important. You don't own all that history."

"I can't," he said. The room had grown dim. He could hardly make out her features. Her fingers ran over his eyebrows, his nose, his ears. His erection had softened. It was too much like what he had heard from Tomiko, after they had lost Dylan. *It's all about you.* "I love you," he said for the third time, but his cock was giving up. He pulled her to him, their legs tangled. In his parents' basement they had lain like this; on the beach; in the backseat of his car. And yet the last time his hand had touched between her legs—he remembered as Brooke's heartbeat slowed—it had been to help her rid herself of a child. At that memory, what was left of his erection shrank like a sea anemone at human touch.

Brooke lifted her head. "But you don't love me," she said softly. "You love the idea of me, just like I love the idea of you. I wanted that idea back, for a while."

"What about *us* back?"

Slowly she shook her head. She sat up and flicked on a floor lamp. In its harsh glow he studied her figure—the heavier breasts, hips that had carried a child to term. "Okay, but," he said. He watched while she rehooked her bra. Desire was a liqueur at the back of his throat. "If you did not believe that this Najda was your daughter—"

"Ours."

"Ours, okay. If you hadn't met her, but had only talked to Isadora. If you had become convinced that what happened in that place—"

"That place is a paintball arcade now. You should see it."

"Maybe I will. While we're strolling down memory lane. But let's say"—he found his hand on her knee, the stiff jeans between them—"you didn't have this evidence of a child who lived. Let's say you only knew that you might have given birth to a living baby, and here I am telling you I pressed that baby's skull too hard." He frowned. "Don't you want to kill me? Don't you think *someone* should kill me?"

Brooke's mouth twisted. "Maybe I'm not all that willing," she said, "to share my own guilt."

"You're going to have to."

"Am I?" Turning, her eyes challenged him. Invited him, again, into a world where the child had survived, had grown into the girl in the wheelchair. Feel guilty about *that*, her eyes demanded.

"Jesus, Brooke," he said. He rose from the couch, took the two empty tumblers to the kitchen, rinsed them and filled one with cold water. When he'd slaked his dry throat, he looked across the wide space to where Brooke stood by the window next to the cupboard, the Scotch tucked away. Desire lay heavy in his veins. They weren't going to make love, not now, not ever. But it wasn't just an idea he'd wanted. It was her. To thrust himself inside her, to drown in the sea of her. He refilled the glass and brought it out. Brooke was gazing westward, at a long orange sunset.

"By your lights," she said, after she had taken a deep drink from the glass, "you have lost both your children."

"I guess I have, yeah."

"Do you have a picture of Dylan?"

He reached into his pocket. "Hang on," he said. He flicked on the light. Retrieving his glasses, he found his wallet on the floor by the couch. From it he drew out the snapshot he'd kept behind his credit cards for three years. "That was just before he went into the hospital for the last time," he explained. "He was never a strong kid."

She held it to the light. He watched as her eyes searched the photo. With pain he remembered the setting—Tomiko and himself on the window seat, the shade lowered behind them to reduce the backlighting, Dylan propped between them with his favorite stuffed monkey. "Beautiful, though," she said.

"He was a stunner."

"And your wife also."

Brooke handed back the photo, but he didn't look at it. He tucked the wallet into his back pocket. They stood quite close; he smelled the slight tang of her sweat, the Scotch on her breath. Past mixed with present—what a cocktail, he thought, what a drug. He lifted his jacket from the floor. "I should go," he said.

"I guess the leaf peepers'll be back by now."

"We'll talk tomorrow," he said. He squeezed the tips of her fingers, and she nodded. But as he headed out on foot, he thought they would not talk—not tomorrow, not the next day, perhaps not for a long while. He could not turn himself in, not now. Brooke would have this other story to tell. And what of his mother, when it all came out? What, for Christ's sake, of his sister?

Rapidly he strode out of the condo complex, around the old soccer field, the high school; across the village green; and into the neighborhood that rose up a long, low hill above the village. The lights were on in the Victorian farmhouse where he had grown up. His car sat in the drive: the girls, back from their mountain adventure. And sure enough, a second car behind his. A old green Dodge Dart, with *TUFTS UNIVERSITY* on the back windshield, the backseat strewn with clothes. Pablo, he thought. For his sister's sake, he smiled as he opened the front door to their chatter and good cheer.

Chapter 24

I think it's time," Brooke's mother said, pouring her a second cup of coffee, "you told me what your visit here is really about."

Brooke chuckled drily. Her mom had returned home yesterday maybe ten minutes after Alex left. Had she wanted Stacey to come upon them like that, making out in the living room? All night she had shifted positions in the pullout, trying to ignore the metal bar that cut across her lower back and trying to figure out what she'd been doing, what she expected. Alex, she concluded, wanted his guilt straight, like his Scotch. A distant action, a lost baby. The cocktail that was Najda and Ziadek and the slurry of the present would not go down with him. And now Luisa had vanished, another consequence. "The purpose of my visit," she said to her mother, "changes on an hourly basis."

"Start from now, then. I'm a quick study."

She was, Brooke thought. However blunt Stacey Willcox's constitution, she had always been able to turn on a dime and get things done. Now she sat on a bar stool across from Brooke at the white counter framing her kitchen. The sun poured through the glass doors from the patio, where pots of bright mums lined the steps. Over crisply pressed pants, Stacey wore a scoop-neck silk tank that hugged her neat torso. It was Sunday, but still she had risen early, pulled herself together. Brooke had not yet combed her hair. She touched a finger to the hot surface of the coffee, then licked it: strong, laced with hazelnut. She met her mom's disquieted eyes. Here, she thought, was as good a place as any to begin a new life.

"I have a daughter," she said. She took a sip of the coffee. "Not Meghan, but another. She's fifteen years old." She heard rather than saw her mother's quick intake of breath. Brooke kept her eyes on the coffee mug—cyan blue porcelain, with a rim of red. Steam rose in genie-like swirls. "Najda is severely disabled, but she is not retarded. I did not know until four days ago that she was even alive. She lives with a Polish family, in a—a development. On the way to Scranton. She needs help. She needs to be at a better school. But I don't know what to do." Now she raised her eyes to meet her mother's. Stacey's brown irises had gone wide. She stared at Brooke as if seeing her for the first time in a decade. "I can't afford a mistake here," Brooke said. "I've only got the one chance."

From an avalanche of questions Stacey seemed to choose one. "This girl—Najda—was born while you lived at home," she said wonderingly. Then just one word. "Why?"

Brooke sighed. She hated, hated to relive any of this. But she had started. "I went to Isadora," she said. "You remember Isadora Bassett—"

"She's a flake. Believes in auras."

"Well, back then she believed in herbal remedies. She told me a certain tea would—would cause a spontaneous abortion."

"Jesus Christ." Stacey's mouth wrinkled in the disdain Brooke remembered from the many times she had fallen short of her mother's expectations. But she recovered. She got the coffeepot and poured them each a refill. Hers she topped with cream and stirred thoughtfully. "Obviously it failed. You had the child." She shook her head, wondering how in God's name such a thing could have happened under her nose.

"I did, yeah. In a motel room." Brooke realized that she was avoiding mention of Alex. But she couldn't put his name to her lips. Eventually, her mom would ask. "I thought," she went on, "it was a late miscarriage. A very late miscarriage. A stillbirth. But I guess the baby just wasn't breathing well. Someone found her and saved her. Only I didn't know. Till now."

Morning light spread across the rim of Brooke's coffee mug. She could not bring herself to meet her mother's eyes. She had told the story, she realized, to the cooling coffee. Finally, breaking the long silence, Stacey said, "I'd have thought you could come to me."

"I know," Brooke said to the coffee.

"I would have paid for an abortion. I'm not religious."

"I knew that."

"Help me out here, Brooke. I want to understand."

Brooke finally lifted her head. Her mother looked fragile. Stacey's skin was beginning to thin. Fifty-two. The actual date was tomorrow. Brooke grasped for a memory, just a snapshot, of when they had felt close to each other, and came up empty. More keenly, she felt it had been she herself, not just her young mother, who had pulled away, who had let the distance enter in. "You remember when you took me to get birth control?" she said. "You remember how I wanted the Pill, and you said I should get a diaphragm instead?"

"Did I? Those pills were a lot stronger then."

"That's not why. You said I needed to take responsibility." Brooke wet her lips. Her mouth tasted of coffee, acidic and bitter. "So I got the diaphragm and I took responsibility. But the thing was sized wrong. It slipped. And I thought you wouldn't believe me, you'd think I didn't use it."

"I always believed you, honey. I trusted you."

"But you were waiting for me to fail. Just like—"

She broke off. She stood, went to the sink; returned with a tall glass of cool water. "Just like I failed, when I was eighteen?" Stacey said when she'd sat back on the bar stool.

Brooke twisted her hands in her lap. "Did you?"

"No." Stacey's smile began tight, then spread. "You're the greatest success story of my life," she said.

"But I lied to you. I became pregnant and tried to abort the fetus and gave birth and abandoned the infant. And I never shared a word of it with you."

"And I never knew. Because I wasn't paying attention."

Brooke didn't argue with that—it was a moment of honesty she had never anticipated. She blinked back tears. She studied her mother. The roots of Stacey's flaxen hair were showing salt and pepper. Stacey's nose lacked the signature bump of Najda's—that had come from Brooke's dad—but something about the set of the neck, and the flat upper lip . . . but no. Brooke knew where Najda's mouth came from. "The father," she surprised herself by volunteering, "was Alex Frazier."

"Well, of course," said Stacey. That was her mother, Brooke thought, acting always as if she were one step ahead of you. "And he's back now. And you're in touch with him. You're getting another chance."

"No. No!" Brooke slipped off the bar stool. She walked a quick circle on the blond carpet of the sitting room. Yesterday's moment with Alex, when she had wanted him beyond all reason, entered her blood again as if through a hypodermic. How quickly desire had filled them and left them empty. When she had told him they were making a mistake, he had not argued. They would talk today, they had agreed. But she expected no call from him. He had blown through her life like a warm, piquant wind. She longed for many things, the past included . . . but she did not long for Alex. Out of all her feelings, what surprised her most was realizing that she had longed for him all these years, up until now.

"Alex does not believe," she told her mother, returning to the counter, "that the child lived. That this child we've discovered is ours. Look," she said as Stacey's brows furrowed, "something hurt Najda. The herbs themselves, or the messy way she came out, or being left for"—she made herself say it—"for dead. I don't know. She cannot walk, or talk properly. Her life's been one long frustration, because of me. But she's here. And I'm here." She felt sure of herself as she spoke, more calm than she had been in years. "And she has a family who loves her, including a mother."

"You gave this child up?" Stacey asked wonderingly. "And now you want her back?"

"No, I told you! Luisa found her. Behind the motel." She hesitated; she was ready to tell her mom about Najda's deficiencies, but not about Luisa's. "And now Luisa's afraid of losing her. Which she won't." She pinched her lips together, holding in fierce remorse. "Najda," she went on, "doesn't need me, not personally. She needs a good school. A school that understands smart kids in uncooperative bodies. She needs a lot of money. And I want to give that to her. I want to give her Grandpa's money."

Brooke's gaze rested on her mom. In Stacey's eyes lay the idea, the ideal, of Brooke Frazier, of that perfect young couple. It was a stubborn ideal. "Alex has money," she said.

"Forget Alex, Mom. He doesn't believe in this."

"And you're sure—"

"I'm sure."

"Well, your grandfather didn't leave much. He didn't leave enough. You think I would still be here"—she gestured around the small, elegant condo—"if my father had left me a fortune?"

Yes, I do, Brooke wanted to answer. But too much was at stake. "What about the quarry? What about the sale?"

"Honey, by the time your grandfather sold that quarry, it was practically worthless. There had been something fishy, you know. With the accounting. Not enough to land anyone in jail. But by the time he paid off his creditors . . ." She held up empty hands.

"Why'd I never know this?" Brooke asked. And then a new possibility dawned on her. "Didn't Alex's dad do the accounting?"

"No one knew it, sweetheart. Not even your father. And by the time your grandpa found out, Ed Frazier was gone."

"You mean Alex's dad—when he had that accident—you mean it wasn't—"

"I don't know. No one knows. Well, all right, maybe Nancy Frazier does, and that's why she's been made of glass ever since. But we can't change the past. It wasn't your fault, or mine, or your dad's."

"I feel awful. Alex never even suggested."

"Maybe it's not a suggestion he knew to make. I'm telling you only because of the money, all right?" Stacey took both of Brooke's hands. She was all reason, all practicality. "We are talking here about the money and what you can do about this girl—if you think she's yours, really. Aren't we?"

Brooke swiped at her eyes. "Yeah. Yes."

"So listen." Stacey's fingers were cool and dry, the touch that had been soothing whenever Brooke had run a fever as a child. "I work with the schools, remember? I know a little something. And one of the things I know is that the state is obligated to provide an appropriate education for each and every child."

"But they haven't." Brooke's head reeled a little, from the news about the quarry. Alex's father . . . had it really not been an accident? Was *that* part of Alex's guilt? Should she have known? "The schools," she managed to go on, her lips numb, "have not provided Najda any sort of education."

"That remains to be seen. I don't know your"—Stacey's lips wouldn't form that word *daughter*, not yet—"this girl, Najda. But if your hunch is right—"

"It's not a hunch! I've seen her! I've talked to her grandfather! She wants to go to college, and if—"

"If your hunch is right," Stacey repeated, "you don't need great wealth." She drew herself up; Brooke's mom was not one to dilly-dally. The quicksand of regret did not lie on the paths she charted. "Brooke, honey," she said. "You need to negotiate the system. You need a good lawyer."

Chapter 25

Luisa stood outside the train station in Scranton, confused. It was the same place—same enormous columns rising from the short flight of steps, same clock above the letters *LACKAWANNA*, with stone eagles on either side. Ziadek had brought them all here when she was little, and they had stood in the grand waiting room and had ice cream from a vendor. Then they had boarded the enormous train for New York. She remembered it all perfectly. And yet here was the station, and people bustling in and out of it, but when she had gone through the revolving doors inside it had all been different. A fountain stood in the center of the tiled floor, yes, and golden marble columns rose from the tile, and a gilt rail ran around the balcony on all four sides. She even recognized the indoor clock, its bright face and roman numerals. Only there were no people waiting for trains, no ticket windows. No one was hurrying. Instead, the people with their luggage stood before a desk, laughing and holding hands. A black man with a little red pillbox hat had been pulling a rack of hanging bags across the smooth floor when he stopped to ask her if she was at the hotel.

"Am I?" she had asked back.

"Are you staying here?" he had said. His lips were full and pink, like the flowers in the enormous bouquet they'd set up in the middle of the fountain.

"I'm going to New York," she'd said. "On the train."

He'd laughed at her, then. He'd said the train didn't go to New York anymore. Not go to New York! Where would it go, then? He'd said this wasn't a station, anymore. It was a Radisson. If she wanted to go to New York, he said, she could take the bus. He'd led her outside, by the elbow. On the street there was construction, big jackhammers tearing up the roadbed and cops directing traffic around. Luisa put her hands over her ears. The black guy touched her shoulder and pointed down the street. "See there," he'd shouted, "where they got the white dog blinking. That's the place." Then he went back through the revolving door.

She stood amid the racket, bright sun streaming onto the workers and wind blowing debris up from the street. Why would they take a train station and make it a hotel? Where had the trains gone? Walking here from the bus stop, she had seen one of the old steam trains they kept for show at Steamtown, chuffing its way across Lackawanna Street. Would they move the new trains over there now?

People brushed past her, going up the broad steps into the station that was a hotel. She lifted her eyes to the columns, the eagles. Then she turned and started down the street.

Last night she had stayed in a motel room outside Towanda. She had spent forty-two dollars of Ziadek's money, she had spent twenty minutes in the hot shower, and she had watched TV until three in the morning. This morning she had slept until noon, when the motel's breakfast was all finished, and the manager had let her have a stale doughnut, but that was all. Then she had waited for the bus into Scranton.

They must miss her by now. They probably missed Ziadek's money, too. She should feel bad about taking it, except it was his fault. He had been about to take a lot more than money from her. Her daughter. She loved Ziadek but she would never forgive him, never. Maybe they would figure that she had taken the bus as far as Scranton. Katarina would drive to Scranton and bring Najda, and they would come look for her at the train station. She wouldn't be there, because the trains weren't there, so they would have to drive up and down the street until they found her. They would tell her how sorry they were and they weren't going to talk to that lady or to those stupid schools again.

The bus station wasn't nearly as nice as the train station. It had a grimy counter with a lady on the other side watching a reality show on her little TV. The three o'clock to Port Authority had broken down outside Elmira, she told Luisa. They expected it in by six thirty; it would pull into New York before midnight. Luisa found a place to wait. Across the room—yellowing posters on the wall, a drinking fountain at one end, gray doors leading to restrooms—a newsstand featured hot dogs revolving slowly on warm metal cylinders, but at four o'clock the guy running it pulled down a grate. As soon as he clicked the padlock, Luisa felt hungry. Around her, people were dozing in plastic chairs, drinking out of paper bags; one tired-looking mom was feeding a little baby. Hoisting her backpack, Luisa went up to the counter. "Can I get something to eat somewhere?" she asked. Her voice sounded hollow.

The lady glanced at the clock—a digital one on the wall, nothing like the clock at the train station. "Newsstand closes early on Sunday."

"I wanted to take the train. They have food on the train."

"Yeah, well, you're out of luck, aren't you."

"Somewhere nearby?"

"McDonald's over on Spruce Street." She glanced at the clock again. "You got two hours, sweetheart. Go for it."

"Where's Spruce Street?"

Now the lady looked at her close. She got up from the table where she was sitting and pulled a map out from a display. With a red pen she marked the route. "You turn left out of the station and go a couple blocks—here, see?—and then left again, past the parking garage and the fitness place. You'll see it by the bank, across from the newspaper building. Do you understand me? Here's the time the bus leaves." She wrote that down. "Do you know your left and your right?" She was talking loudly now. That was how people talked to both Luisa and Najda, and before Najda got those ideas in her head, thinking she was so smart, they used to laugh together about it. Now Luisa just took the map and went out of the station. It was darker outside now, and getting cold. She pulled her knit cap over her ears. She hadn't brought mittens. What if they never came after her? What if she went to New York and it got colder and colder?

She walked farther than she should have, and suddenly she was blocked by all the construction again, in front of the train station that wasn't a train station. She didn't know where to turn; she went up one street and down another, trying to find the right sign. The blocks were empty of people. Finally she asked an old black man walking his skinny dog, and he turned her around. After another block there it was, the golden arches and the bright signs. She was really hungry now. She ordered a Double Quarter Pounder Value Meal and paid for it with Ziadek's money. She sat by the window, looking out on the street. Were they looking for her? They had to be. Najda was probably crying, she was so sorry, she missed her mom so bad. Luisa got a lump in her own throat just thinking how bad her daughter would be feeling. Who would help Najda in and out of the shower? Who would listen to her recite her sad poetry?

Luisa looked at the clock above the counter at McDonald's. Five thirty, it read. What had the lady said about the bus? She pulled out the map she had given her. *6:30* was written and underlined in red right below where the lady had marked the streets. Outside, the light was falling; the sun slipped behind a gray cloud, making everything darker than it should be. Across from the McDonald's was a white brick building, with *Times-Tribune* in fancy black script above a loading dock. The newspaper. Ziadek read it every day. Other newspapers had terrible stories, with big photographs, and people bought them from the rack in the Quik Mart every day. If anyone tried to stop Luisa—she decided, finishing her fries—she would tell the newspaper. She would tell how the lady who looked like Najda had thrown her baby away. True, it had been a boy Luisa had seen, leaving the little bundle in a crate behind the motel, but boys don't have babies. This lady had had the baby, and the baby had become Najda—only that wasn't what this lady had wanted, not back then. She had wanted the baby to die. Now, if the lady promised to go away forever, Luisa would not tell. Or no—the lady would have to give Luisa some money first, then go away. That was a better plan.

She would take the train to New York and then she would wait. That was one thing Luisa was really good at, waiting. She waited for Najda to be finished at the library; she waited for Martín at the Quik Mart to give her something to do; when Najda was little, she used to wait for her to finish sleeping so they could play with Najda's toys. While Najda slept, Luisa would study her pursed mouth, the tiny scallops of her closed eyes, her shallow, regular breathing. Katarina liked to tell the story of how she found Luisa once lifting the baby's eyelid because—according to Katarina—Luisa said she wanted to peek at Baby Najda's dreams. But Luisa didn't remember that. She knew dreams didn't happen in the eyelids.

At five forty, a bunch of guys came into the McDonald's. They were loud and spread out all over the restaurant. One of them, a tall skinny white guy with a tattoo snaking up his arm, leaned over Luisa and nipped a French fry. "Hey!" she said, covering the tub.

"Got to watch the calories, beautiful," he said.

She smiled at that, him calling her beautiful. It felt good to smile. But the man and his friends were being too loud. Two of them stood at the counter calling the serving girl names. "Come on, sugar! Give me a double bitch on a bun! How 'bout some sliders? Hey? Slide me some of that brown breast!" The girl got the manager, a fat young man with a walkie-talkie, who told them both they were drunk and had to leave. Then they stood outside the window, making monkey faces at their friends, until they gave up and skipped off into the night.

"So coked up," said another who remained, two tables over from Luisa. This one had darker skin, long hair. "Fucking goons."

Luisa crumpled up her food bag and stood. "Where you going, little puppy?" said a third guy. He had dark blond hair and a baby face, with small eyes buried deep, the upper lids like little pillows. His voice wasn't mean. It was soft, like a warm towel.

"To the train station," Luisa said, even though there was no train station. She wasn't supposed to talk to them—they were strangers, and drunk—but it felt better to get words around the lump that had appeared, without warning, in her throat.

"Catch a train to the moo-oon," said the skinny one. He flung out his arm. The tattoo was of two snakes, twisting their way up his muscles.

Luisa pushed out the door of the restaurant onto the street. The sky was darkening; a cool wind blew papers across the sidewalk. Streaks of sunset laced the *Times-Tribune* sign.

"What a surprise," said the dark-skinned one, trotting after her from the restaurant. "That's where we're going, too."

"That train must be late," said the baby face in his warm-towel voice. He wore his hair long, too, all twisted into strands, falling over the collar of a dirty leather jacket that he was buttoning up, now.

"Got some time to kill, then," said the first.

Walking faster, trying to keep ahead of them, Luisa had started to cry. She cried because no one had come after her—and they should know where she'd gone, they should know how much she liked McDonald's, they should have found her by now. She cried because the drunk guys were all around her now, and she knew she was caught, she was like a fly in a spider's web.

"Little hooch, honey?" said the tall one. He stuck a paper bag under her nose and Luisa smelled whiskey. She shook her head.

"No, thank you," she said softly. She kept her eyes on the sidewalk. One crack, another, another.

"Come on, puppy, come on here," said the baby-faced one. She liked his voice, and it scared her the most. She couldn't make out his eyes. "Let's take a little rest in here. Come on."

Ahead of them was the construction, bright lights and jackhammer sounds far away at the end of the street. Babyface put his hand in the middle of Luisa's back. He steered her toward an alley. "Little bitch," said the tall one behind her. "Chasin' cars, maybe you catch one."

"Vroom," said the one in the leather jacket.

Alex drove east from Windermere as the sun lowered to the west. He had plugged the BlackBerry into the car charger, to keep it from running out of juice, but he had not heard from Brooke. Nor had he tried to call. He had spent the morning in his big-brother role, fixing pancakes with warm applesauce for all the young people. He had listened attentively to the kid, Pablo, who had indeed found his way to Windermere in order to be with Charlie. That was the case, no matter what story Pablo was creating about heading west in his car, remembering Charlie's phone number, deciding to stop off for the hell of it. An awkward kid with an eyebrow ring and slumping shoulders, Pablo spoke with the extended vowels of a pothead, but his soft brown eyes followed Charlie as she padded around the kitchen. "Whaddaya think?" Charlie had whispered to Alex as they packed a lunch for a morning hike into the Alleghenies. Alex had squeezed his sister's shoulder, told her he thought Pablo was the real deal. And maybe he was. In any case, he wanted nothing more than to take Charlie and her friends on their camping trip and ferry them back to Boston. Alex was off the hook.

Last night he had dreamed, as he often did, of Dylan. In the dream Dylan was alive, not as he had been in his last few months, but younger—a true toddler, with that impish grin showing his pearly row of teeth and the fat dimple in his cheek. Only Alex had made a mistake, had thought Dylan had died, and so he had left Dylan behind somewhere and not taken care of him for days—no, weeks, months, for a span of time that stretched longer as the dream went on and Alex grew slowly aware of how long he had been considering his son to be dead, while all the time Dylan had been alive, his grin slowly fading while his gleaming dark hair waned thin and dull, while his body withered and grew faint, transparent. In the dream Alex was walking, then running, trying to get back to the place where he had left his son because he thought Dylan was dead. Whatever had possessed him, to think such a thing? And now Dylan lay in a coffin, ready to be buried, and he would die indeed, all because Alex had forgotten he was alive. *Is this what you wanted?* someone asked in the dream, and Alex cried out *No! No!* But as so often happens in dreams—and now he knew he was dreaming, and in the chair, but he had to get there, to Dylan, he couldn't stop running now—he made no sound. In his ear came Dylan's laugh, *Da-addy, Da-addy*, like it was all a joke. But Dylan wasn't joking now. Alex's legs churned, unable to move through the thick air, and how could he think his son was dead, and so kill him? *No!* he had cried again, and woken up.

As he hiked Hearts Content after breakfast, Alex had done his best to dismiss the dream, to shrug off the crazy encounters of the day before. That family! Brooke would seize on them as a cause, at least until the pixie dust wore off and she realized it was a false coincidence. The trailer park happened to lie across the highway from the motel. The girl happened to have fair hair and an irregular nose. And the story—which could be manipulative—was that she had been found. And would it allay Brooke's guilt, or her judgment of Alex, to invent this tale of a child crippled rather than a premature infant killed? Not in the end. Finally, when the family took her money and spent it however they pleased, Brooke would come to her senses.

By then, Alex realized as he trudged up the narrow trail, he, too, would have moved on. He was—maybe he had always been—a man in bad faith. He was never going to face Charlie's shock and judgment, was never going to shame himself before his brittle, fragile mother. Maybe, with Brooke at his side, he would have had the strength. He would never know, now; he would keep his crime as his bedfellow regardless of what Brooke did or did not do.

He had left Pablo and Charlie and their giggling friends at the Hearts Content trailhead, poring over maps. By now the four of them were probably at the New York border. He pictured them laughing at a hikers' bar. Maybe tonight, camping in a tent, his sister would make love with Pablo. The thought brought a smile to Alex's face. He had grabbed lunch, driven back to Windermere, sat for a while with his mother as she did the Sunday crossword, and then told her he was heading back to Boston, he had a full workday tomorrow. This was a lie—he had put in, already, for two personal days, planning on his great confession—but being with his mom made him antsy. The year after his father died, she had stopped coloring her hair, which had quickly paled to an ivory white. Blessed with a soft prettiness—Alex had his full cheeks from her—she seemed to have aged three years for every year that had passed since then. She had never worked. These days she left the house only to volunteer at the Presbyterian church or to play card games with older women at the assisted-living place.

"You are my great success," she had said to Alex when she hugged him good-bye.

"I'm hardly that, Mom. I've got a decent job. The rest of my life's fallen apart."

"That was sad. She should have stuck with you. For all they say about Asian women—"

"Mom. Don't start on Tomiko."

"Well." She had pressed a small, soft hand against his cheek. "You're so young, so smart, so handsome. You'll start it all over again. Won't you?"

She had not, to his relief, mentioned Brooke. Nancy Frazier had loved Brooke and felt betrayed by her. And for all her softness, Alex's mom never forgave a slight.

When he pulled off the highway into downtown Scranton, he felt momentarily disoriented. Growing up in Windermere, he almost never went to Scranton. It used to have the station for the train to New York, and the old iron furnaces where the high school brought field trips. Otherwise it was a baggy-pants city—its factories boarded up, its grand bank buildings defaced or up for lease. The area where Jake was overseeing construction had to be in front of the defunct station, now turned into a ritzy hotel for whoever could find a reason to come to Scranton. A few blocks shy of the construction, Alex turned off Lackawanna, the main drag, onto a side street. Straight ahead he spotted a brightly lit McDonald's. He'd bring Jake a couple of hamburgers and a large Coke, keep the guy awake.

"Hear they're doing construction down by the old station," he said to the plump black girl who slid the bag across to him.

The girl shrugged. "They got lights on down there," she said. "You can't drive through."

"I know. Buddy of mine's helping oversee. Should I just hoof it, then, if I want to catch him?" The girl looked at him strangely. "Walk, I mean," he said. "Should I walk over there, or drive?"

"Walk," the girl said. She pointed toward the side door of the restaurant. "Right here, then left. You'll see lights."

He pushed out the door with his two bags. The sidewalk smelled of cigarette butts and stale beer. He would ask Jake if he'd learned anything about that missing girl. He'd explain away the encounter at the trailer park. Brooke was on a mission, he'd say. No, they weren't an item again. They had both happened to be in town for the weekend. Brooke had gotten to know the family when she lived alone—or no, maybe through Brooke's mom, the disability program at the school. Oh hell, he didn't know how he would explain it. He didn't care.

A block past the McDonald's, he heard voices. Rough, slurred. A muffled cry. The street was poorly lit, the brick buildings dark. He drew close. There, in an alley—he couldn't see them clearly, but behind a set of trash cans he made out a jumble of movement and a hoarse laugh. "She's like a little otter, in't she?" said one voice. And another, "C'mon, honey, speak Mongol to us, c'mon, hold still."

He set the bag on top of a trash can. He sprinted into the alley. "Hey," he said. His hands were already balling into fists. "What're you guys doing?"

"Minding our own business!" said a skinny guy who pulled away from the corner where a dark struggle was going on. Alex heard the grunt of sex, a feeble wail from whatever girl they'd gotten their mitts on.

"Get off her," Alex said. He reached in his pocket to call 911, but the phone was back in the car, charging. Damn.

"Go on dude, get outta here." The skinny guy came up to him. Alex could just make out his features, a rubbery face with a squared-off nose and big cheekbones. He stank of booze. "She likes it, we like it, we don't need extras."

"I don't think she likes it."

He took a step forward. The flat of the guy's hand pushed against his chest. "Back off, asshole."

"I said she doesn't like it." Alex swung a fist and caught the guy on the jaw. He staggered back.

"Hey!" A second guy came out of the shadows. His hair corn-rowed, his pants loose around his hips, he hulked over Alex. "What the fuck?"

"Get off her!" Alex grabbed the second guy's shirt to shove him out of the way. Alex was sober and in good shape, but the cornrowed man swung an arm across, slamming his shoulder.

"Please," came a high, weak voice from the corner. "Please, no, no. Help! Zia—" There came a slap and a grunt, cutting her off.

Alex pushed forward, moving the heavy man back toward a wall. He meant to slam his head. Then he would turn to the next one, the one on the girl.

"Bitch," that one was saying, "bitch bitch bitch. Take it now, you little retard, you can take it—"

The heavy man stumbled back. Alex shoved him hard. Just as he got the guy to the wall, his head sang with pain. A sudden, sharp explosion, at the back of his skull. Sparks flew, a ray of white light, a sword-stab of heat. Alex let go the cornrowed guy and wheeled around, just in time to see the first guy, the skinny guy, lift the brick again. Then he went down into darkness.

He opened his eyes to gray, the first light of morning. A damp mist. His head felt like a barrel of water, heavy and sloshing. Something sticky in his hair. He put his hand up and came away with a swipe of blood thick as jam. His arms and feet felt like ice. Slowly he pushed up on an elbow and peered around. One eye was swollen, the eyebrow pressing down on the lid, but he could see. He lay deep in an alley. In Scranton, yes. At the end, streetlights still shone dimly. A truck rumbled by. Alex pushed to his knees and vomited, a thin stinking gruel. Concussion, he thought. He touched his head. On the forehead, a tennis ball; at the back, a handball. As soon as he moved, blood seeped from the gash in his forehead. Slowly he stood. He'd been assaulted. He had to get out, back to the hotel, to his phone, to an emergency clinic, to the cops.

He had stumbled two steps when he heard the groan. With the low, lost sound, the night before flooded back. Quickly he stepped deeper into the alley, shoved aside the bags and boxes blocking his way. There she lay, the woman he'd tried to help. She was little more than a gray form, curled like a crescent moon against the concrete, a black plastic bag thrown over her hips and bare legs. Carefully he knelt by her side. "Miss?" he said. "Can you hear me? Miss?"

"Ungh," came the reply.

Alex strained to see in the scant light. He touched the woman's face. She flinched and turned away. "I'm not going to hurt you," he said.

He saw her swallow and lick her lips. "Ziadek," she rasped.

He had heard that word before—where? What language was she

speaking? "Miss," he said, leaning close, "I'm going for help. Stay quiet for just a minute. Okay? I'll be back. No one will hurt you now. Miss?"

She turned her face toward him then, and there was enough dawn light to see the features clearly. Her eyes were bruised shut, with a dark lump at one temple. Her bottom lip was split open. She stank of semen and spit. But there was no doubting the identity of the face. And in recognizing her, Alex remembered where he had heard the word she used. *Ziadek.* He had seen this woman's photo. This was the woman who had gone missing Saturday from Trails End Estates. This was the sister of Katarina, the daughter of Josef Zukowsky, whom they called Ziadek. This, Alex realized with a gasp of wonder at the twists of his life, was Najda's mother, Luisa.

Chapter 26

No matter how many times Ziadek waved her ahead, Katarina kept coming back for him, urging him along. "We'll get a wheelchair," she said, waving at a nurse.

"No," Ziadek said emphatically. "Go ahead. I know the room number. Go on, now."

Finally she hurried down the hospital corridor, her heels clacking. Ziadek hated the place. Even with oxygen filling his nostrils, he took in the ammonia, the bleach, the medicine smell. He would not end up here himself; he refused to. But at least Luisa was found.

He had first learned she was gone when he came home from Dr. Sanford. Katarina had given him the news in the driveway. He had felt so tired then, wrung out like a rag doll brought in from the rain, he could do nothing but allow Katarina to fix them all soup. Najda was uncharacteristically quiet. She had wheeled herself out to the neighborhood—to the park, he imagined, checking all their old haunts for her vanished mother—then returned to play solitaire and stare out the window as night fell. That first night, Saturday night, he had sat up by the phone. When he felt Katarina tuck the blanket around his shoulders, he had drifted into an uneasy, guilt-riddled sleep. Yesterday he had insisted that Katarina and Chet take him to Mass. He almost never went; he didn't know the new priest. But he bowed his head, the nibs of plastic from the oxygen digging into his nostrils, and he prayed for his girl. That afternoon the police officer came by again. He answered all the man's questions. But he left out the part about Brooke, and he noticed that Najda offered nothing— not that the policeman asked. He just kept looking at Najda funny, the way people did when they couldn't figure out how smart she was. He asked about Ziadek's chess set, and Ziadek showed him. Two thousand dollars missing, from the little drawer you pulled out at the bottom. He had squirreled it away, five and ten dollars at a time, for Najda's schooling.

Last night he had let the others tuck him into bed, but he had woken every hour or so and listened hard to the night. Nothing but the usual sounds, the refrigerator compressor, an owl, distant chatter of a television before an open window. He had pulled himself from bed and dragged his oxygen cart with him four times to the toilet, each time forcing out a thin, reluctant thread of urine. Finally he fell into a muddy sleep, broken by the sharp ring of the telephone. Katarina was already bustling around the house, sweeping out cobwebs and complaining to herself. She grabbed the receiver before Ziadek could pull himself upright. She shrieked with joy, then wept. "Yes, yes," she kept saying. "We're coming right away. Of course I have the insurance information. Just tell me she's all right. Can I talk—? All right then. Yes. Right now."

Katarina would not bring Najda. "You're an ungrateful girl," she said when Najda pulled herself out of bed and buzzed her wheelchair into the living room, her hair mussed and her face drawn tight with worry.

"Where is she?" Najda said, her words cut crisp as carrot slices.

"At the hospital, no thanks to you. Robbed and—and assaulted. Think about that, next time you drop a bombshell on your mother."

"Katarina," Ziadek warned. He had buttoned on a fresh shirt and swished his mouth with Listerine. He stood by the door. "No time for blame right now."

Katarina looked angrily at him. He knew what stuck in her craw—not Najda's treatment of Luisa, but her own boys' treatment of her, how they had gobbled up her love like a good meal and then flung themselves into the world without so much as a glance back at her. "I don't want her coming," she said.

"Najda will stay home for now," he said. So long as he could stand on his own, speak on his own, he held the authority of the house. He looked at the girl. "You keep the door locked," he said. "If you go out, you take your key."

Najda wheeled over to him. She placed her good hand on his wrist. "Sorry," she said. Her fingers stroked his skin, pleading forgiveness. Her eyes had filled with tears that he had not seen on her face since she was a little girl—tears not of anger or frustration, but of pity and sorrow. It was then that Katarina's words sank in. *Robbed. And assaulted.* Feebly he patted Najda's arm. Then they left and came here, to the hospital.

He reached the room, DH-422. Katarina had gone in already. Outside in the corridor waited a young black cop. Next to him sat a white man, also young, but with the lined face and stiff bearing of one much older. His head was swaddled in white bandages, and a purple bruise forced one eye closed. They rose—the injured man with stiff pain—as Ziadek approached. The cop shook his hand, introduced himself as Officer Simpson, said that Luisa had been examined by emergency staff and could he ask a few questions.

"I will see my daughter first," Ziadek said. He was surprised to find himself winded. He had walked slowly. But Dr. Sanford had given him bad news, not the least of which was that he should expect to feel increasingly fatigued. He nodded at the injured man. "This is not—" he began.

"Mr. Frazier found your daughter," the cop explained. "He says the same men who attacked her knocked him unconscious. He's not suspected of anything. We've asked him to stick around. The hospital people are doing some—ah—tests."

Tests, Ziadek thought. They meant sperm, they meant whatever had been forced onto his child while they held her down. He met Mr. Frazier's eye, the one that could open. Something felt familiar, though he had never seen the man before and his features were battered. He supposed he should thank him; without him, what would they have done? Killed Luisa? She lay a few feet away, in that room, hurt beyond repair. He was not in a mood to thank anyone. "Excuse me," he said, and stepped between the two of them, to where Luisa lay.

She would not look at him at first. The money, she mumbled into the white pillow, she'd taken all the money. Ziadek noticed the purple splotches on her neck, on the shoulder that peeked out from the flimsy gown they'd given her, on her temple that bulged out from her round head. Heavily he sat in the little chair they kept by the side of the bed. Across from Luisa, an old woman slept, with tubes going in and out of her. He would not be like that woman, Ziadek told himself. He would find another way.

"Luisa, honey, you've got to give some description of these bad guys," Katarina was saying. Her voice—for Katarina—was unusually gentle. "They did bad things to you, honey. It wasn't your fault. The police need to know—"

Ziadek touched Katarina's arm. When she turned, he shook his head at her. She crossed her arms and stepped away from the hospi-

tal bed, toward the window. Glad to find that his chair had wheels,
Ziadek drew it closer. He reached out a hand and stroked Luisa's
hair. It was still baby-fine, the same type of hair she'd had when she
was a laughing toddler. For the first time, he was glad Marika was
not alive, glad she did not have to see Luisa this way. This had been
her nightmare, that her hapless child would meet with violence. He
would keep Luisa safe, he had promised her. This was America but
they were still a family; they would stay close to one another, a net
of safety. Now Luisa had broken through the net. All the little
speeches Ziadek had run through his head as they tore down here
in Katarina's car seemed to go silent. "What do you want, Luisa?"
he asked. He could hear the quaver in his voice, an old man's voice.

Slowly Luisa turned her head on the pillow. She kept most of her
face mashed into it, but one almond eye opened and blinked at him.
"They took all the money," she said to the pillow.

"I know they did. They took something far more precious than
that. What do you want to happen?"

He was ready for her to say that Najda must not go away. It was
the only desire she had expressed, and to Luisa it must have seemed
a small demand. Ziadek did not know what he would say. He felt
powerless, like a little boy suddenly put in charge. But he felt it in
his gut that Luisa did not need to be told anything; she needed to
be asked. No one had asked her—not Najda, not Katarina or Chet,
not this Brooke who had brought more trouble, not Ziadek himself,
not the animals who had held her down and done such things to
her. No one had asked Luisa what she wanted.

"She doesn't love me," Luisa said. Normally such a statement
would set off a round of wailing accusations, but her tone was flat,
matter-of-fact.

"She isn't very good at showing it," Ziadek admitted. "And she
isn't very happy. Do you want her to be happy?"

"Course I do. I'm her mother."

"When our children are happy," Ziadek said, leaning forward, as if he were sharing a secret, "then nothing else matters. Does it?"

The one eye, blinking, looked suspicious. "I don't know."

"Not loneliness, or sickness, or needing money. That's why we have them. Isn't it? So they will be happy?"

"Ziadek." Luisa took his hand. She turned her head toward him, on the pillow. The skin around her right eye had gone puffy and purple. The temple bulged outward, pulling on her ear. He wanted to weep at the sight. "I'm scared."

"Of those thugs? They won't hurt you again, dumpling. The police will get them."

"Not them. I don't care about them. I'm scared for her."

He nodded. She was so hurt, so fragile, his innocent child; he couldn't argue with her. "That's the hardest thing we do, isn't it?" he heard himself say in his old man's voice. "Live with our fear?"

"I don't want to." She had separated Ziadek's fingers and was stroking them one by one, the way she had done as a child.

"Neither do I," he admitted. "We'll help each other then. We'll be scared for Najda together. It won't be so frightening then. Do you think?"

Behind him, a throat cleared. A young Jamaican nurse stood at the foot of the bed. She held a tray of instruments and salves. "I'm fine," Luisa said to her. "Go away."

"We got to check your vitals, honey," the nurse said. Her smile was warm but firm. "Got to heal you up good as we can."

Slowly, Ziadek rose. He patted Luisa's arm. "I'll be right outside," he said.

"Ziadek, don't go!"

He fought, in himself, the pleasure that came from her needing him. "Katarina can stay," he said. He nodded to the Jamaican nurse and stepped, with as much dignity as the oxygen tank would allow, from the room. "I am ready for you now," he said to Officer Simpson.

The cop asked him plenty of stupid questions. Did Luisa know anyone in Scranton? Did she have reason to know the young men she claimed to have assaulted her? Was she a competent witness? Was there anyone Mr. Zukowsky would suggest they question? Ziadek focused on the English. Sometimes he asked the cop to repeat the question. A beefy, caramel-skinned fellow with a freckled nose, Simpson took notes in a crabbed script on a small pad of lined paper. When he was done, the nurse had still not exited the room. Ziadek leaned back against the wall and shut his eyes. His oxygen had begun to taste medicinal; he supposed it was the hospital air. When the other man, the one who had found Luisa, moved to sit next to him, he felt the air move around him.

"Mr. Zukowsky," this fellow said. What was his name? Farris, Framingham, Frazier, Farmer. Frazier, that was it. "I am so sorry for what's happened to your daughter."

Ziadek cranked one eye open. He was supposed to thank this man, now. For finding Luisa, restoring her. "Luisa is very shy," he said.

"I can tell that, yes."

"She does not talk easily. But you are knowing for the hospital to call us. She tells you?"

"No, actually. She was too upset to talk much. They got the number from information."

"But you know my name? How?"

"Oh—yes. Well." Mr. Frazier reddened and picked at the cuticle of a nail. "I was at your house on Saturday, Mr. Zukowsky. And I saw Luisa's picture. Her photograph. So I recognized her."

Ziadek frowned. Saturday he had been to Dr. Sanford. He had come home to learn Luisa had fled. "You are doing what at my house, Mr. Frazier?"

Onto Frazier's face crept a boyish grin that Ziadek imagined could be charming in another circumstance. Right now it only deepened his suspicion. He glanced down the hall. The cop had stepped away, toward the window, where he was talking into his cell phone. The cop had said nothing about this man's knowing his family. "I didn't think it would be helpful to you," Frazier said, keeping his voice soft, "to tell the police. But I came by with Brooke. She wanted me to meet Luisa's daughter, Najda. I take it you've spoken with Brooke."

Ziadek sat up. His eyes widened. *This* was where he had seen the young man's features before. Not on him; he had never met him before. But on Najda. That grin, the top lip pulled flat across the gum. The broad set of the shoulders and the tapering jawline. He felt a click in his head, like a latch opening. Najda had not gotten those features from Brooke. She had gotten them from this man. From her father. The man Brooke had been speaking with when she left their house that first day. *You're right, Alex. We do have to talk.*

"I have spoken with her, yes," Ziadek said. "She will help us with your . . . with our . . . with Najda." He stumbled over the words, confused. "You have seen Najda," he said.

"I have, yes," said Frazier. His grin faded. "And I want you to know, Mr. Zukowsky—"

"Josef. Call me Josef. Please."

"I want you to know"—he looked directly at Ziadek, and in Frazier's one open blue eye Ziadek saw a thin veil of certainty stretched over a chasm of troubled thought—"I have no intention of interfering with your family. I hope you don't mind my saying. But it's clear that Brooke's interference is what set Luisa off. I am glad I found her, but—"

"Alex. It is Alex, yes?" The boy nodded. Ziadek thought of him as a boy, now—so sincere, so full of concern. "Alex, we know where

Najda comes from. We know this. Luisa, she knows this. It was a bad thing to do, what you did."

"Mr. Zukowsky—"

"Josef."

"Josef, I know Brooke feels guilty about something we—we did. A very long time ago. And yes, yes, I feel guilty also. You can't imagine to what extent. But the child we might have had—the child we had—that's not Najda. I know it isn't."

Now it was Ziadek's turn to smile. "You cannot know such a thing, Alex. This is my grandchild. I change her diapers. Every day I see her face. Now I see you, and I see her"—he pointed to his own eyes, his jaw, his flat cheekbones—"in you."

"You can't." That same jaw, Najda's stubborn jaw, set itself.

"Behind the motel. A wood crate. My Luisa, she shows me. I see in your eyes, Alex. You know this already."

He was shaking his head. "Young people make things up. A girl might say she'd found a child, because—"

"It was not from Luisa, this child!"

"No! No, I'm not saying that. But it's not the child we . . . we . . ." The boy pressed his lips together, as if he were holding something in; and then, as if they had found another exit, a clutch of tears leaked from his eyes. "I *killed* it," he whispered at last, through gritted teeth. "I—I squeezed its head." He held his hands out on his knees, and slowly brought the palms together. "And then it stopped moving. And then, yes, I got rid of the body. I'm much worse than what you thought, Mr. Zukowsky. I'm not some careless guy who left an infant in the rain. I am a murderer."

"It stopped moving," Ziadek repeated.

"Yes." The boy swallowed. All trace of grin was gone. His voice was barely audible. "Its eyes—his eyes," he went on, "snapped open, and stared. That's how I knew he was dead."

"It stopped breathing?"

"Well, she must have. He, I mean. Must have. The color of the skin wasn't right either." Alex sat back in his chair. For a moment he shut both his eyes. When he opened the uninjured one, he looked drained. "I don't want to talk about this anymore," he said. "Not with you. I was just trying to tell you, I feel bad for your daughter, I feel bad for your family, and I won't make it any worse. I came back, don't you see? Just to turn myself in. To be honest about what I did. It has poisoned my life. No point in its poisoning anyone else's."

"But you are not being honest." Ziadek could not help himself. He reached out and put a hand on the boy's arm, as if to stop him from running off. "Honest is 'I am not doctor.' Honest is 'I do not know.' Honest is 'Tell to me, Josef, about this baby, what it is wrapped in.' Do you want I should tell to you what it is wrapped in?"

Alex pinched the bridge of his nose between thumb and forefinger. "No," he said, a little louder.

"Alex." He kept his hand on the arm. He pressed it a little. "Is occasion of joy, no? My English not very good. But I think it is so. My child who I have thought lost is found. My child who I thought dead is alive. Right now"—he inclined his head toward the room where Luisa lay bruised and battered—"we are upset. We are angry. We grieve. But of Najda . . ."

He had run out of breath. He sat back in the chair. Alex pulled his arm away and splayed open his hand. "But I am the *cause* of it, don't you see that? How would you like to look at that girl and think to yourself, 'I did that'?"

For a moment, Ziadek simply breathed. When his pulse had quieted, he said firmly, "My Marika. My wife. She look at Luisa every day. She say, 'I did that.' Then she love her. What she is."

"But I can't do that." That got Ziadek's attention. Sitting up, he met Alex's eyes. Anguish, there. "I am a person," Alex said, "of bad faith."

"But you save my girl," Ziadek said. "You did *that*." He glanced at the white bandages swaddling the boy's head. He frowned. "They suspect you," he said.

"No, no." Alex waved off the question. "They took a swab, sure. Inside my cheek."

"For DNA," Ziadek said. He had heard about DNA and crime on the television. All the cop shows brought it up, one way or another.

"Right. Procedure, they said."

"I get another swab. Najda swab." He reached inside his own mouth with his finger; drew it out, glistening. "Then we know. You want to know?"

Behind him, the door opened. The Jamaican nurse came out. "You can go back in, Mr. Zukowsky," she said. "Would you like a wheelchair?"

"No, thank you," he said with as much dignity as he could manage. He used the wall to help push himself up, then turned back to Alex. "Thank you," he said. He nicked his chin toward the room where Luisa lay. "Thank you for my daughter."

Chapter 27

As the sky paled on Monday morning, Brooke was on the road. Tweedledee and Tweedledum cooed and complained from their cage on the backseat. Still no word from Alex, nor had she tried to contact him. Some day, she thought, they would have another glass of wine. They would talk about Alex's father, about her grandfather, about a past that stretched beyond their own little lives. Right now she had an appointment in Philadelphia, with Sean's cousin, Dominick O'Connor. No way could she go back to Windermere, back to that trailer park, back to Najda's family bearing only her love, her remorse, her yearning. She had to produce some solid piece of atonement; she had to help.

Brooke's mother had promised to find out about Luisa. She knew people in the social service agencies, down toward Scranton and west toward Erie. Even with cash, a provincial woman with Down syndrome could not go far. And Staccy Willcox was resourceful, Brooke gave her that. It was Stacey who had come up with Dom O'Connor's name. Wasn't there that cousin? she had asked, At your wedding?

Doesn't he practice in Philly? I've seen him listed, now and then, on commissions having to do with the schools. Can you go to him? she had asked Brooke, with a look that meant, *Can you tell him what you did?* And Brooke had nodded, yes. Alone among the O'Connor clan, Dominick was the one to whom she could open her heart.

On her way out of Windermere Brooke had bought the *Times-Tribune* and scanned the local headlines for any news of a missing person, or an accidental death. Nothing. She had Jake's card with her, if she wanted to call for news of Luisa from the police. But she had to leave that to her mother. When Luisa was found—then, their work would begin.

He'd be glad to see her, Dominick had said on the phone. He could cancel his lunch and take her to a little hole in the wall he liked. He had said nothing about Sean. From Windermere to Philadelphia was three and a half hours—no farther than from Hartford, where Dom would assume she had started driving.

Whenever she thought ill of Sean's family, Brooke made an exception for Dominick. He had a kind word for almost everyone except the pope and the Republicans in Pennsylvania. Just three years older than Sean, he encouraged him like an uncle. He was tone-deaf himself, but at family occasions he asked about Sean's choral group, and every Christmas he sent a new opera CD. What a politician, Sean's brothers would say when they heard. But Dom's family, according to Sean, had been poorer than Sean's, with Dom's father dead before he was ten and his autistic brother sent off to an institution where the boy withered slowly and died mostly of neglect. Dominick was fired up about social justice, about what government could do to make people's lives better. If he got obnoxious about it—challenging the priest, Brooke remembered, at little Derek's christening—he did so out of hope that a good argument could sometimes change a stubborn mind.

The restaurant was small indeed, but with votive candles and white tablecloths. In her jeans and unwashed hair, Brooke felt like a vagabond. Dominick tried ordering wine, but she shook her head. He was in his element. He squeezed the maitre d's shoulder and settled his weight in the red leather booth, his cuff links glinting from the sleeves of his tailored suit. Quickly Brooke moved past the automatic questions: Sean was fine, Meghan excited about school, Mum just the same, her own job on a little hiatus. Dom ordered food for both of them, sipped his own red wine, and focused his small, bright eyes on her.

Brooke drew courage from her mission itself, and also from the surprise of her mother's reaction. Don't underestimate the people who love you, Stacey had said as Brooke got into her car. Quickly Brooke had exited the driveway, to hide her tears. It was true, what she had said to Alex: She had hoarded her own guilt like a miser, not trusting her brittle but loyal mother to lift even an ounce of the load.

"I have a disabled daughter," she told Dominick now, "from my life before Sean. She is very bright. Her adoptive family is very poor. And my understanding is that the school system has served her badly."

If Dominick was shocked, he hid it well. He kept his eyes, two deep-set chips of blue, trained on Brooke while he lifted the wine again. "How old?" he asked.

"Fifteen."

Curtly he nodded. "You don't need to tell me. They have her in with the nonverbal kids, the kids in restraints, the Down's kids, the whole caboodle."

He drew a small spiral pad from his pocket. On it he took Josef Zukowsky's name and phone number; Brooke's best guess as to who had guardianship of Najda; the name of the school district; the school that Najda hoped to attend. He asked no questions beyond the practical ones. "Crosby," he repeated. "Excellent choice. My partner got funding there for the son of a client out in Allentown. Cerebral palsy, it was. Kid's at Cornell now."

Dominick explained the process. After they had obtained the medical history, they would set Najda up for a battery of tests, which they would then present to the school commissioner while drumming up an expert witness or two. If the school demurred, they would bring legal pressure to bear. These things, Dom assured Brooke, almost never went to court. If he cleared his docket, he could get the process moving within a month.

He signaled the waiter for a second glass of Cabernet. "I don't want this as a family favor," Brooke said as they finished the meal.

"You won't get it that way. I'll send you a bill."

"No, I mean really. My mother's offered to help pay legal fees. And I think—I'm not sure—but I think Najda's father will help as well. Her biological father I mean."

"I figured you meant that." Dom winked. He called for the check. Only then did a drop of his curiosity leak out. "Sean know about this?" he asked. "Because I am lousy at secrets."

"In four hours," Brooke said, "he'll know." She smiled at her cousin-in-law. He had made what she knew to be a difficult task sound like a stroll. "Anyone can know, if they want," she said. "My past may not be pretty, but I'm done with keeping it a secret."

"Attagirl," said Dominick.

Chapter 28

The dogs were milling around the front door, whining. Sean went to let them out. For a moment he stood in the doorway, watching the first yellow leaves of fall drift onto the front yard. His knee ached, where he'd fallen on it yesterday. He couldn't see Meghan, but he could hear the shrieks of the girls in Taisha's backyard. Two nights ago, Meghan had wet her bed. Last night, Sunday night, he'd let her climb into bed with him, where he hummed lullabies to her until she fell asleep, her thumb plugged into her mouth.

He was in no mood tonight to sing. Packing up his desk at Central Printing, he'd lifted the phone to call Geoffrey and beg off from choral rehearsal. Brooke had said she'd be back in Hartford by now and she wasn't—there, he had his excuse. But he knew what he'd do if he stayed home contemplating the shreds of his life. He would slip out to the package store. And so, his stomach clenched, he'd picked up Meghan, fed her an early dinner of bright orange macaroni, and taken her across the street, her knapsack packed with pajamas, toothbrush, and teddy bear, to Brenda, Taisha's mom, who'd agreed to keep Meghan overnight since rehearsal ran until ten. Don't you worry about a single thing, Brenda had said in her Virginia drawl. You just go ahead and sing your heart out.

His heart. It felt like a foreign object right now, floating around somewhere in his chest. This morning, after he'd checked the schedules and ordered a reprint of Hartt School brochures, Larry Dobson had called him upstairs and fired him. No, not fired. Laid him off. There wasn't enough work for two shifts anymore, that was the bottom line. And Larry couldn't let McMahon go; McMahon was his last hope. So he'd promoted his cousin Ernie from the night run to the day shift and gone after Sean. Every time Sean had replayed the scene, through the long bitter afternoon, he had cut loose with a chuckle. There he'd been, in the same spot he'd put so many guys in over the last six months. Declining to sit down while Larry gave him the news. Watching Larry's hand stray over the manila envelope with severance details. Wondering if he should've worked through those two personal days last week, if that would have made a difference. Debating whether to go graciously to the guillotine or kick the guy in the teeth. *That's what guys like me and you do*, he remembered Seymour saying. *Make things easier for the guys doing better than us.*

He wanted to trot across the street and give Meghan a squeeze, but they'd already said good night and she was happy now, not thinking about him. And his knee throbbed. Better not to mess with it. He filled his water bottle and let the dogs back in. Reluctantly, rolling west on Farmington, he put on the CD of the Evangelist again; he forced his vocal cords into service.

Christ, he thought as he parked by the church, he was tired. All he wanted was a way back. Back to where they'd been in August, when Gerry's kid was christened and Brooke was looking forward to new responsibilities at her job. If only he hadn't kept on her case about a second kid! But no. There was something behind that refusal of hers, there had always been something behind it. And even if his jealousy hadn't led him to the booze, even if he'd stayed late at work every day last week, Larry Dobson would still have laid him off. What the hell he was going to do now, he had no more idea than he had of Brooke's whereabouts. He was lost.

The first thing he noticed as he entered the rehearsal hall was the line to the folding table where the white-haired alto who kept the books was sitting. "What's this?" Sean asked a guy named Henley, at the back of the line.

"Paying the piper," Henley said with a mock grimace. "Dues today or—" He drew a line across his throat.

Christ. Sean had forgotten. A hundred fifty bucks the chorale charged. Peanuts, they all agreed, for the experience. Then they joked about forming a union. But what was Sean doing, tossing away dough? He'd just lost his job. His wife was probably looking to divorce him. He might have to take some graveyard shift somewhere, drive a truck, Christ knew what, and then he'd miss rehearsals and be out of the performance.

Thinks he can sing, Mum always said. *Thinks he can afford to idle his time away la-la-la'ing like some retired banker.* He smiled wanly at the thought of his mother's barbs. He'd seen Mum yesterday, at Gerry's new house in the South End, where he'd taken Meghan to play with her baby cousin Derek. Mum and Kate had stayed inside to clean up the Sunday lunch dishes while the brothers sat reading the Sunday paper on the patio, Gerry with a beer and Sean with iced tea. The day had been warm but damp—a storm had blown through the night before, the tail end of a hurricane down south, and fallen branches lay like pick-up sticks below the big maple at the back of the tiny yard. He'd been telling Gerry about the Evangelist when Mum's voice had come through the screen door. "It's the la-la-la!"

she'd said, like always. You figured her for deaf until something came up she didn't like to hear. "Wants the attention!"

That was when Meghan had started climbing the tree, he remembered now. She'd come out from the house, saying that Baby Derry was down for his nap, and she'd scaled the wood fence at the back of the yard to hoist herself onto the lowest branch of the maple tree. He'd told her to be careful. Gerry had asked where Brooke was, why he was getting stuck with the kid even on his weekends. It was to avoid that question that Sean had gone inside, claiming he needed to take a whiz, could Gerry keep an eye on Meghan. The women had finished in the kitchen by then. The afternoon sun was shining on the lemon tree in its huge pot by the bay window, the tree Brooke had chosen for Gerry and Kate, eight years ago. Two fat lemons weighed down its branches. As he took in the sight of the tree—still bearing fruit, he thought, like everyone but him—his mother stepped into the kitchen and headed straight for the cupboard where Gerry kept his whiskey. "Can I get you something, Mum?" Sean had asked.

"You can get me a new life," she said, pouring. "She won't even let me hold my grandchild." Mum's eyes signaled the living room. "'Fraid I'll drop him." She gave a harsh chuckle. Ice cubes plinked into her glass—one, two, three. "Only dropped one, and that was you. Scrambled your brains, I think."

"Knocked 'em right out of my head."

Mum turned to face him. Hers had been a small, pretty face in old photographs. Not sixty yet, her features seemed to draw in toward themselves, like a drying apple. Her chin was reduced to a tiny knob. "Your father used to sing," she said unexpectedly.

"Nonsense. Dad yelled and groaned."

"Before you were born. Used to get paid for it, down in Brooklyn. Weddings, funerals. Sang at my sister's wedding. That's where we met."

"You never told me that, Mum."

She sipped her whiskey. Tears sprang to her soft eyes. "He tried, you know. With the music."

"What d'you mean, tried?

"La-la-la for money. You know."

"He sang professionally?" Sean felt his senses quicken, down to the hairs on his arms. "No one ever told us this. He always worked at the tool and die."

"When I had Fanny," Mum said, "I put my foot down. I said, 'It's lovely sounding, Derek, but it won't feed a brood.' He stopped, then and there. Said he'd never sing a note again." When she slugged the whiskey, she looked ready to bite the glass, just to keep the tears from coming. She set it down on the counter and glared at Sean, as if the story she was telling had been his fault.

"And he never did," Sean said.

"No. And he was never a happy man again. Not till he was brought to his rest."

Not, Sean thought as his mother topped off her glass and left the room, until he drank himself to death. Stunned, he started back out to the patio. From the back of the yard he heard Meghan's voice, calling to him, "Look at me, look at me, Daddy!"

"Where the hell is she?" he'd asked Gerry.

Gerry looked up from the paper. That was when Sean had seen the branch sway in the maple. Had seen Meghan's pink sneaker between the leaves, reaching from one wet limb to the next. Had moved his legs, dreamlike, across the expanse of muddy grass. Had seen one sneaker lift off the branch. Then the branch on which she balanced had cracked with a sound like tearing paper, and like a wide receiver going for the football, arms out, Sean had lunged. He'd caught his daughter's flailing body, all knees and elbows, and they had both rolled through the leaves and mud. His knee—he took the weight off it now, as he stood in the line at the chorale—had twisted under him. Be a couple weeks healing at best. But his daughter, bathed in mud, had suffered no more than a scare.

La-la-la, he thought now. But only if you can afford it. Yesterday he'd had a job to complain about with his brother. Today he was a man adrift. He stood frozen to his spot on the wood floor while other chorale members passed around him and took their place in the line.

"Sean. Hey, Sean," he heard finally, as if everything in the room had gone silent for a moment while Sean's thoughts roared.

He turned. "Geoffrey," he said.

The chorale director cocked his head at him, as if Sean were an interesting zoo animal. "Better stage presence without the whiskers, I think," he said. "You ready to help us with the first movement tonight?"

"I don't know, Geoffrey." Sean's eyes skittered around the room. Thad, the accompanist, was running lightly through the fugue. Suzanne was inclining her head toward the alto next to her—Betty? Bridie? They'd sat together as long as Sean could remember, and long ago when he dated Suzanne he used to glance over and Bridie would nod her head approvingly at him. They had not spoken since that time. "I've—ah—had some stuff going on recently."

"We can use piano cues for tonight. No sweat."

"No, I've got the part down. It's not that."

"Good. Let's talk at the break, then. Hey, you're not in this line, are you?"

"Well"—Sean gestured at the row of good-hearted volunteer singers now snaking around by the windows, waiting to pay—"that's just the thing—"

"Because I thought I told you. Didn't I tell you? You don't pay dues as a rehearsal soloist. In fact I think we've cooked up an embarrassing honorarium, I don't know, five hundred bucks maybe. So should I call on your voice tonight, or—?"

Sean let out his breath. "Well, I don't know, Geoffrey, I'm not sure . . ." he began. Then, as if Geoffrey had sent a delayed broadcast, he heard what had been said. No dues. Five hundred dollars. Which meant nothing, of course it meant nothing, he was a man without a job, without his wife. Still. He began to return Geoffrey's genial, questioning smile, and tears rushed into his eyes. "I can sing," he said quickly, turning his head away. "Better find my seat."

In most ways the music worked its usual magic, rearranged Sean's molecules the way it always did so that by the break he was knit together as a person again, even if he was a person with troubles heavier than he would be able to bear. But there was more. When he stood as the Evangelist and began the legato line, *Und da die Engel von ihnen gen Himmel*—and as the angels were gone into heaven—his voice at first felt shaky and thin, as if the tears he had managed not to shed had watered it down. But then the tenors came in, and the basses, all going to Bethlehem, and he felt himself borne aloft. When he sat again, the rest of the chorale burst into a round of applause, but it wasn't the clapping that touched him. Rather he felt the urgency of it, the way he had thus far only understood the man who reaches for the next bottle, as if a voice inside were chanting, *Do this again, do this again, you have to do this again.*

When rehearsal ended most singers dashed from the hall, but a few lingered—the dutiful, the lonely, the gregarious. Stacking the chairs, Sean stopped to rub his knee above the joint. A bruise or tendon pull maybe, nothing bad. Meghan would have broken a bone at least. And Gerry, father of four, sitting there with the sports section. What a kinky way life had of doling out gifts.

With the room in order, he sat at the piano with Henley and another tenor, a retired podiatrist named Dick Peltier, and they plucked out the tricky passage in the fugue. If they could hear it in their heads, Sean explained to the two men, as *bi-de-bi-de-bum* even as they ran the arpeggios on a sustained *ah*, they could get more articulation. Dick still ran flat when they tried it again, but the pace was better. As Sean shut the piano and prepared to leave, Geoffrey came over from the last cluster of choristers gathered at the door. He nodded at Dick's square frame exiting. "You ought to collect a fee," he said.

"He's fine," said Sean. "Tendency to scoop the note, but that's most of us."

"You get what you pay for. Mostly. Sometimes you luck out." He clapped Sean on the shoulder. "You sounded great tonight," he said. "Intonation, pitch, everything. I'd put you before an audience if I could."

Sean shrugged. He could feel the snug knit of the music already loosing, letting in the sorrow of his life like a cold draft. "I'm glad it helped the group," he said.

"You know, I really don't get it." Geoffrey folded his music stand and set it in the corner. He turned to face Sean, hands on his heavy hips. "You're a printer, right?"

"Was." Sean plucked his jacket from the back of a chair. "Until this morning."

"What, man? You lost your job?" Geoffrey frowned, came close. Sean liked the guy. He was a great musician, and he wasn't a prig like others Sean had seen. But he'd stuck to the narrow path—music lessons, music school, teaching at a conservatory, music director at a church, the chorale—and didn't know much about how the rest of them grubbed their way through the world. "What'll you do now?"

"Too soon to tell." Sean rubbed the back of his neck. What was he supposed to say? He'd thought about drinking himself to death but changed his mind? "Printers are hard hit. You've got desktop publishing, these young guys designing websites. I'm thirty-seven. I'm an old man."

Geoffrey gave a bass snort. "You've got to be kidding me. You're just ripe for a career change. You ever think of going back to school?"

"I've got a family to support, Geoffrey." Even as he said it, Brooke's yawning absence wanted to swallow him up. "I'll figure something out."

"Sean, I don't know if you're dense or just stubborn." Geoffrey drew close. His eyes, small and bright blue, narrowed at Sean. "I've been trying to tell you for months. Years, maybe. You have a gift, man. Now, you may like the smell of printing ink—"

"It was a job, okay? It paid twice a month. I had a good eye for graphics."

"All right, all right. I'm not knocking the paycheck. I'm sorry they cut it. I'm just saying. Carpe diem."

Sean pursed his lips. He was tired. He was grieving. He wanted a drink. The Evangelist had floated away, on his angel wings or whatever transport he used. "I only speak the Latin they put to music, Maestro," he said.

Geoffrey put his hand on Sean's elbow. "Seize the day. Maybe not to be an opera singer, but Christ. You could teach. You like teaching?"

"Teaching's a gas," Sean said, which was the truth.

"Well, you could do that. You could perform locally, you could make this work. Not many people can say that."

"I've got to go."

But Geoffrey didn't release him. "Let's talk more about this, okay?" he said. "You've got some severance?"

"Six weeks."

"Let me get to work on some stuff. Okay? Will you let me do that?"

"I don't think so, Geoffrey. I don't even know if the chorale—"

"Oh, no. No no. We're not talking about that. You are not quitting this group."

"Man, please." Sean loosed his arm, held up his palm. "Not that I don't appreciate."

"All right." Geoff nodded. "Don't mean to push. Just—talk to me next week. Okay?"

"Sure," Sean said, and they shook hands, as if they had some kind of deal. He headed out into the windy night. Geoffrey was a kind guy, he thought, but things had gone easy for him. He didn't understand how things could go hard. At the sidewalk he stood for a moment, feeling the events of the day like clothing he would somehow, eventually, have to fit to his body. He had lost his job. His daughter slept safely across the street from their house. He had sung the Evangelist. He had lost his wife. He needed a drink. Just one. A whiskey, dry and burning.

A car drew up, the passenger window rolled down. "Hey, stranger," came a soft voice. Sean leaned into the open window. It was Suzanne. Her pocketbook, brimming with knitting, sat on the passenger seat; two booster seats filled the back.

"What're you hanging around for?"

"Wanted to congratulate you."

"Well, thanks, but—"

"And to ask why, whenever the tenors aren't singing, you look like you just got handed a death warrant."

Ruefully he smiled. "Is it so obvious?"

"Only to someone with eyes. Can I take you for a drink? Celebrate your solo? Drown your sorrows?"

He dipped his head into the private space of the car. It smelled of spilled milk and the chemical pine scent of the cutout dangling from the mirror. In the yellow light of the streetlamp, Suzanne's features welcomed scrutiny; her smile dimpled a shadow, and her flattish bone structure offered no threat. He nodded toward the back. "Aren't your kids expecting you?"

"I keep the sitter till eleven thirty, in case we run late."

An hour, Sean thought. What would it hurt? And this sweet woman, who had never resented him for raising her hopes, who had plugged along and brought good into the world, would listen to his troubles. She was not the sort to tell him what he ought to have done. She had a disposition to promote his good, or someone's good anyway. His hand moved to the door handle. Then he remembered. "Thanks," he said, "but I'm keeping to Diet Coke, these days."

"Then drown the sorrows in Diet Coke." She picked the pocketbook off the passenger seat and tossed it into the back, into one of the booster seats. "You look like you could use a friend."

Sean did not want a Diet Coke. As he stood leaning into the car, he realized what—besides his wife back, his job back, his life back—he wanted. He wanted a desirous body, an eager and pliant body, to hold him tight and let him pound his frustration into her pillowed warmth. If he let Suzanne's body be that body . . . it would not stop there. In her patient smile he saw her old need, lying dormant. "Just knowing I've got a friend," he said, making himself smile at her, "does me a world of good."

"You sure?"

"Yeah. I've got to get home. Got my little girl," he lied.

"Give you a rain check," Suzanne said.

"'Preciate," he said. Lightly he slapped the door frame, releasing her. He stood back before temptation got hold of him. "See you next week," he said. But she was already rolling up the window.

He regretted it almost as soon as Suzanne's red taillights disappeared around the corner. Hadn't Brooke probably left him, left Meghan, for this guy Alex?

No. Alex didn't know where Brooke was. She had left because he had gotten drunk and abusive.

Then why would she leave Meghan with him?

She had left because she didn't want him, or his child, because he wasn't good enough for her and never had been.

She had left, that was all that mattered. And now he'd had the chance for a bit of comfort, and he had let it drive off.

Starting up his own car, he ejected the Bach Oratorio CD and put in *La Traviata*. He cranked it up to top volume, that tale of love and betrayal, and let the voices wash over him as he drove. Tomorrow he would register for unemployment, stop at a couple of temp agencies, push forward. Tonight he invited sorrow to drown him. When he reached the left turn off Farmington, he was tempted to keep straight, toward the Half Door. But the chorus kicked in and he turned left, and left again into his driveway. And there sat her Subaru, patient as any beast of burden. Inside the house, a warm light in the kitchen. Brooke was home.

Chapter 29

Najda

In years to come, I'll remember my mom's disappearance as the day I began to understand the world. Or as the day I understood I had a family (which amounts to the same thing) because I almost lost them. How many times did Luisa bring me to the library, only to sit patiently while I ignored her, while I took not even five minutes to share with her all the things I was learning? It wouldn't have been hard. Luisa's happy to capture a word or phrase—like *differential equations*, or like that quote from Gödel, "A brain is a computing machine connected to a spirit"—to repeat when she wants to tell people what I'm learning. But before last Saturday, I despised my mom for being slow, for being as stupid as people think I am. So I punished her; I treated her to silence. When I decided I had to find another school, a real school, I never turned to Luisa. I didn't care if she was proud of me or not. I reached past her to Ziadek. And so my mom ran away, straight into disaster.

Katarina won't let me come to the hospital where they've taken Luisa. She'll claim there wasn't time, with the wheelchair and all.

But that's not true. Katarina's furious with me. I deserve it, too. She's gruff but I love her, my aunt Katarina. For years, while Ziadek was working, she stayed home with me and Luisa. She carried us all on her strong back. Now because of me, this awful thing has happened to her baby sister, to my mom.

When they've gone, I stay in the house and weep. Maybe I should wheel out to the short bus and go to school, just to be a good girl for a change, but I can't. One after the other I snap tissues from the box in the kitchen to sop up the tears. My mom isn't dead. There is that, Katarina's said, to be thankful for. But Luisa's been beat up—and raped. That much I know, even though no one's told me. The way she was left in that alley, she has to have been raped. Raping Luisa is like plucking feathers from an angel's wings. That's what I think. Because whatever insults I've hurled at her, I know my mom is the soul of goodness.

I've just started to think about having sex. No one will ever want me, of course. Still, I lie awake imagining myself naked with a beautiful boy. I imagine his touch. It's gentle and hungry. His touch brings me to life in every part, even those parts that normally pay no attention to what I want. Sometimes my hand delves between my legs, and it feels so good, touching there and thinking about that boy. But that's not what's happened with my mom. What she got in Scranton was like a fist in the face. And if we go back further, to when she found me, when she made me her daughter? *That* had nothing to do with beautiful sex. Someone else had the pleasure, and Luisa took on the duties.

When my tears let up, it's not because I feel any better, but only because I've run dry. I drink a tall glass of water. I get myself to the bathroom, where I make a point of not looking in the mirror. If I did, I'd spit at my reflection. Then I wheel outside. I'll wait for them. I'll watch for them, and when they bring my mom home I will slip from my wheelchair and go down on my knees. I will beg Luisa's forgiveness. And I will promise—yes, I will, everyone else has made sacrifices and now it's my turn—to give up on another school. Starting tomorrow, I'll get on the goddamn short bus and go to the special classes. I can stand it, and Luisa can't stand the alternative.

Hours pass. I wheel over to Katarina's empty house and back. I listen for the phone. I go inside and fix lunch; I turn on the TV, but it's all stupid. No point now in reading the books I brought from the library, or looking at the school brochures. I recite to myself the longest poems I know, "Song of Sherwood" and "The Children's Hour." When I get to the part about the round-tower of Longfellow's heart, the eye faucets turn on again. *And there shall I keep you forever, yes, forever and a day, / Till the walls shall crumble to ruin, and molder in dust away!* It makes no sense—he's talking about keeping his children dear to him, nothing wrong with that—but I can't help feeling myself kept in the tower, and my mom moldering to dust.

At three o'clock, I try Katarina's cell phone. No answer. I'd like to howl. She's probably seen the incoming number and refuses to pick up for a spoiled brat like me. I wheel down the ramp again, and then out toward the Quik Mart and the highway.

There, across the busy intersection, sits the paintball place that used to be a motel. Not just any motel, either. The motel where I was born. How old was I when Luisa was allowed to tell me the story? "Like Moses," Luisa used to say, "in the basket." I must have been eight or nine, because Katarina had had a spurt of making Jude and Robby attend Mass, with Luisa and me tagging along. That's where we heard the Moses story. How Moses' slave mother couldn't care for him and sent him floating down the river in a basket, and Pharaoh's daughter found him and named him as her own. I was supposed to think of my birth mother as a good woman too poor to keep me but clever enough to know that Luisa would take the best care of me.

At the traffic light I press Walk. I know the truth, now. Brooke is not a poor woman, a desperate slave. She's a rich-looking lady with my nose and eyes. And she doesn't seem happy with what she did. Maybe she meant to snatch me back, out of the rain and back into the motel, only Luisa was too quick and took me.

No. It wasn't Luisa's fault. She was born the way she is, just like me.

The light changes. Cars screech to a halt. They aren't used to stopping here. As I roll into the front lot of the paintball place, a group of boys come stumbling out. A blast of warm air follows. It stinks. *Awesome*, the boys are saying, *sick, wicked, you dweeb, you moron, get me Jack Bauer.* One of them spots me.

"*Here's* what we needed in there," he says. His gang stops to stare at me. He looks used to commanding them. "A decoy!"

"She here for wheelchair paintball?" says one of the other boys. He punches a third one in the side.

"Ahh, duh, ah hit mahself!" says the last one, a small kid with a big nose and a bruise on his temple. He mimes pointing a gun backward and firing at his own face. Before they can all collapse into giggles, I turn my wheelchair, speed it up, and knock him down.

"Fuck yourselves, assholes," I say. The swear words always come out like this, without a stammer. I wheel around again and continue past the entrance to the place. I don't look back. I've learned that if you strike swiftly and continue, the small spiteful people get so shocked that they don't pursue. My mom has never learned this. If I had been with her, last night, I'd have fended off those men—no matter how big, no matter how evil.

Keep moving, I tell myself, and I do.

The back lot of the paintball place stands empty. Weeds push through the cracks in the asphalt. From inside come a few thwacks, but it's five o'clock on a weekday, and business is winding down. I hear a woman's voice and the slamming of several car doors—one of the boys' mothers, picking them up.

I sit there a long time. A breeze blows through the dead grass of the next lot over. Traffic whines on the highway. Inside this place, fifteen years ago, a girl not much older than me thought she lost a child. Not that she wanted a child—I swallow, hard, around the lump in my throat—but if the baby that came out of her had cried, or kicked, or smiled, she would have taken it to her breast. She would have said, "You're mine, all mine. And your name is . . ." What name? Not Najda. There would have been no Najda. There would have been someone else. The body itself would be different, strong and not lopsided, and her words would come out every time the way they're meant to.

Instead, the baby that was not yet me lay there, limp. So the mother said, "I can't look at her." She cut the cord and took the baby to the back lot and left it. And all the while—as she took the stairs down, as she pushed open the back door, as she found the crate and another crate to protect the baby from the rain (and why protect her from the rain?)—the baby's brain cells were winking out, one by one, like stars. That's what happened. It is up to me to accept it. And to ask forgiveness of my mom.

Tires crunch behind me. I wheel around. On my tongue sit the swear words, to make the boys go away. Almost dark now. A red Prius pulls up next to the paintball, by the Dumpster. A man gets out. He seems not to see me. But when he turns slightly, pulling up the collar of his jacket in the cold breeze, I draw in my breath so loud that he startles. On Saturday, I realize, I saw this same man. He was with Brooke when she came by the house, just after Luisa disappeared. He walked away from all the arguing, and Brooke followed—because she cared more about him than about me. Now he's got a big white bandage wrapped around his head.

"You," I say.

The man jumps as if stung. As he turns to me in the waning light, the color drains from his face. "What are you doing here?" he asks.

I'm not going to be able to make the words come out in the right order. It's too unexpected, seeing this man in this place. I know at once and without any doubt who he is. How did it escape me before? Well, I wasn't thinking about it. About having a father. And then my mom ran off, and I was thinking about her.

So this is the man whose seed got into the girl's body. His blood runs through my veins. "I am looking," I try to say, though it comes out garbled, "for you."

By the way he smiles I knew he's understood me. From the glint in his bruised eyes I think maybe he'll run again, the way he did from our house. But his shoulders only rise and fall in a deep sigh. Stepping over to my spot near the back door of the arcade, he stops to drag an empty paint barrel with him. On this he sits, facing me. A dim light over the back door has come on, so I can see his face. He searches mine for a long time. "My name's Alex," he says at last.

"I know," I say. That was the name she used on her cell phone, last week. Alex. We don't say anything for a long time. He didn't expect to find me here. He didn't plan to lay eyes on me again. It's awkward. Too bad.

"You know who I am," he says at last.

I nod.

"I left you"—he looks around, at the rusted cans, broken bottles, the weedy field—"here. When you were just born."

I nod again. The picture in my head starts to change. Not just a girl giving birth. A girl and a boy. Someone to cut the cord. This boy.

He looks away. He yanks up a weed. He talks as if to himself. He says, "I thought you weren't alive. I swear to almighty God, that's what I thought."

Again I nod. What is there to say, to ask? What if you had murdered me? Would you know it, in your deepest heart? How deep is your heart?

"I used to dare myself," he says, "to come back here. See if you were still here." He swallows hard. "Plenty of nightmares brought me here. That's for sure." He studies his fingernails. "No one was at your trailer," he says when he looks up, "so I came over. An idle thought, you know. And here you are. Christ. All along, you've been right where I left you."

"Almost," I say.

Mostly I hate him. He's like one of those teenaged boys who just quit this place. Careless, cruel. But part of me, not hating him, feels surprise. Not at him, but at myself. All these years I've thought about my real mother, dreamed of her, called for her. I've never thought about my dad. Maybe because I've only had Luisa. But also because when I've thought about what must have happened, it's only made sense to me with a woman giving birth alone. I'd have guessed that the guy who knocked her up never even knew she was pregnant. But now that Brooke's sat in our living room and told her story, I realize that makes no sense, her being alone. If she really thought her baby wasn't alive, she never could have taken me outside in time for Luisa to find me. There must have been someone else.

"You," I manage to get out, and I indicate the wheelchair, my right arm, "This. To me."

"I did that to you, yeah." He presses his lips together and looks at the ground. His upper lip's split and swollen on one side. From under the white bandage, you can make out a purple lump. Somebody got him, and good. His left hand hangs limp from where he rests his arms on his knees. He isn't wearing a wedding band. "I didn't know you." *I don't want to know you*, I feel him thinking, as if I can read his mind. "I didn't understand what I was doing. But I was going to confess it, you know?" He holds his hands in front of him, empty. "I don't know how to confess this," he says.

"Don't," I say.

"Well." He gives an acerbic chuckle. "I didn't commit murder." *Maybe it would've been better if I had.*

So this is it. This is having a father. I've never known I wanted one, and now, just as I feel longing bloom inside me, I hear a siren whine down the highway. I think of my mom again, of Luisa. And the father crouched in front of me seems like an accident, like one of those footnotes in a book that you can skip and still get all the main ideas. I struggle to get a word out. Finally it comes. "What," I say, "do you want?"

He looks startled. "Nothing," he says. "What do *you* want?"

The words jam up in my throat. We stare at each other. I see my eyebrows. My jaw. Clearing his throat, he reaches into his pants pocket and pulls out a little box, like for a ring. He opens the top. "I was going to leave this here, but . . . ," he says. He shuts it, hands it to me. I open it with my good hand. Inside curls a tiny lock of dark hair.

"Not mine," I say. I lift my own wheat-color hank to show him.

"Babies are born with dark hair," he says calmly. He looks right at me. "Then it changes."

I could keep this thing. I could look at it and think of this guy, my father, of how he must have cut a bit of me away before he left me to die. I could do that, and get so mad that everything else stops dead. Or I could give it back.

He hasn't said he wants to be a father to me, or even to see me or hear my story or understand me. Well, okay. At the same time, forgiveness is not what I want to give him. I snap the box shut. I hold it out, pinched between thumb and forefinger. Finally he takes the thing and puts it in his pocket.

He stands up. In the dense twilight he paces up and down the back lot of what used to be a motel. He cups his sharp chin in his hands the way Katarina says I do. I wonder how he got hurt, but then I don't care. I guess he's a handsome man—a lot handsomer, anyway, than Chet or Ziadek. There are handsome boys at the high school but they look right through me. When my real mother was my age, she had this cute boyfriend, because she wasn't in a wheelchair, she wasn't spastic and dyslexic like me. He stops pacing and comes back to me. He pushes his bandage back where it's hunched over his eyes. He takes my right hand in his and turns it one way and the other, like a fortune teller. "I'm not staying," he says. "I'd just make things worse."

"Damn straight," I say. It comes right out.

"But maybe I can—I don't know." He holds my hand. He's got an idea. "You can't be looking out for your mom forever. For Luisa, I mean," he says, though I knew what he meant.

"Why not?" I say.

His eyebrows rise. "You've got your own life," he says. "College."

The tears have me again now. I can feel the words in my head all breaking up. There's no point trying to say anything.

"I've got some money," Alex says. "I'll talk to your grandfather. To Ziadek. Okay? Is this okay? We'll set up a fund. A trust. For Luisa. So she's always got someone to help her."

"Ziadek—" I start to say, and I want to tell him I think Ziadek's going to die, but the words are in pieces.

"Ziadek doesn't have to worry. And your sister—your aunt, I mean—"

"Katarina."

"Katarina, right. She doesn't have to quit her job. You can go to a school that—that can help you." He doesn't know how to say it, a school for crips, gimps, whatever I am, but he's glowing now. He has a plan.

But I shake my head. I try to say I don't care about school any-more, but I think it comes out something like "School give up" or maybe even "Gool skiv up." Either way it gets across because he takes the hand he's been turning over and laces his big fingers in between my thin ones.

"You are not giving up," he says, looking into my eyes. That's all I can make out of his features now, the light shining off his swollen eyes under the bandage. "You've got your mom's stubborn streak. That's how I finally recognized you, you know. Not the nose." He touches mine with the index finger of his free hand. "The pighead-edness."

At this I manage to smile. It's not the first time someone's called me pigheaded.

Alex wants to drive me back across the highway, and I let him. He's awkward helping me into his car, and he doesn't believe me when I tell him I can get the seat belt okay. Banging around with the wheelchair, he gets it folded and into the trunk. As we drive through Trails End, I panic, thinking everyone will be home and angry with me for being gone. But Katarina's car is still not there, and only the outdoor light's lit on our house. Alex parks. He says something else about Luisa. Later I'll learn he was the one who found her, in the alley in Scranton. I'll learn that's how he got beat up.

"Phone," I finally manage to say as he follows my gaze to the house. I haven't heard it ring, but it might. He gets my drift and goes to pull the chair from the trunk. When he opens the door on the passenger side, he crouches to look straight at me.

"I don't live all that far away," he says, taking my hand again. "I don't know what Brooke's going to do. But if you need me—I mean me, not just my money—all you have to do is holler." Reaching into his back pocket, he pulls out his wallet and from it takes a business card. This he tucks into my shirt pocket. As he does so, I see a tear gather in the well of his eye and drop over the lower lid. "Forgive me," he says, his voice cracking.

As I swing my legs free of the car, he puts his strong hands under my arms and hoists me up. His arms go around my back. Lifting me off the ground, he hugs me. I smell his salty skin, his man-odor, some kind of medical cream. We breathe together. I cling to his neck. I don't want him to let me go. But he does, finally, settling me into my chair. I tell him I'll make it up the walk myself. But once I'm at the front door, I turn and he's still standing there. We both stay like that a long time. When he gets into his car and drives away, I feel the way a mountain must feel when an avalanche shears off from its side and the sound slowly dies into silence.

Chapter 30

In the early light Brooke left him sleeping—the deepest Sean had slept since they had married. She uncovered the birds that Sean had put to bed last night. She fed the cats, who gave in and purred madly, rubbing against her legs. She walked the dogs to the park. The air was warmer than in Windermere, the leaves still golden on the trees. Later she would visit Lorenzo in the hospital and bring him an autumn bouquet, orange cannas and Chinese bellflower. Only as she turned back from the park did she dare to check her cell phone. Besides the six missed calls, there was one text message. *Luisa found. Call me. Lex.* The news was a relief, though puzzling that Alex should know, or care. He had denied any relationship with Najda or the Zukowskys. She returned the phone to her pocket. She pulled the dogs with her away from their usual track, across the street, where she rang the bell.

"Mommy!" Meghan cried out. Brooke could just see her from the short hallway, through the high-ceilinged dining room into the kitchen, where she sat at a round table with Taisha, both of them digging into Cheerios. Meghan dropped her spoon, slid down from her chair, and raced to Brooke, who lifted her for a hug. "Mommy Mommy Mommy," Meghan said, patting Brooke's cheeks. Her hands were slightly sticky; her breath smelled of milk and sugar. From outside the screen door, the dogs whined. Meghan frowned. "Don't you ever do that again," she said.

"Go away, you mean?"

"Not ever. I hated you, Mommy."

"But I'm back now."

Meghan dropped her head onto Brooke's shoulder. From the doorway to the kitchen, Brenda watched with a skeptical smile on her face, Taisha wound around her knees. "It was a family emergency," Brooke said to her. "Thank you so much."

"I hope everyone's all right."

"We'll be fine. Thanks to you, too, Taisha."

"Is Meghan coming to school with me?"

Against her shoulder, Brooke felt Meghan shake her head. "I think we'll take her today, honey. But thanks."

"You can tell Sean," Brenda said as she handed Brooke Meghan's overnight bag, "she was dry all night."

Back home, Brooke crouched in the kitchen, holding her daughter's hands. "Were you having accidents?" she said.

"Nuh-uh." Meghan swayed, avoiding her gaze. "Not very much." She looked toward the stairs. "Did Daddy go away?"

"No, sweetheart. He's just sleeping."

"Sleeping? Is he sick?"

Brooke couldn't stop smiling—at her daughter's freckles, her pudgy hands, the way she pushed Mocha away with her hip. Bedwetting, she thought. She would have to pay attention. "Course not," she said. "He's just tired."

"Show him to me," Meghan said. Determined, she pulled Brooke out of the room, up the stairs. Quietly they pushed open the door of the master bedroom. For a moment Brooke imagined, like Meghan, that the room would be empty, another parent decamped. But Sean lay on his side, his head in the crook of his arm, his mouth slack, his chin pale where he'd taken off the goatee, his chest rising and falling in the steady breath of sleep. Even as she pulled Meghan from the room, Brooke felt the imprint of Sean's body on her heart.

Last night, he had come home just as she was hanging the birds from their usual hook in the kitchen, where they twittered their confusion. The dogs had milled around then like water in a vortex, anxiously seeking a safe depth. Sean had moved into their stream and wrapped his firm arms around her. His goatee was gone, leaving his face artless and vulnerable. His kiss had left her dizzy. She had expected recriminations. Instead his hands pressed against her back, her buttocks—later, as they sat on the couch, her arms, her thighs, the lobe of her ear. One after the other, he touched places that Alex had touched, only three days ago. The first caresses forgave whatever it was she had done. The later ones stirred up the desires that had gotten knotted up with Alex and let them unfurl. They had spoken remarkably little. I've been fired, he had said at one point, and Brooke had said, Oh, baby. He hadn't called to tell her, he said, because he knew she wouldn't want him now. He had fixed her with his eyes, the warm color of harvest. She had brought two apples from the kitchen, Macouns, just coming ripe. As they'd talked, they'd bitten into the crisp flesh. The apples had smelled of afternoon sun and honey. Sean had gotten some severance. I'm not broke yet, he had said between bites, and Brooke had corrected him: We're not broke.

He had kissed her again, many times, their mouths tart with apple, as warmly and naturally as if no doubts had lain between them. Then harder, more urgently. As Brooke's head went light, she had heard the tinny ring of her cell phone, but she had ignored it. She had news for him, Sean had suggested when they came up for air. He could taste it. And still Brooke's doubts hovered at the edge of the room, where the cell phone's rings had died away. It could wait, she had said.

"This," she had said, touching his lower lip with her thumb—"can't."

He had lifted her, carried her up the stairs, the dogs following like shadows. With Meghan asleep across the street, they had made full-throated love. Her own hunger astonished her. It was as if that moment with Alex had given her permission not to pick up where they'd left off but to leave them, Brooke and Alex, at last in a story that was finished. With her husband she hungered for everything— his mouth on her nipples, the nest of hair at his sternum, his belly, his ass. All the rest, she thought as he thrust deep inside her, all the rest could wait.

Back in the kitchen, she made Meghan's school lunch while Meghan peppered her with news. They were going to do a Christmas show in ballet, and Meghan was to be an elf. Last night at Taisha's they had had ice cream right before bed, and Taisha's mom said it was fine if you brushed your teeth after. Last Friday Daddy stayed home from work and fixed the swing set in the backyard. And Jackie brought Josefina to school and she was wearing the outfit Meghan gave her and everyone said it was really cute.

She did not ask any more about why Brooke had been gone, or what might have changed. As Brooke drove her to school, she felt herself slipping back into the skin she'd inhabited before. The trip to Windermere—Najda, Ziadek, the Zukowskys, the truth, even the meeting with Dom—appeared the way her past always had, as a disturbing dream, details you banished as you made your way through the day. Why should Meghan's life receive such a curve ball?

"Don't be sad, Mommy," Meghan said, leaning across for a kiss before she let herself out of the car. "I'm not mad at you anymore."

Because, Brooke decided as she pulled out of the lot, balls curved.

She continued down Asylum from the school toward downtown. She had left Sean a note, *Gone to see Lorenzo, back before noon.*

The hospital florist had just opened. No autumn flowers—she should have stopped by the nursery—but she chose a vase with sweet-smelling Adonis and dark pink cockscomb. The names alone would make Lorenzo smile. She found his floor just as visiting hours began. "Hey, friend," she said softly as she entered.

Lorenzo shifted his gaze from the television, which hung from the ceiling. His skin was yellow, his eyes cavernous, with dry, crescent-shaped bags beneath. Could it have been only ten days since she had seen him at the nursery? Even his silvery hair seemed to have thinned. "Thought you'd be here last week," he said reproachfully. His voice had a bronchial rasp.

"I know. I'm sorry. I was out of town. I should have called. Here's my apology, but it's not enough." She set the flowers on his bedside table and pulled away the tissue paper.

"Dream on, girl," he said, cracking a grin at the arrangement. "Those are for the stud next door."

"No. They are for you." She pulled up a chair.

"And my Chianti?"

She put her hand to her chest. "Oh dear, I forgot. Later today. Promise. When they've put you through your paces for the day."

"We're all done." Lorenzo fingered the white sheet drawn up to his chest. He was wearing striped silk pajamas, not hospital issue. "I'll be all done, myself, in six months or so."

"What are you talking about?" Brooke said. Panic seized her at the bone.

"It's not a surprise, really. The statistics were there all along. But denial's a big thing, you know." Lorenzo's eyes, as he managed to meet Brooke's alarmed gaze, were shallow pools. "I'm afraid of the pain," he said. He reached for the glass on his stand and sucked water through a straw. "They say they give you enough drugs so you don't feel it. But I tend to scream a lot."

"Isn't there something they can do? Chemo, radiation . . . would they try surgery?" As Lorenzo silently shook his head, Brooke stood up and took a turn around the private room, with all its cards and flowers, sat again. "Where is the pancreas anyway?" she said. "Do you really need it? Can't they cut it out?"

"It helps digest food," said Lorenzo patiently, "and no. It's metastasized, my dear. I should have come in months ago, when I first felt a little achy. We're too late now, I'm afraid." He reached out his hand, with its elegant fingers, and patted Brooke's arm. "They can do a thing called palliative chemotherapy," he said, "but I'd lose my hair and die anyhow."

"Oh, Lorenzo." Brooke began to weep. Of all that had happened in the previous twenty-four hours, this news was the least expected, the one blow that toppled her emotional house of sticks. "I can't accept it," she said. "I cannot sit here and talk to you and accept this."

"You don't have to. It's only me who has to accept."

"Anything you need—anything you want me to do—"

"There is a thing, actually." Lorenzo's voice went raspy. He sucked more water through the straw. "Had my lawyer in on Friday. He drew up some papers. I told him I was sure you'd be by. I mean, the nursery's falling apart without you."

"That can't be true." She tried to smile, but the tears wouldn't let her.

"They're probably planting marijuana in the greenhouse. I don't know. I'm stuck here. Take a look at that file, there. On the windowsill."

Brooke pulled a tissue from the box by the bed and blew her nose. She brought the folder over. It was thick, filled with neatly fastened copies of a contract. The label on the tab read *Lorenzo's Nursery Trust*. She handed it to Lorenzo, but he pushed it away. "Open it," he said. "Read."

From the first page, she knew. The trust had already been established. During Lorenzo's lifetime, she was named as its executor. Upon his death, when probate was complete, she became its beneficiary. There were no outstanding liens on the Hartford location; the Simsbury site carried a mortgage that would be settled with the sale of certain investments upon Lorenzo's demise. He was giving Brooke the nursery. "You can't do this," she breathed.

He had pushed himself up in the bed. A flush of color had come into his cheeks. "Only way to stop me," he said, "is refuse to sign. Then you don't get invited to my funeral."

"But this is so . . . I'm not even a member of your family, Lorenzo."

"Sure you are. You're my girl." He leaned forward then, and wiped a tear from her cheek with his thumb. "You oughta know by now," he said, "we got blood between us. Christ. You're about the only family I got."

She brought a copy of the trust home. Sean was in the backyard, ripping out weeds. "You've got a better eye than I do," she said.

He stood and dusted off his pants. "A man needs work," he said.

"We might both have as much of that as we can handle," she said.

She got an old blanket and they sat on the grass while she showed him what Lorenzo had written. Sean lifted the pages by the corner, not to get them dirty. He hummed and nodded. "Poor fellow," he said.

"Six months, they're giving him."

"They gave my father nine, and he took five. But that was the drinking." He handed the deed of trust back to Brooke. "Would you ever have guessed," he said, "that my father wanted to be a musician? That he gave it up for Mum, and for us?"

"He was a depressed man. You always said that."

He nodded. "And Mum knew it. She feels guilty about it to this day."

"Well then, why does she—"

"Exactly. She was always afraid I'd try, and then be kept from trying. I told her that you—" He broke off. His hand strayed past the blanket to the grass, where he gripped a large dandelion and got it up by the root. When he returned his gaze to Brooke, she could feel the heat coming off him. "I want to go back to school," he said, "for music. I want to make my life with you and Meghan, and as a musician. A teacher of music, a singer. And I won't bother you about a second child, and I'll never drink again."

"Oh, Sean," she said. "Sean." She cupped his face in her hands. Gradually she managed to lift him up, to bring him next to her. She curled her long legs against him. She bent her forehead against his. "You started to say this," she said, "before. Then we got off track."

"Are we on track now?"

She kissed his smooth chin, where the goatee had been. "You know what I have," she said.

He sighed. "Secrets, probably."

"I have a CD—no, I'll say it all. A constant disposition." She kissed the chin again. "To promote." The nose. "Your good." She brushed his lips.

"We won't have much money."

"We'll have the nursery."

He nodded. She could feel his pride rising within him, could see

him wrestling it down. Reaching past her, he pulled another dandelion, its white root like a bone. She took a deep breath. "Yesterday,"
she began, "I went to see your cousin Dominick."

"In Philadelphia?" His eyebrows went up.

"It was on the way back from Windermere." She held a beat.
"Where I learned that I have a daughter. Who survived everything
that I threw at her."

It was the third time she had told the story in as many days. She
had almost grown comfortable with it. She was able to create a character of herself, the foolish seventeen-year-old girl who believed a
supposedly hip older woman about a remedy for a condition she was
too ashamed to admit. As before, when she came to the moment in
the Econo Lodge, she insisted that she did not feel the baby move,
or breathe; that its color had been gray, its limbs lifeless. Yet as she
repeated the memory, the baby seemed to come gradually to life,
and her awareness—not now, but back then, as the girl in the motel
room—grew. The horrible thought crossed her mind that she had
known, that she had let Alex take the baby from her not because it
was dead but because it was alive and she wished it dead.

She shuddered. That way lay madness. She swallowed hard; she
moved the story forward, to Alex's reappearance in Hartford and
her trip to Windermere, to Luisa and Josef Zukowsky, to Najda's
condition and Najda's dreams.

All the while she was speaking, Sean sat cross-legged on the
blanket. Now and then his hand strayed to another weed, or to
stroke Lex's ebony head. Whenever she paused, he nodded. "And
then?" he asked three or four times.

"And then," she finished, "I managed to reach Dominick. He's a
lifesaver, Sean. I think he can really do something for Najda. And
whatever I might want—like time traveling, to fix the whole thing—
my focus has got to be on doing something. Doing it now."

She had expected fury from her husband, or disbelief, or even the kind of shock that only whiskey would sort out. She had not expected what his face displayed, which was pure relief. "Come here," he said after a long silence. "To me."

He rose onto his knees and lifted her to hers. His arms went around her back, warmed by the midmorning sun. They rocked back and forth. Above their heads a mockingbird called. Sean gave off traces of the Irish Spring soap he always used, mixed with fresh dirt and grass; he gave off the scent of his own skin, as unique to Brooke's sense of smell as she had heard a mother's milk was to her baby. As she let her head sink onto his shoulder, her eyes released tears that dampened his neck and collar. They sank onto the blanket. Long and deep, they kissed—a kiss different from last night's, a kiss that asked nothing. One of Sean's hands slipped under Brooke's jersey and cupped her breast. "Forgive me," she said.

"Nothing to forgive."

"I cheated you. Seven years and more. I've been half a woman to you. I was just so afraid—"

He cut her off with another kiss. Then he murmured against her cheek, "Being afraid isn't anything to forgive."

"But if I hadn't been such a fool. If I'd faced what I did squarely."

"Then you'd be with Alex," Sean said, "and not with me."

She twisted her torso, squinting against the sunlight to gaze at him. Her face, she knew, betrayed the truth he'd hit on. "I was with Alex a little," she said, "in Windermere. Not—you know. But almost."

She saw the jealousy rise like smoke inside him; saw him work to snuff it out. "I wasn't really asking about that," he said.

"But I had to tell you."

His eyebrows lifted and lowered; he nodded. He projected an odd, surefooted calm. "What I was really asking," he said, "was if you want to be with me, now."

"Of course. But I haven't . . . it hasn't been the way you deserve."

"I'm not asking about the old Brooke. I'm asking about the new one." With his ring finger he traced an invisible line on her forehead. "You've got plans, you've found this daughter, you don't have to hold anything back anymore—"

"I want to have another child with you."

Sean dropped his head back onto the blanket. He looked up at the deep blue of the autumn sky. He smiled ruefully. These, Brooke knew, were the sweet words he had hungered to hear. But he had borne losing her once already. "If you want our life," he said, reaching up to touch her hair, "if you really want our life together, you'll do more than just tell me all this stuff." He paused. She waited. The mockingbird dove; one of the dogs snapped at it and grabbed air. "You'll bring me to this daughter of yours," Sean said. "To these people who've cared for her. Whatever there is to do, we'll decide to do it. You and I. Not just you. Us."

Brooke held her lower lip in her upper teeth. She gazed at him a long while. Then, gravely, she nodded.

Chapter 31

The week Alex got back to Boston, Charlie begged him to come to her Halloween party. "There'll be other old farts there," she said. "My roommate Amber—you remember her, she came to Windermere—she's dating this grad student in physics, he's like thirty, and he's bringing his roommates. I want you to see my costume."

"Do I have to wear a costume?"

"Don't be a stick. Of course. And you can't dress up as a banker."

He went as a Japanese *oyama*, with a kimono he'd bought in Kyoto and an obi Tomiko had given him on their honeymoon. The kimono was dark blue with a golden dragon snaking up the center back and twin dragons on each side of the chest. When he first went to Japan, he wore it around his apartment and felt very tall and cool and pseudo-Asian. The obi, black with occasional gold threads, had belonged to Tomiko's grandfather. He hadn't touched either in years. He thought momentarily of chalking his face, but abandoned the idea. Over his half-shaved head he dropped a black Kabuki wig

he picked up at a costume shop in Somerville. He wore his old cloth
tabi on his feet, which froze as he walked from his car to his sister's
apartment.

Pablo was there, too, dressed as a Yankees player, while Charlie
wore Red Sox. From time to time, as the party heated up, they pretended to wrestle each other. Alex thought his sister looked fetching
in a baseball uniform. She wore a pink baseball glove on her left
hand, making it look vaguely like a lobster claw.

"Good thing Brian's not here, though," he said as Charlie staggered from a bout of staged fighting to the ragged couch where he
sat. "He'd go after your boyfriend with a baseball bat, just for being
on the wrong team."

"Brian! Geez. You should've brought him. I remember him! He
used to tickle me until I peed my pants."

She was a little stoned. She also had about her the glow of a
woman falling rapidly in love. Around them, in the living room, an
assortment of Sarah Palins and various animals and even a guy in a
banana suit danced to the Monster Mash. As he waltzed by in his
pinstripes, Pablo leaned down to give Charlie a wet kiss. She wiped
her mouth with the back of her hand when he was over at the keg.
"It was Windermere that started it, you know," she said, turning
back to Alex.

He pulled his kimono over his knees. Already he'd taken off the
wig, which itched. "Our hometown's a romantic place."

"Not for you, apparently." She gazed at his bruised face, and he
wished he'd gone for the makeup. For a week the suits at the office
had been ribbing him about bravado and knuckleheadedness. Everything he'd told them about the stitches that tattooed the shaved side
of his head was true. He'd stopped to get Mickey D's for an old cop
buddy in his old hometown, had started down a side street, had
heard a woman screaming and gone to her rescue. Knight in shin-

ing armor, they each said, and each time he winced, thinking of Brooke. "You didn't say you were leaving the hike," his sister went on, "to be a hero."

"Not my intention, exactly."

"Don't do it again."

A smile twisted his mouth. "Did you get to interview those women?" he asked, to change the subject. "The ones protesting Planned Parenthood?"

She nodded. "Pablo came with me."

"So you're both joining Right to Life."

"Don't be stupid." She batted at him with her lobsterish mitt. "Pablo was great. He argued with a couple of those women. He said, 'What makes you think these babies even want to be born? If they've got souls, maybe they're hovering in the ether somewhere having a fine old time. Life all by itself isn't all that great, you know.' "

"Is that your argument? For your paper?" Alex felt the beat of the music as someone turned it up for a second round. *Spirit babies*, he thought.

"I think I'll write about assisted suicide instead." Charlie blew a bubble with her gum, then sucked it back. "More cheerful. Don't you think?"

"I wouldn't know."

She batted him with her glove again and stood up. "Cute kimono," she said, swaying. "The boy with the dragon tattoo." Then she turned away.

"I have a daughter," Alex said, but Charlie didn't hear him. Later in the evening, one of the grad students, a big-bosomed postmodernist dressed as Dow Jones—everything jaggedly plummeting, like a series of lightning streaks, across horizontal lines—shared her joint with Alex and they made out for a while on the rickety back balcony. Her hand slipped beneath the folds of his kimono. Still, he left the wig behind and drove home alone. That night he dreamed, again, of Brooke. Waking, he made up his mind. He had to get away.

It took him four weeks to put in for a transfer. In early November, he met with a lawyer in downtown Boston and set up a trust for Luisa Zukowsky. Into it he deposited the fifteen thousand dollars he had socked away, mostly for Dylan, during his years in Japan. He arranged for an automatic transfer of a thousand dollars from his checking account every month. After his death, assuming she was of age, Najda Zukowsky would administer the trust. He sent the paperwork to her, care of Josef Zukowsky. When he got back to his apartment after sending all the documents, he pulled the ring box out of the drawer in his kitchen and sat for a long while, drinking Scotch and contemplating the curled lock of Najda's baby hair.

When time began to hang heavy, he went to see Fabrice in accounting. About the soccer league, he explained. Fabrice was a Haitian guy, dreadlocked and muscular. When he heard Alex had played in college, he put him in at fullback. Every Sunday they played and went out for beers—a motley assortment of former jocks, some with bad knees and some with coke habits. Three times, Alex agreed to meet a couple of the single guys later in the evening, at a nightclub in Jamaica Plain. They swapped life stories—the second time, Alex told them about Dylan, and it was easier and better than he'd expected—and looked for women. The third time, he went home with a chunky composition teacher, but when he left in the morning he didn't leave his phone number.

Brussels was the most likely place. Gray and potato-faced, known for chocolate and beer. Stodgy, one of the guys at the office said, but Amsterdam was two hours by train. When Alex told Charlie about his plan, just before Thanksgiving, she called him an asshole. She was breaking up with Pablo by then and had taken to outlining her eyes in black liner, which ran when the tears spilled out. Not until after Christmas, he assured her, but she threw her napkin at him anyway and stormed from the restaurant.

"She'll forgive you," Brooke said when they finally met. Alex had stopped calling her by then. He was never going to give her what she wanted. He was never going to say to her, Yes, Najda is our child, and I did this to her, I almost destroyed her. He had seen, in that alley in Scranton, what such honesty led to—a runaway mother, a violent end. Trying to repair the damage of the past was like wishing on the monkey's paw: Your last wish would be to put the damage back exactly where it had been.

But on Thanksgiving weekend the phone had chimed and it was Brooke's number, and he hadn't stopped to think before picking up. They met at the nursery she was creating, in Simsbury. Two months earlier, the place had been a mud zone, with mountains of mulch looming over spindly trees and paths discernible only by the lengths of wood laid zigzag from a small cracked parking lot. Now, though the place was bedding down for the winter, it looked ready to bloom. Sean had made the difference, Brooke said. Lorenzo had hired him, for now, while he prepared for the Hartt School, the conservatory. Today Sean was interviewing with the graduate committee; next week, he would audition. Meanwhile he had built the greenhouse and rejiggered the website. Alex sat with Brooke in a heated building that would house retail gardening supplies at one end and a florist at the other. It smelled of sawdust and caulk, but shelves were already up around the walls, a C-shaped counter at the front. They sat in a pair of folding chairs, drinking cheap wine from plastic cups.

"If Charlie forgives me," Alex said, "it's because I'm her only brother. That doesn't make it right to keep putting oceans between us."

Brooke chuckled. She was freer, more energetic—*bubbly* was the word Alex would have used had it not been impossible to apply to Brooke. "You're not as powerful as you think, Lex," she said. She reached out a foot to tap his ankle. "Charlie's twenty-two. When she was seven, maybe, you were God. Now you're a free lunch and a shoulder to cry on."

"I'd like to be that shoulder, though."

"Then don't go." When he didn't answer, she leaned forward. Here it comes, he thought. "You know who she is, Alex. I feel like I can't even say her name in front of you. Even when having her in our lives is the great, most fantastic surprise—and all because you—"

Alex put his hand up. "Look, they got my DNA," he said.

"What do you mean? Who got it?"

"Scranton police. They were just doing their job," he said when Brooke rolled her eyes. "My point is, if you or the Zukowskys or anyone wants to know if I am that incredible girl's father, you are welcome to the information."

Brooke shook her head. She contemplated her wine. Then she looked up, her eyes questioning. "Don't *you* want to know?"

He shrugged. "Knowing wouldn't change anything," he said. "It wouldn't change my responsibility for whatever happened to a baby that I know—that I knew—was alive at the moment I pulled her from between your legs. It wouldn't change the composition of her family. Her mother is still Luisa Zukowsky."

"Who cannot help her."

"You'd be wrong about that." He rose, toured a set of empty shelves, and sat down again. He had avoided looking at Brooke directly, but now he made himself. She had cut her hair. With the cooler weather, and no more need to dig holes, she wore a sea-green cashmere V-neck that lay softly across her collarbone. He watched the vein beat in the hollow of her neck. "I'm not doing nothing," he said. "I'm not running away."

Brooke turned to look out the window. The trees were bare, a tangle of limbs against a gray sky. "I remember it all differently now," she said after a long silence. "I remember movement. Sometimes I even remember her breathing. Her tiny belly against my chest."

"Memory plays tricks, Brooke. I used to think I went abroad straight from BU, that I never saw my dad in those months before he drove off the cliff. But there's a photo in my mom's house, me and him. My suitcase is by the car. The tiger lilies behind us are in bloom. I'm holding the Japanese flag. I saw my dad that very month, and I still can't remember a thing about it."

"Your dad," Brooke said, still looking out the window, "committed suicide."

"Yes, he did."

"Because of the accounts. Because he'd done something to set the quarry up for bankruptcy."

"He felt too guilty to live, that much I'm sure of."

"Guilt," Brooke repeated. "It's a killer."

She turned back to Alex. Between her eyes—luminous now, with a spark he'd thought extinguished—ran a furrow of doubt. Why not tell her about the trust fund he had set up, for Najda's mother? She would fling her arms around him then, welcome him to the club of believers. They would keep talking, meeting, planning together; and he could not bear it. So no, he would not tell her, not until he lived far away and in a new life. "Her name is Najda," he said slowly. "And she will be as okay as anyone in her situation can be. And I will learn to live with what I did to her. But at least, this way, I cannot harm her more."

They rose and walked the perimeter of the nursery. They talked of lighter things. In the darkening afternoon, they lingered by Alex's car. "What about happiness?" Brooke asked.

"That's a funny question for you to ask me."

"I would never have made you happy, Lex. I was too"—she unfolded her arm and waved a hand feebly—"whiffly."

"No, you weren't. You were too afraid. You didn't trust me." His words sounded harsh, and he regretted them. He reached a hand to the back of Brooke's neck and pulled her head to his chest. "You trust Sean now, though. Don't you?" He felt her nod. "So that's new. And I'll be new, one of these days. I've just got to work on it."

She lifted her face. Tears moistened her cheeks. "Far away," she said.

"It's easier," he said.

The next day, at the soccer scrimmage, a cold wind blew across the field, bringing the first stray flakes of snow. Alex felt his skin flush; ricocheting off his hip, the ball stung. Cold sweat gathered in the small of his back, and smacking the ground felt like hitting rock. When he scored, his teammates slapped him on the back and the butt. Just like high school, one of them said at halftime. Another said, Except for the knees. And Fabrice, the Haitian guy, chimed in—it wasn't the knees so much as the shit they were all working out. Right here, on this field. Amen, they all said. Then they trotted back to the field and tried to win.

Chapter 32

Najda

My legs hurt, from the walking. Alison, the PT here at Crosby, says it's a good hurt, even if the pain keeps me up at night. She massages the muscles above and below the knees. I get exercises to do, leg lifts with weights and pulleys. The left side's coming along fine, of course—it's the right, where all the muscles are smaller and don't cooperate. In the water, I'm fine. Even my right arm moves, though I can't keep the fingers together to make a real stroke. I love the pool here. Light floods in the picture window facing south, and the water bounces it to make blue waves on the walls and ceiling. Sounds echo. Some of the kids here are what they call multiply disabled, which means they are genuinely retarded along with everything else, and in the water they are so happy. There's this one kid, Spicer, whose head stays in a brace on land, but with his teacher holding him so he can float on his back, he waggles it around. You can just imagine how that feels, the cool water at the base of his skull after it's been in a clamp all day.

I walk with braces, for balance, along a track between two rails to keep me oriented. This morning I demonstrated for my family. They're here for Family Day, which happens every March. I thought Katarina was going to start crying when she saw me. She grabbed Luisa's hand and sort of squealed. Ziadek just sat in his chair and nodded, like he knew I could do this all along. And my mom—well, she looked confused. It's hard. I know that now. Luisa had it all worked out, that she took care of me, and then I go making new rules, taking care of myself. She loves me and it's hard for her. And not to be condescending, but I'm proud of her that she came today. I thought she wouldn't. I was afraid she wouldn't. I'm going to lose Ziadek. I don't want to lose my mom.

Alex, my counselor, says my disabilities won't keep me back, but my temper might. Funny that he has the same name as my supposed dad. He's completely different—chubby, bearded, full of nervous tics like the way he keeps knocking that kinetic-motion thing on his desk into action. What little I saw of my supposed dad suggested he was the still, watchful type. I call him that, *supposed*, because there's no proof. Last fall, when Jennifer first came to help my mom start to manage by herself, everyone was pretty grateful to that other Alex. Katarina told me he had taken a DNA test. If I wanted to get my DNA, they could tell for sure if he was my dad.

He's not my dad, I told her. No matter about the DNA. He wants to help Luisa, great. But I don't need him, I don't need to know if I've got his genes.

As far as my temper goes, Alex—Alex of Crosby—is right. I'm impatient. People here talk about wanting to be normal. I don't want to be normal. I want to be amazing. Last week they showed a couple of episodes from that English TV series with Stephen Hawking. Now, he is amazing. But how did he get so curious about black holes and quasars, things we'll never experience? Me, I want to unlock the brain. My brain, specifically. That's the narcissism of youth, Alex-of-Crosby says. But then other brains, brains in general. What does it mean to damage them? Where do they heal with scars, like scalded flesh, and where do they not grow back, like an amputated arm? Neuroscience—that's what I'll study, in college. Which means a lot of science now, bio and chemistry, and it makes my head ache, all the words scrambling in front of me. I can do it, though. I'll bet Stephen Hawking gets headaches, too.

Dinner in an hour. From my dorm window I can see the E. J. Crosby building, where my folks are getting some kind of discussion, a slide show, an upbeat talk. My mom won't be able to follow much, but I noticed she bought a new coat and new shoes to come here; she really wants to look like a mom. Ziadek will fall asleep; that's the meds. And Katarina will ask weird questions, like: What if we fall off one of the horses? Or: Are we learning how to make change?

I'm learning to make change, Aunt Katarina. You bet.

I love my family. I'm trying to get used to the idea that Ziadek's going to die, but it doesn't work. I need him to tell me, again, that it's okay. That he feels lucky. I told Katarina I want to come home in his last week. I want to hold his hand. She says she can't guarantee anything, that he could go anytime. If I insist, I'll have to come home right now. And I won't do that.

I push the window open a little—they overheat this place—and hear my favorite horse, Squeaky, whinny from the field where grass is just starting to push up out of the mud. The horses are mostly for the autistic kids, so they can develop empathy, but I ride Squeaky to learn balance. Afterward, I brush her coat, and her flesh shivers a little as I pass the brush across her hindquarters. It makes me think about being stroked like that, about being touched. Maybe one day.

The books on my shelf are full of romance. Brooke sent them, with a note. She said she had loved these books when she was my age. They belonged, she wrote, to my grandfather. They're all vintage hardcovers, with beautiful pictures on the front, flowing watercolors of women in long sheer dresses and men in armor or vests embroidered with crosses. Myths, basically, about chivalry and quests for holy objects that have no use unless you believe in magic. Visions appear in the air. Women cast spells. Wizards age backward. Knights throw each other off horses and are trampled.

I'm not going to insult Brooke, but I have no use for these tales. My grandfather is Ziadek, and he told me stories about the old country, about the war. If Brooke comes to see me here, I'll blow the dust off the books and thank her, but I won't read them.

For so long, I think as I look out on the twilight, the lights in the Crosby building, I waited for my mother. Then she came, and I still miss her. I miss her like a part of me that I might have known once, but I've forgotten. Or like a twin who was always there during my childhood—running through long grass with her tall blond mother, listening to her romantic tales at night, hearing her songs—and now she's gone forever, dead or simply run off. No matter how well I come to know Brooke, I will always miss my mother in this way.

And I will always belong to my mom, to Luisa. There she is now, pushing Ziadek's wheelchair as they leave the building. She looks up toward my window and I wave, but she doesn't see me. Last time she was here, she brought me a chess set, a beautiful wooden one. It cost almost all her earnings from the Quik Mart, I think. You can play with your teachers, she said. They're smart. And I said no, I wanted to play with her. Ziadek didn't come that time; he was too sick with the chemo. Today, before they leave, maybe we'll have a game. Luisa can move Ziadek's pieces for him. She'll like that, counting to bishop four or queen two. Her hands on the smooth wood of the rooks with their crenellated tops, the queen with her little button of a head. Her hands with their close-clipped nails, the straight crease across the inside of the palm. They saved me, those hands. And here they are, the knock on my door. I push myself upright, clutch the bookcase for balance, take one step. Then another.

Chapter 33

Lorenzo lingered for almost six months. Every time Brooke went to see him he claimed he was at rest, he was ready. But even the hospice nurse said he had fight in him. The day before he died, Brooke found him propped in bed, staring down at his legs, which had developed a tremble that wouldn't quit. "I don't know, I don't know," he said in the high, feeble voice brought on by the morphine.

"What don't you know?" Brooke asked.

"What I'm supposed to do."

She took his thin hand. "I don't think you have to do anything," she said.

Ziadek, back in Windermere—she thought of him as Ziadek now, everyone called him that—was holding up better, though Brooke suspected that he, too, would be gone by summer. At least he had hung on long enough to see Najda settled at the Crosby School, and Luisa beginning to heal.

The week before Christmas, Brooke had brought Sean and Meghan to Windermere. With trepidation she had arranged for them to meet Ziadek, Najda, and Katarina at the T.G.I. Friday's on Route 6. Luisa had refused to come. Meghan had just lost two teeth within a week, and insisted on bringing them both along to show her grandmother and her new "cousins." The meeting had been awkward. Najda was due to start at the Crosby School after the holidays. Katarina alternately quashed any excitement about this development and struggled to present her family as a self-sufficient unit, allergic to charity. Quickly she targeted Sean as a possible ally against relations between the two families. But Sean had the gift of geniality—he was delighted to meet her, to meet Najda, to have the privilege of knowing Ziadek, of whom he'd heard so much. Now and then, Brooke had felt the warm pressure of her husband's hand in the center of her back, like a support on which she could lie back and float if she needed to. And Meghan, luckily, had regained her chatty self. She insisted on climbing into the wheelchair, on Najda's showing her how all the controls worked; if she noticed that her new cousin moved strangely or had trouble with words, she let that go in favor of novelty.

Ziadek had lost his hair to the chemo by then, and scarcely ate. But he took Brooke's hands in his own, once the meal was blessedly over, and said in a rasp, "He has done this thing. Your lawyer. We need to pay him."

"No," said Brooke. "You don't."

"Luisa. She—she is not ready." He pinched the transparent clamp that held the tube of oxygen to his nostrils. Already Brooke could trace the plates of his skull, the hollows for his pale eyes. He attempted a smile. "She is liking this coach you send, this Jennifer."

"I didn't send Jennifer, Ziadek."

"No, no, I mean the boy sent her. The boy who save Luisa."

"Alex?"

"Alex." Ziadek managed the smile, showing his long teeth. "Good boy, Alex. He watch for her, for Luisa."

"Are you sure it was Alex? He paid for a coach? What kind of coach?"

"Life coach." He humphed; the rice paper of his eyelids fluttered. "Funny word, *coach*. He pay for many things, your Alex. Luisa sends him pictures. A good boy," he repeated. He squeezed Brooke's hand.

I am not running away, Alex had said. And maybe, Brooke thought, he wasn't.

Najda herself was different—more reserved, more watchful. When she spoke of the Crosby School, her eyes shone. "I swim," she said of the visit she'd had there. "Say they walk maybe. Me, I mean. Walk!" She admired Meghan's teeth. She shook Sean's hand. She allowed Brooke to fit an early Christmas present, a red wool coat specially made for wheelchair users, around her shoulders. But there were no hugs. She did not call Brooke *Mother*. She did not mention Alex. Luisa's ordeal had obviously shaken Najda, had changed her outlook. Perhaps, Brooke thought, Najda had come to think differently about this long-awaited mother who had returned to put her together like Humpty-Dumpty.

"It does no good to press her," Sean had said on their way back to Hartford from Windermere.

"I'm afraid she'll start hating me."

"Not if you don't start hating yourself."

"I know. I know."

Back and forth, that winter, they went over the familiar ground: what Brooke could and could not forgive herself for; why she refused to blame Alex for anything; what she wanted for Najda, what she wanted from Najda. "I've got to stop burdening you with all this," Brooke said more than once, when their talk had gone past midnight and Sean stayed up after to study music theory.

"She ain't heavy," he would croon, cornily, each time. "She's my lov-err."

Their days arranged themselves differently, now. The daffodils
were up. The Simsbury location was opening in two weeks. Sean
had dived into a full load of classes and spent thirty hours a week at
the nursery. Besides the website, he had designed a new logo for
Lorenzo's, plus the banners and brochures that announced the new
site and management. He had helped Brooke compose a page com-
memorating Lorenzo; already, Brooke had received a half dozen
e-mails from his relatives as distant as Italy, thanking her for the
photos and memorial. Meghan was back to ballet and also playing
spring soccer. Brooke liked to pick her up after a day of greenhouse
work. They would vie for who was muddier.

Today at Lorenzo's they were putting out the first boxes of pansies. The indoor shop was filled with bell-shaped lilies and purple
tulips for Easter. Five days of steady warmth had melted the last of
April's snow, and cars splashed through great puddles in the parking lot. As Brooke stepped out from the greenhouse where she was
incubating the starter vegetables, a loud blast of hip-hop veered into
the drive. Shanita had called from the Simsbury location a half hour
ago, and here she was already, to pick up pansy reinforcements.

"Hey, Boss Lady," she greeted Brooke as she stepped down from
the truck. Her boys crowded the passenger seat, worrying their Play-
Station Portables.

"Told you not to call me that," Brooke warned.

Shanita inspected the pansies. "I used to tell Lorenzo," she said,
"I don't know why folks call queer men pansies. They look nothing
like these little faces, here."

"You never said that."

"You not the only one with an inside track."

It was still taking some adjustment, this new relationship since
Lorenzo's death. Brooke had said nothing about it beforehand, and
in the first week Shanita had threatened at least five times to quit

before she'd take orders from her old buddy. Now they handled it with these dumb jokes and subtle digs. Brooke pulled on her gloves and helped carry flats of pansies to the truck bed. She wore wading boots every day in the slush, and still came home with mud on her jeans.

"Hey, boss," Shanita said as they loaded the last set. "You're wobbly."

"I've been on my feet all day, Shan."

"I don't mean that." Hands on hips, she stepped back and stared at Brooke's belly. "You got a little passenger in there, don't you?"

The air was still cool, but Brooke's face flamed. "I can't believe it shows."

"I've got a practiced eye. How far along?"

"Just a couple months. I've only put on six pounds!"

"Well, that's a sack of potatoes, and they're all in one spot. Guess you don't have to raid Africa for your baby now, huh?"

"Shanita." Brooke set the pansies in place. "It was never about that. It was just about me, about . . . old fears."

"But you don't tell me you're with child. I need to guess at it. Now you're the Boss Lady, where's my friend at?"

Brooke faced her old confidante. What a cyclone the last six months had been! But she couldn't allow the swirl of her life to leave Shanita in the dust. What had she claimed, to Dominick, back in October? She was *done with keeping it a secret*. "Let's knock off early today," she said. "Let the guys close up. I'll buy you a glass of wine."

"I got to get the kids home," Shanita said—sulking, a little, not wanting Brooke to take her for granted. And she was right, Brooke thought.

"How about I come over then?" she said. "I'll bring the wine. I'd like to see your new place."

"If you don't mind boxes," Shanita said.

One by one, Brooke thought, one by one, she was unstitching the shroud of her past self. There remained tight stitches to undo, strong seams resisting, risks to run.

Shanita drove off to Simsbury. Brooke moved through the greenhouse, misting. People always came looking for herbs and lettuce before the season was well enough advanced. One element she hoped to add, once Shanita had the Simsbury operation up and running, was a tasting room. If the nursery forced some of the plants a bit early, they could offer a spread of pesto from their own basil and garlic, a small cup of sliced strawberries, a salad of fresh arugula drizzled with cold-pressed olive oil, which they could also offer as an impulse buy. Last fall, tossing their lives in the air like a deck of cards, she and Sean had talked about his career—what he could do, realistically, in music; what made him happy. In the end, he had turned to her. "When we met, you were working with plants," he said, his amber eyes warm on hers. "You said they were easy to talk to. I think maybe they didn't ask you any questions."

"True enough," Brooke had confessed. "And I could get the job without going to college."

"Do you miss it?"

"Miss what?"

"College. The life of the mind. All those clever things you'd have been so good at, the way your friend Alex is good at them."

She couldn't help the small thud in her heart. "Don't go getting jealous of Alex again," she said quickly.

"Don't go getting defensive." They had been in bed; he pulled her close and kissed her earlobe. "What does Brooke want, now that she's not in hiding anymore?"

She had lain quiet a long while. Finally she said, "I love the nursery. Maybe I wouldn't have chosen it, if things had gone differently for me. But I can't imagine other work, another career. I make things grow. I help people find a kind of beauty they can care for. Lorenzo's leaving us a gift and a challenge. I want what we have, Sean." She laced her fingers through his chest hair. "Isn't that funny?"

A rap at the greenhouse door interrupted her thoughts—Eddie, one of the ponytailed guys who'd resurfaced for the spring season. He and his buddy Jasper were strong and steady, but they knew no more about plants now than when they started a year ago. "Customer, Brooke," Eddie said. "Guy wants a whole garden's worth."

The man standing with his son on the damp mulch looked familiar. "I'm Brooke," Brooke said, striding toward him in her waders. "We've just got plants out that can take a frost right now. Don't be fooled by three days of sun."

The man scrutinized her, then broke into a smile. "I can't believe I haven't bumped into you again," he said. "I'm your old boyfriend, remember?"

Brooke's hand froze in a moment of wild confusion.

"Tad Horgan," he said, squeezing and then releasing her hand. "And this is Jason? You said I reminded you of your old sweetheart. My legs did, anyhow." He made a lame attempt to pull up the cuff of his pants.

"Da-ad," said the boy.

"I remember now." Instinctively, Brooke put a hand on her belly. No one but Shanita would be able to tell yet that she was pregnant. But the slight swelling reminded her how far she had traveled since August. "You must have thought I was flirting with you."

"Can't blame you, with these legs. Made a point of covering up this time."

The laugh Brooke tried to hold in came out as a snort. "And is this guy following in his dad's footsteps?" she said when she had recovered.

"Playing soccer? You bet. In fact, I think we've seen that champ of yours on the field."

"Dad, she's on my team!" Jason shook his father's elbow. "She passed the ball to me last Saturday, remember? And I scored?"

"Scored, huh?" said Tad. "Cooties gone, I guess."

"So what brings you to Lorenzo's, Tad?"

He sighed. "My wife wants landscaping. And she wants it before the pool season opens and I disappear."

Pools, Brooke remembered—Tad installed swimming pools.

"And *I* said no pansies!" Jason added.

"Well, we've got a lot of pansies," Brooke admitted. "But there's dianthus, too, and snapdragons, and of course the spring bulbs, but you're too late for those."

She took them around the grounds. She *had* flirted with Tad Horgan, last summer. How far away it seemed, that time when a pair of muscular legs put her in mind of Alex Frazier. Tad seemed a nice guy, quick to let things pass. And when she thought of Alex, she no longer thought of his teenaged body but of the e-mails she'd started getting, every couple of weeks since January. Brussels, he wrote, was a strange, twisted place in a disguise of dullness. He was brushing off his high school French in hopes of getting away from the Americans. He had a little place in the Ixelles district, near some good jazz haunts. If the rain ever let up, he might check out the old-men's soccer scene. He struggled with depression, sometimes. But he was happier than he had been in Boston; he could imagine settling—he did not say marrying, but the hint was dropped—in Belgium. He did not mention the money he was sending Najda, and Brooke did not ask. She did report what she had heard from Ziadek about Luisa's coach, and she described Najda's victory over the school system, her new life at Crosby. To these updates Alex never responded directly. But the e-mails kept coming, like green shoots emerging in springtime, hints of a garden they might one day call friendship. Soon, Brooke thought, she would divulge her pregnancy. And she would tell Sean—yes, she would—that she was writing Alex.

She waved Tad off with a trunkful of sweet William, snapdragon, and even some macho-looking dark pansies. With Jasper and Eddie, she covered the flats of flowers against the night cold. Before she locked up, she called home. "Mommy, Mommy," Meghan said when she picked up. "Katarina called. And Daddy says I can take piano lessons instead of ballet." Meghan had lost another tooth and had trouble with *s. Lessons* came out as "lethenth." Brooke adored it.

"I thought you liked ballet," she said. "Why did Katarina call?"

"I don't like it anymore. Madame made me sit on the piano. Daddy plays the piano, he says he'll teach me to start. In case I don't like it. Jackie plays the violin. She goes to Suzuki. When are you coming home?"

"That's why I called. I'm meeting a friend after work. I'll be home a little late. Are you and Daddy okay?"

"Daddy's doing homework. Can I take piano?"

"If Daddy's willing to get you started, sure. Why did Katarina call?"

"I don't know. Can we call the baby Katarina? If it's a girl?"

"I'll have to think about that. Why do you like the name Katarina?"

"Because she's strong. And she has red hair. Or else we could call her Tiffany."

"If it's a girl. Can you get Daddy to the phone a sec?"

Katarina had called, Sean explained, to report that Ziadek would visit Najda one last time, then go into hospice. He could last as long as a month; he could be gone in ten days. He had asked to see Brooke. "She wasn't thrilled to be relaying any of this," Sean said. "But she loves her dad. She's carrying out his wishes."

"I'll go then. Over the weekend maybe. You?"

"He didn't ask for me. I'll stay here with Meghan. She's got soccer."

Brooke sat on the stoop of the flower shop as the sky darkened. The smell of spring hung in the air—old molds unearthed, thawed manure, upturned soil. She had begun, just barely, to believe in her good fortune. What a resilient daughter she had in Meghan—a kid who spoke out, who acted out, who let you know what she wanted, even if that changed from hour to hour. And Sean. She had sat at the back of the hall during the chorale's last rehearsal before tech week, when Sean as the Evangelist led the rest of the singers through the Bach oratorio. What courage he possessed, and grace. And he loved her. With all her failings and flaws, he loved her beyond measure.

Then there was Najda, who might forgive her one day and the next bring her to judgment. But she had hope, a future, a chance at happiness. Who was it, who had said the past wasn't dead—that it wasn't even past? The spring stench of living things waking from the fetid earth made that truth plain enough. The same held for the way Brooke felt, in moments like this, when her thoughts floated and came to rest on the daughter she had discovered. The ache in her heart never went away. It visited her again and again. It would occupy its wounded space as long as she lived, as long as she and Alex and Najda held the past in their bodies.

And in her own body, tiny life. There were no spirit children. She knew that now. They neither waited to be born nor hovered in the ether, making judgment calls. There were only children, rushing into this world in a tumult of blood, seizing their brief season.

A sliver of moon appeared above the line of spruce at the edge of the nursery. Brooke rose and started her car, to visit Shanita at her new home.

The Lost Daughter

Discussion Questions

1. Discuss Alex and Brooke's shared experiences and how the past haunts each of them. How have they each tried to distance themselves? How have the events at the motel taken a toll on them since?

2. Sean's desire to have a second child causes splintering tension between him and Brooke. Do you understand or sympathize with his pain, reasoning, or persistence? Why or why not? Is it this tension that drives him to drink?

3. How do Brooke's life and future plans change after the birth of Najda? What drives the new decisions she makes—from her choice about college to her overall attitude?

4. How would you describe a mother? How does Najda's understanding of what a mother is evolve in the book?

5. Even though adoption is commonplace today (and, as the author reminds us, it finds a well-rooted model in Moses' early story), stigmas still face adopted children and their families. Why do you think this is? How do these families respond or compensate?

6. Discuss Luisa's role as Najda's rescuer, advocate, and parent. What kind of unique challenges does she face in raising Najda, who has disabilities herself? Does she experience any limitations? As a

parent with Down syndrome, how does Luisa provide for and raise her daughter? How does her family work together to help her?

7. Compare the men in Brooke's romantic life: Sean and Alex. What kind of life does each offer Brooke? What kind of behavior does each elicit from her? Does she give something up when she commits to her marriage?

8. What does Brooke feel is at risk in telling Sean the truth—about her past actions, Alex's new role in her life, her investigation?

9. Why does Alex insist on coming clean to the authorities? What good does he think it will do? And once he learns the truth from Brooke after her search, why does he have such a hard time accepting the evidence?

10. Do you think Brooke and Alex should have been charged with a crime? Why or why not?

11. A few of the main characters wish for rescue in the novel, as suggested by Brooke's fascination with tales of knights and maidens, and Najda's dreams of being saved by her unknown, "normal" mother. How do these desires change by the end of the novel? Why?

12. How do Brooke, Sean, and Alex evolve over the course of the novel? What does each of them confront as the past comes to light? Do you think they can finally move forward freely with the truth now out in the open? Why or why not?

13. What do you think lies in store for each of the characters? Do you think Najda has forgiven her biological parents for their actions? Have they forgiven themselves?

NOTES

Notes

Notes